# One

**V**icky Clay could still see. Not well, not clearly, but in a vague and hazy way, as she might recall a dream. She was aware of her dusty, old-fashioned hotel room as a patchy mix of shadow and yellow lamplight. To her side, just at the edge of her peripheral vision, she could make out the blurred, fleshy line of her husband's naked shoulder.

She could hear—not Meade Clay's breathing, for he was strangely quiet—but the dull buzz of people laughing and talking downstairs. She heard them well enough to recognize a voice or two, yet they seemed strangely distant, as though miles away.

What she was aware of most was an odd tingling sensation throughout her unclad body—not on the surface of her skin, which was oddly numb, but beneath, within, as though a low-voltage current was running through her. It was a hot, humid Virginia June evening. She had been very sweaty when she and Meade had finished making love. Now all sense of warmth was gone. Yet neither was there cold.

What had she done that night that could make her feel this way? Nothing very healthy maybe, but nothing unusual, nothing she didn't do all the time, especially during the spring racing season.

A horse Vicky had trained had won the big steeplechase event that afternoon, the victory getting her very excited, all juiced up, wanting a man, though not her husband. She'd wanted someone more special, the handsome, courtly Captain Showers. Every woman in Dandytown wanted him. Or else, perhaps, one of the important men from Washington who were there for the races.

*1*

But she'd gotten nowhere with any of them. Her husband had kept hanging around, scaring them all off. Meade had been drinking and in a foul mood, and had been arguing and fighting with her all day. Finally, in the driveway of the inn, in front of some of the most respectable people in Dandytown, he had given in to his frustration and hit her. She had screamed at him that she hated him, that she wished he was dead, and she'd meant it.

But she'd started drinking herself, and eventually got so drunk she'd gone to their room with him, just to have someone between her legs. When she got like that, she'd sleep with anyone. She'd even tried taking on a horse once, as she'd heard Catherine the Great of Russia had done, on a hot night when she'd been all alone at Meade's place and raving mad and all flipped out on wine and drugs. The damned beast had almost killed her.

The next day, she'd let it gorge itself on feed and water and then galloped it in the heat until it had dropped and died.

She and Meade had done more than get drunk this evening. He'd had some good cocaine in his veterinarian's bag, and they'd both snorted up a couple of lines each before pulling off their clothes. She'd wanted him quite a lot by then. She'd felt flush and racy when they'd hit the bed, pulling her legs up tight, lifting her hips, urging him into her.

He'd given her what she'd wanted, exhausting himself, and for the first time that long, hot dusty day she'd felt at peace. As he rolled off, she'd stretched out her short, muscular legs and squeezed her thighs together and then completely relaxed. She'd closed her eyes, and drifted away into a warm, dreamy sleep.

Now she was awake again, but in the strangest way. She could see, and hear, and feel the peculiar tingling.

But she could not move.

She could open and close her eyes, could turn her head, ever so slightly. But her arms and hands and fingers wouldn't budge. She demanded of her legs that they move, that one foot lift and cross the other, but nothing happened. Except for the tingle, her bones and tissue seemed so much nothingness.

Vicky thought—hoped—that she might somehow still be asleep, that her dreaminess was an actual dream from which she would soon awake. But a woman's sudden, clear, loud laughter coming from the room below seemed to rebuke her for her foolish, forlorn notion. She was awake. Everything was very real.

And she could not move. She strained. She willed herself to stir

*2*

with such horrendous effort she feared she might hurt herself inside. She saw her arm shift and fall to her side. But nothing more.

Vicky now became very frightened. She tried to speak but heard only a weird, gurgling exhalation. Again she tried, but all she could produce was the same monster noise. The strain of her vocal effort made her feel faint.

What the goddamn hell was wrong? What had happened? Had Meade bound her to the bed? She could feel no strap, no cord. From what she could see of her own naked flesh—the curves of her breasts, her forearm and motionless hand—there were no restraints.

There was a gentle, almost imperceptible motion to her chest— the tiny, rhythmic act of breathing. She calmed herself, concentrating on the sensation. She was small, but very strong, as full of stamina as a good distance horse. Whatever had gone wrong with her, she was resisting it, holding up, her strength surviving. Perhaps this would pass, this strange and awful thing. She must be having a bad reaction to the mix of alcohol and cocaine. It happened. Some people died of it. She was strong. She was not in a coma. Her heart was working. She was breathing, though sound now came to her ears all fuzzy, buzzing and fuzzy. Fuzzy Wuzzy was a bear. Fuzzy Wuzzy had . . .

Her mind locked on the sudden, remembered image of a horse she had put down a few weeks earlier, after it had failed a mere three-foot timber jump. It had stumbled and fallen, spraining a foreleg. Furious with the feckless, balky beast, she had treated the injury as Meade might a deadly fracture. None of her husband's various poisons were at hand to inject into the creature, but she had found some "elephant juice"—etorphine—an analgesic that full strength could be eighty thousand times as powerful as morphine. A careful, measured dose could extend a horse's endurance wondrously, could smother all the pain and strain of a hard stretch drive.

She had given the animal ten times the normal dose, yet it had taken so long to die. The shot had instantly paralyzed it, rendering it a lumpy pile of meat and bone and hide upon the grass. But its eyes had remained alive. They had bulged, staring at her with fear and fury.

Did her eyes look like that now?

Another thought. Horrible thought. Searching the memory. Remembering a tiny, stabbing pain. Where? In a funny place. In the side of her buttock. A quick, sticking prick of pain. Like a thorn or nettle. Just below her hip. It was what had awakened her. She'd

*3*

thought it was from a sharp stitch in the bedspread, but that was wrong.

Something now was moving in the room, a shape emerging from the gloom of a corner. It came near, and became a face. Curious face, staring intently, as Vicky had stared at the dying horse. Dead horse.

The face turned away. Hands reached over her husband, lifting his arm, opening his hand. Vicky saw an object—long and thin and shiny. A syringe. It was placed in her husband's hand and his fingers were curled over it. Then hand and needle were gently lowered. Disappeared.

Needle. There had been a prick of pain in her hip.

She heard a word, softly spoken, spoken as two distinct words. "Good bye." A farewell. A finality. Then silence.

The shadowy face returned, peering close. Then a terrible smile. But no further word. The face withdrew. For a long moment, there was nothing. Then one last sound. The dull thud and click of the door closing.

Vicky tried to cry out, raging, begging for the face to return, but this time she could not even produce the gurgling. So she shouted inside, to herself, furiously, wrenchingly, hopelessly, hatefully.

"Elephant juice." She must have been given elephant juice. She was suddenly as terrified as a child who had just reasoned out mortality, the inevitability of the end of all life. The certainty of what was happening to her was awesome. And maddening and inescapable.

It was done.

It was as irretrievable as a bad jump realized in midair. She was dying. She was dead. Vicky Clay, twenty-six years old. Finished. Ended. In a very short time, she would be nothing. Forever. Forever and ever and ever and never again. What she had done to so many horses had just been done to her. She wanted so fiercely to scream.

How long would it take? How long could it? Hours? Minutes? Lying stiff and still and soundless. Imprisoned in her own corpse. Next to this wretched man, this rotten son of a bitch. Just inches away. Already dead? At peace? Or dying like herself? Was he as miserable as her? Or happy and gloating and satisfied? Was this his doing? The son of a bitch. The bastard. The self-righteous, whining motherfucking cocksucking loser asshole bastard dirty sonofabitch. She hated him with white-hot, incandescent hatred. She hated the face she had just seen, hated not knowing why this was being done to her, hated, hated, hated. HATED!

Fury and despair combined within her like a combustible mixture, exploding in a sudden burst of desperate struggle.

Her head lifted, and in a last, flailing thrust, her torso rose and twisted. She fell over on her side, one arm and hand now pressed against Meade's skin. Her fingertips felt nothing, but she sensed the pressure against them.

She lay motionless for a moment, waiting for the oxygen to accumulate again, her face next to the leathery flesh of his neck just millimeters away. The light was dimming, growing dark around the edges of her vision. Only little wisps of life left. She gathered the very last of her energy, and directed it now as will, forcing a motion of her fingers, a motion fueled only by the grimmest determination and purpose. She would not simply stop, simply end, simply vanish. She would leave something behind. A name. Keep mind on name. A brand. A name. Leave the name. Biting and scraping and digging. Again and again. Darkness complete. Silence. She lost all sense of time. Hours, minutes, days, it was all the same. But she was going now. Slipping down the slope, slipping beneath the sea. Drowning in infinity, spinning into nothingness. Only her fingers alive. Digging and scraping, in spasms. Then still. Very still. All gone. All was . . .

# Two

There was a crisis in Belize. Not a hell of a lot of excitement. Not World War III. Belize was barely a country. If the British hadn't clung to it for so long as a little banana colony, it would have become part of Mexico or Guatemala long ago. But now there was trouble there, and Mexico and Guatemala were probably part of it. Belize was nothing. Guatemala was next to nothing. But Mexico was a big deal. So Robert Moody was worried. The president might not be very concerned, even though he had won the Texas Democratic presidential primary largely with the Hispanic vote, but he didn't have to be. He had Moody for that.

What had happened in Belize happened all the time in Latin America. Some cabinet minister had been ambushed in his car and the government was blaming Guatemala. Some Guatemalan citizens had been arrested and the Guatemalan government was threatening retaliation. There had been some shooting on the border and between Belizean police and unidentified parties. The nasty stuff appeared to be over in a few hours, but it remained an official crisis nonetheless, with the U.S. embassy in Belmopan put on full security and a couple of navy destroyers standing by off the coast near Belize City. A National Security Council crisis management team had gathered in the White House situation room. The NSC had standing orders to do this at the first sign of any trouble. In the next election, Moody was not going to give the Republicans any chance to call his Democrats international softies and wimps.

But where was *he*, Robert Moody, the goddamned White House chief of staff, for crying out loud? *He* was standing here in a

Virginia country inn in a fool place called Dandytown seventy miles from the capital and talking about these high-priority matters with some sleepy National Security Council duty officer over a pay phone. He'd boot a subordinate halfway across the Washington Ellipse if he caught him or her discussing a national security matter over a pay phone.

"This line's not secure," Moody informed the man on the other end.

"Not secure. Understood, sir."

"You're sure the president's been informed?" Moody said. He pressed the receiver close to his ear. He was in the Dandytown Inn's central hallway, the crowded noisy bar to one side and the crowded, noisy dining room to the other. The steeplechase weekend had drawn people from all over Virginia and Maryland, and even the inn's lobby was full of them, talking and laughing, all very loudly.

"Yes sir. General St. Angelo gave him a full report."

"And?"

"That was all, sir."

"What was the president's response? Does he want me to come in? What did he say?"

It would take Moody a good hour and a half to get back to the capital, unless he called for a helicopter.

"He just said to keep him informed of developments—as they occur, if they occur."

The president was up at his seashore retreat in Wellfleet, on Cape Cod, taking another of the long weekends he insisted on no matter what else was happening in the world, communing with nature as though he were Henry David Thoreau and not the leader of the mightiest nation on earth. When he got in these moods he'd completely isolate himself from Moody and the rest of his staff, taking with him only a secretary and a small Secret Service detail. He'd urged Moody to go on a similar retreat.

"Get off by yourself for the weekend, Bob," he had said, in that paternal, patronizing, upper-class way of his. "Get some rest. Stay off the phones. Enjoy yourself. Our greatest work lies just ahead. I want to be able to call on your full energies."

If it weren't for Moody's "full energies," the man wouldn't have been elected in the first place.

"What about the secretary of state?" Moody asked.

"We tried Geneva, sir," said the national security officer. "Can't locate him. He's gone mountain climbing."

For a fleeting moment, Moody thought of zooming into

Washington—chief of staff to the rescue—taking charge of whatever was going on in Central America while the nation's principal diplomat, a Dartmouth mope named Charles "Skip" Hollis, was off in Switzerland supposedly attending a United Nations conference, but essentially engaging in a little junketeering to indulge his fondness for rock climbing, more likely some foothill than the Matterhorn. Though a friend of the president's and a man born to wealth, the secretary of state was an empty-headed chump who couldn't tell Belize from Spanish Harlem. He was one of the president's biggest cabinet mistakes and a lot of people in Washington expected him to be out of office by the end of the year. If the Belizeans and Guatemalans started having at one another, and Moody was in place doing Hollis's work for him, it could be just the nudge that was needed.

But it would also be a little obvious. And besides, it was hard to tell just what the hell was going on down there in Central America.

A little jab wouldn't hurt, however.

"Has anyone talked to the Belizean ambassador?" Moody asked.

"No sir."

"Well, have someone send him a message from the White House, authorized by me, warning that any harm done to U.S. citizens or property will be viewed seriously. Send another one to the Guatemalan ambassador."

"Yes sir."

"And find out what the Mexicans are doing."

"Yes sir."

"And keep me informed."

"Yes sir."

"Now switch me up to Wolfenson. He should be in my office."

"Yes sir."

As Moody waited to be transferred to his principal aide, he noticed a tall, very slender man in riding clothes standing in the shadows of the hall nearby. The fellow had silver hair and looked close to forty, yet he wore the black riding boots, white breeches, and blue blazer that marked him as one of the steeplechase jockeys. Could jockeys be that old? This steeplechasing was nothing at all like any horse racing Moody knew about.

"Can I help you with something, friend?" Moody asked the man. The fellow was more than six feet tall, very tan in the way of these horse country outdoorsmen, and handsome, though his nose appeared to have been broken and he had a slight scar on the side of his face. Moody had seen him before, probably in Washington, but couldn't recall exactly where.

"I'm just waiting to use the phone," the man said.

"Well, I'm talking to the White House."

"Oh yes. Of course. Terribly sorry." He moved back, taking a position in the doorway of the bar, politely out of earshot.

His speech was refined—that odd, old Virginia aristocratic accent that Moody had heard too much of in his life. It had the same Old English origins as the speech in his native West Virginia, but it was not at all the same. He knew this man, but from where?

Suddenly Moody felt self-conscious, especially about his dress. This was a country weekend, and he was wearing a suit, a dark, Brooks Brothers pinstripe that stood out like a clown costume in contrast to the more casual sport coats and blazers of the wealthy locals. His new wife, Deena, had chided him when they were getting ready for dinner, saying the boardroom suit in these surroundings made him look like a redneck dressed up for church. She had said it in her playful, jesting way—little ol' Southern accent thick as her perfume—but as usual she was woundingly close to the mark. Moody was a man born in the hollows, and for all his fine education and millions, it still showed. His lank, black hair, pink, raw-boned face, sharp chin and long neck—none of it seemed to go with the expensive garb he favored, or with the immense power he enjoyed.

What did impress people about Moody—what invariably intimidated them into respectful silence and circumspection—were his burning dark eyes, full of his intelligence and, not so occasionally, his anger and meanness. He glared at the tall, silver-haired jockey. The man looked away, and then at his watch.

"Mr. Moody!" said a new voice on the phone. "How's your weekend going?" Wolfenson's eagerness was as annoying to Moody as the security officer's lethargy.

"Anything going on I need to know about? Aside from the shoot-'em-up in Central America?"

"No sir. Well, Senator Reidy called. Said there was a problem with the Earth Treaty, but he was handling it."

The handsome jockey was watching him, frowning slightly.

"What problem?"

"He said he was having some trouble with Senator Sorenson, that he might be backing away from his commitment. He said not to worry; he'd take care of it Monday."

**9**

"Monday! The goddamned committee may take a vote on the thing Tuesday morning! Where is Sorenson?"

"I don't know."

"You don't know? Then why are you there? Where's Reidy?"

"He said he was spending the weekend on some boat. He called from Annapolis."

"Find out what boat! Have him call me!"

"Yes sir!"

Moody hung up without a further word. The gentleman jockey straightened.

"It's all yours," Moody said, as close as he would come to apologizing for keeping the man waiting.

"Thank you, Governor," the man said, politely.

The fellow was at least aware of the fact that Moody, before he had become the president's chief of staff, had been the Democratic governor of the state of Maryland, much as that seemed to matter in Virginia.

"S'all right," Moody said.

The people of the horse country were as tribal as the Scottish clans and as feudal as medieval England. The ruling families—Lynwood Fairbrother's in Dandytown, the Arundels in Middleburg, and the Mellons in Upperville—were as powerful in their way as the barons of the Magna Carta. Their wives and daughters controlled the social life of their communities absolutely, presiding over the rituals and pageantry of the steeplechase races, horse shows, and fox hunts like queens and countesses at court.

The breeders, trainers, and riders were nobility, too. Kitty Beveridge of Middleburg and Alixe Percy of Dandytown had won so many firsts in area horse shows that the ribbons strung from their stable tents at area competitions resembled the battle pennants flying at medieval tournaments. Young Patrick Worrall of the Sheppard-Worrall stables had taken two Virginia Gold Cups before he was twenty. Speedy Smithwick of Middleburg had won more than a hundred races. Captain David Spencer Showers, the silver-haired rider Moody had encountered by the telephone but not recognized, had won more than thirty major events, despite a foreign service career that had kept him abroad for years at a time.

Horse country was a kingdom unto itself, running through the Piedmont and rolling foothills of the Appalachian Mountains from South Carolina all the way up to New York's Hudson River Valley. Virginia was the heart of this kingdom. The other states within the realm had their own aristocracies, but none were so proud or ancient as the Old Dominion's. Speedy Smithwick was not only many times a champion; one of his forebears had sold Robert E. Lee his legendary horse Traveller. The Dandytown horse farm Captain Showers struggled to maintain had been in his family since before the American Revolution. In Washington, he was just another midlevel State Department bureaucrat. Here in the horse country, he was a chevalier, a knight, a mounted noble.

The famed steeplechase course designer Raymond Woolfe had once written: "Steeplechase horses are the bravest and most severely tested of their species (now that the war horse is obsolete). They are in a real sense, the last horse warriors. Their riders, by the same token, are the last of the tournament knights. In a world getting short on tradition and individual spirit, steeplechasing still offers men and women a rare opportunity to roll the dice for that fleeting taste of glory. The stakes laid are the ultimate, life itself, but in a single day, in a single encounter, they can thumb their noses at the everyday routine and dare to do what most of their fellows shy away from for a lifetime. Through the danger they feel their mortality, an uncommon sense of what it is to be alive, and they feel that it is a prize worth the risk."

A woman had once given that quotation to Showers before a major race. He still carried it, as fighter pilots might a lucky piece.

After taking his turn at the phone, Showers went into the bar, embarrassed when his entrance prompted a scattering of applause. He had ridden in two races that afternoon, winning one of them and losing another only after taking a bad fall on a timber jump. He was walking now with a slight limp.

The most enthusiastic applause came from two women at a corner table, Alixe Percy, his neighbor and lifelong friend, and young Becky Bonning, who lived on Showers' farm and helped him with his few horses.

"David!" said Alixe, her broad, booming voice loud enough to be heard by everyone in the room. "Where the hell have you been? Upstairs with a lady?"

Alixe was a large, bluff, cheery, and reflexively profane woman whose family predated even Showers' in Virginia. Her vast, sprawling horse farm, the next up the road from his, was one of the largest estates in Banastre County, almost as big as Lynwood Fairbrother's. She was Showers' best friend in the horse country. In their youth she had been something more than that. Sun, weather, work, and strong drink had coarsened her beauty, which had once been considerable. Alixe was into her fifth bourbon whiskey of the night, though by no means ahead of everyone else in the room. Back in Washington, especially among the foreign officers at State, wine and mineral water were now the rule. Here the custom still ran to whiskey and gin—on celebratory nights like this, by the bucket.

Showers was in no mood for wine or mineral water. After making a slight bow to the ladies and pulling up a chair, he ordered a straight scotch from the girl who hurried up to take his order.

"I was down at the barns," he said to Alixe. "Asleep. By myself. The doctor gave me something for my knee and it knocked me out."

"Leg still hurts, eh?" said Alixe. "A few more spills like that and you'll have to retire to carriage driving, like that geezer Prince Philip."

"Are you all right?" said Becky, with almost wifely concern. "We went ahead and ate without you."

"I'm fine," he said. She seemed excited. It couldn't have been just because of his winning an unimportant race.

Becky Bonning was very young, barely more than twenty, a stocky, pleasant-faced girl with sun-bleached hair pulled back in a ponytail. Her features were a trifle too horsey for anyone to call her pretty, but she came close, especially when she was happy and animated. She had large, quick blue eyes, and an enormous smile, which she turned on Showers as he sat down. Becky was probably the best rider in the county, though she competed only in horse shows, her interest in racing limited to Showers' efforts. Fanatical in her devotion to animals, she was troubled by the danger and cruelty inherent in steeplechasing, and utterly despised the blood sport of fox hunting, even though Showers belonged to the Dandytown Hunt.

The captain—Showers carried the title as a member of the Virginia National Guard—stretched out his injured leg, wincing slightly.

"I am getting too old for this," he said.

"You didn't have a bad day," said Becky. "You had a win."

"I'm not going to pay off the mortgage winning three-thousand-dollar purses for other owners."

"Depends on the fucking race, dear heart," said Alixe. "Did Fairbrother talk to you about riding Moonsugar in the Dragoon Chase tomorrow?"

The Valley Dragoon Chase, with a $15,000 purse, was the biggest race of the weekend. Showers' father had won a Virginia Gold Cup, but never the Dragoon Chase, and never the Old

Dominion National Cup, the biggest race of Dandytown's fall season.

"He talked to me about it," Showers said. "Hasn't made up his mind."

"That's a big horse," said Alixe. "He'll need a big rider."

Showers flexed his leg. "He needs one who can stay in the saddle."

"You'll be all right," Becky said. "You just spend too much time behind a desk."

The waitress brought Showers his scotch. Becky watched carefully as he took his first sip.

"I have a surprise for you," she said. "We're rid of Billy. He's agreed to the divorce. He's coming for the last of his things tonight."

Billy Bonning was her husband. Becky had run away from home to marry him, or used him as an excuse for running away from home—in any event, her first big wrong decision as an adult. Showers had let them live on his farm, a mistake in the case of Billy. He was not only a lout, but collected guns and swords and watched X-rated horror movies late at night on a VCR when Showers was away in Washington. Sometimes Vicky Clay came over to watch them with him. She was Bonning's sister.

"Thank God," he said.

"Tell him the other surprise," Alixe said.

Becky beamed. "You're going to buy a horse at the auction tomorrow night."

He smiled. "I can't afford the horses I own now," he said.

"It's a stallion. From a very good line. Do you know how good a line? His third dam was Queen Tashamore."

She uttered the last two words brightly, as though they were a magic formula guaranteeing eternal happiness.

Showers lowered his glass slowly. "Third dam" meant the stallion's great-grandmother. Queen Tashamore was the last horse Showers' father had let go when he'd finally been compelled to sell off all his bloodstock to pay off debts. She was the finest brood mare the Showers family had ever owned.

"I didn't notice any such horse in the catalogue," he said.

"He'll be in an addendum they'll put out tomorrow night before the auction. Vicky Clay told me about him."

"Vicky?"

"She heard Bernie Bloch talking about him, saying he'd go for a low bid. She didn't know why he was interested, but she thought you'd be. Queen Tashamore!"

Bloch, a Baltimore billionaire newly come to steeplechasing, was sitting with a group of sycophants at a big table in the center of the room. Vicky Clay was his trainer. Vicky's brother Billy had just gone to work for Bloch as well, after Showers had ordered him off his farm.

"Bernie Bloch wouldn't know Queen Tashamore from Flicka," Alixe said. "Common, common, common."

"If Mr. Bloch is interested in that horse, there's no point in my trying to bid on him," Showers said.

"You don't know that!" said Becky. "He might not bid at all. And if you don't someone else might pick him up for five or ten thousand. How would you feel then?"

"Since I don't have five or ten thousand, just fine. Becky, I haven't even seen this horse."

"Let's go look at him."

"Not tonight."

"In the morning."

He smiled. "All right."

"The captain may be tired in the morning," said Alixe. "Her Ladyship approacheth, with a slight list."

She was looking past his shoulder. He turned, a little anxiously, to see a woman coming toward them with wobbly step but great purpose.

Her name was Lenore Fairbrother, and, if Dandytown had a reigning monarch, she was it, though less a Queen Victoria than a Charlotte the Mad. Some twenty years younger than her almighty husband, Lynwood, she would have been of consequence in the community even if she was not married to the town's richest man. A native Virginian born to land and horses, if not all that much money, she was a remarkable beauty famous for it not only in Banastre County but Richmond, Washington, and London—cities she had invaded and conquered through clever marriages, including one to a knighted barrister, and her legendary parties, one of which had lasted a full week and been the cause of three divorces. Though now Fairbrother's wife, she had kept the title "Lady," and insisted everyone use it, at least now and again.

An almost anorexically thin woman, tending to boniness, but possessed of most wonderful bones, Lenore had very fine English features and wore her long, ash blond hair held back from her face with a gray silk hair ribbon that matched the color of her eyes. She

*14*

was wearing a summery floral print Laura Ashley dress with lavender sash and shoes, the ensemble a little too young for her and much more suitable for the royal enclosure at Ascot than rural Virginia. She carried a drink in one hand and a beribboned picture hat in the other, as though for balance. She had known Showers since childhood, but it had seemed odd to many in Dandytown that he had been one of her many husbands. Not her sort. Practically no money.

"David, you wretched swine," she said, stumbling to his chair. "You haven't spoken to me all day, even though I cheered for you till I was hoarse—as hoarse as a horse."

He started to rise, but she abruptly sat down in his lap, causing him to wince.

"What's the matter, darling?" she asked. "Did I hurt your little thingie?" Her accent was more than a little English, though she hadn't moved to that country until she was thirty. She was now nearly forty, and her beauty, of a sudden, was beginning to go.

Showers flushed, but said nothing. She sipped from her drink, peering over the rim of her glass at the other women at the table.

"Hello, darlings," she said. "Are you as bored tonight as I am?"

"I've never been that bored in my life," Alixe said.

Becky just stared at Lenore bleakly. Showers seemed decidedly uncomfortable.

"David," Lenore said, after sipping again. "I've simply wonderful news. Lynwood wants you to ride Moonsugar in the Dragoon Chase tomorrow."

Showers studied her carefully. Lenore often made up good news—and bad. "Are you sure? He seemed to have doubts."

"I am absolutely, positively, certainly sure," she said. "He decided at dinner. He was going to tell you himself, but he's wandered off someplace. In any event, my dear boy, you're to come to our stable in the morning."

"David," said Becky, sounding like a little girl denied a promised trip to the zoo. "We're going to the auctioneer's in the morning."

"Well, whoop de doodle do," said Lenore.

Showers hesitated. "We'll go there, too," he said.

"Now for my reward," said Lenore.

"Your reward?"

"For persuading him!" she said, looking very mischievous. "You don't think he'd pick a broken-down old has-been jockey with a gimpy leg like you without a little persuading?"

Showers said nothing, aware of how many in the room were

watching them. Lenore leaned back unsteadily a moment, then flopped her picture hat onto his head and bent beneath its brim to kiss him.

Becky left the table without a word.

"Who the hell is that guy?" Moody asked.

He had rejoined Bernie Bloch's party at the big table in the center of the barroom. His wife, Deena, was chattering happily away with Bloch's wife, Sherrie, and other guests, allowing Moody an interlude to gaze unguardedly at the goings-on at Showers' table.

"Don't you know him, Bobby?" said Bloch, a bald, overweight man with huge bags under his dark eyes and the breezy manner of an affable New York cab driver. Improbably dressed in a bright Madras plaid sport coat, lime green pants and blue Lacoste polo shirt, he was Moody's former business partner and oldest friend. His assets totaled more than, as he would put it, "a unit"—one billion dollars, fifty times Moody's net worth.

Moody, still staring, shook his head.

"He works for you," Bloch said. "For your administration, anyway. He's with the State Department. Captain David Showers, the Sir Galahad of these parts."

Moody's memory, usually excellent, had lapsed in this case, but with a little effort, he made the connection. An image of Showers in a dark diplomat's suit finally came to mind. The man had indeed been in the White House, attending a meeting Moody had called on the Earth Treaty. He'd been introduced as Spencer Showers, the Spencer likely a middle name. The Ivy League types at State loved to use their middle names, as though it made them special—an American nobility.

Moody recalled further that Showers had seemed fairly sharp, answering intelligently all the questions put to him, and making a sensible suggestion about enlisting the aid of the Canadian embassy in encouraging more support for the bill. Why hadn't he recognized him? There was too much to remember, running the White House. It was much worse than being governor.

"Where does he get off calling himself 'Captain'?" Moody asked.

"He is one," Bloch said. "In the National Guard or reserves or something."

Moody had been a marine captain in Vietnam, where he'd won the Silver Star. He was still a lieutenant colonel in the reserves, but no one in the White House ever called him "Colonel," though he'd let it be known that he wouldn't mind.

"Who's the woman on his lap?" Moody asked. He had seen her at the steeplechase course that afternoon. She was hardly as voluptuous as Deena, but something about her attracted him. She had a few years on her, but was still a beauty, sleek, like a fashion model, and probably very rich.

"That's Lynwood Fairbrother's wife," Bloch said.

Deena suddenly stopped her chatter. Following Moody's gaze, she observed Lenore Fairbrother quite intently.

"Do I know Lynwood Fairbrother?" Moody asked.

"You ought to. He's a player. The biggest name in steeplechasing out here. He also races horses on the flats, up at Pimlico and Belmont. Saratoga, too. He and his wife are part of that Mary Lou Whitney set."

"He's just a horseman?"

"Shit no. He owns more coal mines than I do. And a couple of big banks. He was up for ambassador to England when the Republicans were in office, but they withdrew his name because of his wife. She's got a bad reputation in England. Too many lovers. Too many drinks."

Moody stared at her solemnly, and then not so solemnly. He looked away when he realized Deena was watching him.

"Bernie," she said. "What happened to that little red-haired girl who works for you? She seems to have abandoned us."

"Vicky Clay? She's probably out in the stable screwin' somebody. We won't see her again until morning."

"But you have a big race tomorrow."

"Don't matter. She's got that stallion into the best shape I've ever seen him. Bet your money on Bernie Bloch."

Showers, pleading his injured leg and the need to rest for the next day's race, finally managed to escape from Lenore, bidding a hasty good night to Alixe and others in the bar, knowing that the partying would go on for hours. "Depravity is so dreadfully boring," Lenore liked to say, "but there's nothing else to do."

As Showers expected, Becky was waiting for him in his Jeep Cherokee.

"I wasn't sure you were coming," she said.

"Of course I was coming."

"Shall I drive? Save your knee?"

"Thank you."

His farm was just three miles west of town, on a narrow, curving, hilly road that required a driver's full attention. He didn't feel like talking. She did.

"Do you want me to leave, now that Billy's gone?"

"Certainly not," he said.

"Everyone will talk."

"They always talk."

"I guess you've no one else to run the farm."

"No one else I'd want to run the farm. I wish I could pay you more." He touched her knee, but only briefly.

"I'd do it for nothing. You know that."

What she meant, he knew, was that she'd be happy to run the place as his wife, that there was nothing that would make her happier. He didn't know how to cope with such devotion, let alone repay it, but Becky should know better. He was bound to another. He had been for nearly twenty years.

"Someday you'll have your own place to run," he said to Becky. "And a husband and children to help you."

"I want to stay on your farm," she said.

She had been born Rebecca Gibbons, the daughter of a well-off Washington psychiatrist. He had first met her when she was a little girl riding in junior equitation competitions at the Dandytown Colt and Horse Show. She had spent much of her adolescence hanging around him and his farm. When her father had bought her a $150,000 horse for her sixteenth birthday, she had boarded it on Showers' farm, despite the long drive from Washington.

When she'd turned eighteen, she came to Showers' place to stay—as a runaway, with Billy Bonning, her husband of a few days, in tow. She'd married Billy less for love and his good looks than as a means of preventing her father from ordering her back home—and off to college.

Showers didn't like Billy Bonning. No one in Dandytown did. He and his sister Vicky were from a local family that dated back to the Civil War but had never amounted to anything before or since. Their father owned a small vegetable and cattle farm and junk car business. One uncle ran a gas station and tavern in Dandytown and another was a horse handler up at the flat-track race course in Charles Town, West Virginia. The worst thing anyone could be called in Dandytown was "common," and the Bonnings were considered the preeminent example of that. The other term used was "trash."

Because of an ancestor who had been a commissioned "lieutenant" in the band of Confederate thieves and brigands known as Mosby's Rangers, the Bonnings had been able to gain admission to both the Sons and the Daughters of the Confederacy, and Billy had made good use of the connection in prowling the periphery of the Dandytown social circuit in search of rich, gullible girls. He was a handsome fellow—blond, freckled, and muscular—and cut a good figure even in the cheapest rental dinner jacket. A lot of young women had gone to bed with him, but few had let him get near their money.

Showers had not been happy when Becky and Billy had appeared on his doorstep, but had let them stay, informing her father that he was doing so. The man had actually seemed relieved, apparently expecting that Showers would serve as a sort of chaperon. He supposed he had.

Under their arrangement, Becky cared for the horses, while Billy did the heavy work on the place. Not all that much was required. Showers owned only a brood mare that had foaled that spring, plus his fox hunting horse. Becky had her show horse, and there were three or four boarders in the stables. In return for the couple's labors, Showers paid them a small stipend and let them live rent-free in what had been the farm's servants' cottage, allowing them full run of the main house when he was away in Washington during the week or traveling abroad.

As Showers had feared, Billy had begun treating the place as his own, throwing parties for some of the younger horse people in the area and humiliating Becky by trying to hustle some of the prettier or richer young women. Billy had even put a daguerreotype of his Mosby's Raiders ancestor on the mantel. Showers had taken it down. He'd three times thrown Billy off the property—twice for stealing and once for hitting Becky. It was Showers who had urged Becky to divorce him and buy him off if necessary to make a quick, clean break of it.

"You said Billy agreed to a divorce," Showers said. "He's willing to sign papers?"

"Yes," she said, keeping her eyes on the twisting road. "We're going to see a lawyer in Culpeper next week."

"How much does he want?"

"He asked for a hundred thousand. I offered him twenty-five. He said he'd take fifty, plus the pickup truck."

"I'm afraid I can't help you, not with that kind of money."

"You don't need to. Daddy said he'd write the check. Only he wants me to go back to college."

"It's not a bad idea."

"I don't need a degree to ride a horse."

He didn't answer her.

"I just don't want to leave here," she said finally.

"Well, the University of Virginia is an hour away," Showers said. "If you can't get in there, Northern Virginia Community College is even closer."

"That would be all right with you?"

He hoped she wasn't misunderstanding. "Sure."

She drove a little faster.

The front gate to Showers' farm was hanging open, which annoyed him. His border collie, Hardtack, was a roamer, and was probably now out coursing across the fields in the darkness. The pickup truck Billy had claimed as his own was pulled up in front of the house by the main porch. As they parked next to it, killing the headlights, the screen door opened and Billy stepped outside, two or three rifles and an old cavalry sword cradled in his arms. He opened the door to the cab of his truck and set them gently inside. Weapons were the only things Billy treated gently. In the back of the truck was a large cardboard box and two old suitcases.

"You don't have anything of David's in there, do you?" Becky said.

"Fuck you," said Billy, and he disappeared inside.

"You'd better look through it," Becky said to Showers.

"That's all right," Showers said, loud enough to be heard within the house. "If anything's missing, I'll simply have him arrested."

"Fuck you, too!" shouted Billy from the hall.

A moment later, he struggled outside with another cardboard box, smaller than the other, but apparently heavier.

"Do you have everything from upstairs?" Becky asked. "All those horrible magazines and movies, including that one with the woman getting her throat cut?"

Sweating, Billy dropped the box into the back of the truck with a thud. He turned and leaned back against the rear fender, lighting a cigarette. He was dressed in boots, blue jeans, and a T-shirt, his normal outfit when he wasn't costuming himself as one of the local swells.

"I've got everything," he said.

"Where are you staying?" Becky asked.

"With Vicky and Meade. You can bring my mail there."

"I'll have the post office forward it. I don't want to touch any of those filthy magazines you call 'mail.'"

"You just make sure I get everything that's mine."

"And you just make sure you're at the lawyer's office on time. I don't want to be married to you one second longer than I have to."

"You seen Vicky?" Billy said. "I tried her room at the inn but she didn't answer the door. Can't find her anywhere."

"You didn't look in the right bedroom," Becky said.

Billy glanced at Showers. "Guess I know which one to find you in from now on."

Showers took a step closer to him, his knee hurting as he did so.

"Leave now, Mr. Bonning," he said. "I don't want to find you on this property again."

Bonning grinned defiantly. "Then maybe you ought to spend more time around here, Captain." Though he'd only just lighted it, he flicked his cigarette onto Showers' porch as a further gesture of contempt.

Becky went to extinguish it. Showers simply stood his ground.

"You're a jerk, Billy," Becky said.

"Fuck you," he said, getting into the cab. He paused to light another cigarette, then hit the ignition and gunned the engine, roaring in reverse onto Showers' lawn. Tires spinning, he ground the truck back onto the driveway and then down the lane to the road. A cloud of gravel dust hung in the air after he had gone.

Showers sat down on his steps, stretching out his injured leg.

"Do you want a drink?" she said. "I'm going inside to make sure he didn't leave anything behind."

"All right," Showers said. "A little scotch and water."

Two drinks on the night before a race was a lot for him. He would go to bed soon.

She put her hand on his shoulder and squeezed, a friendly gesture, but also a wifely one. "I'll be right back."

He slouched back against one of the tall white porch pillars, almost slumping, he was so weary. The day's racing had been very arduous, and, if he was not yet old, he was well past tireless youth. Halfway through his life. Perhaps.

If half done with life, what were his triumphs? The dusty ribbons and trophies cluttering his tack room? To be sure, he had a tack room. Perhaps that was triumph enough. He had somehow kept the farm, and a few horses, in stables meant for forty. After fifteen years in the foreign service—a decade and a half of carrying messages, sending communiqués and dispatches, relentlessly gathering ignored or ultimately forgotten facts—he still had his job; had in fact attained the high bureaucratic station of deputy assistant secretary of state for oceans and international environmental affairs. But what were his accomplishments? In all that time, the only meaningful enterprise to which he had devoted his labors was the Earth Treaty, the newly proposed global environmental charter that the president had made the chief priority of his administration—though few were giving it or the accompanying enabling legislation much chance of passage.

Showers had no wife. His parents were dead. A sister, who had come to hate the South, even the modern South that northern Virginia had become, lived an exile in Vermont and had not visited him in years. There was no one else except a dissolute newspaper-man cousin and Becky and Alixe and a few other friends. What difference would it make if he were to vanish from this place? If he were to climb into the Jeep and roar off into the night as Bonning had and never be heard from again?

He'd never do such a thing, of course. His frivolous, indulgent, careless father had paid little attention to his upbringing except for his riding, but his grandfather, a fierce old gentleman sternly representing all previous generations of Showerses, had from his early childhood on taught him principles. Simply put, they were honor, duty, family, and resistance to change. Showers had bound himself to them, but the last one had been difficult.

It was a moonless night, and the scented summer darkness was very close. The light from the house windows stretched in broad yellow panels across the lawn but barely penetrated the trees beyond. Fireflies flitted in the soft gloom, and there was the buzzing and bumping of other, larger insects.

There was never silence on such nights. Showers could hear the raspy croaks and peepings of frogs down by the creek, and the myriad sawing sounds of grasshoppers in the high pasture grass. A few wakeful birds mewed and called in the nearby tree branches. A dog barked somewhere, and then another. In the woods, other animals spoke, barely heard, unidentifiable.

These were supposedly tranquil, peaceful sounds—all part of the pleasure of life in this gentle country place. Yet it was, he realized, a sham, a romanticized confection. The reality was that the glow of the female firefly was a deadly lure, attracting males with which to mate but also others on which to dine. The birds were telling each other to stay away, to go to hell. The frogs were devouring masses of insects and the insects were devouring each other, and snakes and swooping owls and bats and bobcats were devouring everything they could. All of God's creatures, killing and eating each other, as they did every night and every day all over the earth. Man rhapsodized over this and called it nature, called it beauty, called it life.

Some near or distant day, perhaps some night like this, he would die, just like some firefly snatched on the wing. And generations after his death, this farm might be a suburban parking lot, or a barren plain, or a radioactive wasteland. No Earth Treaty could stay the explosive moment, a billion years hence, when the sun and all around it would flare cataclysmically and die. The few bright stars visible in the night haze; how many were just the expended, far-flung, slowly traveling light of now dead suns?

His thoughts surprised and depressed him. They had intruded upon his consciousness without invitation, like a nightmare into his sleep.

He was getting old. He needed a son, a daughter, a wife. Life was a great burden to bear alone. He was glad when Becky brought his drink and sat down beside him.

A soft, gathering breeze stirred the warm air and the smaller branches of the trees, making the summer scent more intensely fragrant. He sipped his drink and felt a little happier.

"Thank you," he said.

"Billy forgot one of his tapes," Becky said, holding up a videocassette. It was marked with a plain white sticker that bore only the word VICKY. "God only knows what's on it."

"Give it back to him when you meet with the lawyer," he said.

"Should we look at it?"

"No."

"I'm curious."

"Becky, just get him out of your life, as soon as possible."

She set the cassette down on the step and leaned back, her blouse pulling tightly against her large breasts.

"You're going back to your apartment in Washington Monday?" she asked.

"Yes. Of course. Have to." The ice clinked in his glass.

"Wouldn't it be nice if you didn't, if you stayed on here and just ran the farm?"

"Without my government salary, I'd lose this place."

"You could work up a business training and boarding horses. Alixe could help you with money."

"Becky, I've worked all these years to pay off my father's debts, not pile up new ones."

"My father could give us some money."

"We've been through all this before, Becky."

They sat quietly a moment.

"Now that Billy's gone," she said, "do you still want me to sleep in the cottage?"

"That would be best."

"What difference does it make? We're all alone out here. People will be saying things anyway."

"It makes a difference."

"You don't want me."

"Becky."

"Well, you don't."

"You're very dear to me, Becky. I couldn't manage this place without you. Let's just leave it at that. Let's not complicate things."

She drew her knees up and rested her arms on them, looking at her hands. She then removed her wedding band, studied it, and tossed it in the bushes.

"All right, Captain Showers. Whatever you say."

He heard an automobile coming along the road. Headlights suddenly appeared, swerving left and bouncing as the vehicle turned into his drive. Showers thought and feared at first that it might be Billy returning, bent on more trouble, but the vehicle was much lower than the pickup truck. It was a long, fancy motor car, a black Jaguar. When it came to a stop and the headlights went out, they could see the driver clearly.

"Go to bed, Becky."

"I guess that's where you're headed now, isn't it, Captain?"

"Just go to bed. Please. Good night."

She rose and leaned to kiss his forehead, then went to the end of the porch and down some side steps, disappearing into the shadows. The Jaguar's door slammed shut. Lenore Fairbrother stood a moment, her hand against the car for balance. Then, with a wicked smile, she reached to the back of her dress and began to come forward. With a wriggle of her shoulders, her dress fell to the ground. She stepped out of it and kept walking, reaching back this time for the catch of her brassiere.

She had on no stockings. By the time she reached Showers, she was wearing only shoes. She knelt before him, perhaps six feet away, like a supplicant in some Eastern religion.

"Lenore, please." He was so tired.

"Please?"

"Please don't. Not now."

She sat back on her haunches, her pale breasts catching the light.

"Why not?"

"I just don't think it would be the best thing you and I could do right now."

"But David, darling. You and I have made love all over Banastre County."

"That was a long time ago—and now you've married to Lynwood."

"More or less. But so bloody what?"

"Lynwood is my friend. It makes a difference."

She squirmed to make herself more comfortable. "Bosh. Come on, Captain. It will limber you up for tomorrow."

He only sighed.

"Like the first time, David. When I was such a blushing young virgin. Here in the grass. 'Oh white woman whom nobody loves, why do you walk through the fields in gloves, when the grass is as soft as the breast of doves?'"

They'd been only twenty then. She hadn't been a virgin, and two years later, she'd left him for a moneyed older man from Philadelphia. Showers had no money. It took him many years to get over the sadness, but he'd wished her well.

"Please, Lenore."

"Please, indeed. You owe me quite a debt, sir. Lynwood wouldn't have let you ride Moonsugar if I hadn't prevailed upon him with my lovely charm."

"You may choose to believe that."

She began to laugh, then stopped. Her voice became soft and melancholy, almost poetic. She always knew what got to him.

"When I lay there, such an innocent girl, my hair spread in the grass, you swore an oath to me. You pledged yourself to me forever. My lover and my champion."

For all the heat and smell of whiskey, for all his weariness and distress, the beauty of this odd moment was not lost on him—a lovely woman even lovelier in her nakedness, kneeling before him in the soft summer night, offering him the oblivion of abandon; escape from all the wretchedness and emptiness of that day, of all his days.

"It would be quite dishonorable to deny me, after all those fine words long ago." She rose and came forward. "Someday I'll prove to you that Lynwood Fairbrother is not your friend."

He set down his glass, and let her come into his arms. Nothing his grandfather had taught him had prepared him for Lenore. No one ever denied Lenore anything—not when she really wanted it.

He touched and held her breast. They kissed, her warmth one with the summer night. His hand slid to her waist and hip and below. And then he froze.

"David . . ."

"No." He released her and moved away. "For God's sake. I'm going to ride his horse tomorrow."

"Oh, please, David. Please? Pretty, pretty please, darling? I know how much you want me. Your thingie's very hard. I could feel it, David." She moved close to him again. "I must have you tonight. Tonight, tonight, another night of nights, to remember forever and ever and ever. Please?"

He stood up. "Stop it, Lenore. If you don't, I'll call Lynwood and have him come and get you."

"You wouldn't."

"I would. I'll just tell him you're drunk again and making a fool of yourself. Again."

"He never cares."

"I care. I can't stand it when you're like this."

The word "it" was in lieu of "you."

She folded her arms, an unhappy child. He expected her to say something nasty. She had a large repertoire of biting remarks suitable for such occasions. But she fooled him.

"David. I love you. You know that. Who have I ever loved but you?"

"You left me, Lenore. I asked you to stay and you treated it like an amusing joke."

"But David, you were so poor."

"So there we are."

They sat quietly for a long moment. A sudden noise proved to be Showers' border collie, bounding up the drive. He entered the reach of the house lights and stopped, looking at them, then bent back his head and neck to scratch.

"Oh, dear, dear David," Lenore said, rising. "You're such a prig."

With a sashaying walk, she returned to her car, getting into it and driving away without a second's backward look.

She left all of her clothes on his lawn.

# Three

The bodies of Vicky Clay and her husband lay undetected on their bed until late the next morning. The young chambermaid at the inn left their room until last, knowing it was occupied by Vicky and fearful, from embarrassing experience, of what she might well encounter were she to enter it earlier. Once, though there had been no DO NOT DISTURB sign hanging from the door and no response to her knock, she'd come in on Vicky sitting stark naked on the master of the hunt's face.

The first race of the day—a pony chase for young riders—began at eleven. A few minutes before, presuming everyone would be at the steeplechase course, the maid finally tried the Clays' door, but, glimpsing the naked forms on the bed, she closed it quickly, not returning for an hour. The next time, noting that the bodies were in exactly the same position, she hesitated on the threshold, saw how still and sickly yellow they looked, and became very worried. Peering more closely, she saw the bloody scratches on Meade Clay's back and the hypodermic in his hand. Frightened, she fled downstairs to the front desk.

The desk clerk, a young man not much older than the maid and like her a student at the University of Virginia, went unhappily upstairs to investigate. He came down again very quickly.

"They must have OD'd," he said, hastily dialing the phone. "I wonder what in the hell they were using."

"Are you calling the hospital?"

"Hospital? They're dead. Cold as ice. I'm calling the sheriff. God."

The line was busy. Nearly everyone in the Banastre County sheriff's department had been assigned to traffic and crowd control at the Dandytown steeplechase course that day.

"They must have been making love when it hit them," the young man said. "You should have seen the way she clawed his back."

"I saw," said the maid. She slumped down in one of the lobby chairs, and began to feel very ill.

The early June day was brilliant, the warm air full of the scent of grass and blossoms, the colors of sky, meadow, and green woodland so vivid and perfect the scene might have come from an antique painting. Only the line of expensive cars parked along the rail of the VIP section of the racecourse testified to the contemporariness of the moment. The mounted race officials in their hunting pinks, the jockeys in white breeches and racing silks, the gentlemen spectators in their elegant jackets and ladies in flowery summer dresses and picture hats—they all could have been figures in one of the framed equestrian prints so ubiquitous on the walls of Virginia horse-country houses.

Robert Moody appreciated the painterly scene. What preyed upon him was that he did not belong in it.

He was standing in a group of well-dressed people by the open trunk of Bernie Bloch's big Rolls-Royce Corniche parked at Bernie's "box" along the rail, a roped-off patch of grass in a prestigious location near the ornate wooden tower of the officials' stand. Bloch had paid a substantial amount of money for that box, but no amount of money, it seemed, would have sufficed to make the race fans in the adjoining boxes behave in friendly fashion to him and his guests. Moody had said good morning to an elderly woman in a flowered straw hat seated on a folding chair just across the rope divider from him, but she'd paid him no more attention than she would have to a buzzing fly. Perhaps she was hard of hearing, though he doubted it.

This was only Moody's second day of steeplechase but he was really coming to hate these people. Years before, when his daughter May was a little girl taking riding classes, he'd accompanied her to a few horse shows in Maryland, but he'd never mingled with the horse folk much, not even when he was governor of the state. They seemed inhabitants of another culture, another race. It wasn't simply their clothes or wealth or accents or obsessive habits. It was their attitude of difference, their unassailable nonchalance and perfect lack of self-consciousness, an unstudied poise that sustained them even when they were staggering drunk—even when they'd lost a big race. They lavished fortunes on their animals but never seemed to mind losing. It confounded him. Moody was a winner. He'd won at everything he'd put his hand and mind to—the law, real estate, politics, the Washington game. America made sense because it was a country that had always honored winners. These people only honored themselves, win or lose.

Moody rubbed his chin, wondering how soon he'd have to shave again. When he was feeling insecure like this, he sometimes shaved three times in a single day, scraping away at the damnable blue-black shadow that never left him.

It amazed him that his daughter could resemble him so greatly, yet be such an extraordinary beauty, an actress who had been celebrated in Hollywood as much for her looks as for her talent, which was considerable enough to have won her a Tony when she was working on Broadway.

May's long hair was as dark as his, as were her eyes, though her complexion was pale, like her mother's. Her features bore many hints of his, but showed more of the Irish in their ancestry. Slightly irregular, they lent her beauty a touch of wildness. He had called her "my little wild rose" when she was changing from girl to woman, when she still doted on him. He carried an old photograph of her from that time in his wallet.

Moody photographed horribly, but May had never taken a bad picture. He used to brag about her constantly, back when she was still talking to him, before he had left her mother.

Moody's hand came away from his face wet with sweat. He had bought the gray flannels and expensive tweed jacket he was wearing especially for this weekend—copying the style of horse people he had seen in *Town and Country* pictorials, forgetting that it was now the brink of summer, and that the swells and toffs he'd seen in the pictures were dressed for a different season—not this heat.

He wondered how many were noticing his discomfort. Probably everyone who saw him.

Anxious about Central America—the Guatemalan and Mexican armies had gone on alert—and the gathering threats to the president's pending Earth Treaty, Moody had been on the phone much of the morning. Secretary of State Hollis had been reached and informed of the Belize situation, but, with the president remaining on Cape Cod, had decided not to return.

Moody's people had tracked down Senator Reidy and Senator Sorenson and Moody had persuaded them both to meet with him at

**29**

the White House early Monday morning. During the night, there had been an oil tanker spill off the north coast of Florida, but that was good news. It would help the Earth Treaty.

Bloch walked up, handing Moody a gin and tonic. He'd been preparing drinks for his guests from the fairly elaborate bar he'd set up in the trunk of the Rolls.

"You look hot, Bobby," Bernie said. "Take off your coat. Relax a little. We're here to have fun."

Moody accepted the icy drink, nodding his thanks, but made no effort to remove his jacket. He'd read a lot of Thomas Wolfe when he was in college and there was a passage in *The Web and the Rock* that had never left him. It was about a visit by the young hero to a friend's very wealthy family in New York's Westchester County. The patriarch of that clan had insisted that a gentleman never removed his coat in public. Moody now never took his off, even when the president was in shirtsleeves.

"I'm all right."

"My trainer hasn't shown up. I wonder who she was screwing last night."

"She may have just been with her husband."

"Come on, Bobby. You know what she's like. You've given her a little poke yourself."

Moody looked away. "What are you talking about?"

"Last month, when we were all in Baltimore for the Preakness." Bloch gave him a friendly jab in the shoulder. "S'all right. Why do you think I keep her around? She's hell on my horses but she keeps my friends happy. Keeps me happy, too."

"She's a nice girl."

Bloch laughed. "She's a lot of things, but nice isn't one of them." He paused, lowering his voice. "I wouldn't fuck around with her anymore, Bobby. She's a cocaine junkie. She's done a little time on drug charges. A man in your position doesn't need that kind of trouble."

"I think you're exaggerating my interest in her," Moody said quietly.

"I'm glad to hear that."

"Why did you hire her?"

"I'm not too popular out here. She was the only trainer I could get who's any good with jumping horses."

"Shouldn't someone be looking for her?"

"She'll show up. She's probably just sleeping off her bad night."

He glanced at his other guests. "I gotta mingle. You should too. You're the politician, right?"

"I'm off duty."

"You've never been off duty, Bobby. Not in all the years I've known you."

Bloch moved away. He was wearing a lightweight baby blue blazer over a yellow Lacoste polo shirt that clung comfortably to his overlarge belly. Bernie always looked comfortable. Moody felt as miserable as he must look. The tweed seemed to bite through the back of his shirt like a weave of thorns.

His wife, Deena, was at the track rail, talking cheerfully with Bloch's wife, Sherrie, and another couple. Catching Moody's eye, she gave him a quick smile and tiny wave, then returned to her chatter. She didn't look as though she belonged here, either, though she'd tried. Her much festooned, wide-brimmed hat was too elaborate, her platinum hair too bleached, the pink of her dress and shoes far too bright and the bodice too flamboyantly low cut—the sort of clothes one would expect to see at a racetrack in Miami.

But she was happy, in what she considered "her element"—rich people, expensive cars and playthings, a very social setting. If anyone looked down on her, she pretended not to notice. She was Southern, originally from Kentucky. Women like her were good at that.

Fifteen years younger than Moody, she'd been a good wife to him thus far, as compliant and attentive in their public life as she was in their bed, always willing to do what he deemed correct or necessary or politic, his agreeable junior partner in the Washington game, where she was treated like a very major player by everyone except the first lady and her circle. What haunted him was the fear, bordering on certainty, that she would flee him in a moment should he lose his position—faster than that if he should lose his money. He was her third husband, and she was only thirty-eight.

The nation had elected at least one president who was a compulsive womanizer and another who had been divorced. It had never elected one with a wife who'd made a career of marriages.

Moody retreated to one of the white folding chairs set up to the side of Bloch's Rolls, being careful not to lean against the back as he sat down. He sipped his drink, impatient for the next race to begin, impatient for the entire racing program to be over.

It wasn't as though he'd been treated as a pariah. The race announcer on the official's stand had announced his presence along with other important guests and celebrities over the public address system. A number of people had come up to greet him or introduce themselves. But they were just Washington graspers—a lot of them rich, powerful Republicans of the sort ever on the hunt for friends who might aid them in the maintenance of their success and station in Washington, friends even in a Democratic administration like Moody's. They were here as guests. They didn't really belong, either.

In the distance, beyond the farthest rise of meadow, he could see the pale, hazy line of the Blue Ridge Mountains. Beyond them was the rugged, endlessly hilly terrain of the state of West Virginia. A hundred or more miles west of the border, lying in the fold between two long mountain ridges, was the wretched, ramshackle coal town where Moody had grown up—near it, the grubby little ramshackle village where he'd been born. He hadn't been back to either for more than two decades. Now they seemed oddly near, as though he could just get up and walk over that ridge on the horizon and be there.

He had wanted to go back, sometimes. Twice he had actually started the trip. But each time he had succumbed to a superstitious foreboding and turned away. It was as though the decaying little towns with their unpainted buildings and vacant stores and auto-strewn front yards might somehow reclaim him, enfold him in their poverty and ugliness, and never let him leave again.

His first wife, Geneva, May's mother, had gone back. He had made her a very wealthy woman by West Virginia standards with his divorce settlement—one of the richest women in the mountains—but she lived comfortably rather than grandly, using her money mostly to make a difference in the community. Moody had read in some government report or another that coal mining jobs in West Virginia had diminished by half since 1980. Through Geneva, his money was helping—a little.

The Earth Treaty, waiting for him back in Washington like an execution order condemning an old friend, could eliminate the rest of those jobs, if the Senate ratified it and the Congress passed the accompanying environmental legislation that would enable the government to comply with the treaty's strict terms. West Virginia coal was about the dirtiest in the nation.

Moody picked up his racing program, turning past the Mercedes-Benz and perfume and champagne advertisements to study the field for the next race, the Valley Dragoon Chase, a three-mile run twice around the course, over timber—unyielding three- and four-foot-high wooden fences that in a race the previous fall had killed a rider and three horses.

Bloch's mount, a big chestnut, was called Sherrie's Dream, a name that had prompted a lot of jokes about Bloch's wife's sex life. Bernie had said his biggest competition in the race was Lynwood Fairbrother's gray horse, Moonsugar. The rider listed in the program was Captain David Showers. Moody looked over at the paddock. Showers and the other jockeys were preparing their mounts for the race. He'd changed from his navy blazer to the pink and green racing silks of the Fairbrother stable. Showers was taller than the other riders, but not by much.

Moody thought for a moment of summoning Showers over at some point in all this equestrian pageantry. Make him stand obediently in the midst of Bloch's little Rolls-Royce circle here. Ask him how the State Department was coming with the various treaty analyses he had asked for. Dismiss the man after he gave his answer.

It was a bad idea. The arrogant charade would be recognized for what it was. Showers might not even respond, making Moody look like the chump. Moody had noticed a number of people out here like "the captain." Nobodies in Washington. Somebodies in Horse Land. One young woman was nothing but a press assistant in one of the Smithsonian museums, yet she had walked right up to the officials' stand as though she owned the place. The British ambassador had nodded to her as she passed, almost a bow. Moody recalled her last name. It was one he had seen in a local Washington society magazine. She had passed by him, too, without saying a word, even though the head of the Smithsonian was a friend of the president, and his phone calls came through Moody's office.

Having taken care of his other guests, Bloch returned, lowering himself heavily into the chair next to Moody's. He took a healthy swallow of his drink, belched, and then wiped his mouth with the back of his hand.

"Like it out here, Bobby?" he asked.

"I've been in the country before," Moody said, a little testily.

"This is a long way from West Virginia."

"Where I grew up, we didn't know people like this existed. I didn't meet any until I got to the University of Virginia."

"Most of them are all right. They're players, you know?"

"Republicans."

"Maybe, but players. You gotta play with the players." Bloch scratched his belly. "They like making money as much as we do."

"I've made my money, Bernie."

"You're not going to be in the White House forever."

Bloch's words had too many meanings. Moody searched his mind for a different subject, but was spared the effort when a woman who had come up behind them put her hand on Bloch's shoulder. Both men looked up, a little startled. It was Lenore Fairbrother.

"You're Bernie Bloch, aren't you, darling?" she said, her odd, almost English accent very strong. "I'm told you keep absolutely cases and cases of gin in that big vulgar car of yours. Could you be a dear boy and bring me a drink? I finished mine waiting in the damned potty line."

Bloch got clumsily to his feet. "A pleasure, Mrs. Fairbrother. A pleasure." He took her glass and went over to his car like a servant bidden.

"And you are?" she said, turning to Moody. Her lovely eyes seemed to have trouble focusing.

"My name is Robert Moody."

"Which is your horse?"

"I haven't any horse. I'm here as a spectator."

"No horse," she said, glancing over to the paddock, where the riders in the next race were now saddling and mounting up.

"I'm from Washington," Moody said. "I'm the president's chief of staff."

His remark, uttered as though in defense of his horselessness, sounded stupid.

"Chief of staff," she said, with a smile that was a quiet way of laughing at him. "Well whoop de doodle do."

Bloch hastened back with the refilled glass, saving Moody from a response. For an instant, he'd felt like hitting the woman. He'd never done such a thing, but his West Virginia father had.

He had another urge, too. There was more to that mocking smile than ridicule. It struck him also as a challenge, possibly even an invitation. This was a real lady, as much a thoroughbred as any of the horses in the paddock. He found himself even more excited by her than he had been the previous night, though he wished she were more sober.

"Thank you, dear boy. So terribly nice to meet you, uh, chief."

She took an unsteady step backward, sipping her drink, then turned in a great swirl and set off for the paddock.

Sweat was dripping off Moody's forehead and nose. He wiped it away.

34

"Hell," he said.

"Don't let her bother you," said Bloch. "She's like that all the time."

"She doesn't bother me," Moody said.

Bloch looked at his watch. "Not long now."

Moody watched the Fairbrother woman enter the paddock, stepping daintily over some horse dung. Bloch's jockey was already in the saddle, with two grooms attending to his mount.

"Aren't you going to talk to your rider?" Moody said.

"I never go near my horses, Bobby. Only when they're in the winner's circle."

The ground behind the VIP boxes sloped upward to the top of a long ridge that ran the length of the course. It had been the site of a sizable cavalry skirmish in the Civil War, a small if briefly fierce engagement won by the Confederates, who had caught their Union foes encamped on the summit and chased them from their tents and campfires across the plain and into the woods. A small historical marker by the highway memorialized the obscure event.

Tents were pitched on the summit again—not military but festively striped civilian tents offering shade from the sun and expensive refreshment for the guests of the wealthy racing folk and corporate sponsors. With their pennants and banners fluttering in the occasional breeze, they seemed almost medieval pavilions, as might be erected for kings and nobles attending a tournament.

Tables and chairs had been set up on the grass in front of most of them, the sanctuaries cordoned off by rope and marked by signs, politely warning, INVITED GUESTS ONLY. Robert Moody had no such invitation. As he did not know and would not for a moment have expected, his daughter May did. He had thought she was out in California, but she was in Virginia that afternoon, sitting there, looking down on him. She had come to Washington to sign a contract to play Rosalind in *As You Like It,* which the Folger Shakespeare Theater was presenting again that fall. One of the big financial contributors to the theater, a banker named Steven Granby, had taken her out to the steeplechase for an afternoon in the country. Her father was the last person she expected to see there. She would have thought he'd be at some congressional barbecue or hard at work at his office—not among all these horses and aristocrats. She'd known that in accepting a role in Washington she'd run the risk of encountering him again, but she'd imagined a different scene—his coming to the theater as an apologetic supplicant, asking permission to visit her backstage, permission she might not grant. She had been in town only two days, yet there he was, seated in a folding chair by the rail just below her, with that horrible Bernie Bloch, a man who made the sleazy little tyrants who ran movieland seem saints.

Granby, her host, was a nice, slightly star-struck, not unhandsome middle-aged man, as bent on showing her off as he doubtless was in pitching a little woo, maybe getting her into his bed. She had quickly discouraged both these aspirations, extracting his promise to return her to Washington before dinner.

May had looked forward to this outing in the country, but now she felt altogether miserable. It had been a shocking, painful surprise to find her father there. If it weren't for the embarrassment it would cause, if Granby hadn't been so enormously nice to her, she would have insisted on leaving at once, pleading the heat or headache or almost any excuse. Except for a brief, angry conversation over the phone when she was in California, she hadn't spoken to her father in nearly three years. Though the anger was gone, the hatred and resentment remained.

To her immense relief, he hadn't noticed her. He had glanced in her direction once or twice, but evidenced no recognition, apparently taking her for just another figure in the crowd, as she intended. Like many in her profession, she had learned the tricks of disguise. She was wearing very dark sunglasses, a light chiffon scarf over her head, and a wide slouch hat over that—the brim pulled down over her eyes in mysterious Marlene Dietrich fashion. Her host had introduced her to his friends only as "Miss Moody," and they had reacted with no more excitement or interest than if he had said "Miss Smith."

If these were people of taste and intelligence, they would hardly be familiar with her last few films, so dreadful they might not even be in video rental stores. May Moody, at the age of thirty, appeared to have lost her stardom, though she had never quite understood exactly what that was, or why it was.

"Are you having a good time, May?" said her host, resting his hand briefly on her shoulder.

"Marvelous," she said, flatly, and turned away from him to look at the jockeys getting ready for the race. Finally, he took his hand away.

Lynwood Fairbrother had promised Showers a $7,500 bonus if he won the Valley Dragoon Chase, precisely half the purse. The sum was nothing to him, but everything now to Showers. He and Becky had gone to the auction pavilion that morning to look at Queen Tashamore's great-grandson and now Showers ardently wanted that horse. Except for his great-grandmother, the stallion's ancestry wasn't terribly impressive, but the big animal was magnificently formed, an athlete who looked both fast and strong. According to his papers, he was five years old. With training, Showers might at last have a competitive steeplechase horse of his own. That the animal would restore the Tashamore line to the Showers' blood-stock was simply serendipity. It made the opportunity to buy the stallion seem divinely provided, if the price remained low.

The manager of the auction house said no one else had asked to look at the stallion, not even Bernie Bloch, despite his talking about the horse to Vicky Clay. Showers had a few thousand dollars in the bank. If he was able to take that $7,500 bonus from Fairbrother, he might have a chance to bring the animal home that night. This was a relatively small auction—not like Saratoga or Lexington—and a lot of the sales were for less than $10,000. There was a good chance this horse might have no other serious bidders.

The Dragoon Chase would be a most meaningful contest. No Fairbrother horse had ever won it. Neither Showers nor his father had ever won it. His knee still hurt and he was a little groggy from the night before, but he was truly up for this race.

Becky was holding Moonsugar's bridle for him as he rechecked the girth. Fairbrother's horse was big, seventeen hands, and very scopey—capable of any jump on the course at the fullest stride. But the gray gelding was young and inexperienced, prone to nervous-ness and fits of temper. He could become quite obstreperous if passed by another mount.

"I wish it were a little cooler," Becky said. "And a little breezier. He really doesn't like this heat."

"He'll be all right," Showers said.

"What about you?"

"I'm fine."

"You could have used more sleep."

Without responding, he took the reins from her and mounted. It was no business of Becky's what had happened last night—or hadn't.

Moonsugar began sidestepping, prompting Becky to snatch the bridle and hold the animal fast, taking control of the horse—and Showers.

Showers had known this racecourse all his life, had ridden it in a score or more of races, and had walked it again that morning. He studied it now from the saddle. To win, he would have to take the lead early and let Moonsugar run full out, hoping not only that the animal's endurance would last the distance but that it wouldn't kill itself in the process. The horse had only one speed it was happy with, flat-out, and once committed to it, there was no holding it back. Showers would have to work hard to collect the animal before each jump.

"This will be his best race," Showers said.

Becky frowned. Lenore Fairbrother, her owner's badge and ribbon readily admitting her to the paddock, had joined them, bringing a drink.

"Stirrup cup, my brave captain?" she said, offering up the gin and melting ice.

"After the race, Lenore," said Showers, uncomfortably.

"Very well, dear boy, then kiss my hand."

She raised her free one up to Showers' knee. He hesitated, knowing that the many eyes upon him included her husband's, then leaned forward and brushed her fingers quickly past his lips. Becky was looking at him as though the promised $7,500 was payment for his entertaining Lenore the previous night.

Moonsugar took another side step, throwing Lenore off balance and causing her to drop her glass.

"Oh, shit," she said.

"Time to go, Lenore," Showers said. He gathered in the reins, preparing to move off onto the course.

"Wait," Lenore said. "Take this." She snatched a piece of ribbon from her hat, handing it up to him.

"What am I to do with it?" he asked.

"Tuck it in your belt, dear boy. As you go bounding along, it will make you think of me. 'Valor, brave knight. You fight under fair eyes.'"

"Don't you think that's a little medieval?"

"Just like you, dear boy." She hiccuped.

He shook his head, smiling indulgently, shoving the ribbon into his boot top. With the merest flick of rein, he got Moonsugar into motion, heading onto the race course. Horse and rider towered above all around them.

"I've got ten large on this race," Bloch whispered to Moody as they moved from the chairs to the rail. "Sherrie's Dream to win. Gotta get something for what this is costing me."

"Ten thousand dollars? I thought people here only made two-dollar bets."

"My bookie in Baltimore is laying it off for me."

"I don't want to hear about bookies, Bernie."

"Relax, Mr. White House. You're not involved."

Deena came between them, hooking her arms in theirs. "What a beautiful sight," she said.

There were fifteen racing horses out on the turf, gathered nervously at the starting rope, looking like a cavalry troop about to begin a charge.

Deena was holding on to her husband and Bloch tightly, her eyes glittering with her excitement. "You should have us out here more often, Bernie," she said. "This is great."

Moody wondered which rider she was staring at, and why she was clinging to Bloch as closely as she was to him.

A recording of kettle drums was played over the loudspeakers, increasing to a crescendo. Suddenly it stopped, the starting rope dropped, and the line of horses and riders shot forward. The mount to Showers' left, a big coal-black thoroughbred named Inkydink, leapt into the lead. Moonsugar snorted after him, but took time in getting up to his stride, allowing a number of other horses to pull ahead as they pounded along over the meadow grass toward the first jump. A big chestnut bulged in on Showers from the right, the animal's hindquarters almost touching Moonsugar's right front shoulder. Moonsugar veered left, tossing his head in frustration, pulling into Inkydink's wake but crowded on the other side by another horse falling off the pace. In that position, they came to the first fence, sweeping over it as though lifted by the same hand.

Moonsugar cleared the obstacle with encouraging ease, but the wall of horsetails and rumps ahead had closed. Leaning into the oncoming turn, as the course descended into a shallow swale, Showers kept his mount in place, cursing this sabotage of his race plan. They splashed over puddled mud at the bottom and then dug into the turf of the ascending rise beyond, bits of dirt from the horse ahead stinging into Showers' face. Moonsugar's power carried him up with little strain, but they could make little headway.

At the next jump, the chestnut horse to their right faltered slightly, allowing Showers a chance to spring forward a length and ease to the outside, but he was still stymied. Moonsugar's strength would rot back here unless the field broke open, or he found some other path.

After the third fence, a murderous four-footer set at the climax of the turn, he made a decision, pulling his horse in front of the chestnut and then sliding far out to the right. It cost him time. He could see the lead horses pulling away as they thundered onto the back meadow, but, ticking over the fourth jump near the end of its rails, he found clear grass stretching invitingly ahead. He relaxed his pull on the reins and felt Moonsugar respond, as though he were pushing on a speed lever. One by one, the horses to his left began to slip behind him. After two more fences, he began to edge Moonsugar back into the center of the course.

He was lying fifth, sailing along unimpeded. It was quiet on this side of the course—no sound but the collective thud of the gallop. Showers might have been engaged in nothing more earnest than a Sunday fox hunt. He felt good, realizing he now had a chance. It was a long race, and Moonsugar was a horse for the distance. He stood high in the irons for a moment, stretching his injured right leg, then settled to a faster seat, letting his horse reach with his stride.

On the ninth fence, a rider went down, his mount bolting ahead, goaded by the flicks and glancing blows of the wildly flying empty stirrups. Showers looked back and saw the jockey roll to the side and rise to his knees, well clear of the pack. His concern for the jockey held his attention too long. He almost missed the approach to the next obstacle.

Moonsugar managed it easily without help or direction. The riderless horse was plunging along in fourth place, and they gained on it swiftly. The ground dipped and the course jogged a little to the right before curving left into the north turn. The timber of another jump flashed beneath. The third-place horse was faltering a little now, trailing Inkydink and Bernie Bloch's Sherrie's Dream, another chestnut, by two or more lengths.

Muddy clods scattering in the air, they came around toward the crowd now. The general admission spectators were at this end, jammed in a mob along the rail. Three jumps further along was the VIP section, fronting a long straight stretch without hurdles. Once they were onto it, Showers gave his mount full head, thwacking him twice with his light whip. They had another circuit of the course to go, but Showers put Moonsugar into what amounted to a stretch drive. If he didn't get his horse in front here, he never would.

With quick glances, Showers searched the stream of faces along the rail for Becky's. He couldn't find her, but noticed Lenore

Fairbrother all right. She was standing on the hood of her Jaguar, cheering him on with a raised glass.

The roar from the crowd drowned out the hoofbeats, becoming an overwhelming din. The third-place horse slipped behind him. Within four or five strides he began to pull even with Sherrie's Dream, and then slowly moved ahead, the other jockey looking worried and puzzled as he went by. The man finally gave whip to his horse, but it was too late. Showers gained a length, and then another. Moonsugar rolled along at top speed, happy in his effort. He went into the turn just trailing the leader, Inkydink, gaining ground with each of the next two hurdles. Both horses went over the fence after that together, stirrup to stirrup.

From then on, it was a two-horse race. The other jockey, a young man named Jimmy Kipp, appeared upset, confused to see Showers showing so much speed with so much race to go. He seemed hesitant, as though seeking some sure measure of his horse's remaining strength.

Showers gave Moonsugar the whip, just once. The animal jolted ahead, pulling a half length into the lead, then more. He was going full throttle now. Showers looked back to see that Kipp had decided to do the same.

As though stuck together, nose to tail, Inkydink trailing now, they lunged and bounded over the fences of the next turn. Moonsugar was winding a little, ticking the top rail of the jump at the end of the swale, his breath coming in snorts. Showers heard the same sounds from Inkydink, heard a similar grunt as both horses landed hard from the next fence, plunging on into the backstretch.

The damned cloying heat! Moonsugar smelled strongly of it. His coat glowed with sweat. Showers dripped with it. Only the brisk wind of their passage kept it from flooding his eyes. The pain in his right leg was becoming serious, and his left was beginning to cramp as well. Almost forty. So old and foolish to be doing this.

But still he felt wonderfully exhilarated. His mind was clear and clean. He succumbed to a giddy joy, to an uncharacteristic gloating pride. If there were such things as ghosts, then his father's was with him now. And his grandfather's, all his ancestors'.

Another fence. Moonsugar tiring. Inkydink, too. At least half a mile to go. The pain reaching into his ankles, spreading along his thighs, climbing his spine. The last turn ahead of him, its first jump coming at him in a rush.

He pulled his horse to the left upon landing, leaning closer to the rail, forcing Inkydink to the right. There was a rough furrow of turf running diagonally from the next obstacle. It would slow Kipp if he hit it squarely from his position, slow him more if he shifted to avoid it. Had Kipp remembered it?

If he had, he paid it no mind. Inkydink kept pace over the rail, hitting the ground beyond with a galumphing thud, recovering clumsily. Kipp whipped him back into place, lying just at Moonsugar's haunch.

Showers took time for a last quick look at the field. It was far behind, still bunched up in the backstretch, with a few horses strung out at the rear. Sherrie's Dream was the only other horse in contention, the jockey whipping him frantically.

Moonsugar's glistening neck and veiny head were thrust forward, fully extended, lifting for the next jump, then pushing out again. His eyes were wild. His breaths came like the pounding of heavy machinery. He was all ego now. His flaring nostrils seemed to smell the finish.

Two more fences to clear, and then a hundred yards or more of open turf to the end. The crowd was screaming.

A bad tick of the right foreleg on the first of these last jumps, doubtless causing stinging pain. But a good landing. Fast into the approach to the next. Inkydink still pressing, coming closer. Showers could see his black head, his bulging eyes. Ahead the grass, clean and green and divinely inviting.

Kipp moved nearer still, infuriating Moonsugar. All of Showers' concentration was given to getting him over this last barrier. His thoughts were all to the fore. Moonsugar was scattering his attention, worrying to the side. As they took off, he kicked right, striking his rival, hoof hitting hide and bone.

Up they went together, but Inkydink kept rising, his head high, mane flying. The animal veered, broaching the jump, hind legs smacking against the rail, his body rotating like some huge stone. Kipp went forward onto his mount's neck. Showers reached out to shove him back into the saddle. Someone had done that for him once, saving him from a terrible fall.

But there was no preventing this one. Kipp slipped from his grasp. Clear of the fence, Moonsugar, confused by Showers' movement in the saddle, landed badly and staggered, then sank and rolled. Showers flew into the air, turning, watching like some hovering bystander the hideous aftermath of Kipp's collision with the earth, the other jockey's leg disappearing beneath his horse's back. Both their screams were so awful Showers couldn't tell which was the man's and which the beast's.

*42*

Showers hit the ground on his side, one leg caught twisted beneath the other. He rolled over, frantically pushing himself up. Sherrie's Dream was just seconds away, the knot of following horses still at some distance.

Showers got to Kipp just as Sherrie's Dream flew over them, somehow missing them in a herculean leap. The next horses were coming in a thunder of hooves. Showers grabbed Kipp's wrist tightly with both hands and heaved them both backward toward the edge of the course. Kipp shrieked. Shutting the sound from his mind, Showers pulled once more, collapsing back on the grass as, in a flying stream, the rest of the field thumped and galloped by.

Then it was strangely quiet. He got back up to his knees, straightening his back. Kipp was very still, probably unconscious from shock. The man's right leg was bent at a terrible angle, the sharpness of bone protruding from his boot top, blood pumping into the grass. Across the course, Inkydink was down on his side, snorting and coughing. Over by the rail, Moonsugar stood very still, oddly calm. Sadly, Showers saw that the animal's foreleg was raised high, as though he was preparing to paw the earth. Except he kept it there, his leg muscles tightly clenched.

Every part of Showers' body now hurt. His ankle was swollen and numb. He sank back, looking up into the gentle blue sky. If his father's ghost was watching now, he'd doubtless be laughing, or crying. He knew what Fairbrother would say to him: "You damn fool! You had it won!"

May Moody had watched the accident with disbelief and horror. Now she felt a great rushing anger. What was the damned stupid point of racing over these deadly wooden fences? Why not gallop over land mines, or a field of pikes and spears? If the riders were out to prove their idiotic male courage, why subject the poor innocent horses to this bloody folly?

One horse was standing with great dignity, but was obviously injured and in pain. The other was down, helplessly trying to get up with forelegs alone, braying its agony. The first rider lay grotesquely crumpled, barely moving. The other jockey, miraculously, got to his feet and leaned back against the fence. He removed his riding helmet, his silver hair bright in the sunlight.

May had liked the look of him when she'd watched him mount in the paddock before the race. Though cursing him for the accident, for participating in the race, in the slaughter, she felt a rush of amazed admiration for him. He'd recklessly risked his own life to save the other's. He'd thrown away the race. Who would have asked him to do that? Of all the men she had ever known—lovers, pals, colleagues, kin—she doubted that any of them was capable of such a thing.

That was not fair. Her father had braved death to save the lives of three of his men in Vietnam. That's why they had given him the Silver Star.

An ambulance had pulled out onto the course and was trundling along the grass toward the injured. Bumping out ahead of it was a pickup truck hauling a small trailer with what looked to be a tent folded up in it. The track announcer had called the unofficial results and was now talking about the finish time, noting it was off the record. He said not a word about the accident.

May had leapt to her feet when the first horse and rider had gone down. She now took a few steps forward, removing her sunglasses to better see what was happening.

The pickup truck got to the scene first. Two men jumped out and hurried to the trailer, lugging out poles and canvas. As May watched incredulously, they began setting up a huge screen around the carnage, masking it from the spectators. The ambulance pulled up behind the truck and the attendants hastened forth with a stretcher, disappearing behind the canvas. More vehicles pulled up, including a Jeep hauling a horse trailer.

"Are you all right, Miss Moody?" said her host, Granby. "You seem awfully pale." He looked pretty ashen himself.

"I'm fine."

"Can I get you something to drink?"

"A drink? God, no." It had been more than a year since she'd had one of those, a very long year.

To her amazement and outrage, there was laughing and cheering in Bernie Bloch's box down the slope from her. To his credit, her father looked somewhat unhappy, but Bloch was beaming. So was the blond woman whom May recognized as her stepmother. She was hugging Bloch, though his wife was standing awkwardly next to him. Their horse had won. Damn all else.

The track announcer, his voice only slightly subdued, reminded people that there were still three races to run on the day's program and that in a moment the trophy for the Valley Dragoon Chase would be awarded to the victor in the winner's circle. He said there were a number of distinguished guests among the spectators and that he hoped they'd come to the officials' stand for the ceremonies.

Another horse trailer was being brought up. The injured horse that was still standing began edging away at its approach.

May turned to Granby and touched his arm.

"I'd like to go now," she said quietly. If this ruined his afternoon, hers already had been.

"Of course," he said, with gallantry. "Just let me say goodbye to someone."

The track announcer called out the names of some of the VIPs invited to the winner's circle. One was a famous mystery novel writer and former jockey. Another was a U.S. senator. It surprised May, though it shouldn't have, to hear her father's name announced.

Then came words that sliced into her like a knife.

"We not only have the White House chief of staff with us today," said the announcer, his voice booming all over the meadow, like God's. "But I'm told we're also graced with the presence of his lovely daughter, the talented actress May Moody. We'd all be grateful if she would join her father up here as we award this year's Dragoon Chase trophy to the owner of the winning horse, Bernard Bloch, a sportsman newly come to steeplechasing but one who's already made a tremendous contribution."

People all around May were staring at her. Down in the group around Bloch, her father turned to look. So did the blond woman who was now his wife.

May fled, almost tripping over a tent rope, pushing through some spectators and hurrying behind the tent and away from the course. The parking area where her host had left his Mercedes was on the other side of a fenced-in pasture with several unsaddled horses in it. She didn't know which lane to take around it, but plunged on. When the one she chose proved to be blocked by a closed gate, she retraced her steps and ducked under a rope barrier. She remembered that the Mercedes was locked. Granby was nowhere in sight. She didn't want to stand there, visible to all. Panicking, she looked frantically about, noticing finally a small wooden building farther along the ridge with a white board bearing a red cross on its wall. The aid station. She bolted for it.

There was only one attendant in it. He seemed much too young to be a doctor.

"I've got an injured man coming, miss," he said as she stepped inside. "Are you in a bad way?"

"I just feel faint," she said. "The heat."

He studied her a moment, then motioned toward a cot by the

corner. "Why don't you lie down there. I'll get to you as soon as I can."

She did as bidden, removing her hat and scarf and then slowly reclining. She did feel a little dizzy. She certainly felt sick. Her heart was pounding.

The injured man was not the horribly injured victim of the bad jump but the silver-haired jockey, who came in limping badly, assisted by a young woman in riding clothes. The attendant had him sit up on an examining table. None of them paid any attention to May.

Outside, a siren could be heard, loud at first, then diminishing, then gone.

"They're taking Kipp direct to the hospital," said the attendant. "You sure you don't want to go there, Captain?"

The jockey shook his head. "I don't think anything's broken. I can stand on it. After a fashion."

The medic worked the leg back and forth, gently. "I don't know, Captain Showers. That ankle's pretty bad. I want to take a look at it." He hesitated. "I'm afraid I'll have to cut off the boot."

"Is that necessary? These are my favorite boots."

"It'll hurt like hell if I try to pull it off."

"Let's have a go at it," said Showers. "It can't be that bad."

"I'll help," said the girl who'd come in with Showers.

May's eyes widened as she watched them struggle to remove the boot. The silver-haired man grimaced and swore, but did not cry out. The other two paused.

"Keep pulling," Showers said. "Let's get it over with."

The boot came off. The medic set it down, then removed the man's sock. The ankle was terribly swollen. The medic probed the flesh and moved the foot.

"It's not broken, but it's a pretty bad sprain. I'll tape it up."

The jockey looked at the girl. "How's Moonsugar?" he asked.

"They have two vets with him."

"I hope one of them's not Meade Clay."

The medic laughed.

"Fairbrother's with Moonsugar, too," the young girl said.

The jockey frowned.

"It's his decision, David," the girl said.

"I could kill myself for doing that to him," Showers said.

"If you hadn't, Jimmy Kipp would have been killed."

Showers shook his head sadly. "I hope he doesn't have to die."

"Maybe he won't, David."

**46**

"Not if we have a good go at saving him. Go to Fairbrother, Becky. Ask him not to do anything until he talks to me. Until I see the horse."

"All right, David."

"And could you bring me my shirt and jacket? This may be the last time I wear these." Showers pulled off his racing silks. His neck and face were very tan, but his chest was not.

"Don't talk nonsense, David. We're all counting on you to win the Old Dominion National this fall."

The girl left. As the medic leaned over Showers' foot with his adhesive tape, the jockey tapped his shoulder. He was looking at May.

"Have you attended to her?" he asked.

"Not yet."

"Please take care of her. I can wait."

May shook her head. "I'm all right," she said. "I just want to lie here awhile."

"You're quite sure?"

"Yes."

She closed her eyes, listening as the medic went about his business and the two men talked about the more seriously injured jockey. He had suffered a dangerous compound fracture, but his other injuries did not appear to be life threatening. He'd been taken to a hospital several miles away.

"Kipp's a professional rider, isn't he?" said the medic. "Horse shows and all that?"

Showers sighed. "He won't ride again."

"There's other work."

Showers looked down at his own leg, swinging it.

Lenore Fairbrother entered, tripping on the step. She caught her balance, looked around, then rushed to Showers' side.

"My darling, darling David," she said, taking up his hand and kissing the palm. "My God, I thought you were going to be killed."

"I'm fine, Lenore."

"Your beautiful leg's not broken?"

"Jimmy Kipp's leg is broken. I think for good."

"That little fairy is damned lucky you were there," Lenore said.

"For God's sake, Lenore! Moonsugar caused the accident. He clipped Inkydink going over the timber. It was my fault."

"Nonsense, David. Bloody nonsense."

Lenore fell silent as Becky returned, carrying Showers' shirt and jacket. She was accompanied by an older man, who was elegantly but casually dressed in gray trousers, checked sport coat, white button-down shirt, red silk ascot, and khaki sun hat. He stood before Showers, not speaking for a moment. The medic moved away, busying himself by a medicine cabinet. May was watching intently now. It was all like a play.

"I'm sorry, Lynwood," said Showers.

The older man put his hand on Showers' shoulder. "David, I couldn't be prouder. What you did was in the finest tradition of the Dandytown Hunt. This will go into the history of Virginia steeple-chasing. I can't tell you how terribly pleased I am to be associated with you today."

"I've left you with a very large empty space on your trophy shelf."

"The cup's a formality," said the older man. "We can attend to that next year. You won the race today. Everyone saw you do it. It's an irrefutable fact. That you did this honorable thing instead of continuing on to the finish, that changes nothing. Mr. Bloch has a very hollow victory."

"His horse won the Dragoon Chase, Lynwood. He won it fairly, just as fairly as we would have won it if I'd left Kipp behind and gone on to the finish."

"But you didn't, David. You didn't. And that's the whole point." The old man reached into his jacket pocket and pulled out a folded piece of paper. "Here you are. Just as I promised. I made it out before the start of the race. Never had a doubt about you."

Showers unfolded the paper. It was a check.

"But I didn't finish."

"Please, old boy. Not another word. Now, how are you? Banged up badly?"

"I'm fine, Lynwood. What about Moonsugar?"

The older man hesitated. "Not good, I'm afraid. There appears to be a fracture. We're going to have to put him down."

"No. You can't."

"We must. It happens in racing, as you know very well. I'm sorry."

"He can't be that bad. He was standing calmly. Please."

"I haven't time to deal with him, David. I'm going to London this week. We have horses to pick up in Southern Pines. It can't be done. Not without an awful lot of cost and bother. Both vets say he can never race again."

Showers looked down at the floor. "Let me try."

"On your farm? In your condition? Just you and Becky?"

"Please, Lynwood. Let me try."

"He's a gelding, David. We can't even put him to stud."

"Please."

Lenore put her arms around the older man, staring intently into his eyes.

"Lynwood. Give him Moonsugar. He's nothing to you now. He's everything to David. If anyone can save him, David can. Let him try."

The old man sighed. "This could cost you a considerable sum of money, David."

"Understood."

"Oh, very well. You're such a stubborn man. He's been tranquilized. I'll have him taken to the vet's barn. You'll have to see to setting the leg yourself."

"Thank you, Lynwood. I'm much in your debt."

"I'm in your debt, sir. Honorable work. Well done." He put his hand to Showers' shoulder again. "Well and finely done."

Lenore was very flushed. As her husband turned to leave, she darted up and kissed Showers' cheek. "See you at the inn tonight, darling," she whispered—loud enough for the others to hear. "We're going to have quite a party." Then she followed her husband out the door.

Becky's eyes were gleaming. "You're crazy."

Showers asked the medic for a pen. Taking it, he leaned over the table, writing something on the back of the check. Then he handed it to Becky.

"I want you to go to the hospital and give this to Jimmy Kipp," he said. "You can use my Cherokee."

The gleam vanished. Becky was thunderstruck.

"David, this is for $7,500! You need this money. For the auction tonight."

"I'm not going to the auction. I expect I'll be spending the night in the vet's barn, with Moonsugar."

"David, you can't be serious. If you miss the auction you'll never get that horse. I got the number. It's 17A. They'll start the bidding on him sometime after nine o'clock. You've got to be there! You told me how much you want him!"

"I don't have money to bid on that horse."

"You do with this!" She held up the check as though it were a holy vessel.

"That's for Jimmy Kipp."

"Please, David. Don't do this!"

"Becky, you're not my slave. If you don't want to take that to the hospital, I'll do it myself later. But I'm not going to the auction. I'm going to be with Moonsugar."

The girl was tearful. "I'll do what you say. But you'll be damned sorry for it."

When she was gone, Showers stood up, with some small success putting a little weight on his injured ankle. "At least it's the same leg I banged up yesterday," he said, pulling on his shirt. "If worse comes to worst, I can hop."

The medic went to a metal locker and took out a pair of crutches. "If you're going to walk, Captain, use these. I'd stay off that ankle as much as possible for a couple of days."

His shirt buttoned and his blazer on, Showers took the crutches, stopping to adjust them to his height. "Bloody nuisance."

May sat up. "Can I help you?"

He halted, as though he'd forgotten she was there. "Help me? Oh, no. I'm quite fine. Thank you very much." He bowed to her slightly, then swung himself out the door.

He'd forgotten his boot and racing silks. May snatched them up and, darting past the puzzled medic, followed the jockey.

"You left these," she said.

"Oh. Thank you." He stopped, injured leg bent, and reached for her bundle.

"Please," she said. "Let me carry them for you."

"Well, if you insist," he said. "Thank you very much. It's not far. Just down there." He swung off toward a long low building on the other side of some corrals, then paused. "Are you all right? You were feeling poorly."

"I'm fine, really. My name is May Moody," she said, giving him her best smile.

"David Spencer Showers," he said. "You're the movie actress they announced over the public address system, aren't you? You should be up at the winner's circle."

"No I shouldn't. Not with that winner."

An amused expression came over his face, but diminished into sadness. "A terrible spectacle today. I'm sorry you had to see it."

They ambled slowly along, May clutching the dirty riding clothes to her chest. She was astounded by this man, not simply because of his courage and sacrifice, but because of the ease and swiftness with which he had made these enormously consequential decisions. May knew producers and directors back in Hollywood who could spend weeks in mental mumbling over the most trivial details. She would

**50**

herself sometimes fret for days over whether to repaint her living room or ask for a change of a few words in a script. This man had chosen to risk his life, abandon a sure triumph, give away a large sum of money, give up a horse he obviously wanted to buy very badly, and devote a lot of time, effort, and money to another horse that was likely going to die anyway—and he'd done this all in a matter of a few minutes, without hesitation.

She was at a loss as to what to say to him. Idle chatter was not very appropriate. As they walked, she contented herself with stealing glances at him, wondering why he wasn't doing the same with her. He was much younger than she had thought at first. His hair color and the long scar on his face had added years that weren't there. He was also quite tall. She was five feet six, and had to look up to him.

As they neared the barn, two stable hands came out, followed by a large woman in riding boots whom Showers introduced as Alixe Percy. She took Showers' clothing from May, and began talking about the injured horse. The jockey thanked May again, then started into the barn. May suddenly felt very sad for him, realizing how miserable the man had to be beneath all his manners and sangfroid. Such a beautiful day had been made so awful—so quickly.

May found her escort waiting unhappily for her by his Mercedes.

"I don't want to go back to Washington just yet," she said. "I'd like to go to that horse auction tonight. Would that be all right?"

Granby looked surprised, and not altogether pleased.

"Whatever you wish, Miss Moody."

Bernie Bloch had led his group from the winner's circle back down to his Rolls-Royce. He poured last drinks all around, and then began packing up his liquor chest. There were three races still to be run but the only one that mattered to him was over and he was ready to go back to the comforts of the Dandytown Inn. Robert Moody realized that this would be taken as bad sportsmanship by the locals, but he was ready to go himself. He'd been completely unnerved by the twin shocks of seeing his daughter after so long and then having her flee from him—in front of everyone.

He decided he'd spend the rest of the day on the telephone. In fact, if Bloch was planning on making a big night of it out here, Moody thought he might slip away back to Washington. He'd had enough of this place, and these people.

"Are you going to look for your daughter?" Deena asked, quietly.

"No."

"That wasn't very nice of her to go running off like that."

"She still sees things her mother's way."

"What's she doing in Washington?"

"I don't own the town, Deena."

"Are we going to have her underfoot this summer?"

"Don't worry about it."

"Wasn't it wonderful, what that Captain Showers did?" said Sherrie Bloch.

"If my jockey pulled a stunt like that I'd kick his ass into the next county," said Bernie, slamming down the trunk lid.

"You ought to send the man a bottle of champagne," his wife said. "He's the only reason you won."

"Shut up, Sherrie."

There was a stirring among some of the spectators farther down the rail. People were turning to one another, talking excitedly. Whatever the news, it traveled rapidly from one to another, spreading out through the crowd. The excitement was audible, almost palpable. Moody saw Lenore Fairbrother. She listened as someone spoke to her, then began laughing. She looked over at Bloch's group, her laughter uncontrollable.

"What the hell is her problem?" Bernie said.

"I'll go ask," Moody said.

She began moving away, but he caught up with her quickly.

"Excuse me, Mrs. Fairbrother. What's going on?"

"Death, dear boy," she said, her laughter subsiding. She put her hand on his arm. "Vicky Clay. Your friend's trainer? She and her husband killed each other. Fucking! Your poor Mr. Bloch's won his race and lost his bimbo!"

She began to laugh again, until a man came up and pulled her away.

The assistant commonwealth attorney, Wayne Bensinger, a dark-haired, thin-faced young man wearing glasses, a short mustache and an ill-fitting tan polyester suit, was only three years out of law school. The most serious felony he had ever prosecuted was an armed robbery of a convenience store in which a counter clerk had been wounded by flying glass when the perpetrator's firearm had accidentally discharged, shattering an overhead light fixture. The perpetrator, a nineteen-year-old first offender, had been sentenced to eight years. Virginia juries could be tough. Bensinger, who had a wife and an infant daughter, sometimes worried about the young robber—about what might be happening to him in the state penitentiary, what the boy might do when he got out.

The last homicide in Banastre County had happened many years before. A local horse trainer, who had been sleeping with the wife of a wealthy farmer, had shot the man to death in his own bedroom. The trainer had claimed that the husband had found him in bed with the wife and gone back downstairs for his gun. When the husband returned, the trainer had hit him over the head with a boot, taken the pistol away, and shot the husband twice. The trainer was quite popular in the county, especially with the ladies, and the farmer was not. The trainer was convicted of a charge of unlawful use of a weapon and given three months in the county jail. He was acquitted on the homicide charge.

In an aside, the judge had faulted the sheriff for shoddy police work. He had lost evidence—the boot—allowed fingerprints on the murder weapon to be smudged, and failed to take a sworn statement from the wife, the only witness to the crime.

The sheriff, Richard Cooke, was still in office. Arriving at the inn more than an hour after the maid had discovered the bodies of the Clays, he had assumed like everyone else that the two had overdosed on drugs and alcohol, but wasn't going to take any chances. He called the state police to have evidence technicians sent to the scene and, while waiting the nearly two hours it took for them to arrive, had his deputies take Polaroids of the bodies, the contents of Meade's veterinary bag, the room, the corridor outside, the lock on the door, and even the view from the window—to show that no perpetrator could have gained access to the chamber through it.

Cooke also began taking statements. He drew up a list of all the inn's guests and employees, adding the names of all those known to have been in the inn at any time that evening. It was a very long list.

He started with the employees. There were delays. A deputy had to be sent to the next town to buy a sufficient number of blank tape cassettes to record the statements. The man was dispatched again to buy fresh batteries for the recorder. But the sheriff was insistent. Everyone would be interrogated.

The interviews were conducted in the office of the inn's manager. People were allowed to go about their business in the inn—return to their rooms, use the bar and dining room, lounge about the lobby. But they were not allowed to leave the premises until they had given their statements.

Commonwealth Attorney Bensinger sat with the sheriff for most of the questioning, jotting down notes to himself or doodling, not

**53**

altogether sure whether Cooke was following proper procedure, or whether all this was necessary. During the interrogations, he heard a great deal about Vicky Clay's love life and self-destructive habits, but little that was useful in determining how she had ended the night dead. She'd been in the bar much of the evening, arguing with her husband, flitting from man to man, drinking compulsively. She'd last been seen a short while after nine o'clock. The stories were largely the same, though there were still many left to question.

Robert Moody was among them. He had gone directly to his room to shower and change clothes, remaining there to work his telephone. If Sorenson was weakening, other senators might be even softer. A phone call coming out of the blue on a Sunday could stiffen them up, the White House reaching anywhere, at any hour, to offer friendship and make its wishes known. In the Bush administration, the president himself would be doing this job. Moody's boss found such intercourse just too, too distasteful. More and more, the man was reminding Moody of Woodrow Wilson. Not that that was such a bad thing. Wilson had depended on his Colonel House as absolutely as Moody wanted his president to depend on him.

Moody was going to deliver on this damned Earth Treaty, on the accompanying Earth Bill, on anything else the president had in mind. He had promised himself this triumph, just as he had promised himself that he would be governor, that he would one day be a millionaire, that he would marry Deena Atkinson, though at the time she had been married to someone else.

In all, he reached twelve senators—nine of their own and three liberal Republicans. Every call was worth it. He could sense every one of them straightening up a little at his crack of the whip. A few asked for some things in return that Majority Leader Reidy had never told him they wanted. A couple were a hell of a lot softer on the treaty question than Reidy had indicated.

Moody also checked on the Belize situation. There had been no more arrests or killings, but the Mexican government had dispatched some troops to its southern border, placing them in position to enter either Belize or Guatemala.

Moody ordered that a stern warning be sent to the Mexican embassy to cool it—a message made in the president's name but signed by him.

Moody felt good when he was done with his calls. Deena had gone downstairs long before him. He found her in the bar with

Bernie and Sherrie Bloch. Bernie was drinking a martini, and was very angry.

"These goddamned hayhead cops," he said. "They're keeping us here until we all give statements about Vicky. I've got to get over to that horse auction."

"Bernie's taking us over to Wintergreen for dinner," Deena said. "To the Inn at Little Washington." It was probably the finest restaurant in Virginia.

"Not until I buy this horse," Bloch said. "It's one of the early hip numbers. It won't take very long. But these bastards are stiff-arming me."

"I'm not sure they have a legal right to do that," Moody said. "Did you tell them who you are?"

"You bet your ass. But it doesn't cut any shit with them. Hell, they're making Lynwood Fairbrother stay. Though he hasn't complained any. If he did, they might knock off this crap."

"Why don't you just get up and leave?" Moody said.

"I tried. Front door, back door. Got stopped by these Smokey the Bear dipshits both times," Bloch said. "Look, I don't want any trouble with the Virginia law. I just want them to listen to reason. I don't know what the fuck happened to Vicky. She's a goddamned junkie. Anything could happen to her. I just gotta get to the auction. I gotta buy that horse."

"Why don't you call the auctioneers? Have them hold off until you get there?"

"I tried. They won't do that for a buyer. A seller can pull a horse out of the line, but not a bidder."

"Call the seller."

"The seller's in New Jersey. The auctioneer's acting as his agent, and he acts like he's never heard of me."

"Well, I don't think they can do this," Moody said. "If they want you as a witness, they have to subpoena you, but they can't hold you like this unless you're a suspect."

"Shit," said Bloch. "Maybe I am. Maybe we all are."

"I'll take care of it," Moody said.

The White House chief of staff pushed open the door to the manager's office as though he were entering his own. The sheriff, a deputy, and a dopey-looking kid in glasses and a suit were talking to a bellhop. Moody's sudden appearance startled them, and angered the sheriff.

"You're going to have to wait your turn, sir," he said. "We'll get to you as soon as we can."

"Do you know who I am?" Moody said.

"Yes sir. You're the ex-governor of Maryland. This is Virginia, sir. And I've got a homicide case here with two corpses."

Moody went to the desk, planted his hands firmly on the top, and leaned forward, glaring into the sheriff's eyes.

"I am chief of staff to the president of the United States, mister. I am a federal officer with the entire U.S. Secret Service at my disposal. I am dealing with a number of very important matters at the moment, including a crisis in Central America, and I am going to have to return to Washington. Aside from the fact that the wrath of God is going to come down on you if you obstruct me in any way, I am also an attorney. I am familiar enough with the law of this commonwealth to know that you have no legal right to detain me or any of these people unless you have sufficient evidence to place them under arrest."

"Everyone will be free to go as soon as I get a statement from them. If they try to leave the premises before that, I'm going to treat them as suspects, or arrest them for obstructing justice."

"The hell you are."

"I'm doing it. I called Judge Merrick."

"I'm leaving. If you wish to question me, my office address is 1600 Pennsylvania Avenue, Washington, D.C. I suggest you get a subpoena."

He stood up straight. "All right, sir. You can go. We don't want to interfere with the president's business."

"I'm taking my wife with me. And my friends."

The sheriff hesitated, then looked at Bensinger.

"You're the investigating officer," Bensinger said, a little flustered. "Right now, I'm just observing."

"Sorry sir," said the sheriff, "but they'll have to stay. Your wife was seen talking to Vicky Clay in the women's room last night. Your friend Mr. Bloch was seen talking to her outside his room. We have some questions for them."

"Then call them in now and get it over with!"

The sheriff became implacable. "They wait their turn. After this man, I'm going to talk to Mr. Fairbrother. I've already kept him waiting too long."

Moody took a deep breath. He had two Secret Service men waiting outside by his car. Push could come to shove. Moody had been pushed by the likes of the British prime minister and the head of the United Auto Workers, but he'd always won the shove.

Still, the president would be disturbed by such a public incident, especially one involving a possible crime and a law enforcement officer, however insignificant. In the man's own words, he'd be appalled.

"You're going to be very, very sorry about this," Moody said to the sheriff, as he headed for the door.

"We'll be talking to you," said Cooke.

Bloch looked up expectantly as Moody returned to their table in the bar.

"Sorry," Moody said, looking first at his wife. "He'll let me go, because I said I've got official White House business—which I do, as a matter of fact. But I'm afraid you're stuck. Why don't we just have dinner here again?"

"I don't give a damn about dinner!" Bloch said. "I want that horse! I gotta have him."

"What's wrong with Sherrie's Dream?" his wife asked. "He won the race."

"Be quiet."

They all sat unhappily, sipping their drinks, looking as glum and irritable as everyone else in the room.

"Bobby," said Bloch, finally. "You're free to go?"

"Yes. And I'd better. My place is in the White House tonight."

Bloch pulled out his checkbook and started to write. "I need a big favor, Bobby. I'd like you to go to the auction for me. It won't take long."

Moody had no idea which of them owed the other the most favors, but certainly he owed Bloch a few. He might still be practicing law in Cumberland, Maryland, if it weren't for Bloch.

"I don't know anything about buying horses, Bernie."

Bloch signed a check with his hurried scrawl and tore it out of the book. "I've made it out and everything. All you have to do is fill in the amount. I wrote down the horse's hip number here. It's 17A. They'll call it in order, right after number 17. Don't bid on 17. Make sure it's 17A. It should be a good-looking horse. A bay, I think. Very dark."

"You haven't seen it?"

"I know all about it. I don't have to see it."

This seemed more than a little odd to Moody, but he didn't question his old friend's peculiar ways. He took the check, folded it carefully, and placed it in his wallet. "How much do I bid?"

"Whatever it takes. It shouldn't be much over ten thousand, maybe less. If Wayne Lukas were here, I'd worry, because he puts a lot of store on what kind of an athlete a horse looks like when he buys. He's pulled big-money winners outa nowhere. But he won't be around. The buyers here will be looking at pedigrees, and this horse doesn't have much."

Moody knew that Lukas had trained winning horses for the Kentucky Derby and other big flat-track races. He wouldn't be involved with steeplechase.

"Why do you want this one so badly?" he asked. "The world is full of horses."

Bloch grinned. "I got a tip. This one is special. Now, that horse is going to belong to you the instant the bidding's over, but you shouldn't have any problem getting them to hold it there for you until I can get Billy Bonning or somebody over there with a horse trailer to pick it up."

"You want me to sign for it? As the new owner?"

"As my agent. Don't worry about it. Just a formality. What matters is that I get the winning bid down."

"What if it ends up costing a lot of money?"

"Bobby. Please. A lot of money, I got."

Moody's driver and Secret Service bodyguard were waiting by his official car, which was parked prominently by the inn's front verandah. If they'd been bored, they now looked fully alert, perhaps in anticipation of returning to Washington soon. Moody handed his briefcase to the bodyguard to put in the car's trunk, then slid into the back seat.

"We're going to a horse auction," he said to the driver.

"Not Washington, boss?"

"If we were going to Washington, I'd tell you."

"And Mrs. Moody?"

"If she were coming, she'd be here."

There were several sheriff's deputies standing along the inn's circular driveway. One of them stepped back respectfully and gave a small salute as Moody's black sedan passed by.

Moody repeated the directions Bloch had given him. The auction pavilion was on the other side of town, adjoining the grounds of the Dandytown Horse Show. It was a short drive.

As they turned through the gate, following several other arriving cars down a lane between rows of parked vehicles, there was a quiet beeping sound. A small green light flickered on Moody's telephone console. His bodyguard picked it up and uttered the word "Straw-boss," which was the Secret Service's code word for the White

House chief of staff. The man listened a moment, then handed the receiver to Moody.

"It's the White House, sir," he said.

Another National Security Council duty officer was on the line.

"New development in Belize, sir," he said. "More trouble. Involving U.S. citizens."

"Shooting trouble?"

"Affirmative. We have a confirmed fatality."

Moody put his hand over the mouthpiece. "Stop!"

His car slid to a halt in the gravel. In a large open space beside the pavilion, Moody could see horses being led.

He put the receiver back to his ear. "Has the commander in chief been informed?" he asked.

"General St. Angelo is doing that now, sir."

Moody hesitated, but not for long. "Tell him I am en route to Washington. I'll be in my office in an hour."

His driver was already turning around, honking to make other cars move out of the way.

"I'll have the latest situation reports waiting on your desk, sir."

"Have General St. Angelo waiting there, too." He paused, frowning. "Something else. I'd like you to place a call to my wife at the Dandytown Inn. Tell her there's been an emergency and I'm returning to the White House. Tell her I'll call her as soon as I can."

"Very well, sir."

"Something else. Tell her I'm unable to wait for the horse."

"The horse, sir?"

"She'll know what I mean."

He could call her himself, of course, but he knew she'd only complain. The chief of staff of the president of the United States was not about to be nagged. He wasn't going to be held up by some screwball horse deal of Bernie's, either.

"That's all. Thank you." He hung up, leaning back against the seat. When at last they bumped up onto the highway again, and were heading east, his driver glanced over his shoulder.

"We're not going to make it back in an hour, boss."

"Give it your best shot."

May Moody's gentlemanly escort seemed a little hurt that she offered no explanation for her sudden decision to stay for the horse auction, but he proved helpful enough, arranging a seat for her near the auctioneer's podium and obtaining a copy of the catalogue for her.

She noticed several people looking at her as she took her place, but she was unsure whether it was because they recognized her as a celebrity, or because she was an unfamiliar face to them. So many of these people seemed to know one another well.

May had repeated the hip number, whatever that was, of the horse Captain Showers wanted over and over in her mind: 17A. There was no such number listed in the glossy catalogue, but she found it in the pages of a hastily printed addendum stuck in the back.

She had been to art auctions before, but was unsure of the procedure here. At art sales, people were provided with cardboard paddles to indicate their bids. As the horse auction got underway, bidders were signifying their intentions by raising their hands. The auctioneer recognized one or two men who did no more than nod their heads.

The catalogue page devoted to Hip No. 17A was full of esoteric references, beginning with a barn and stall number and the name of the seller: "Tampico Enterprises, Newark, N.J. Ltd., Partnership No. 1, Tampico Enterprises, Agent."

Then followed the words, "Bay Stallion," the animal's birthdate, and a diagram of the horse's family tree, dating back three generations.

After that came listings of the racing victories and horse show records of the sire, the sire's other offspring, and those of the horse's first, second, and third dams. In the entries for most of the other horses in the catalogue, these race and horse show records were fairly extensive. Those for 17A were quite skimpy. Two of the dams had nothing listed at all.

She glanced through the front of the catalogue, noting several pages of legalese that seemed not a little forbidding:

There is no warranty express or implied by the auctioneer, sponsors, owner or consignor, as to the racing soundness, merchantability or fitness for any particular purposes of any horse offered in this sale. All horses are sold "as is" with all existing conditions and defects except as set forth . . .

Should any dispute arise between or among two or more bidders, the auctioneer shall forthwith adjudicate the dispute, and his decision shall be absolute, final and binding on all parties . . .

Title passes to buyer at fall of the hammer. All risk of injury to the horse becomes buyer's risk on passing of titles. Horse will be held for buyer by consignor until buyer makes settlement as provided . . .

Any controversy arising out of a claim arising under conditions eighth, ninth and eleventh shall be settled by arbitration between the buyers and consignor . . .

May lowered the catalogue to her lap and took a deep breath. She had the money to do this. She had just sold her house in Malibu Canyon for $2.5 million and had deposited a cashier's check for $250,000 in her account. She had other funds as well. Her career may have skidded off the track, but she was far from broke. Ten or twenty thousand was nothing. She had friends—she used to have friends—who would drop that in a single afternoon of shopping in Beverly Hills.

In a year or two, she might think differently. Her career could be in such a mess that she'd need every cent of ten or twenty thousand. She'd earned herself a reputation with producers for being difficult—irresponsible, unreliable, even crazy. That was behind her, but she had to prove it. That's what she had come to Washington to do. The Folger was the finest Shakespeare company in the country. Though its actors were paid only a little more than $600 a week, they were disciplined professionals of the highest standard. If she could hold her own with them, if she could win some favorable reviews with her performance, she'd prove her point. She'd be back in her league. She'd never again be reduced to accepting roles in horror-chiller films, just to keep working. That was why she was going to subject herself to spending so many weeks in her father's city.

The bidding was going very quickly. The horses were brought out one by one to the little sawdust ring in front of the auctioneer's podium and seemed to spend less time there than actresses performing at an audition. One had an opening price of $1,000 and sold for exactly that in a few seconds. Several sold for $30,000 or more. One went for $128,000, scaring May to death.

But she had to go through with this. She was tired of making promises to herself she never kept. It was crazy—the sort of irrational act that would convince her moviemaking friends that she'd gone completely cuckoo.

Her escort nudged her gently. "Your horse, Miss Moody. They're calling its number."

She glanced down at the catalogue entry, then looked quickly back to the podium. The animal was handsome, very dark, with white markings on his forelegs and one rear leg. He danced out to the little ring, sidestepping skittishly as the groom tried to hold him still.

The auctioneer spoke glowingly of the animal's ancestry—going on about "winners' blood," as he had about all the entries so far—but no one in the audience around May seemed at all impressed.

"He's beautiful," said her escort, "but he seems a little temperamental."

The opening price was $10,000. Timidly, May raised her hand. The auctioneer, looking to more likely quarters in the audience, appeared not to notice her. Irritated, she thrust her arm up high.

"Ten thousand dollars," the auctioneer said. "Do I have eleven? Do I have ten thousand five? Ten thousand one hundred?"

The horse whinnied and suddenly rose on his rear legs, pulling the reins from the groom's hands, pawing the air with his forelegs. A hoof struck the auctioneer's podium, causing it to rock back and forth. The gavel came down hard.

"Sold! For ten thousand dollars."

With the help of Granby, who was a banker and familiar with complicated transactions, May managed to get through the purchasing procedure, which was conducted in the auction house office. She signed several copies of several papers, and was handed a batch more—certificate of ownership, veterinarian's statement, others she didn't understand at all. These were stuffed into a large manila envelope, which was placed in her hands after she slid her check for $10,458—including miscellaneous costs—across the counter.

Then she and Granby were led to a barn and told to wait outside. A few minutes later, a groom appeared with the horse. Still nervous and skittish, it seemed monstrous. The only tack that came with it was a halter. The groom handed her the reins. It was then that the enormity of her foolishness struck home.

"Nice horse," said the groom. He turned to walk away.

"Excuse me," she said. "Is there any way I can have him delivered?"

The youth halted. "Delivered?"

"Delivered. Sent to someone."

"We don't do that, ma'am. We just sell them. It's your horse."

"But I don't have a trailer or anything."

Granby looked embarrassed. "Could you hold him for us, until we're able to get a trailer?" he asked the groom.

"Sometimes we do that. I'll go ask my boss."

"I don't even know where his farm is," May said quietly, after the groom had gone. "I didn't think any of this through."

"Whose farm?" said the banker. "I'm afraid I don't understand what it is you want to do."

"Captain Showers. The jockey we saw this afternoon. I bought the horse for him."

She bit her lip. For a brief, panicky moment, she thought of just leaving the horse there and never coming back. It was something the old May Moody would do.

Another young man was walking toward them, with an ambling but purposeful gait. He was dressed in jeans, boots, and T-shirt and had a cigarette hanging from his lips. He had blond hair and struck May as handsome.

"You Moody?" the young man said to the banker.

"I'm Moody," May said.

"You're supposed to be a man."

"I'm not a man."

"No, you sure as hell aren't." His eyes wandered from her face to her body, then lifted. "Well, I'm here for the horse."

"Are you with the auctioneers?"

"The auctioneers? No, I'm Billy Bonning. I'm with Bernie Bloch. I'm supposed to pick up the horse. I've got a trailer right over there."

For a moment, May thought she'd been rescued from her predicament, but the name Bernie Bloch stopped her. Bloch wouldn't know she'd come here tonight. He'd have no idea she'd just bought a horse. "The" horse.

"You've made a mistake. This is my horse."

The youth took the cigarette from his mouth and flicked it into the grass.

"Look, lady. You're Moody. You just bought the horse. It's hip number 17A, right?"

"Yes, but—"

"Well, quit wasting my time. I've had enough things go wrong on me today." He snatched the halter from her and began leading the animal away.

"Stop! That's my horse!"

The young man kept walking. The stallion was tossing his head, as though sensing the tension around him.

"Did you hear her?" said the banker.

"Fuck you, buddy."

"Goddamn you, Billy Bonning! Not another step!"

The thunderous voice was a woman's. She stepped out from the shadows of the barn and strode toward them. She was wearing riding clothes and, as she came into the light, May recognized her as Alixe Percy, the woman who had greeted Showers when he went to tend to the injured horse at the racetrack barn.

"Butt out, Miss Percy," said Bonning, who had stopped in his tracks. "I'm just trying to do my job."

"Does your job include stealing horses? I saw her buy this stallion. She was the only bidder. Now just what in the hell do you think you're doing?"

The youth's arrogance began to drain away. "Bernie Bloch sent me to get this horse."

The Percy woman, who was as broad in the shoulders as she was in the hips, stepped in front of him and took the reins.

"I don't know what your goddamned Mr. Bloch is up to, Billy my lad," she said. "But you tell him this is not his horse. Tell him to find another state to play horseman in. For God's sake, boy, your sister's dead! Why aren't you tending to that instead of coming out here and causing trouble?"

"You're the one who's causing trouble, Miss Percy."

"I'm going to give you one minute to depart these premises, Billy. If you don't, I'm going to find a sheriff's deputy and have you arrested for the attempted theft of a horse. You go see to your sister's arrangements. And don't you bother this woman again."

"The hell with you!" snarled the youth. He kicked at the turf, then started back toward his truck. "Fucking bastards!"

May was trembling. Bonning scared her, though she wasn't quite sure why. The Percy woman turned to the horse, stroking his nose and calming him. Then she looked to May, smiling gently, attempting the same result.

"Don't worry about him," she said. "A mistake was made. He's just too damned stupid to realize it. Common as dirt, that boy."

She stepped closer. The horse moved with her. May felt odd with their three heads so close together. Granby was standing uncomfortably a few feet distant, his impatience fairly visible now.

"David Showers told me about you, Miss Moody—how he met you in the aid station," Alixe said.

"Yes."

"Did you know that he wanted to buy this horse? That he would have done if he hadn't given his race money to that injured jockey?"

"Yes. I heard them talking about it in the aid station. That's why I bought it. I, I want to give it to him. A sort of surprise. I mean, I don't want him to know it comes from me. I just want him to have it, for all that he did today. Does this sound crazy? I suppose it does. I don't even know the man. I'm sorry. I just wanted something good to come out of today. And now I don't know what to do."

"Like you say, you hardly know him. I'm his closest neighbor and one of his oldest friends. If I thought he'd accept such a gift, I would have bought it for him myself. He's not much on charity—for himself. He paid off all his father's debts without asking a dime from anyone."

"I didn't mean it as charity. It was just an impulse." She glanced up. The horse seemed to be staring at her. He was a very beautiful animal. May felt close to tears. "I don't know what to do. I've bought this horse. I don't even have a place to put him."

The Percy woman studied her for a moment, then nodded, as if to herself. "All right. I think there's a way we can do this. I'll take him off your hands."

"But I want him to go to Captain Showers."

"Of course. But we have to go about this a little obliquely. First thing, I'm going to have to buy him from you. It'll be a hell of a lot easier getting him into David's barn if we start from mine."

May still felt troubled. "I want to pay for the horse."

"I understand that. Your secret gift. But transferral of horse ownership is a trifle complicated, especially with good bloodstock. Let me pay you a sum, say a thousand? And you sign the papers over to me. We can go in the office and find a notary."

Granby cleared his throat. "I am a notary."

He looked very pained. May wondered if she could trust him—either of them. She trusted absolutely no one in L.A.

"Not so much money," May said. "Make it a hundred dollars."

Alixe Percy shook her head. "That'll seem too strange for words, my dear. A thousand's a more likely sum, though I daresay this animal looks like he's worth a hell of a lot more than the ten thousand you bid. I don't know how you got him so cheap."

"Okay," said May, anxious to be gone. "A thousand. You'll let me know what happens?"

"I'll invite you out the first time David races him." She patted the horse's neck, then fumbled about in the pocket of her jacket, pulling out some papers, cigarettes, a few odd dollar bills, and finally a checkbook.

"This is very nice of you."

"Anyone who wants to do something for David Showers, that's someone I'm always glad to help."

# Four

obert Moody reached the White House in time to find General St. Angelo, the president's national security adviser, still in charge at the White House situation room, commanding a motley, ad hoc crisis management team he had scraped together from weekend staff at the Pentagon, State Department, and Central Intelligence headquarters across the river in Langley. Except for a woman Spanish-language expert from the NSC Latin American section, the room was filled with men, their ties loosened, coats removed, and sleeves rolled up, all of them looking more bored and weary than tense. The scene reminded Moody of some Baltimore political back room during a long vote count, rather than the nerve center of the most powerful military force on earth.

Maps, intelligence reports, diplomatic dispatches, and scrawl-covered notepads littered the conference table, with coffee cups set among them like the playing pieces of a game. At least the team wasn't using computers. Moody hated the idea of the nation's security apparatus being run by computers, as always seemed to be the case in the Pentagon war room. General St. Angelo liked to think, not interpret analyses. He was a first-rate national security adviser.

"Update me," said Moody, pulling up a chair next to the general.

"The Mexican government has sent protests flying everywhere and moved some armored recon units down into the border area, mostly around the highway crossing at Ciudad Chetumal," St. Angelo said. "They also put their air base there on alert. The Brits have sent a strongly worded protest to Guatemala City and put their troops in Belize on alert. Otherwise the situation remains the same as when we last reported. Stable for the moment, but potentially dangerous."

He was a quiet-spoken West Pointer. Like Moody, he had seen combat and been decorated in Vietnam. It made for a bond between them that few in the White House command structure could share.

Moody nodded. He picked up the latest communiqué from Belize and glanced over it as he listened.

"The American citizen who was shot was trying to get off the streets and got caught in some crossfire," said one of St. Angelo's aides. "The embassy has the body. He's been identified. A missionary."

"Catholic?" said Moody, still reading. In Central American political terms, that would mean liberal, maybe leftist. It could also mean trouble—like the murdered nuns in El Salvador.

"Protestant. Pentecostal or something."

"The president's been informed?"

"Of everything," said the general, unhappily, "but he hasn't been very interested."

"We'll have him interested in time for the morning press briefing," said Moody. He dropped the communiqué back on the table and, despite himself, yawned. A couple of others at the table reflexively did the same. He glared at them.

"What are our assets?" Moody asked.

"Covert?" asked one of the men from Langley.

"Not spooks," said Moody. "Troops and hardware."

"Elements of a destroyer flotilla in the Gulf of Honduras that will shortly be in boom-boom range of Belize City," said St. Angelo. "Otherwise, nothing nearer than Key West."

Moody pulled one of the maps close, blinking as he studied it. "Near enough," he said. He leaned back, rubbing his eyes. "This is only a suggestion. You can put it under the heading of precautionary measures. But I'd like to see our sternly worded messages backed up with a hint or two of American resolve. We must have a banana boat or two onloading at Belize City. I wouldn't mind seeing a few marines landed there to provide dockside security. I'd like the marine guard at the embassy reinforced—by chopper, a lot of big, noisy, nasty-looking U.S. marine Jolly Green Giants. I don't know what you have on the ramp at Key West, but I think an overflight of the capital area by U.S. military aircraft might be useful, too. Rooftop stuff. Chetumal, Belize City, Belmopan. And maybe Guatemala City."

"Okay, I think a reconnaissance flight or two might be in order," said St. Angelo, nodding.

The State Department man, a weekend desk officer, looked troubled. "With all due respect, sir, don't you think this is overreacting? And provocative? Historically, Belize has been a British problem. It's still a British protectorate. Technically, the Belizean chief of state is the queen of England, no different from Canada or Australia."

Moody turned his dark eyes on the man like a tank commander training his gun. The uppity little son of a bitch wasn't even an assistant secretary.

"I don't give a shit about history," Moody said. "And as far as I'm concerned, the British count about as much in this situation as fucking Luxembourg. I don't know what's going on in this piss-ant little country, but whatever it is, it's going on two hundred miles from the goddamn Mexican oil fields at Tabasco. I suspect all this amounts to is a little south-of-the-border political gunplay that got out of hand, but I don't want it to get so far out of hand that we have Mexicans and Guatemalans shooting at each other. And I don't want any of those lunatic guerrilla groups down there deciding this is a great time to start shooting at everybody. Our job is to calm things down, and a couple of F-14s flying low enough to give haircuts can have a tremendously calming effect, isn't that so, general?"

"They'll keep some heads down."

The State Department man was close to sputtering. "I think Secretary Hollis should be informed of your decision," he said.

"I'm sure he will be informed, just as soon as you can get to a phone," Moody said. "But I want it on the record that I've made no decision. I'm not the commander in chief. I've made a suggestion concerning routine precautionary measures that might be taken to protect American lives, property, and interests pending a final determination by the president. Understood?"

The State Department man flushed.

"Do you understand me?"

"Yes."

Moody glanced around the table, his eyes settling finally on the CIA's representative. "The intelligence product on this sucks," Moody said. "Can we get some fresher stuff?"

"Consider it on the way."

Moody pushed his chair back. "Let's all get some sleep and reconvene here at, say, seven A.M. I'm sure the president's going to be calling a meeting of the NSC sometime in the morning. In the meantime, I'll bring him up to date."

By "in the morning," he meant when the president returned to the White House from his vacation.

He stood up, feeling very, very good.

Sometimes, when he was working late at night, Moody left the White House by going through the rooms on the state floor, using the main entrance instead of the less conspicuous doors of the West Wing office lobby. Walking along the mansion's long, red-carpeted Cross Hall, with its marbled walls and pillars, venerable portraits and stately furnishings, gave him a reassuring comfort, a sense of belonging in his job. He liked the notion of the past presidents looking down on him, perhaps approvingly. Occasionally, he'd duck into the Red Room, where Dolley Madison used to play whist with drinking companions late into the night. There was a sumptuous painting above the mantel of Dolley's young South Carolina cousin, Angelica Singleton, who had married widower Martin Van Buren's son and was easily the loveliest first lady ever to have graced the Executive Mansion. Moody liked to stand there and gaze at her, much as he might were she alive.

As he approached the Red Room this night, he heard voices. For a moment, he feared the president had returned, but they sounded like strangers. One voice he suddenly recognized, however. The pitch was high and the accent affected, a little like a bad nightclub comedian doing an impersonation of George Plimpton. It was Peter Napier, a would-be Washington socialite who had been a high-ranking errand boy in the campaign and was now on the staff of the party's national committee. The man was a little weird and a total phony, but he'd proved very useful, willing to do whatever was asked of him. Moody recalled having once allowed the man a White House pass, but he'd thought it was temporary.

Moody stepped into the doorway. Napier, startled, stopped in midsentence. He was with a well-dressed, middle-aged couple and a handsome boy Moody presumed was their son.

"Good evening, Mr. Moody," Napier said brightly. He was in his thirties, and had a plump, shiny face, pointy nose, and seriously receding dark hair. His smile was eager. Moody didn't like him, but recognized the need to have people like that around. Someone had to fetch coffee, carry messages, and retrieve drunken politicians from their whorehouses.

"Good evening." Moody was curt.

"I'd like you to meet Mr. and Mrs. Hamlin. He was campaign finance chairman in Ohio? And this is their son Kenny."

The boy, maybe nineteen or twenty, smiled as eagerly as Napier.

"Pleased to meet you," Moody said, without enthusiasm. "May I speak to you a moment, Mr. Napier?"

The smile widened. "Sure thing, chief."

Moody didn't go far out of earshot. "What the hell are you doing in here?" he asked.

"Conducting a VIP tour. Senator Reidy asked the national committee to arrange it and I volunteered to do it."

"Are you on the White House access list?"

"Well, sure. You put me on it yourself."

Moody made a mental note to have the man's name removed. "You and your VIPs are going to have to leave," he said. "We have a crisis management team working here tonight."

"I'll have them out of here in two minutes, Mr. Moody. Nice to see you again."

Napier darted back into the Red Room. As Moody started down the hall again, he heard Napier say, "I'm awfully sorry, folks, but there's a major international crisis underway and we're going to have to cut this short. But I think you'll be able to say you were in the White House at a very historical moment."

Moody shook his head, and hurried out the door. "If those people aren't out of here in five minutes," he said to the guard, "get them out and escort them to the gate."

"Yes sir, Mr. Moody. Good night."

Moody owned two houses—a big, sprawling mansion outside Baltimore and a beachfront place just north of Ocean City—but after marrying Deena and then taking the White House job, he had bought an apartment in the Watergate complex, convenient to both his work and the capital's social life. His driver had him home very quickly.

Their housekeeper had gone to bed, but had left messages on the hall table saying that both Deena and Bernie Bloch had called. He decided to call them back in the morning. Both were doubtless upset with him. He needed some peaceful sleep.

He switched his regular phone to an answering machine, but activated the direct line from the White House, a secure, closed system to which only a few had access. Then he made himself a nightcap and stepped out onto his long, curving balcony, which looked out over the Potomac at the dark shape of Roosevelt Island. Beyond its high trees were the glittering high rises of the Rosslyn section of Arlington. Upriver were the heights of Georgetown and its hilltop university, the tall twin spires of its chapel a European silhouette against the hazy night sky. Though it was late on a weekend summer night, there was enough traffic on the nearby Rock Creek Parkway to make the city seem to throb beneath his feet, like the constant if almost imperceptible tremble of a ship's engines felt through the deck—a sensation of power. It was quite pleasing. The Virginia horse country seemed a million miles away.

Peter Napier got his charges off the White House grounds onto Pennsylvania Avenue without too much embarrassing haste, and then accompanied them on foot to their hotel, the majestic, beaux arts Willard, two blocks away. The mother seemed very tired, prompting Napier to invite them all for a nightcap in the Round Robin Bar, calculating that the son might accept but they would not. In fact, the boy suggested just that when his parents declined, but the father somewhat sternly reminded him that he was underage.

No great matter. The boy had expressed an interest in serving as a Senate page, and Napier had promised to see what could be arranged. He'd see the boy again. He'd look forward to that.

When they parted, Napier made a point of saying that he would have to get up very early in the morning in case the White House called. After all, he said, there was a major international crisis. He was glad they didn't ask where, as he didn't know.

Deena Moody was furious with her husband for ditching her in Dandytown the way he had—for making her face the sheriff and all the dumb but humiliating questions all alone. She'd get back at him for this in some truly nasty way at the first opportunity. Deena was a woman who earned her living by marrying men, and it occurred to her she was close to due for a promotion. That, of course, was a decision to be made after the next convention, when the president would make his call on a running mate for the next election. If he dumped the vice president for Moody, a possibility that at least one or two political columnists had already begun to ponder, that, she supposed, would be promotion enough. In the meantime, she was getting very tired of her husband's job.

The Blochs were going to drive her back to Washington in the morning. In the meantime, she thought she might as well find some way to take advantage of her husband's absence. A couple of men in the inn's bar had tried flirting with her, but Deena was not at all interested in that. Sherrie Bloch, rattled by the deaths of the girl trainer and her husband, had gotten quite drunk and was spewing forth a lot of unkind revelations about her husband. These could be useful, indeed. Deena sat sympathetically with the woman, stretching out her own drinks and listening patiently. Sherrie was complaining that Bloch had sometimes used the Clay girl for sex. Deena already knew that. She wanted to know who else had jumped in the hay with the dead girl. She had a pretty good idea her husband had. Women were probably his only weakness, but it was a big one.

Sherrie said her husband was extremely upset about something that night. Deena knew it wasn't because of Vicky Clay. Except to complain about the sheriff's handling of the investigation, Bernie Bloch had paid practically no attention to that little matter. Vicky might as well have been a horse who had died. Maybe less than that, since she didn't cost him anything. What did it take for Bernie Bloch to value a woman? What would she have to be, or do? How had this dumb, mouse-voiced bimbo gotten her hooks into him, and kept them there for so many years?

Sherrie was so drunk she probably couldn't stand, but not enough to stop talking. They'd been joined by three others, a silly-looking couple as drunk as Sherrie was, and a young man whose type Deena instantly recognized, the kind who hung around money like a fruit fly hovering over a bowl of grapes. Deena wanted no part of him. Not now. Creeps like that were for a woman's old age.

She stood up. "Sherrie, honey. I've gotta go see somebody. You all right?"

Sherrie waved her off. Deena took that as a blessing.

Bloch was in the bedroom of his suite, sitting lumplike on the edge of his bed, staring morosely at the floor. It was several hours since he'd gotten the bad news about the auction from Billy Bonning, and Bloch had given up trying to get through the White House switchboard to Bob Moody, who had left instructions not to be interrupted by anyone. Bloch had his friend's direct office number, of course, but that just ran on and on unanswered. Calls to Moody's Watergate place had reached only a housekeeper and then an answering machine. Bloch couldn't understand how Moody could have done this to him—whether his old pal was angry about something or had just suffered a mental lapse. He decided it must have had something to do with the White House. That job was changing Bobby Moody, a lot more than Bloch liked.

He'd tried without any success to track down Moody's daughter, but she and the damned horse seemed to have completely vanished. He'd find her eventually. Movie stars and race horses didn't just disappear. In the meantime, he had another call to make, one that was hours overdue. One that he'd be happy to wait a hundred years before making.

Bloch dialed the number slowly, like someone calling a doctor for the results of an important lab test—only it was he who had the bad news.

When his party finally got on the line, Bloch paused, then jumped into it. He played poker that way, bet or get out.

"This is Bernie Bloch," he said, as confidently as possible. "There's been a problem. I wasn't able to get to the auction. I don't have title to the stallion—yet."

He leaned back, holding the receiver away from his ear. The other man's voice was unpleasant, and loud.

"Give me a break here, will you?" Bloch said. "The police wouldn't let us go. My trainer and her husband are dead. Drug overdose or something, but they kept us all here for questioning."

He was sweating. His shirt was soaking.

"Look! They wouldn't let us go! Did you want me to stir up the cops in addition to everything else? . . . Yes, I did send someone in my place. A good friend. Only there was a mix-up. His daughter ended up with the horse."

The other man's voice raged inside the receiver's earpiece.

"Yes, I know where the horse is!" Bernie said, getting angry himself now. "It's with her. I'll take care of everything—in the morning . . . Look, you gotta understand. There are police all over the place. Local police. Sheriff's police. Cops who know about horses."

The voice on the other end became less hostile—or at least, more circumspect.

"I'll call you tomorrow," Bloch said. "It's all going to work out fine. Like always. Trust me."

Hanging up, he sat there a long moment, rocking back and forth slightly with his eyes closed. Fatigue and fear had numbed his brain. He needed to think, but couldn't.

There was a gentle rapping at the door of the suite, so faint that for a moment Bloch wondered if the person was knocking at the room next door. Expecting that it would be his wife, and wondering if she'd done something stupid like losing her key, he swore, got up, and went into the sitting room. Swinging the door open rudely, he found himself looking at the blond, tan, and pink spectacle that was Deena Moody.

"Bernie," she said, her southern voice a little breathless and husky. "What have you been doing up here?"

"Business," he said. "Your husband really fucked me up."

She moved past him, her expensive but too strong perfume making him a little dizzy. "How's that, Bernie?"

"I really wanted that horse. He should have told me he wasn't going to make the auction."

"I'm not too happy with him tonight, either, darlin'."

He shut the door, making sure of the click of the lock. Having Deena Moody in his hotel room at this hour wasn't exactly something he would have expected. But nothing that had happened that day had been expected.

"I'll work it out," he said. "It's probably no big deal. Your husband's a busy man. I forgive him."

"I don't," she said. "Can I have a drink."

"Sure," he said, a little uneasily. "A little scotch?"

"Yes, please. And I hope you'll join me." She sat down on a couch. "Your charmin' wife is way ahead of us. Gallons ahead. I'm not sure she can make it up the stairs."

"She gets that way sometimes," he said. "More and more lately."

When he brought Deena her glass, she held it, but did not drink. He leaned back against the arm of a nearby chair, rubbing his belly, a nervous habit.

"So, you enjoying the weekend, Deena?"

"Up until tonight."

"I like it when we can all get together," he said.

"You and I never get to talk much."

"Always happy to see you."

They stared at each other for a long moment. He was amazed at how awake and alert she looked at this hour, at the directness of her gaze.

"I like you, Bernie," she said, softly. "I've never had a chance to tell you how much."

"I like you, too, Deena. I was really glad when Bobby decided to marry you. His first wife and I, we didn't get along too well."

Another silence. Her eyes never wavered. She took a deep breath, her breasts heaving against the low neckline of her dress.

"Life is short, Bernie. We shouldn't pass up its opportunities. You're not a man to pass up an opportunity, are you?"

"Well, not often."

She put down her glass. "I like you, Bernie, and I'm mad as hell at my husband."

"Deena . . ."

"We're both grown-ups. You're about the most grown-up man I know."

His mind reflexively began calculating—possibilities, odds, problems.

She stood up. Her kiss took him by surprise. Afterward, a funny, happy look came into her eyes—like an artist pleased with the effect of a brush stroke.

"What do you think, Bernie?"

"Sherrie could come through that door any minute."

"I don't think so, sweetheart, but we probably don't have a lot of time. It can't be the way I'd really like it. But it can be somethin'."

"Deena, I don't know. I . . ."

She reached for the back of her dress. "I'm going to take off my clothes. I want you to see me, Bernie."

Her movements were well practiced. Her dress slid to the floor with a hushed rustle. The rest came off quickly.

She looked even better than he had imagined, and he had thought about that many times. Few women her age could manage to look like that.

"Don't move," she said, coming close again. "You're not going to have to do a thing."

The first touch of her tongue struck him like an electric current. He looked down the gleaming smoothness of her back to the roundness of her bottom, then closed his eyes.

Bob Moody had just caused him a major amount of trouble. It ought to cost him something.

Deena was just pulling on her dress when the key turned suddenly in the lock. Bloch, still emerging from his bliss, had not yet dealt with his pants and the door opened before he could. The dread certainty that it was his wife became surprise as Lenore Fairbrother stuck her head into the room.

"Oh dear," she said. "This suite is most definitely occupied."

Bloch turned around, struggling furiously with his zipper, swearing. "Do calm down, Mr. Bloch, darling," Lenore continued.

"Sinning is the rule here on race weekends. If you hope to be a regular you're going to have to get used to that."

Deena, her dress more or less in place, looked frantically about for a route of escape. Finding none, she decided to retreat into indignation. Her voice got very Southern.

"How dare you walk in here like this? Where did you get that key?"

Lenore pulled it from the lock. It was on a large brass ring with many others.

"My dear husband, who owns most everything in Dandytown, also owns this inn," she said. "You may consider me room service. I'm sure you didn't order her, but I'm bringing you an unconscious and quite terribly drunk woman who's been misbehaving in the bar. Your charming wife, I believe. Two helpful gentlemen are just now carrying her up the stairs."

Bloch gave up on his zipper and simply pulled out his shirt, yanking it down around him. He was calculating how much he was going to be in this woman's obligation.

"Could you get out of here, Mrs. Fairbrother?"

"Of course, dear boy." Enjoying herself immensely, she glanced at Deena, who was reaching into the bodice of her dress to straighten her bra. "You two will probably want to make yourselves more presentable, so I'll delay the two gentlemen for a moment."

She stepped back into the hall, then hesitated, returning her face to the doorway. She was probably as drunk as Sherrie, but quite in control of her speech.

"I shall have your wife brought in now, Mr. Bloch," she said. "If you should like her taken away again, just call the desk. Or if you like, just put her out in the hall. Nighty night."

Alixe Percy had fallen asleep waiting on the porch of Showers' house while waiting for his return, slumbering so deeply she didn't hear the approach of his Jeep. Seeing her collapsed in one of his wicker chairs, Showers sent Becky off to bed, then hobbled up the porch steps and eased himself into an adjoining chair. He was so tired he could think of nothing to say, and just sat for a long moment.

Alixe was snoring, quietly, but without promise of cessation.

"Alixe," he said finally, just as quietly.

The snoring continued.

"Alixe!"

She snorted, her head snapping forward, then looked quickly about her, smiling when she saw him. She looked at her watch.

"My God, man," she said. "You've been out half the night. You and the fair young Becky been out in the hay?"

Showers sighed wearily, closing his eyes, "No, Alixe. We've been with Moonsugar. It looks good. I really think he's going to make it. I think I'm going to be able to give Fairbrother back his horse."

"He won't want it. You know how he is about damaged goods. No, David, whatever else you did out on that course today, you won yourself a horse. If he comes through it well enough, you may be able to use him in the dressage ring."

Showers stretched out his injured leg. "Just what I need, another mouth in the barn to fed."

She hesitated, then decided there might be advantage in his sleepiness.

"That stallion out of Queen Tashamore's granddaughter went pretty cheap tonight," she said.

Showers only stared at the woods.

"Ten thousand," she said. "Someone from out of state."

"They got a bargain, unless there's something wrong with it."

"Looked good to me."

"Looked good to me, too. There are other horses."

"I may be able to pick it up even cheaper. I don't think this was a really serious buyer."

"Not Bernie Bloch?"

"He didn't even show. Vicky Clay must have been wrong."

"In too many ways."

"Poor little wretch. If she hadn't killed so many horses, I'd feel sorry for her."

"I feel sorry for her."

"You feel sorry for everyone, David, including a lot of people who'd be a lot better off if someone just gave them a kick in the ass once in a while. Including a Lenore Fairbrother I could name."

"If it weren't for Lenore, Lynwood might have put Moonsugar down."

"That's Lenore, a regular Mother Teresa." She stretched and yawned. "David, if I can get this horse, are you still interested?"

"No, Alixe. I'll have my hands full with Moonsugar. And this treaty is going to take a lot of my time."

"Well, I'm going to see if I can't do a little horse trading anyway.

I've got room in my stable, and I think that's more horse than she wanted to buy."

"She?"

"The buyer. I think I may be able to work something out. If I do, and you change your mind, maybe you and I can do some horse trading."

"Not anytime soon."

Alixe slapped her knees and stood up. "Hell, David. It's been hours since I've had a drink. You want to join me?"

"No, thanks, Alixe. I've got an early day."

"All right, dear heart. Just remember, my bottle's always open."

She laughed, feeling good. "Good night, dearie. Take care of that leg."

He watched her stride off into the night.

Somehow, he managed to get himself upstairs, setting his alarm for an hour so early that going to bed seemed a pointless formality. After undressing, he lay back against his old-fashioned country pillow, turning his thoughts to the day to come, wondering if he could handle the long drive to the capital in his Jeep. At the very least, it would be extremely painful, but there was nothing else to be done. It was his job. Jumping horses was his pleasure, and no excuse for truancy.

He closed his eyes. As sometimes happened, the day's events rushed by in hurried memory, and he could almost hear the pounding of horses' hooves. He saw Jimmy Kipp's blood again, spattered over the grass. He saw Kipp's injured horse rise and fall and die. But he fell asleep with a pleasant image in his mind, the face of the dark-haired woman he'd encountered in the aid station. He could see her in the most perfect detail. He supposed all beautiful movie stars affected one that memorably.

# Five

Secretary of State Hollis had made the kind of mistake Moody would expect from a loser.

Hollis's first attempt to climb the small but respectable Swiss mountain called Der Mädchenberg had been foiled by rain and slippery surfaces and his own fear. His second effort was curtailed when his Swiss guide unexpectedly developed stomach cramps. In two days, Hollis was due at the United Nations conference in Geneva that was his ostensible reason for coming to Switzerland. That left time for one more attempt—if he was quick about it—and he'd rashly decided to make a try. He had climbed a number of decent little mountains in the United States and around the world, but never a genuine Swiss Alp. He wanted to go back to Washington with a photograph of himself standing on the Mädchenberg's summit, just as his big-game-hunting predecessor James Baker had returned from so many diplomatic missions with wild animal trophies—missions that had little other real purpose.

What made the little Mädchenberg so respectable was a formidable rock face that, with three breaks, rose in an otherwise nearly sheer wall for more than two thousand feet on the mountain's north slope. There were seven overhangs to be surmounted, and a dangerous traverse across a deep, diagonal crevasse. The secretary of state would have reason to be proud of his photo.

Hollis and his guide, recovered from his cramps, were camped on a fold of ridge high up on the Mädchenberg when the call came over the two-way radio about the crisis in Belize. Informed by staff who had remained behind in the village that the situation was under control and that the president had not requested his presence, Hollis had elected to stay and complete his climb. He was so desperate to do it he probably would have fended off a call to return from the president himself.

Hollis was a man of fifty-eight who vigorously kept himself in the physical condition of someone a good fifteen years younger. He was an experienced if not inordinately expert climber who had scaled New Hampshire's 6,200-foot Mount Washington when he was only fourteen. But his skill could not compensate for his haste.

The rains returned the morning of his final ascent. Attempting to keep to schedule, Hollis moved too quickly clambering up over the rock face's second overhang. His hand slipped, then his foot, and he fell backward, head first.

He was well roped. His guide, in the lead, had set his pitons well. Had Hollis dropped straight down, he would have easily survived, except for bruises from his harness. But when he began to lose purchase, his efforts to hang on were so frantic that he pushed out when he fell. After the rope snapped taut, he swung back against the wall like a weight on a pendulum, spinning as he swung. Instead of striking the rock cliff with his feet, as a truly expert climber might have managed, he collided head first. The guide, perched on the overhang just above, heard a shout and then a popping thud.

The secretary had hired a helicopter to take photographs and videotape footage during the ascent and then pluck them off the summit once the climb was done. The pilot/photographer captured the entire tragedy. After he and the guide had brought Hollis's body down, he sold the pictures to an American television correspondent from Geneva. They were on CNN in a few hours.

Usually, Moody was the first high-ranking official in the White House to be told of such momentous events. Any staffer who failed to inform him first could find himself or herself suddenly transferred to the Department of Housing and Urban Development, or some worse bureaucratic purgatory. But at the early morning hour at which the news arrived, Moody was closeted in his West Wing office with Senators Reidy and Sorenson and had threatened beheadings if he was disturbed by anyone except the president or General St. Angelo.

Instead of taking his guests to the informal circle of armchairs he kept by his office fireplace—an arrangement more conducive to relaxed and informal conversation—Moody remained behind his huge antique desk, placing his two guests in stiff-backed chairs in front of him, like subordinates making a report.

Senate Majority Leader Reidy was a rough-hewn but unusually handsome man, politically experienced, legislatively clever, at ease in leadership, and very, very smart. He had a picture-perfect family, a doctorate in history, a respectable military record, was a familiar face on the Sunday morning television news interview shows, and had done important favors for virtually every major politician in his party. He had waited until just the right time to make his move for the presidency. It had utterly dumbfounded him to have lost early in the Democratic primaries to the cold, visionary, pompous Massachusetts aristocrat who now occupied the Oval Office. Reidy had not accepted the pundits' conventional wisdom that his failure was entirely due to his refusal to take a strong, forthright stand on any of the contentious issues that had dominated the campaign—especially the environmental ones that his rival had forged into a personal crusade. Reidy bore a deep, bitter resentment bordering on hatred toward everyone responsible for his defeat—except, of course, himself.

But he was a skilled, professional politician, and surface affability was very much a part of his job and his method. Though he despised Moody, he always shook his hand warmly, calling him "Bobby." Reidy was a westerner from one of the mountain states, and informality came easily to him. A Stanford graduate and onetime Rhodes scholar, he was nevertheless fond of wearing cowboy hats and telling off-color jokes. He was as ruthless a lawmaker as had ever survived and succeeded on Capitol Hill. As had once been said of Lincoln, those who underestimated Reidy quickly found their backs against the bottom of a ditch. Moody didn't trust him much, but admired him.

Sorenson was a much younger man, a well-meaning midwestern liberal open in his hypocrisy. He was a strong advocate of major cuts in the defense budget, except as concerned the procurement of army trucks and small navy patrol craft, both of which were manufactured in his state. Like many of his constituents, he was a strong-minded environmentalist—except as concerned open-cut logging and pollution from paper mills.

His pitch to Moody that morning was a long lament about the effect the president's Earth Treaty and accompanying Earth Bill would have on those of his constituents employed in timber and paper manufacturing. Their plight had given him doubts, he said.

He wondered if the president's environmental package wasn't too much, too soon.

Moody didn't like Sorenson at all. He was a man who compensated for his small stature and bland physiognomy with thick-soled shoes, dapper dress, and a very carefully styled TV anchorman's hairdo. The young senator was also a jogger and a devotee of health foods. As a guest at one of Deena's more socially ambitious dinner parties—catered with an elaborate French menu—Sorenson had consumed only the vegetables. As a boy in West Virginia, Moody had eaten vegetarian meals only because his family couldn't always afford meat.

But Sorenson was important. Ratification of the Earth Treaty and passage of the tandem implementing legislation would require every possible vote. Approval by the Senate Foreign Relations Committee was the first big stone to be rolled over. Two or three of the Republicans on the committee had indicated their support of ratification, but it was paramount that the Democrats vote unanimously. Sorenson was the only waverer. Thus far. His defection could lead to more.

Glancing at his watch, Moody noted that the president would be returning in less than half an hour.

"Excuse me, Senator," he said, interrupting Sorenson, "but we don't have time for any more of this starving lumberjack bullshit." He grinned, as though to imply his rough talk was intended as "real man" bonhomie, but the startled Sorenson was not disarmed.

"The provisions of the Earth Treaty are not negotiable," Moody continued. "Consequently, those of the implementing legislation aren't either. Sorry, but that's the way it is. The president made a promise to the American people and he's not going to back down on it—not for you, not for me, not for anyone."

"But—"

"Read the polls, Senator. They're still holding better than two to one for the treaty. Been that way from the beginning."

Moody leaned back in his chair, resting his big hands in his lap. "This is not to say we have nothing to talk about. You need a little something to make the folks back home feel good about you if you throw in with us. So what do you want?"

"I don't understand."

"Look, Senator. I served in a state legislature. You served in a state legislature. You understand perfectly."

"Well," said Sorenson, looking as uncomfortable as a child on a department store Santa's lap, "we've fought pretty hard to keep that

Amtrak link open from Chicago, but you guys cut it from the budget."

Moody made a notation. "The budget's still on the table. That can be rethought."

"And you froze highway trust funds we were counting on for interstate bridge repairs. Plus the airport runway extension."

Moody scribbled further. "We can take a look at that."

Reidy cleared his throat. "I trust you fellas are keeping in mind that Appropriations and the Commerce, Science, and Transportation Committee will have to sign off on these things."

"And you'll be happy to see that they do, won't you, Senator?" Moody said.

Reidy glowered at him, but let the remark pass.

"Anything else, Senator Sorenson?" Moody said. "Let's not get too greedy. This is a pen I'm holding, not a magic wand."

"Is the president going to campaign for individual senators?" Sorenson said. "Speak at fund-raisers?"

It was what the president hated most about his job—about politics. "Maybe a little," Moody said. "I'm not sure how much he'll be out your way."

"That's the last thing you want," said Reidy. "The Earth Bill is not exactly what your labor unions and business PACs have been praying for."

"Anything else?" Moody said, letting some impatience show.

"Well," Sorenson said, with a quick glance at Reidy. "My wife's expressed an interest in serving on the Kennedy Center board. But, uh, the Senate leadership, well, I guess there's a waiting list."

"The very next vacancy," Moody said, writing that item down with a flourish. He had already promised Deena the next Kennedy Center vacancy, but Sorenson would have to come first. Perhaps a way could be found to create two vacancies. The administration had ambassadorships and commission appointments to trade.

"And, as I think of it—" Sorenson began.

Moody cut him short, setting down his pen.

"You've been quite reasonable about this, Senator," he said. "I appreciate that. I'm sure the president will, too, when I try to talk him into all this."

"That's it?"

"Isn't it?"

They sat in silence a moment, then Sorenson stood. "Maybe I'll hold a press conference to announce how I'm going to vote."

Moody wondered if he had been hijacked. If Sorenson was as

worried about the threat to logging and paper mill jobs in his state as he said, he sure as hell wouldn't be holding a press conference.

He got up from his leather swivel chair and extended his hand. "If there's anything more we can do, let us know."

Reidy accompanied Sorenson to the door, but remained behind. When he and Moody were alone, he went to the windows to the rear of Moody's desk. The view was of the Ellipse and the Washington Monument, the obelisk's edges sharp in the brightness of the early morning light.

"I tell you, Bobby, you keep buying votes this way and there won't be enough money left in the budget to pay for a single emissions control inspector."

"Don't get the wrong idea. My generosity has its limits. But his vote's important. I want to get some momentum going—and that means every swinging Democratic dick on the committee. What's your count on the Republicans?"

He continued to sit facing forward, even though Reidy was behind him. He was not about to turn around and speak his piece looking up at the Senate leader.

"Hell, Bobby, I think when push comes to shove you'll get nearly all of them, except for a few right-wing looney tunes. The Earth Treaty's motherhood. It's not like the days when Reagan could say fuck you to the world and tear up the United Nations Law of the Sea Treaty. Anyway, that was all about sharing the wealth from undersea magnesium nodules, for God's sake. This is air and water, trees and Bambi. Sorenson might find some way to drag his feet in committee, but he still wouldn't dare cast a nay against ratification on the floor."

Moody drummed his fingers on the desk. It had once belonged to Teddy Roosevelt, a man whom Moody much admired, despite his aristocratic background.

"So we should just call the whole package up for a vote and then all go to the seashore?"

"That's not what I'm saying, Bobby."

"Take your seat, Dan. Your coffee's getting cold."

Reidy hesitated, then reluctantly did as bidden, ambling back to his chair. He leaned back, propping his highly polished loafers up on the desk top. He gazed appreciatively at Moody's framed photograph of Deena as he spoke.

"But I'm talking about the treaty, not the whole package," Reidy said. "The treaty's pretty easy. It's just a promissory note. Ratifying it won't cost anybody their jobs. It's just an agreement to enact the

Earth Bill—at some time in the future. But if you push them through together in one package, the way the president wants, I can see things grinding to a halt, a real long halt. That's where those good polls of yours begin to crumble, when they start closing coal mines and landfills and power plants."

"That isn't what you saw a month ago."

"Things change. The economy's getting sickly again."

"The Earth Bill sailed out of the House."

"I wouldn't call a seventeen-vote margin sailing. More like crawling. It's got to go through at least three Senate committees, and there've already been fifty-eight amendments proposed for it. The final decision's going to be made in a House-Senate conference committee, and I could rewrite the whole goddamn Constitution with the right kind of conference committee."

"What are you saying, Senator?"

"You've got to persuade the president to break these out separately. Move fast on the treaty now, but hold off on the Earth Bill. Get yourself a big flashy victory on ratification, then use it as a lever to get what you really want—and need." He paused. "It would help if you could get Japan to sign the damn treaty, and Taiwan and Korea—not to speak of Russia, England, and Mexico."

"We're working on that."

"You gotta get Japan aboard. No American's going to want to give up his job for the nice little trees while the Japanese are breathing smoke to keep all the Toyotas coming. You've got the Germans with you. They're taking as big a leadership role as we are. Why not the Japanese?"

"The president's been talking to them."

"I'm sure he has, but what's he been saying?"

"We'll take care of the diplomacy, Senator. Your job's your esteemed colleagues. When you say 'hold off,' how long do you mean?"

Reidy shrugged. "Late October, November. Not all that long. But I've got an idea about the Japanese, something that could scare them shitless, if it's handled right." He reached into his pocket, pulled out a single sheet of folded paper, and laid it out flat on the desk in front of Moody.

"What the hell is this?"

"Just read it."

Moody did so, then made a very sour face. "This is fucking nonsense, Dan. There is no White House plan like this, not even in those end-of-the-world contingency files. The president would never threaten the Japanese with this shit. It's a declaration of economic war. If they retaliated—if they pulled their money out of our banks—it would be the biggest fucking mess you've ever seen. The president would kick me all the way to the river if I ever suggested anything like this."

Reidy smiled. "Of course he would. I'm not saying you should do any such thing, or that he should say anything to the Japanese, or that anyone should type up a White House memo."

"But this says there is one."

"Read it again. This is a confidential letter on Democratic National Committee stationery, signed by a junior staffer and addressed to the party's state finance chairman in California, asking how he thought such an ultimatum would go down with all the Japanese-owned American companies out there. It only says that the staffer understands there is such a White House memo—a White House plan. He's worried about the political repercussions."

"The first thing that finance chairman would do is call the president."

"No he wouldn't. He'd call you. But this will never get to him. The idea is just to float it past the Japanese. Let them get a whiff of it, that's all. Enough to scare them. Make them think there's big trouble brewing, without challenging them out in the open."

"This staffer whose name you've got on it, Peter Napier. He's just some goofball errand boy. I had to shag him out of the White House last night. He was giving some fund-raiser a goddamn personal tour."

"The Japanese don't know any of that. His title's legitimate. It will look like real good intelligence."

"How much does this Napier guy know—about what you have in mind?"

"Practically nothing. I told him it's a phony I just want to use on a couple of senators, to keep them in line, to show them the president's hanging tough."

Moody drummed his fingers on the desktop, biting down on his lower lip. "And how do you propose floating this past the Japanese?"

"I thought I'd go to the smartest man in Washington and let him figure that out."

"Who?"

"You. You've got the whole administration at your disposal, Bobby. You must know some up-front guy in the Trade Office or at State who deals regularly with the Japanese, some guy you can trust to do the right thing. A guy at a low enough level so it wouldn't look like this was coming directly from the White House."

Moody drummed his fingers again. "I suppose anything's possible."

"Think about it. And think about what I said about moving on the treaty first."

A faint ticking noise caught their attention. In a moment, it grew to a throbbing clatter, steadily increasing in volume. Both men looked to the windows. A cluster of dots appeared in the distance beyond the Washington Monument, their size expanding until they were visible as helicopters.

"Hail to the chief," said Reidy.

"Thanks for your help, Senator," Moody said. "You'll be the first to know what the president decides on the treaty move. But I don't think I'm going to bother him about this."

He put the phony memo in his pocket. As Reidy started toward the door, Moody reached for his telephone. "Get me General St. Angelo," he said to his secretary. "Now! And when I'm done with him, get me Secretary Sadinauskas."

The president was already in the Oval Office by the time Moody finished getting his briefing from the general. Charging down the corridor, he walked right in. Moody was the only member of the staff who could enter the president's office without announcement, and he did so then. Immediately, he wished he hadn't. The president's unhappiness was almost palpable.

The president did not even greet him. He sat in his big leather chair, staring at his empty desktop, his cold mood holding Moody to a simple "Good morning, sir."

The president looked at him sadly, but did not speak. The helicopters took off again in a flurry of noise.

"Good morning, Robert."

The man said nothing more. Moody wondered if his boss was angry or worried over the handling of the situation in Belize.

"I just got a report from St. Angelo, sir," Moody said. "The crisis is as good as over."

"What are you talking about, Robert?" The president's mournful voice sounded like old hollow wood.

"In Belize."

"Belize. Oh yes."

"The Mexicans and Guatemalans have backed off. The Belizean government's going to open an inquiry into the shooting of our missionary. The guerrillas have gone back into the bush. Our only casualty was the missionary."

The president leaned slowly back, and closed his eyes. " 'The worst is death, and death shall have his day.' Death is having his day."

He sighed, and swiveled toward the windows overlooking the Rose Garden.

"He was a noble, honorable man, Bob. The finest friend I had in school. The finest friend a man could ask for."

"The missionary?"

"The missionary? No. I'm talking about Secretary Hollis. Skip's dead, Bob. Didn't you know?"

Moody lowered himself into a nearby chair. He was stunned. And furious. Why hadn't anyone told him?

"I'm sorry, sir. I didn't know. What in the hell happened?"

"They informed me as I was getting off the plane at Andrews. There was an accident, a climbing accident. He was mountain climbing in Switzerland. I told him he needn't go to that conference in Geneva. But he insisted. Skip was that way. Never a shirker. Always plunging ahead."

"A hell of a guy." Moody's shock had worn off. His mind was racing.

"The best. I'll never be able to replace him. Never."

"I'm sorry. No one told me. I was in a meeting with Senator Reidy, on the treaty."

"Skip believed in the treaty. Deeply. His death is a big setback for us."

Moody swallowed hard. Hollis's death would have about as much effect on the treaty as the New York Yankees losing the pennant. He framed his next words carefully.

"Reidy thinks it looks real good for the treaty, sir. We had one possible defection. Senator Sorenson. But I got him back into line this morning. Just now."

The president said nothing.

"In fact, it looks so good Reidy thinks we ought to move immediately on ratification, even if it means waiting awhile on the implementing legislation."

The other turned slowly in his chair. "Wait?" He uttered the word like an obscenity. "Wait? This is the most important legislation ever to come before Congress. It means the salvation of our planet!"

"I understand that, sir. I'm not sure I completely trust Reidy on this score. I made it very clear to him that we won't tolerate any unwarranted delay. But I think he's right about moving at once on ratification. A quick victory like that would take some wind out of the opposition. And it would serve as a beacon for the countries that haven't signed yet."

"Far too many of those."

"And," Moody continued, "it would be a wonderful tribute to Secretary Hollis. A fitting memorial."

The president began rocking gently in his chair—an old habit. "It would indeed, Bob. Yes, it would."

"I'll see to it then, sir."

"Yes."

"Move immediately on ratification."

"Indeed. We'll go on that."

Moody rose, then hesitated.

"Sir, I came in last night to help General St. Angelo with the Belize trouble."

"You're no shirker either, Bob."

"I, I mean we, we deployed a few military units here and there. Small ones. Just to show the flag. Help keep the peace."

"With salubrious effect, I gather."

"Yes sir."

"Very good. I don't know how this place could run without you."

Moody started for the door, then halted again.

"Sir, do you want Undersecretary Richmond to sit in for Secretary Hollis this morning? You have a cabinet meeting at ten. I presume you want Richmond to run things at State until you name a successor."

"I don't even want to think about a successor just now."

"But you do want Richmond at the cabinet meeting."

"Cancel the meeting, Bob. Cancel everything. I've got to write a letter to Skip's wife. Wonderful girl. I knew her when she was at Smith."

Returning to his office, Moody stopped at his secretary's desk, planting his hands hard on its surface and leaning over to glower into her pale, apprehensive eyes.

"Anne," he said quietly, "why didn't you tell me immediately that Hollis had been killed?"

"You were with Senator Reidy, Mr. Moody. You said—"

"Didn't it occur to you that I might want to know?"

"Yes, sir, but I didn't think—"

"You didn't think? Then why are you here?"

He slammed his office door behind him.

Hollis's death had thrown the State Department into chaos, the secretary's now vacant office the calm eye of a hurricane of frantic telephone calls, hastily called meetings, and useless bustling about. A stranger looking upon the scene would have thought war had been declared or that the president had been shot. In the labyrinthian corridors of the lower floors, department bureaucrats stopped for hushed conversations, most addressing the same concerns: Who would be the next secretary? Would there be a major shake-up? If the deputy secretary got the job, would everyone move up the ladder? Would more ambassadorships be opened to career diplomats?

Showers, arriving just before lunchtime, tried to ignore all this. He had heard the news of the secretary's fatal accident on his car radio. It had startled him, but he knew very well there was nothing he could do to affect the rush of events that would follow, not even those that might personally affect him. He doubted there would be much impact on the Earth Treaty. Hollis had been the least effective secretary Showers had ever served under. All the policy decisions concerning the treaty had been made in the White House.

His limp was still painful, but he was managing with a cane. To those who asked him about his injury, he simply responded that he'd had a riding accident. That he had lost or won a major steeplechase race out in Virginia meant nothing to these people. His equestrian life was just another hobby, like the late secretary's mountain climbing or Showers' secretary's aerobics classes.

She gave him a brave little smile as he entered. "Awful news about Mr. Hollis."

"Yes. Terrible thing."

"Are you all right?"

He glanced at his leg. "I'm fine. Just getting too old to be jumping horses."

"Your two meetings this afternoon have been canceled. The energy secretary called. He wants to have lunch with you. At Duke Zeibert's. One o'clock."

"Today."

"Yes."

Showers had been planning to eat at his desk. "All right. Fine."

"I'll call his secretary."

He nodded his thanks, then limped on into his office. It was midsized, and had a view of the Mall, the top of the Lincoln Memorial visible just above the trees. The walls were mostly decorated with Currier & Ives prints of fox hunting scenes. In his long foreign service career, Showers had worked mostly with maritime and oceanographic matters, yet had never had much interest in boats or sailing. His mother's people in Rhode Island had been sailors. His cousin Jack Spencer had won as many small boat races in his youth as Showers had steeplechase events. If he hadn't become a newspaperman, and such a heavy drinker, Spencer might have competed in the Olympics, or the around the world Whitbread race, or even the America's Cup.

Trophies. Medals. Prizes for games. They were such sacred totems in his family. But who else cared?

The principal decoration in Showers' office had nothing to do with games. It was a large, floor-mounted globe, set in an antique wooden frame. He kept it positioned upside down—something he had learned from Elliot Richardson when the former cabinet secretary had served as U.S. ambassador to the Law of the Sea Conference and Showers was a young diplomat just assigned to his staff.

Richardson had sat on his couch, doodling owls on a notepad as he talked on and on about the importance of the conference, then he'd unexpectedly gotten up and gone to his globe—one much like Showers'.

"I keep it like this so that people will understand," he'd said.

Viewed from beneath, the earth was nearly all ocean, with smidgens of continent appearing at the edges, like unimportant islands.

Globes, of course, bore no representation of the earth's atmosphere, and thus could not depict the quite frightening hole eaten in the protective ozone layer by the seasonal polar accumulation of man's aerial poisons. This year, the hole had reached dimensions exceeding the area of the Antarctic land mass.

Showers went quickly through his mail, extracting two thick reports that he'd been expecting from the Environmental Protection Agency. He'd already seen summaries of their findings, but needed the voluminous data they contained for reference during the week's briefings and staff meetings.

The conclusions were as frightening as the current degree of ozone depletion. One report was an estimate of the annual accumulation of solid waste in the United States. Back in 1989, there had been dire predictions that the nation would be generating more than 216 million tons of useless and noxious garbage annually by the year 2000. The turn of the millennium was still a few years away, but that tonnage had already been reached. Beaches were being closed that summer from Lewes, Delaware, to Block Island.

The other report contained a highly technical survey of pH levels produced by acid rain in upstate New York lakes. It sadly reminded Showers of a time more than a decade before when he had visited a Canadian counterpart in his office in Ottawa. The man was seriously ill and was being made to take a medical retirement from his job. He despaired over this, because he had accomplished so little and such a monstrous lot remained to be done. Showers recalled him standing at his window, a frail, forlorn figure staring out at the vastness of Canadian wilderness stretching away to the north.

"It's all dying," he said. "You may not believe this, but one day your own Lake Champlain will be dead."

According to the pH-level report, Lake Champlain was now terminally ill.

Showers placed the reports in the large wooden file box of official horror stories he kept on the top of his desk. He and his assistants called it their "hell box." It was getting very full.

He was due at lunch. His date wasn't merely with a cabinet officer, but an old friend.

The government of the United States could no more function without its Washington restaurants and watering holes than a garden could bloom without the commerce of bees.

As had been true since the earliest days of the republic, when Secretary of State Thomas Jefferson had supped with Secretary of the Treasury Alexander Hamilton at the table of their common boarding house, the discreet and convivial atmosphere of the capital's bars and dining rooms allowed for a freedom of discourse and candor impossible in formal, recorded meetings or monitorable telephone conversations. It was in these places, not offices and hearing rooms, that alliances were cemented, enemies wooed, plots hatched, and secrets shared.

The restaurant was a great leveler. Seated across a table, cabinet secretary and reporter, ambassador and committee staffer, four-star general and White House aide, could abandon protocol and speak as equals. Usually, each needed something from the other. Occasionally, they met simply as friends. It was on this basis that Energy Secretary Waldemar Sadinauskas and foreign service officer David

Showers shared a warm handshake and sat down at a quiet corner table at Duke Zeibert's, a New York–style steak and gravy eatery that had probably given birth or administered death to more legislation than any committee room in the Capitol.

Sadinauskas was a big, unpretentious, rough-mannered and disarmingly amiable former congressman whose occasional crudeness and proletarian tastes masked a keen intellect and expansive knowledge of world affairs. Many an old-school Washington Brahmin had underestimated this man at his consequent peril. A Lithuanian-American from one of the coal valleys of Pennsylvania, he had never graduated from college but had richly educated himself through voracious and highly eclectic reading. He had served seven terms in the House, rising to chairman of the House Energy and Commerce Committee and second-ranking member of House Foreign Affairs. He'd been snapped up by the president for this cabinet post.

Sadinauskas and Showers had met back in the 1970s during the rancorous "cod war" between Iceland and Great Britain. Despite the sporadic violence the conflict had engendered at sea, the State Department had dismissed the dispute as a "Mouse That Roared" fish fight beneath its concern at a time of increasing cold war tensions and continuing crises in the Mideast. Showers, then a very junior diplomat assigned to the U.S. embassy in Reykjavík, was firmly convinced that little Iceland was clearly in the right in its fight with its big, imperious neighbor, and further, that it was desperate enough to throw the U.S. Navy out of its key air base at Keflavik if NATO ally Britain did not relent in its fishing depredations. He also felt that Iceland's declaration of a two-hundred-mile territorial sea would become the world's norm, as swiftly proved to be the case.

Sadinauskas, stopping in Iceland in the course of a fact-finding tour of northern Europe, was impressed with the young foreign service officer and his arguments, and, returning to Washington, he'd pressed Iceland's case and his own concerns with his colleagues on House Foreign Affairs and with a friend of his who then happened to be secretary of defense. For the sake of NATO unity, Britain was persuaded to give up. Sadinauskas became what politicians would call Showers' "Chinaman."

"So, what do you think, Dave? Is Hollis's death going to change anything for you?" said Sadinauskas, after ordering braised ribs and dumplings.

Showers smiled. He hated being called "Dave," but accepted it from his old friend. It was preferable to being called "Spencer," as the more pretentious of his State Department colleagues insisted on doing.

"I'm too far down the greasy pole for it to make any difference. Hollis wasn't a bad sort. Would have made a good ambassador, I guess."

"To a country with no mountains." Sadinauskas sipped from his martini, then leaned back in his chair, settling his weight like a sack of something that had been set down.

"Last time we got together," he said, getting down to business, "you told me you hoped you'd get something important to do in this treaty thing."

"You know my career. The Earth Treaty is the only really meaningful project I've worked on since I joined the foreign service. Hell, it's the fate of the world. We're on the brink of killing more people than we did at Hiroshima."

"You got yourself assigned to the intergovernmental council Moody put together on the treaty."

Showers smiled again, ruefully. "I carry other people's reports to meetings at the White House and read from them when called upon. On rare occasions, I'm asked my opinion of other people's ideas. I also testify at Senate hearings, telling committee members things their staffs already know. Though sometimes I wonder. Last week I was asked why the tides are always twelve hours apart."

"How does it look? For the treaty."

"You tell me."

"I'm interested in what you think."

"I still think it's rather a long shot. I wish it were otherwise, but I can't believe the treaty's something the United States Congress will easily accept. In the short run, it means the loss of too many jobs. The Hill never worries about the long run."

Showers reached for his drink—a Diet Coca-Cola.

"What if they cut the treaty loose from the implementing legislation and push for ratification now?" Sadinauskas said.

"The treaty's worthless without the implementing legislation."

"The whole thing's worthless if it stays tied up in committee. Anyway, that's what the White House is going to do. The chief of staff put out the word this morning. The treaty now. The Earth Bill in the fall."

"I suppose Mr. Moody knows what he's doing. I ran into him this weekend, out in Dandytown. He's not what you'd call a courteous man."

"No, but he's a smart sonofabitch."

"Do you trust him? He has some rather strange friends."

"Moody's loyal to the president. The most loyal guy he's got, after you and me."

Showers flushed. "I do my duty."

"I know you do. That's why I've come to you with this." Sadinauskas took another gulp of his martini and then reached into his coat pocket, taking out an envelope. He set it on the table.

"What do you think the chances are of the Japanese signing the treaty?"

"I think they'd sooner stop selling us cars."

"But it would really sew things up, if they signed."

"Certainly the other Asian exporting countries, Taiwan, Korea, they'd have to go along. And it would certainly help with Congress. But it's not likely. I've dealt with the Japanese in at least a dozen fishing disputes. And on the International Whaling Commission. They're not amenable to diplomatic persuasion. It's against their code. I don't know how you'd budge them."

Sadinauskas pulled a piece of paper from the envelope, unfolded it, and slid it across to Showers.

"There's always something, Dave. There's always something."

It was a photocopy of a Democratic National Committee memorandum, from an aide identified as Peter Napier. It said the White House was considering punitive measures to be taken against Japan if that country refused to support the Earth Treaty. The list was very long. It included a proposal to subject Japanese autos to the same painfully thorough port of entry inspections that American cars were put through before allowed into Japan. There was another, calling for sale-for-sale trade parity on all goods. Yet another suggested an outright ban on all Japanese fishing within two hundred miles of all United States territories and protectorates, including every island flying a U.S. flag in the Pacific. There was even a proposed international boycott in retaliation for Japanese whaling depredations.

"It wouldn't work, Waldemar. This would be Pearl Harbor in reverse."

"You're right. If the president came out and announced it as an ultimatum, it would backfire. They'd lose too much face. They still haven't gotten over having to humble themselves in front of General MacArthur on the *Missouri*. But if we were subtle about it—had some other way to get the message across to them—not so directly."

"Obliquely."

"Yeah, obliquely. You know, the Korean War didn't end just because Eisenhower gave in on the prisoner of war issue, allowing the Chinese and North Koreans to take all their POWs back, whether they wanted to go or not. He played the atomic card. Not out in the open, but 'obliquely.' He rolled out some of those atomic cannons in Korea, where Chinese spies could see them. He stockpiled some nuclear shells for them, and let the Chinese spies see that, too. He never said a word, but the Chinese got the idea."

"You want the Japanese to get the idea, without coming out and telling them."

Sadinauskas nodded, looking as wise and clever as an ancient Oriental sage.

"Is the president serious—about this?"

"He must be. I'm not supposed to tell you this, but it came to me from Moody himself."

"All very diabolical," Showers said.

Sadinauskas nodded again. "We need a way for them to find out about this memo on the quiet, so it comes to them, not as an official threat, but as a piece of prime intelligence."

"Have the CIA leak it to them?"

"The CIA hasn't the credibility."

"So what then?"

"You."

"Me?"

"Haven't you got some Japanese counterpart you've been working with for a while, someone you like and trust, someone who trusts you?"

"Yes. Of course. At my level, we're all fairly much committed to what we're doing."

"Pick a good candidate and find a way to show him that."

Showers studied the paper again. "Under what pretext?"

"Your concern. This could knock Japanese-American relations into the toilet, undo all your good work."

"Isn't this more than a little duplicitous?"

"For crying out loud, Dave, you work for the State Department."

Showers stared at the paper as though it were a soiled thing.

"Look," Sadinauskas said. "The U.S. has never gotten anywhere in this world trying to appeal to other countries' better nature. The Germans and French are with us on this thing only because, with all the Green parties in their domestic politics, they have no choice. Their people are fed up with all the trees dying. The Japanese just don't give a shit. It's not like they were Russia or the Chinese, with all those mouths to feed. They're like the goddamned English. They think they're special. They see no more reason to go along with this than they have with trade agreements or fishing limitations. We have to provide a reason for them to give a shit."

Showers started to push the paper back toward his friend. "I think this is much too subtle for them."

Sadinauskas pushed it right back. "Nothing is too subtle for the people who got America's kids addicted to Nintendo games," he said.

The waiter brought their food. Showers had ordered only a salad, but his plate was as abundantly heaped with it as the meat, gravy, and dumplings dish Sadinauskas had chosen.

"Tell you what," Sadinauskas said, taking the memo and refolding it. "You just hang on to this for a week or so. Think about it. I won't ask you to do something you don't want to do. But we're not going to get this treaty adopted just by climbing onto a horse and shouting 'charge!' If you want a little recognition after this is over, well, as far as I'm concerned, you're long overdue for an ambassadorial appointment, and I've got friends all over the place who can make that happen—especially if the White House is in your debt."

"I'm not after recognition. I just want to make a difference."

"This will make a difference. Think it over. Get back to me tomorrow."

Showers put the memo in his breast pocket, just as Sadinauskas turned to greet three men who were coming by their table. One was a congressman. The other two were lawyers—in Washington, another term for lobbyists—for a firm that represented a very large oil company. They carried on as though they all had been friends since grade school. Showers, as always, was polite.

Moody, as was his habit, took his lunch at a small table set up beside his office fireplace. He ate hurriedly, then returned to his desk, resuming his work before the waiter from the White House mess could clear away the dishes.

On his expensive, leather-bound blotter was a single piece of paper—what had been the president's schedule:

8:00 A.M.    The president receives intelligence briefing with the chief of staff and the national security adviser. Oval Office.

| 8:15 A.M. | The president receives national security briefing with the vice president, the chief of staff, and the national security adviser. Oval Office. |
| 8:45 A.M. | The president meets with the chief of staff. Oval Office. |
| 10:00 A.M. | The president attends cabinet meeting. Cabinet Room. |
| 11:50 A.M. | The president telephones school pupil who has "saved a blade of grass" in nationwide environmental crusade. |
| 2:00 P.M. | The president participates in briefing for regional reporters. Room 450, Old Executive Office Building. |
| 3:00 P.M. | The president meets with treasury secretary. Oval Office. |
| 3:25 P.M. | The president participates in presentation of the national education goals poster. Oval Office. |
| 3:30 P.M. | The president participates in ceremony to honor winners of elementary school recognition program. South Lawn. |
| 4:30 P.M. | The president meets with chief of staff. Oval Office. |

Except for the morning meeting with Moody and the telephone call to the school pupil, an Illinois boy who had won a prize for a science project involving organic mulch made from bathroom waste, the president had canceled the entire schedule. But Moody had not canceled the events. Enlisting the vice president to undertake the ceremonial chores, he had himself presided over a meeting of the cabinet and the briefing sessions, and would shortly undertake the one-on-one with the treasury secretary, who was worried about the strain that global pollution-control measures would place on the International Monetary Fund. Moody would tell him to shut up and do as he was told, like a good member of the team.

In a magazine article appearing years after the Ford administration had slipped into history as a footnote to Watergate, former White House chief of staff Donald Rumsfeld had listed a set of rules for those who followed him into that job.

One was, "When in doubt, you have no choice but to move decisions up to the president."

Moody had never once been in doubt.

Another was, "Don't play president—you're not. The Constitution provides for only one president." The Constitution had not provided for a president who would cancel important cabinet meetings and national security briefings so he could pen a short note of condolence to the widow of an old school chum.

*99*

Another of Rumsfeld's rules was, "Be able to resign. It will improve your value to the president and do wonders for your performance." Moody saw no need whatsoever for improvement in either his value or performance, and could conceive of only one circumstance under which he would be willing to leave his job.

He had been thinking about it for months, but never had the possibility so concentrated his mind as it had that day, ever since the moment when he'd learned of Hollis's death.

For all its power and responsibility, its endless hours and toil, its enormous risks and constant testing, the job of White House chief of staff led nowhere. For anyone who harbored presidential ambitions—and, deep in his or her soul, anyone who'd ever been elected to anything harbored at least some wild fantasy of that—the most direct route to the president's chair lay through the inconsequential and often ridiculous office of vice president. For a public official like Moody, who'd never had the exposure of a run in national politics, the best hope of gaining that lay in cabinet office.

Thomas Jefferson and Martin Van Buren had first done duty in the cabinet before ascending to the vice presidency, and thence to a greater glory beyond. Rumsfeld and James Baker, who'd virtually run the country while serving as chiefs of staff, had both chafed at the thanklessness and anonymity of that post, and had craftily switched to the cabinet—Rumsfeld to secretary of defense and Baker to secretary of state—where both had performed brilliantly and became at least presidential contenders.

Like Baker, Moody meant to become vice president, and knew that meant becoming secretary of state first. The president had been elected on the single issue of the environment, and had staked his all on the success of his treaty initiative. If Moody could deliver his boss that, he could ask for the world and the president would give it to him. Moody had been surprised—indeed, stunned—at the depth of loyalty and affection the president had maintained for Skip Hollis. But now Hollis was dead, and the way wide open. Ratification of the treaty could clinch everything. He had no other way.

Showers' newspaperman cousin Jack Spencer was only a few years older than he, and, unlike Showers, his hair still retained much of its natural sandy color. But he seemed a considerably older man. Early in his career, Spencer had been a police reporter; later, a foreign correspondent. Between wars and crimes, he had walked in a lot of blood. If some stories about him were true, he had even killed a couple of men—a government soldier in El Salvador and an Irish Republican Army Provo in Ulster, the latter as he was attempting to bomb Jack's hotel in Dunmurray.

He had been working for some years now as a columnist for one of the smaller supplemental wire services in Washington, and his time at this had aged him more than anything—the craven hypocrisy of what he called the spectacle of the American people trying to govern themselves engendering a contempt and cynicism that had lined his face far more deeply than any of the fearsome violence he'd experienced. He'd once been married to a rich, frivolous woman who had made him miserable, but he was just as miserable now that they were divorced. Another woman he'd loved deeply had been murdered. He later discovered that she'd been a Central Intelligence operative who had been using him, but that only worsened his grief.

He no longer sailed. Off or on duty, he now spent much of his time in bars. Showers met him in the Round Robin, just off the lobby of the Willard Hotel. Restoring the lounge to its turn-of-the-century antique magnificence, the hotel management had hoped it would attract the newsmen and -women from the nearby National Press Building, as it had in the days of Mark Twain, but heavy drinking was an anachronism with such people nowadays, and the bar's customers ran largely to hotel guests and tourists. Spencer preferred it that way. No one bothered him.

He was as tall as Showers, and even thinner. Standing hunched over the bar, he seemed smaller than his true size. He looked askance at Showers' cane.

"Is this a new State Department affectation, or did you take another little tumble out there in horseman's paradise?"

"The latter," said Showers. "The whole weekend was a shambles. A horse was killed. One of the riders broke his leg and is out of action for good. And a trainer and her husband died of a drug overdose."

"Sounds pretty typical for your set. Did you win anything?"

"One small race. I lost the Valley Dragoon Chase, the one my father always wanted to win. I sprained my ankle in the process."

"Tragedy all the way around. My mother always said you people were stark, staring mad. I hope you got laid at least."

Showers said nothing. Spencer was drinking a manhattan, and not his first. He was the only person Showers knew who still indulged in those things. Showers ordered a Diet Coke.

"You said you needed my advice," Spencer said.

Showers handed him the memo Sadinauskas had given him. Spencer lighted his pipe, and read through it carefully.

"Is this real?"

"I'm not sure."

"If it is, it means the president is about to demand that the Japanese start buying Zenith television sets. I know his head goes ding dong when he shakes it, but is he this nuts?"

"I haven't talked to him. This was passed on to me by someone in the administration. They want me to find some suitable Japanese diplomat and let him see this—get the message across that way. It's intended as an encouragement to get the Japanese to sign the Earth Treaty."

Spencer handed it back. "I don't know what advice I can give you. I don't know any suitable Japanese diplomats. I don't know any diplomats who are suitable for much of anything—yourself excepted, of course."

"That's not the problem. I know a fellow in their fisheries section. The thing is, I don't think I want to do it."

"Show him this memo?"

"That's right. I suspect it's a bluff. I think they just want to make use of the credibility I have with these people to make them think the threat is real."

"How lucky for the White House to find an actual honest man in Washington. Honest men tell the best lies."

"An honest man wouldn't do this."

"Did they order you to?"

"No. It was all very unofficial, more like a request for a favor."

The bartender brought Showers' Coke. Spencer pointed to his now empty glass.

"Do you think this could help with the treaty?"

"Yes. I suppose it could. I have to be honest about that."

"So you're left with a rotten choice, eh? Stick to your principles and maybe hurt the treaty, or do the sleazeball thing and help the worthy cause."

"Yes."

"I'll tell you, cousin. If that's the way it looks to you, you probably ought to say the hell with your job and sign up with the Sierra Club or the Fund for Animals. Nothing sleazy or slimy about those guys. They always stick to their principles. That's because they don't have to make any choices."

"Why should I resign? There's nothing in my job description about this sort of thing."

"You know what I've always said about wars? They're not won by heroes and great generals. They're won by the fools who make fewer dumb mistakes than the fools on the other side. Well, treaties and laws don't get passed by heroes, either. They get passed by sleazeballs who make fewer mistakes than the other side's sleaze-balls."

"If I want to make a difference in this I have to become a sleazeball, is that it?"

"If you want a nice word for it, call it pragmatism."

"I don't like it."

"Well, that's my advice. Let me see that memo again."

"Why?"

"I want to look at that name." He read it aloud. "Peter Napier. Never heard of him."

Moody was in the carpeted main hallway of the West Wing, talking to one of the president's legislative aides, when his secretary came up to tell him Bernie Bloch was on the line. Moody didn't mind his friend calling him at the White House, as long as it wasn't very often and Bloch was careful about what he said. But he didn't like being summoned to the phone. And he was sure he wouldn't like what Bloch had to say.

He thought for a moment of telling her to take a message, but he didn't want Bloch any more angry with him than he doubtless already was.

"Hello, Bernie. I hope this is important."

"You know what it's about." He sounded surprisingly calm.

"I'm really sorry about having to leave like that last night, Bernie, but we had a few fires to put out here. First things first, you know? Anyway, I had one of my guys call Deena. Didn't she get hold of you in time?"

There was a pause on the other end.

"Not in time, Bobby. The horse went to someone else. Your daughter."

"May? You're kidding."

"Not kidding. She and the horse took off to someplace I don't know where. And I'm fucking stuck."

"Bernie, this is a White House phone."

"I really wanted that horse, Bobby. Had my heart set on him. I figure maybe she did it because I'm your friend. It was a way to put the screws to you."

"I never talked to her, Bernie. She took off before I could even say hello. I'm sure she had no idea you had an interest in that horse."

"I'd like to get in touch with her, Bobby."

Moody was not about to let that happen. May was hostile enough as it was.

"I can't help you. She hasn't spoken to me in three years. She lives out in California, you know."

"I know. Her phone's unlisted. I tried. I thought maybe you could give me her number."

"Sorry. She moved some time ago. I don't know where she is now. She might still be in Washington."

"Maybe Geneva could help me find her. Do you have Geneva's number out there in West Virginia?"

"She won't give it to you. She won't even talk to me. I'm sorry, but I can't help you, Bernie. Now if you don't mind, I'll catch you later. We have a few things going on here right now."

"Bobby, I'm asking you as a friend, as your best friend."

One of the first things Moody had learned about Washington was that every time you picked up a government phone, you ran the risk of a tape recorder clicking on somewhere.

"You're my friend," Moody said, "but I've got a boss, too. We'll talk about this later. All right?"

"Not so all right."

This horse racing was getting to Bloch's head.

"Later, Bernie."

To Moody's surprise, Deena was exceedingly nice to him when he got home a little after nine that night. She didn't bring up the weekend in the country at all, and didn't object when he asked to skip a party at the British embassy she had been looking forward to attending for weeks.

In bed, she gave him her full special treatment. Afterward, settling softly into sleep, he indulged himself for a moment with a thought of what it would be like to be serviced in that manner by Lenore Fairbrother. He suspected she wouldn't be cold and aloof and passive, as he had once thought was the case with all women of her class. She'd be different from Deena, though; not so skilled and clever, more wild and crazy.

"Bob?" said Deena, moving close to him. "I've been thinking about May."

"You and Bernie. He called me at the White House today. It's a little weird. May bought that horse he wanted."

"I heard. But that's not what I was thinking about."

Moody lay there, fully awake now. May and Deena had once had a nearly violent confrontation, before his divorce from Geneva had come through—back when May was still buying vodka by the half gallon, and topping it off with pills.

"It was a real shock running into her out there," Deena said.

"That it was."

"She's still as beautiful as ever."

"Maybe more."

"This may sound crazy, but I think she'd like a reconciliation. I think she'd like to end this war between you two."

"Not a chance. You saw how she ran off."

"But why did she come to Washington, then? This is your town."

"She's going to do a play at the Shakespeare Theatre, like it said in the *Post*."

"But why Washington? Why not New York or some other city?"

"She'll be near her mother."

"Nearer to you."

"You're dreaming, Deena. If she wanted to make peace with me, she would have called. I think she took this Shakespeare job just because she went to Juilliard. The theater has a big connection with Juilliard. A lot of kids from Juilliard do plays there."

"I'd like to call her, Bob. Someday, I'd like her to accept me as your wife."

Deena had a big thing about movie stars. She loved being around them. Having one as a stepdaughter—a stepdaughter who didn't treat her like dirt—would be a big deal for Deena.

"I don't think that's a good idea."

"I'd like to try. What can it hurt?"

"No, Deena."

She sat up. "I'll write her a letter. Do you have her new address?"

Moody wanted to get to sleep. "She gets mail through her agent. Nick Aaronson or something. He's with Coast Talent Associates, in Santa Monica. But she won't answer you. I guarantee it."

"Thank you, darlin'."

She lay back and curled up against him, her flesh warm against his side. She only snuggled with him like this when she was very pleased with him.

# Six

t took Showers several days to reach his decision. In the end, it was so simple he felt foolish. The treaty would mean little without ratification by the United States. It would mean just as little without the Japanese. He would do what was asked of him. No one had suggested that he commit murder. It wasn't as though he was in the bombardier's seat aboard the *Enola Gay,* bound for Hiroshima. He had merely to lie, and he might find a way to avoid even having to do that.

He arranged to meet his friend Mr. Kurosawa of the Japanese embassy for lunch at the Gangplank Restaurant, near Capitol Hill on the embankment of the Washington Channel marina, the closest thing the District of Columbia had to a city waterfront.

It was rare for foreign officers at Showers' level to take people to lunch in Washington on official business. Were he and Kurosawa overseas, he could spend as lavishly as he pleased, but within the United States, the State Department was chary with its expense accounts.

This wasn't exactly official business. He was paying for the lunch out of his own pocket. The Gangplank was pleasant, and it was cheap. It was also appropriate. The Potomac was very bright and blue and beautiful that day, the hulls of the moored sailboats a brilliant white in the sunshine, the screeching of the wheeling seagulls overhead seeming to urge him on, chiding him to keep up his resolve.

Kurosawa was head of his embassy's maritime section. For most of the lunch, they talked usefully about an Alaskan waters fishing dispute that had been preoccupying both their offices for months. Showers suggested that the United States might now be willing to agree to a compromise, allowing the Japanese an increase in their catch quota if they would reduce the size of the territory they claimed as international waters. This was a small breakthrough, as heretofore neither side had been willing to relinquish anything. There had been no official change in U.S. policy, but the assistant secretary Showers worked for had mentioned that Secretary of State Hollis's death had removed an impediment. Hollis's sympathies and interests centered on Europe, and he had been contemptuous of the Japanese. Showers' boss and Undersecretary Richmond, now acting secretary of state, favored conciliation, and wanted to get this long-standing dispute off the books. The possibility offered Showers a good pretext for this meeting.

Kurosawa seemed pleased to hear what Showers had to say on the matter, but not really surprised. With good reason. The Japanese had all manner of high-priced American lobbying firms on their payroll, their operatives at work all over Capitol Hill. They'd probably learned of the change in thinking before Showers had been informed of it. Showers' disclosure at least provided confirmation of their intelligence.

"What do you hear about the Earth Treaty?" Kurosawa asked. "Is it going to be a close vote?"

Again, the Japanese were far better informed on this question than Showers was. They'd had people lobbying against the treaty from the first moment it hit the Senate.

"You never know until the votes are counted."

"We hear the president is going to move for a vote on the treaty first, and bring up the enabling bill later. This is true?"

"I've talked to the president just once since the inauguration. It was at a White House Christmas party. He wished me a Merry Christmas."

Kurosawa smiled. Showers liked the man. He was very interested in horses, and they occasionally rode together in Rock Creek Park. They'd also had long talks about the sea, how it was the common blood of all nations.

The man was still smiling. There was no better moment for what Showers had to do. He reached into his pocket.

"Do you know anything about this?"

The smile disappeared very quickly as the other man read the memo's contents.

"Who is this Peter Napier?"

Showers shrugged. "Someone with the National Committee."

"If this is true, David, it would be most unfortunate."

"You've heard nothing about it?"

"No." He gave the word a Japanese intonation, making it sound almost like a bark.

"Then I'm sure it can't be true. There are always rumors going around. Perhaps this fellow was just foolish enough to put one down on paper."

"How did you come to have this?"

"One of my superiors got hold of it." Here the lies began. Showers quickened the pace of his words. "He asked me to check it out. I thought you would know if anyone would. The National Committee wouldn't tell us anything. The White House people I talked to acted as though I had lost my mind."

"It is unbelievable."

"I think that's what I'll tell my boss." He reached for the memo, but Kurosawa held on to it.

"May I borrow this, to make further inquiry?"

"I'd rather you didn't. That could get me in a lot of trouble."

Kurosawa gave the paper another quick read, then handed it over.

"Very interesting." He signaled to the waiter for the check.

"I invited you," Showers protested.

"Oh no, please. This is very good news you bring me about the Alaskan matter. Happiness is to be repaid."

He signed the credit card form with great haste. Showers offered him a ride to the embassy in his Cherokee, but Kurosawa politely declined. He all but ran out into Maine Avenue to hail a cab.

Limping back to his Jeep, Showers hesitated before unlocking the door, then took out the memo and tore it into very small pieces, dropping them into a trash basket on the embankment.

He had thought he'd feel quite rotten at this point, but instead there was an odd exhilaration. He quickly realized what it was. Except for his brief but serendipitous involvement in the long-ago Anglo-Icelandic cod war, this was the first time in his career that he had actually caused something to happen.

It took the efforts of Alixe Percy, Becky Bonning, a veterinarian, and two grooms to get Moonsugar moved from the steeplechase course barn to Showers' stable, but the horse survived the trip well and settled comfortably into his stall. The vet's diagnosis was that the fracture was more a hairline crack than a real break, and that it was fortuitously placed. A few inches closer to the ankle, and there would have been no prescription but death. The horse still favored the leg badly, putting no real weight on it. But he could stand, and did so without complaint. It would be weeks before they'd even trust him to an amble around the stable yard, but every indication was good.

"That goddamned Lynwood Fairbrother was two seconds away from putting him under," Alixe said, as they stood in the stable after the veterinarian had departed. "I'll speak no ill of Lenore after this."

"I wish David could be here," Becky said, stroking Moonsugar's head. "I don't understand why he has to stay in Washington so long."

"It would be fine by me if the British came and burned the place down again," Alixe said. "Useless damn pile of marble, that city." She stuck her hands on her wide hips and squinted out the open stable door. "As long as I've got the horse trailer hitched up, let's take care of some other business. Let's get that fine big bay stallion I bought over here into David's barn where he belongs."

"You're sure this is the time do it?"

"Hell, yes."

"What do you think David will say?"

"He'll piss and moan and give us all sorts of noble shit about not accepting charity, but I'll work on him. Maybe I can get a couple hundred dollars out of him and persuade him to let me carry him for the rest if he'll sign the papers. If he balks at that, I might just ask him to train the big beast for me for steeplechase. The main thing, Becky, is to get that animal under this roof. If we're ever going to get the good captain to come back and run this place properly, it's all got to start with this horse. Keeping up the Queen Tashamore line, that's a family obligation. And that man loves obligation the way I do Virginia Gentleman straight bourbon."

"Sometimes I think that's all he loves."

"How's your divorce from Billy coming?"

"We signed the agreement. I just have to wait for the court decree."

"Billy didn't give you any trouble?"

"He wants out. My father cut me out of his will, you know. He wrote me a letter saying he couldn't change it back again as long as I was married to Billy. I guess you might say he didn't love me for myself."

Alixe snorted. "That bastard. I held no love for that horse-killing tramp sister of his, but they sure as hell took the wrong Bonning feet first out of the inn."

"He was my husband, Alixe."

"You just put him out of your mind now. If he bothers you, let me know. If I ever catch that sonofabitch out around here again, I swear there's going to be a hunting accident."

Every opening of a new exhibition at Washington's National Gallery of Art was invariably accompanied by a gala black tie dinner, honoring each show's organizers, contributors, and underwriters. The museum's trustees, director, top staff, and major donors usually made up the better part of the guest list, along with a sprinkling of important federal officials and members of Congress. Because so many of the donors were wealthy widows, the list was often fleshed out with a few male art critics and local celebrities, and enough socially prominent Washington bachelors to provide sufficient dining companions for the superfluity of ladies.

In this capacity, Showers was in fairly regular attendance at these affairs, held almost always in the Gallery's ultramodern East Building, designed by I. M. Pei. The Gallery had been established by the Mellons of Upperville, the principal family of the Virginia horse country, and Showers' father had been a generous contributor before he'd run out of money, considering support for the institution a requisite part of a horseman's noblesse oblige. Showers had no money to give, but was happy to help out as an extra man.

The exhibition that had just opened was one of works on paper by the Austrian artist Egon Schiele. The menu that night, accordingly, was delightfully Viennese. The guests included not only the Austrian but the Canadian ambassador, as the latter was a noted collector of Schiele's drawings. The protocol called for arriving guests first to view the exhibition, pause for cocktails on an upper balcony overlooking the East Building atrium, then descend to the main floor, where candlelit tables were arranged around a central fountain and potted shrubbery in the manner of a Vienna summer garden. While they ate, the guests were to be entertained by a string quintet playing short pieces by Mozart. Many considered these National Gallery evenings more glittering occasions than White House state dinners. From time to time, even the president came.

He was not there that night, but his chief of staff was. It was Robert Moody's first exposure to any of Washington's multiplicity of art museums. As governor of Maryland, he had attended a few functions at the Baltimore Museum of Art, but had paid no attention to the objects on the walls. Now he was given no choice. Upon entering the East Building, he and Deena were swept along the reception line and then guided upstairs by young women in evening gowns and directed into the show.

Moody and his wife stood uncomfortably a moment, feeling as though more eyes were on them than on the pictures, until Moody at last spotted a congressman he knew from New Jersey. Abandoning Deena, he walked quickly to the man's side.

"Hello, Charlie," he said. "What the hell brings you here?"

"My committee's got the National Endowment for the Arts appropriation up. I guess this is a way of greasing the skids."

They studied the picture at which the congressman had been staring.

"What do you make of that?" Moody asked.

"It's a picture of some woman. It doesn't look like he finished it." The congressman leaned to look at the wall text next to the work. "Her name's Schiele, too. Probably his wife."

"It's his sister, actually," said a voice from behind them.

Startled, especially by the familiarity of the voice, Moody spun around to find himself looking at "Captain" David Showers, seeming a little less heroic in the uniform of black tie. A few days before, he couldn't even remember the man's name. Now he was running into him everywhere.

"Good evening, Mr. Moody," said Showers, shaking hands. "Good evening, Congressman."

"Hiya," said Moody. "His sister, you say?"

"Yes. He did a number of portraits of her. Schiele's output was enormous, even though he died fairly young, during a flu epidemic at the end of World War One."

"Is that why he didn't finish this picture?" Moody said, trying to sound knowledgeable.

"It's finished," said Showers. "Schiele was something of a minimalist. He didn't often do backgrounds."

An awkward silence fell. Finally, Showers spoke again.

"I understand we're moving ahead with the treaty."

Moody glanced at the congressman, who was not exactly an administration stalwart, then glared at Showers. He disliked the use of the inclusive "we."

"*We* haven't said what we're doing yet."

"Some new reports came across my desk today," Showers said. "There's a frightening one from Australia. At the rate they're experiencing skin cancer because of the ozone depletion in the

Antarctic, they expect that nearly ninety percent of the population will eventually get some form of the disease."

"The sun shines a lot down there," said the congressman. He looked around, saw someone he could talk to, and quickly excused himself. Environmentalist talk made him nervous. People talked about his state as though it were some sort of death trap.

Showers looked to Moody. "I met with a man from the Japanese embassy today."

"Yes? Well, that's part of your job, isn't it?"

"I showed him the National Committee memo."

Moody simply stared.

"He looked quite startled," Showers said. "I'm sure he informed his superiors immediately."

"I don't know what you're talking about."

"Sir?"

"I said, I don't know what you're talking about. Don't know anything about it."

"But Secretary Sadinauskas . . ."

"Hell of a guy, Wally. A real team player." He shook Showers' hand. "It's real nice talking to you, Showers, but I better get back to my wife."

Moody found Deena out on the long balcony with two other high-ranking administration wives, sipping champagne and chattering amiably as she watched late-arriving guests mounting the stairs. She was still being inordinately sweet to Moody, and took his arm as he came beside her. With her were two women Moody had never seen before along with Jane Stoltz, wife of the agriculture secretary. They wore high-necked gowns, in frumpy contrast to Deena's expansive, much exposed bosom. They were talking about the president's wife, complaining about her reclusiveness. Mrs. Stoltz had had to stand in front of her that afternoon at a National Forest Service tree-planting ceremony at Mount Vernon.

"Save a blade of grass, plant a tree. That's her thing," said Jane Stoltz. "You'd think she could take an hour out for it."

"Maybe she just didn't want to get her hands dirty," said one of the other women. She gave a short, squeaky laugh.

Deena was eyeing the crowd with sweeping glances—a fighter pilot scanning the skies. Suddenly her eyes widened, as though in surprise or alarm. For an instant, Moody wondered if she had spotted the president. Turning quickly, he saw that it was only

Lynwood Fairbrother and his wife. Lenore was wearing an emerald green dress and small tiara, easily the most elegant woman there.

Deena turned away. The Fairbrothers, reaching the top of the stairs, proceeded along the balcony toward what looked to be a group of very wealthy friends. Seeing Moody, Lenore veered away, directly toward him. Her husband continued plodding ahead.

"Chief, darling!" she said, and kissed Moody on the cheek. "How very, very, very nice to see you again. You'll like the arts crowd. Just as depraved as the horse crowd, but ever so much more discreet about it."

Deena stared coldly, her eyes narrowed.

"Good evening, everyone," Lenore continued, her hand still on Moody's shoulder. "Are you having a wonderful time? Egon Schiele is such a delightfully obscure artist. Pity they have only his pretty things up. Most of his work was frightfully obscene. Oh dear, there's Bunny Mellon. Must run and see her. So nice to see you all here. Next time you come, Chiefy darling, you must bring your lovely friend Mr. Bloch. The Gallery would just love to have some of his money."

She swept away, waving to friends. Moody was sure his face was crimson.

Deena looked like someone who had narrowly escaped being run down by a speeding motorist. "What are they doing here? This isn't a horse barn."

"Mr. Fairbrother's on the board of trustees," said Mrs. Stoltz. "He's gives gobs of money to the museum's acquisition fund."

"I'm much more interested in the Kennedy Center," Deena said, almost smugly.

Moody had put through the paperwork on the nomination of Senator Sorenson's wife to the Center's board that afternoon. He excused himself, saying he wanted to go back and look at the art.

Showers sat dutifully through the after-dinner speeches, then excused himself and slipped away into the night. Lenore had stopped by his table to whisper something about staying over in town instead of driving back to Dandytown with her husband, but Showers was no more in favor of that than Lynwood would be. Fairbrother was a fanatical Anglophile who ran his horse farm in the style of an English country manor. He excused his wife's flirtations and occasional sleeping around because that sort of behavior was the long-standing habit of the British upper classes. He allowed it under his own roof because that was in the tradition of English country weekends. But he would not tolerate anything so provocative and humiliating as Lenore's resuming her old romance with Showers. He trusted Showers not to let that happen. He'd told Showers that he did. Showers had given his word that it would not happen. Lenore seemed as bent on getting him to break his word as she had been on losing her virginity to him those many long years before. It was a game with her, he was sure. Lenore loved winning games.

Showers' small apartment was near the Washington Channel, more than ten blocks from the National Gallery. He decided he'd walk at least part of the way. His limp had diminished and he no longer needed a cane. The night was pleasantly warm, and the image of himself as a solitary figure in evening clothes nervously appealed to him. Loneliness and emptiness had become the principal features of his life.

He stood on the museum steps a moment, looking up at the bright, full moon. The Mall and the ghostly public buildings were bathed in its iridescence. It suited his mood.

Showers had wholly pledged himself to Lenore only to be rewarded with the unending prospect of frustration and impossibility. He had kept his promise to his father to save the family horse farm, but to no purpose. It was a place without any real function. It wasn't likely it would ever again have one until he sold it, or died.

He had also dedicated himself to the public service of his career, but, as he now realized, all those years were essentially pointless. He'd been a messenger. All he had done in his rendezvous with Mr. Kurosawa was bring the man a message, and a spurious one at that. Moody hadn't even accorded him the courtesy of acknowledging the deed, let alone thank him for it. He'd simply been dismissed, like a waiter who had nothing more to bring.

He had nothing more to bring to anyone.

Faced with the emptiness of his life, his cousin Jack had turned to drink and bitterness. Showers had dutifully accepted the void, without recourse to painkillers. He supposed his grandfather would be proud of him.

May had gone to the movies with her agent, the only man she knew in Los Angeles who was straight and yet wouldn't try to go to bed with her, although he'd attempted that once or twice in the beginning. The film, a sneak preview, was awful, Robert Redford and Jane Fonda, together again, in roles far too young for them and far too demanding of their talents. May would have torn up her audience survey form were it not for her superstitious feeling that the fates would not look kindly on such a spiteful act. In her own last picture, she'd been attacked by giant slugs that had left slimy trails all over her body. The fact that the director had once won an Oscar, and that the story was based on an old French horror tale, had not lessened the indignity. She wrote something generous on the form and dropped it in the box in the lobby.

"You want a drink?" her agent asked.

"A Coke."

"I need a real drink after that garbage. You want to drive up the PCH?"

Her agent lived on the Pacific Coast Highway in Topanga Beach, the closest he could afford to Malibu with clients on May's present level.

"No. There's a restaurant I like near my new place. Il Cielo. It has an outdoor terrace. We can look at the moon."

When May had moved from her big house in Malibu Canyon, she had taken a small apartment on Burton Way right on the Beverly Hills–Los Angeles line. It was a six months' lease that would be up in October. Things might be much different then.

Her agent had a Mercedes convertible, also leased. She wondered why anyone in Los Angeles bothered taking title to any possession. Things were always being bought and sold, people moving up, moving down, success following failure, and failure success. Her own car, left that night at the curb outside her building, was a banged-up old Volkswagen convertible she had bought when she'd first become a big star in hopes it would keep people from recognizing her. Its anonymity served her as well in failure as in success.

As they drove by it, something about it caught her attention. She glanced back as they continued down the street, but the nature of the distraction now eluded her. The car seemed all right. It was parked exactly where she had left it.

At the restaurant, they took a table outside, by the hedge that separated the establishment from the sidewalk. It was laced with small Italian lights, making her think of Christmas. A torch set on a cast-iron rod flickered nearby.

There was a violinist at Il Cielo, a long-haired fellow dressed all in black named David Wilson. He looked New Age, but his music was lush and pure and sweet, especially when he played "You Are Too Beautiful," which seemed to be his theme. He turned to it again when he noticed her enter, as he had done on several nights. It was far too romantic for someone as lonely as she now felt.

"You sure you want to do this?" her agent asked.

"Stick with Coca-Cola? You're damned right."

"No, I mean go back to Washington. All that Shakespeare shit."

"Kevin Kline and Michelle Pfeiffer do Shakespeare."

"Between movies."

"You don't like fifteen percent of six hundred a week."

He made a face. "Universal's casting that Kevin Costner ripoff Indian flick. You'd be perfect. All that long black hair."

"I'd get three scenes, right? Carrying firewood, fucking the male lead under a bearskin in the firelight, and running around the teepees screaming during the massacre."

"It might be a big hit."

"Into the video stores in two weeks. And I probably wouldn't get the part. There are an awful lot of actresses not getting work in this town. God, I saw Elizabeth McGovern at an audition last month."

"I'm just afraid if you go out there, you won't come back."

"I'll come back. I'm not ready for retirement yet. Not on these terms."

"You going to see your father?"

"I told you. I already saw him when I was out there to sign the contract. It was horrible."

"No. I mean, are you going to get together with him again?"

"I think I told you that, too. Hell, no."

"Your stepmother called me today. I wasn't going to tell you. It was supposed to be a surprise."

The night air seemed suddenly cold. "What was supposed to be a surprise?"

"She's writing you a letter. I gave her your address."

May closed her eyes and shook her head. Then she leaned back and looked up at the moon. It seemed close enough to touch, but so impassive, almost forbidding.

"I told you not to do that," she said. "For anyone."

"Hell, babe, it's your family."

"That woman is not my family."

She sipped her soft drink, but suddenly it tasted flat and metallic. She supposed anything that touched her lips at that moment would.

"I'm tired," she said. "I want to go home."

He dropped her by the walkway that led to her building's glass-doored entrance. As he roared off back toward Santa Monica Boulevard, she hesitated, and looked at her car again. What had caught her eye before was now very obvious. The interior light was on. The curbside door was hanging slightly open.

Swearing, she hurried up to it. She was about to slam the door shut, when she noticed the litter on the floormat—registration, insurance card, some old repair bill receipts, a small box of Kleenex. Her glove compartment lid was hanging open. Swearing more, she jammed the papers back inside and closed the door. Nothing seemed to be missing. The trunk was still locked.

Her building, a small Art Deco construction with curved corners and glass-tile borders, contained only four apartments. There was no doorman. She ascended the stairs to her door slowly, preparing to run down again at the slightest sound.

The door was closed and locked. Opening it slowly, she gasped.

Everything was in disarray. All her desk drawers had been pulled out. So had those in the kitchen. Her bedroom looked like a store after a clearance sale, with her underwear scattered all over the floor. They'd found the hiding place where she'd put some of the jewelry she'd taken out of her safety deposit box. Her emerald necklace and earrings were missing. So was her strand of fake pearls.

May sank down on her bed and shuddered, then snatched up the phone and called the police—not that it would do any good. This was another omen. She had to get out of L.A.

# Seven

I n Dandytown, religion generally was something decided by one's ancestors. The Fairbrothers, Alixe Percy, and most of the Dandytown gentry were the Episcopalians their grandfathers and great-grandfathers and great-great-grandfathers had been. The Showerses had for generations been the town's leading Presbyterians. David's father, despite his exuberant fondness for the community's traditional sins, had served as an elder, as his father and other forebears had done.

The church of the Bonning clan was Baptist. They attended it infrequently, and in meager numbers, but a funeral for one of their own drew them all out. Some twenty-five Bonnings and relations now stood around the grave site as the preacher intoned his familiar phrases. Vicky's mother was the only one of them crying, but then her daughter had been bringing tears to her eyes for the better part of her life.

Meade Clay's people, North Carolinians, were not present. They had taken his body back to their homeland like a reclaimed possession, relieved that death had at last separated him from his notorious wife.

The red brick church stood on a hillside north of Dandytown, overlooking the two-lane highway that led to Berryville. The churchyard spread up the hill behind it, reaching into the shelter of several large, leafy oaks. The graves were mostly grouped in clumps, family by family, but a few were scattered on their own.

The view was of the eastern slope of the Blue Ridge, its summit line soft in the summery haze. The beginnings of afternoon thunderheads were visible rising farther to the west, but here the sun was bright. Were it not for the occasion, it would have been a most pleasant and cheerful day.

There were few outsiders present—two or three of Vicky's fellow riders, some grooms and walkers, the bartender from the inn. Vicky's employer, Bernard Bloch, wasn't there, of course, nor was anyone representing him. Instead, he'd sent flowers.

Showers and Becky stood quietly at some distance from the others, as far as they could get from Becky's estranged husband, Billy Bonning, who kept giving them nasty looks. There were rumors that Billy had already picked up another woman—wealthy, ugly, and fifteen years older than he—someone from Charlottesville.

Becky was there only because Showers had insisted on coming. He had just driven in from Washington, stopping at his farm only to drop his bags and pick up Becky, who could just as easily have done without witnessing the laying of Vicky into the ground. Showers had not asked her to accompany him to the funeral, but he'd made it seem such an obligation for himself that Becky was reluctant to stay behind. She shifted her weight impatiently from foot to foot, brushing flies from her face, wishing all concerned would hurry.

The funeral was not without a mysterious moment. During the Bible reading, Showers sensed some movement behind him and glanced back down the hill to see Lenore Fairbrother, hatless and wearing a summer print sundress, perched like a mischievous ghost on a tombstone, smoking a cigarette. When he looked again a few minutes later, she was gone. Sometime after that, he saw her Jaguar speeding away on the two-lane below, heading back to Dandytown. Lenore had not liked Vicky Clay. Though they'd been tempted by many of the same sins, Lenore found her crass and vulgar, lacking taste and style. They'd sometimes quarreled in the bar of the Dandytown Inn. At least twice, Lenore had had Vicky thrown out. Perhaps this was her way of seeing to it for good.

Showers stared sadly as they lowered the casket into the grave. He had long held the hope that whatever dreadful inner fires had been tormenting the girl would burn themselves out, leaving her free to find a more peaceful way through life. But she'd never found that deliverance, nor even sought it.

He'd liked her. His family had treated her like trash, but when Vicky had been younger, a fresh-faced, spunky, pretty teenager winning firsts and best-in-shows all over the county, he'd found her appealing, full of promise, if only her wildness could be tamed. He'd tried to make a protégée of her, as he had with Becky, but it hadn't taken. As fiercely demanding as she had been as a trainer, Vicky was herself untamable, utterly lacking in self-discipline. It was as if she had been born with a genetic deficiency. In the end, there was nothing to be done about it—one could only watch it run its course.

Now she lay in a box in a hole, with clods of Virginia soil pattering down upon her—God taking back a mistake.

Showers forced himself to think about the horses she had killed. He could imagine them stacked in a great heap that would overwhelm the little grave. In every irony, there was justice.

The ceremony ended awkwardly, with the minister running out of words. After an uncomfortable silence, people began to move about, unsure of what to do next. When it was clear that the formal proceedings were over, Showers went dutifully to pay his respects and condolences to Vicky's mother, who received him coldly.

Sheriff Cooke and Wayne Bensinger, the assistant commonwealth attorney, had also come to the church, but hung back by the parking area, making clear that they had not come as mourners. As people began returning to their cars, Showers found the sheriff waiting for him by the Jeep.

"A moment of your time, Captain Showers?" said the sheriff. He was out of uniform, dressed in an ill-fitting tan suit and maroon tie.

Showers nodded, and limped along with Cooke to a rail fence. There were cows in the pasture on the other side, standing or lying about beneath a large-branched oak.

"Too bad the funeral had to be delayed so long," the sheriff said. "But we couldn't release the body until we got a final autopsy report. Someone lost that first lab test and they had to go back for more tissue."

"I'm sure the family understood," Showers said.

"You heard about the results?"

Showers nodded. Becky had told him all about it on the way out to the churchyard. Showers gathered that no one in Dandytown was talking about anything else. "Horrible way to die."

"Why would he use a drug like that on her?" the sheriff asked.

"I don't know. Perhaps it was all Meade had at hand."

"He sure didn't like her very much. The pathologist said she lived for more than an hour after getting hit with that shot."

"It's very sad."

The sheriff looked away, scratching his nose. Bensinger was out of earshot.

"The inquest is scheduled for Monday," the sheriff said, finally. "It won't take long. It's pretty open and shut. Murder-suicide. Had one of those fifteen, twenty years ago—down in Edgarsburg. Only that was gunshots."

"I remember it."

"Like I say, Captain, won't take long. We took statements from just about everyone in town. Got everybody who was at the inn when it happened. Except you."

"I'm sorry. I've been in Washington."

"Yes sir. I understand. You're a busy man these days."

"Would you like me to testify at the inquest? I'm supposed to be back in Washington Monday. They're expecting a Senate committee vote this week on the treaty I've been working on. But this certainly takes precedence."

"We don't want to keep you away from important business, Captain. But I need to get some kind of statement on the record, since you did show up at the inn later. And you did know the victims. I've got to file a report with the state police, and I don't want to leave anyone out."

"Whatever I can do to help."

The sheriff took a small tape recorder from his pocket and turned it on, holding it between them.

"Captain Showers. Can you account for your time between five and nine o'clock the day of the incident?"

Becky was standing nearby, watching them intently.

"Yes. I was at the steeplechase course, in the jockey tent. I'd been given a painkiller after I took a fall in one of the races and it made me sleepy. I didn't want to drive until it wore off, so I lay down for a while."

"Did anyone see you there?"

"Yes. Jimmy Kipp was still there, and I think another rider. At least when I went to sleep. When I left, there were still some grooms around."

"You were seen talking to Vicky Clay before she came back to the inn. What was that about?"

"It was a personal matter, Sheriff."

"She's dead, Captain."

Showers frowned. "Does this have to be on the record."

"Put it however you want."

"I believe the young lady felt some attraction to me. She made a proposal I felt obliged to decline."

The sheriff grinned. Damned few men in Dandytown had declined Vicky Clay's "proposals."

"Do you know anyone who might have had a grudge against the Clays? Somebody who might really have had it in for them?"

At one time or another, that would have included much of the county.

"You said murder-suicide."

"That's the way it looks, but I've got to cover all the bases."

"Sheriff, I don't know anyone, no one in Dandytown, certainly, capable of anything like this."

"Uh, one more thing, Captain. Meade Clay worked on your horses. Was he left-handed or right-handed?"

"As I recall, he was left-handed." Showers shrugged. "He may have been ambidextrous, but when he did sketches of horses for Coggins reports, he used his left."

The sheriff clicked off the little machine. "Well, okay. Thank you very much."

"That's all?"

"Yes sir. Just wanted to complete the record. Sorry to bother you out here."

"I would have been happy to go to your office."

"Oh, I expected you'd be here. I was kinda curious as to who else might turn up. Should have known it would only be you and Becky, except for all the Bonnings."

The sheriff must have seen Lenore. Showers let that pass.

"Sheriff, do you have doubts that Meade killed Vicky and then took his own life?"

"I don't, no. Like I say, I'm just covering all the bases. I think we can close the case all right. But if the state police have any more questions, I want to make sure I've got everything on the record. Have a good day now."

When he and Bensinger had started toward their car, Becky came up to Showers, looking quite worried.

"What was that about, David?"

"He's just doing his job. Some questions about Vicky."

"What did he want to know?"

"Where I was when Vicky died."

"What did you tell him?"

"The truth."

Becky took his hand. "Let's go home.

Returning to his farm, Showers went directly to the stables without stopping to change clothes. Becky and Alixe had kept him informed of Moonsugar's progress by telephone, but he'd found it difficult to believe the horse had recovered as well as they had said. In the first few days, he had expected the worst possible news every time the phone had rung.

Moonsugar seemed glad to see him, and nuzzled the back of his neck. Showers ran his hand along the horse's neck and back, then crouched and gingerly lifted the animal's injured leg. Moonsugar became a little skittish, but did not interfere.

"He can't put much weight on it yet," Becky said.

"We're damned lucky."

Showers stood up straight. Patting Moonsugar's head again, he left the stall and went to a shelf near the tack room, where the vet had left a list of medications.

"This dosage seems rather strong."

"It's working, David. I gave it to him myself."

He squeezed her shoulder affectionately, then turned at the sound of a horse's whinny, coming from the other end of the barn. The stalls down there had been vacant.

"What's that? A new boarder?"

"You might say. Come take a look at him."

The big bay was moving about, agitated. Showers couldn't tell whether his unhappiness was due to his confinement or being kept so far from the other horses.

"Isn't he beautiful?"

"Is this the colt out of Queen Tashamore's granddaughter? Alixe said something about buying him."

"Yes."

"What's he doing here?"

"He's yours, David."

"Mine?"

"Alixe'll explain everything. I'll have her come over."

Showers gave her a dark look. "When you call Alixe, tell her to bring her trailer."

Alixe came on foot, walking over on the path through the small woods that divided their properties. Showers had put a bridle on the bay and had led him out into his stable yard. The stallion seemed happier outside, and even handsomer.

"Saddle him up, David," Alixe said, her voice booming. "Or have you hocked all your tack?"

She was carrying a large manila envelope—the horse's papers.

"I appreciate your generosity," Showers said politely. "But I can't accept the gift."

"Who the hell said anything about a goddamn gift? I mean to sell him to you."

"Alixe. This horse is worth at least a hundred thousand dollars. Probably a lot more."

"Then this is your lucky day, because I picked him up for a paltry thousand, and that's all I want from you."

"A thousand? That's impossible."

Alixe pulled some papers out of the envelope. "It's all here. All legal."

The bay was looking at Showers.

"Who did you swindle?"

"Didn't swindle a soul. It's as I told you. The buyer had an impulse at the auction, and then thought better of it. Changed her mind."

"You said the auction price was ten thousand. Who would let go of nine thousand dollars just for a change of mind?"

"Someone with a lot of money and not much horse sense. We get a few like that out here."

Showers stepped closer to the stallion, stroking him.

"Who is she, this buyer?" he said.

"Doesn't matter."

"Alixe. Her name's on the papers."

" 'Spose it is."

"Well, who is it?"

"It's that actress you introduced me to, May Moody, the governor's daughter."

"She bid on this horse?"

"Yes. Only bidder."

"And then she just let him go?"

"Those Hollywood people do things a lot stranger than this. But who cares? Here he is."

Showers stood silently a moment. "Alixe, I simply don't have the money."

"You have a hundred dollars?"

"Yes."

**124**

"I'll take that, and your brood mare for collateral. I'll give you two years to train him and another to race him. If you haven't paid me the remaining nine hundred by then, then you put him to stud and I get the first foal. But I expect you'll have paid me off long before then. Paid me off and won the Old Dominion National."

Showers bit down on his lower lip. "If this horse belongs to anyone, it's Miss Moody. Before we start thinking about races, I'd like to make sure she doesn't want it back."

"A noble thought, David, but she made it pretty damned clear she doesn't want it."

"You're sure?"

"Got it from the horse's mouth, m'boy. Now are you going to accept my offer?"

"Yes. I'd be foolish not to. Have the papers drawn up."

Alixe grinned. "Already did that. Let's go into your kitchen and sign them."

When Showers had signed his name in all the proper places, he started to push the papers away, then pulled them back, leafing through them until he came to the horse's registration again, studying the accompanying sketch. He frowned. Watching him, Becky did, too.

"What's wrong, David?"

"This horse has a bad Coggins. The drawing's not right," he said, referring to the annual veterinarian's report required for every horse—always accompanied by a sketch.

"Veterinarians aren't exactly Edgar Degas, Captain," said Alixe.

Showers turned the sketch toward her. "This shows white stockings only on the forelegs. That bay has a stocking on the right rear leg, too. And the blaze on the forehead isn't quite right, either. His is much more elongated."

"A lot of fucked-up vets around, David," Alixe said. "Who did it? Anyone we know?"

Showers turned to the page with the veterinarian's signature.

"I'm afraid so," he said. "It was Meade Clay."

Alixe was pouring herself a drink. "Are you sure?"

"Take a look."

"I'm sure he just made a mistake, David," Becky said.

"This horse is from New Jersey," Showers said. "What's Meade's name doing on the Coggins?"

"Vicky used to go up there," Becky said. "With Bernie Bloch. Sometimes Meade would go along."

Showers pushed back his chair. "I want to take a look at that stallion's upper lip."

Unlike European bloodstock, every registered American horse bore something far more useful than a brand—a number tattooed on the underside of its upper lip. The practice had done far more to eliminate horse theft than all the summary hangings of yore.

The number on the lip matched that on the papers. Showers examined the flesh around the tattoo carefully. It was cleanly pink. There'd been no surgical attempt at alteration or erasure.

"You see," said Becky.

"Meade Clay was as much a boozer and pill popper and coke sniffer as his wife," Alixe said. "I imagine there were days when he had trouble signing his own name."

Showers was looking at the stallion's teeth, not happily.

"This horse is supposed to be five years old, Alixe," he said. "I don't think he's half that."

"I think you're getting damn particular. The numbers match. He's the right color. He's a damn fine animal. You're certainly not getting cheated. If Meade did a sloppy job or made a mistake, what difference does it make? He sure as hell can't tell us about it now."

"Something isn't right."

"Maybe Dandytown Bloodstock made a mistake," Becky said.

"Auction houses don't guarantee horses," Showers said. "But they guarantee that they don't make mistakes. I've never heard of Dandytown Bloodstock making one. Not a big one."

"I think you've been working too hard, David. If you don't want the horse, fine. I'll take him back. I'm getting tired of all this goddamn nonsense."

Showers put his arm around her shoulders. "I'll keep him, Alixe. Please don't misunderstand me. I'm damned grateful. Everyone knows I would have lost this place long ago if it hadn't been for you. But I think there's something wrong here. I'm just not sure this is a horse out of the Tashamore line. I don't want to be a party to a questionable transaction. Not with a horse this valuable. I don't want you to be, either. Or Miss Moody."

"He's ours now, David," Alixe said. "Yours. All perfectly legal. What do you want to do, drive up to New Jersey and ask those people if this is the horse they put up for auction?"

"Bernie Bloch was interested in it," Showers said. "Vicky told Becky that. Maybe he knows something."

"That was just Vicky's prattling," Becky said. "I doubt she was

**126**

telling the truth. She seldom did. Bloch didn't even come to the auction."

"He couldn't," said Alixe. "That damn-fool sheriff had everyone under house arrest out at the inn. And Bloch sent Billy after the horse. He tried to take it away from the Moody girl."

Showers kicked at a clod of earth. His shoes, highly polished that morning, were covered with dust. He wanted to get out of these clothes, into some breeches and boots.

"Alixe, who's the best judge of bloodstock you know? Someone whose word you absolutely trust?"

"That would be Heather Freeman over in Berryville, or maybe Kerry Donahue."

"Would you ask one of them if she'd mind coming over some time this weekend and taking a look at him?"

"I'm sure Heather would be delighted. She's the nicest and most helpful horsewoman we've got out here."

They couldn't reach Miss Freeman, but Kerry Donahue came out that afternoon. She examined the animal carefully, and then walked and trotted him around Showers' ring through a few figure eights. She even jumped him over a low rail that had been set on a couple of blocks. Her conclusions were everything Showers didn't want to hear but expected: The animal was closer to two years old than five. He had received very little schooling and had never been jumped. The Coggins looked suspicious indeed. And the horse was of such quality that she would have paid a hundred thousand for him in an instant.

Showers thanked her warmly. To repay her, Becky elected to go back with her and help exercise her horses. After they had gone, Alixe slapped Showers on the back in friendly fashion.

"We'll clear this up in no time," she said. "What I think you might end up with is the right horse but some fucked-up papers."

"This isn't the right horse."

She left him to make her weekly run up to Winchester for supplies. Showers, weary, went up to his room and, without bothering to take off his boots, lay down on his bed. A deep slumber came with the closing of his eyes.

He awoke to darkness. Day had become night. He found himself still alone in his house. There was no sign of the old Toyota Becky had bought to replace the pickup truck her husband had taken as part of the divorce settlement.

A light was showing in the window of the servants' cottage that was now Becky's quarters. It could mean her return or simply that she had forgotten to turn it off in the morning. Like many who lived in the country and were often away, they kept lamps on all night against visits by prowlers. Showers walked slowly over to the little house, his injured leg stiff from all that sleeping. He knocked on the frame of the screen door.

"Becky?"

No answer.

He gently pulled open the door. This was an unpardonable intrusion, but it was his cottage. He had not been in it for weeks. If nothing else, he wanted to see whether Billy Bonning had taken anything he might deem a souvenir.

The furnishings and wall prints, all inexpensive, seemed to be in place. The small living room was quite cluttered—horse magazines and newspapers spread over the coffee table and floor, a couple of soft-drink cans left on the table, a pair of dusty boots lying on the rug, a bag of snack crackers on top of the television set.

There was a VCR connected to it. She must have just bought it, because Billy had taken the one she used to have.

Showers stepped closer. A red light showed that there was a tape in the machine. He noticed a cassette box and picked it up. The label bore the word VICKY. It was the tape Billy had left behind the night he'd moved out, the tape Showers had asked her to return.

He stared at the box, feeling guilty. Finally, he put it back where he had found it. Where on earth was Becky? She had promised to be back for dinner.

There was a phone in the cottage's tiny kitchen. He went to it, called information for Kerry Donahue's number, then dialed it. She said Becky had left to return to Dandytown more than an hour before.

Showers went back to the machine. If nothing else, the tape might contain something of interest to the sheriff. He hesitated, then turned on the television set and pushed the VCR's Play button. The screen came to life in midscene.

It was, in truth, pretty much what he'd expected. There was Vicky, naked, in the midst of making love—in unique fashion. She was on a very rumpled bed, on her knees, rear to the video camera, straddling another naked form, sitting far forward, over the other person's face, gyrating. The other person's knees were up, but the breasts were visible and the vaginal area wantonly exposed.

*128*

Showers wasn't shocked to see it was a woman. He'd heard that about Vicky, too.

He stood there, watching in consummately guilty fascination, waiting for the two bodies on the screen to part, for the one beneath Vicky to sit up and reveal herself. It would not have surprised him to see Billy enter the picture. There had been rumors about that as well.

He hit the Stop button, then clicked off the machine. The disgust he felt was overpowering—disgust with what he'd been watching, disgust with himself. Whatever the tape contained, it was Becky's private property. This little house was her legal domicile, accorded her as part of her meager compensation for her employment. He had no right to be here.

Leaving everything as he had found it, he crossed the yard to the main house, going directly to the kitchen. He called Alixe, but she had not returned. On impulse, still curious about Lenore's appearance at the funeral, he dialed the Fairbrothers, hoping she might answer. Instead, it was a servant, who informed him both Fairbrothers were out.

He had another idea. The Los Angeles information operator consulted her computer, then rather rudely informed him May Moody's number was unlisted. Pacing his kitchen floor, he remembered the papers from the auction house. Searching through them on the kitchen table, he found what he sought. May Moody, an address on Burton Way. A phone number.

After three rings, her voice came on the line—as clear and melodic as he had recalled, but recorded; an answering machine. He started to hang up, but there was a click, and her actual voice interrupted the recording. She sounded edgy and unhappy, disturbed by the interruption.

"Miss Moody? This is David Showers, out in Virginia."

There was a pause. When she spoke again, she sounded calmer, less displeased.

"Oh yes. Captain Showers, right? The horseman."

"Yes."

"Excuse me," she said. "But how did you get this number?"

"I'm sorry. I didn't mean to intrude. I found your number in the papers."

"What papers?"

"From the bay stallion you bought at the auction out here."

She hesitated. "The horse. Yes. What about him?"

"Well, you sold him to Alixe Percy."

"Yes. What did she tell you?"

"Only that you bought him and then sold him to her on the spot. You had second thoughts or something."

"I just didn't know what I was doing. He seemed so pretty. I didn't stop to think that I'd have no place to keep him. And no time to ride him. What did she say?"

"She knew I was interested in the horse. He comes from a line that was once connected with my family. So today she sold him to me—not for a great deal of money."

"She sold him to you?"

"Yes."

"Well, I'm glad he's got a good home."

"He'd be better off with her, actually."

"Don't you like him? I thought he was beautiful."

"Too beautiful."

"What do you mean? Don't you want to keep him?"

It would do no good to bring up his doubts about the horse's pedigree. This woman was so nice. Not at all like his preconceptions about movie stars. Not at all like her irascible father.

"I just wanted to make sure you—I mean, are you certain you don't want this horse? I believe he's worth a great deal of money. A lot more than I'm paying Alixe for him, a lot more than she paid you."

"Don't you want him?"

"Yes. Of course. He's wonderful."

"Well, like I said, I'm glad he's got a good home."

He sat in silence for a moment. He could hear her breathing.

"Look, Captain Showers. I've got some people here. An insurance man. My apartment was broken into and I had some stuff stolen. There's all this paperwork."

"I'm awfully sorry."

"I'll be back out there soon. I'm starting rehearsals for a play. In Washington. At the Folger."

"The Shakespeare Theatre."

"Yes. Maybe I can come out to your place, and see the horse. See how he's doing."

"That would be marvelous. Please. Anytime."

"The horse you were riding. The one who was injured . . ."

"He's doing fine. The break wasn't as serious as we thought. He's in my stable now."

"I'm really happy to hear that. I'm afraid I really have to go. There's a policeman here, too. Thanks for calling."

"Yes, I—"

**130**

"Goodbye now."

"Goodbye."

His dog was at the front door, barking furiously. Showers thought it might be Becky, but quickly discounted that possibility. Hardtack never barked at her. He never barked at cars, always waiting to determine who it was getting out.

Showers went out onto the veranda, the dog, still barking, darted outside with him.

A horse came bolting out of the woods at full gallop, followed by two others. They cantered crazily around the stable yard for several turns, then careened on around the side of the barn.

Showers looked back in the direction from which they had come. Above the trees was a weird orange glow, growing brighter.

He took off, running as best he could, Hardtack bounding ahead.

There were two main stable buildings on Alixe's farm, long rectangular barns set side by side, adjoining her main exercise ring. One of the barns was engulfed by flames, which had fully consumed one end and were spreading rapidly through the entire structure. The other barn was as yet untouched, but was threatened by the blizzard of sparks spewing into the air.

Someone had gotten at least some of the horses in the burning building out of their stalls, and they were running loose all over the grounds. A couple of grooms were chasing after them, trying to herd them into the ring. But the pasture gate was wide open, and, in ones and twos, they were making their way through it into the open. A man Showers recognized as a house servant was uselessly directing a stream of water from a plastic garden hose into the now towering flames. Two others, Alixe's cook and a housemaid, stood unhelpfully nearby, staring at the fire in shock and stupefaction.

"Forget that!" Showers shouted at the man with the hose. "Soak down the other building! Hurry up! Cinders are landing on the roof!"

The man, more used to orders than independent thought, hurried to do as bidden. Showers turned to the women.

"Did you call the fire department?"

"Yes!"

"Well, get some more hoses and help him! Keep that roof wet!"

He hurried away, stumbling over a mound of earth as he hastened to the pasture gate, lifting and pulling it closed, just as two of the animals came pounding furiously up, veering away as their avenue of escape closed before them. Fastening the gate closed, scraping

*131*

his knuckles on the rough iron latch, Showers looked back to the stables. He could hear horses kicking and bellowing inside the building that was as yet untouched by fire.

Alixe's huge front yard was enclosed by fencing—as good as a corral. A farm truck with a horse trailer on its hitch was parked alongside the barn. Showers went to it, found keys under the floor mat, where he knew Alixe kept them in her farm vehicles, and drove the rig away from the building. Bumping over the yard, he took it around in a circle to the side of the stable building that faced the front yard, pulling to a stop perpendicular to the fence, the truck and trailer blocking the lane that ran between it and the stable. Then he kicked and bashed down the top and middle rails on one small section of fence. He'd created a corral.

He was taking too much time. The smoke and heat were bitter. Coughing, he hurried into the near stable. The frightened horses inside were raising bedlam in their stalls. One had kicked through a stall door and half pushed himself through it. Showers snatched up a halter and started his desperate work, one by one catching hold of the animals and dragging and hauling them out of the barn and into the sanctuary of the front yard. He had gotten four into it by the time the Dandytown volunteer fire department arrived. With the help of the grooms and one of the firemen, he had all of the animals out of the barn and in the enclosure by the time Alixe roared up.

"What the hell is this?" she bellowed.

Just then the center section of the burning barn collapsed with a great crash of timber and a hiss of exploding, spewing flame. Becky's frightened face appeared next to Alixe's.

"We were at the inn," she said. "What happened?"

"I don't know," Showers replied. "It was burning when I got here. You've got loose horses all over. Some of them got out through the back pasture."

"Shit!" Alixe said. She repeated the word over and over. Becky went running after one of the horses still in the yard.

The firemen had run a hose to Alixe's pond and two powerful streams of water were arcing from their pumper into the collapsing barn.

"What do I do?" Alixe said. "What the hell do I do?"

Showers didn't know what to say. His own front gate was open. The horses that had run into his yard could be out on the highway by now.

"We have to get after the loose ones," he said. "They'll be all over the county if we don't."

More vehicles were pulling up from the road. Horse people, coming to help.

"Everyone who was in the bar must be coming over," Alixe said. "Fat lot of fucking good they're going to do. They're all drunk. Shit. So am I." She turned to a groom. "Don't stand there! Round up some of the calmer mounts and get some saddles on them! And get some flashlights!"

Becky trotted by, riding a horse bareback, her hands clutching the mane. The flames from the burning stable building continued to subside, as much from lack of fuel as from the quenching water.

"You up to riding, David?" Alixe said.

"Yes, of course."

"Well, let's get after them!"

They worked on horseback and on foot through the night and well into the early morning. One horse had crashed through a barbed wire fence into a brush pit and injured itself so badly it had to be shot. All the others, except for two, were recaptured and brought to safety. Most had gotten no farther than the back reaches of Alixe's farm or the woods behind Showers' place, though three had made it out onto the road and were found at sunrise, grazing on a lawn nearly a mile distant. Two others were still missing. After sending Becky and the others who had been helping them back to get some sleep, Alixe and Showers made a last circuit of the meandering fence line encompassing their properties, then turned their tired mounts back to her stables. The sun was rising high, already hot.

The one building had been completely destroyed and a long connecting shed badly damaged. Otherwise, the farm survived intact. Alixe counted herself lucky.

"Never a fire," she said. "Never in all these years. I always figured if I got one it would be a hell of a lot worse than this."

"It's bad enough," Showers said, remounting. "I wish I'd gotten to it sooner."

"Listen, m'dear," said Alixe, reaching from her horse to slap his shoulder. "If it hadn't been for you, I might have lost the whole damn thing."

They trotted into the stable yard. Smoke was still rising from the piles of ash and charred timber. Most of the firemen were gone, but the sheriff and a few of his deputies were on the scene, gathered

*133*

around something in the ashes that Alixe feared was one of the still missing horses.

It wasn't. The charred, skeletal, smoking body was that of a human. A deputy, using a rake, rolled it out of the acrid debris. The face was hideous, teeth exposed in a macabre, fleshless grin, empty eye sockets huge and staring. One of the other deputies turned away, gagging. Showers had once served a tour of duty in Central America. He'd seen such bodies before.

"That must be Joe Smitts," Alixe said. "He's been missing all night."

"He saved your horses," Showers said. "He got them all out."

Alixe turned to her other grooms, who were standing nearby.

"And just where were you gentlemen when all this started?"

They looked at each other sheepishly. "We were in the show barn," said one. "A little card game. Joe heard the horses acting up, and went to check on 'em. I guess that's him."

Sheriff Cooke took the rake and nudged the head of the burned man a little.

"He must have fallen under the horses," he said. "The side of his head is caved in."

They went to her kitchen. After Alixe produced a bottle and glasses, they sank into two of the antique wooden chairs set around her huge round oak table. Alixe took a large slug of her whiskey, coughed, and then leaned back her head.

"There're two horses still unaccounted for," he said.

"Something funny here, David," said Alixe. "I only own two bay horses. Only two in all that stock. Now, we didn't exactly take a careful census out there, but I don't recall seeing either of them in our roundup. I'll bet you anything, David, those two missing horses are my bays."

"The Queen Tashamore horse is a bay," Showers said.

"He is that." She emptied her glass with another gulp and then slammed it down hard on the tabletop. "He is that, Captain Showers. Billy Bonning tried to get his hands on that horse at the auction. Billy works for Bernie Bloch, and Bloch wanted that horse."

Showers rubbed his chin. "I'm too tired to think straight," he said.

"Well, I'm not. I've got a dead boy out there. And at least one dead horse."

"Alixe, Bloch is certainly not my idea of a horseman, but he

**134**

wouldn't set fire to a barn just to get at that bay. The man is worth a billion dollars. He can afford any horse in the country."

"Billy Bonning would do it. That wretch would do anything if you paid him enough. You know how quick a barn can burn. How could one groom get all those horses out of their stalls without any of them even getting singed, and then end up a piece of roast meat himself?"

"He was injured."

"Right. Stepped on, the sheriff said. By the very last horse? If the barn was already on fire when he got there, half those animals would have perished. Most of them would have. I'll bet you anything that fire was started after they were all out of their stalls."

"A parting gesture."

"More than a gesture." She poured more whiskey. "They were covering their tracks. Hoping all the horses would run off—as they might have done, if it weren't for you."

They sat drinking without speaking. Finally, Showers stood up. "The sheriff probably hasn't left. Let's go talk to him."

"No, no. That lard-bellied cracker would just think we were nuts. I don't want to bring in the law until an insurance investigator takes a look at this."

"There's something else we can do. I'll go over to Dandytown Bloodstock and see about this Coggins report."

"You do that, David. I'm going to find out where Billy Bonning was last night." She stood up. "And we better give some thought to moving that new bay stallion of yours to someplace other than your barn."

Ned Haney was as much a member of the Dandytown horse country aristocracy as Showers and the Fairbrothers. His family had founded Dandytown Bloodstock in the 1880s and had been conducting semiannual auctions there ever since, in addition to operating a feed, stud, and general livestock sales business year round. Ned divided his time between Dandytown and branch operations in South Carolina and upstate New York, and was often in Europe. But he was always in town during the steeplechase and fox hunting seasons. He and Showers had known each other since childhood. They trusted each other.

"It's a bad Coggins, no doubt about that," said Haney. "We've had a few of those over the years from that particular vet, rest his soul. Usually we catch them but, hell, David, we ran an awful lot of horses through here in that auction." He flipped open a notebook on his desk. "Two hundred and seven head, including the private sales. But everything else seems to be in order. And the party with a grievance—if there is a grievance—is this May Moody, not you or Alixe. If there's a claim to be filed, legally it has to be done by her. And, speaking of irregularities, Alixe bought that bay and sold him to you without obtaining a veterinarian's certificate for either transaction."

Haney leaned back in his wooden swivel chair. He had dark hair going to gray and a very English face. He was married to an extremely attractive horsewoman from South Carolina, who spent much of her time there. There was talk of other women in his life. Lenore's name had been mentioned.

"It isn't that I want a claim pressed against you, Ned. I just want an investigation. This is a counterfeit horse. I'm sure of it. Alixe has very strong doubts about the animal, too."

"You said the lip tattoo is correct. There's been no alteration."

"We don't know where that stallion was foaled, no matter what it said in your catalogue. There are countries where they don't tattoo registration numbers. England is one of them."

"You're suggesting that animal was smuggled into the country from abroad, brought down here, and then put up for sale at public auction open to all comers?" He went to his notebook again. "It only brought ten thousand."

"That's about all the Queen Tashamore pedigree is worth now, the way the line's been bred. That stallion is worth much more than that pedigree. It's a different horse, Ned. Alixe and I figure it's a two-year-old. You listed it as five."

"Even if true, why would anyone go to all that trouble for a mere ten thousand dollars?"

"If there had been more bidders, the price might have gone a damn sight higher. The sheriff kept a lot of people back at the inn because of the Vicky Clay murder—including Bernard Bloch. I'm told he was interested in the horse."

"He paid a quarter of a million for the last horse he bought from me. Going by the papers, this stallion wouldn't be in his league."

Showers fought back drowsiness. His long, hard night without sleep and his morning drink with Alixe were beginning to catch up with him.

"What do you know about the seller? That outfit in New Jersey?"

Haney shrugged. "Not much. They've only been in business a few years. They're flat-track people. Won quite a few races in New York."

"Why would they come down here to sell a horse? Why not use Fasig-Tipton up at Saratoga, or one of the other big concerns?"

"We're not that small, David." Haney smiled, then shrugged again. "Perhaps there really is something wrong with that stallion—a congenital defect that Meade Clay somehow managed not to notice. Perhaps they thought they could dump it on one of us country bumpkins down here. That's been tried before, though we've always caught it. But you say he seems in good shape."

"Very much so. He's magnificent."

"If you want to file a claim on those grounds, that's another matter. But you know the conditions of sale." Haney picked up one of his catalogues and read from it. " 'Any horse sold in this sale which has a condition that must be announced as provided before time of sale, and is not so announced, shall be subject to return to consignor with refund of purchase price and reimbursement for reasonable expenses for keep, maintenance, and transportation of the horse from fall of the hammer—' "

"I know that by heart, Ned. So do you."

Haney waved away the protest. " '. . . provided that within seven days after date of sale the auctioneer receives written notice from the buyer and a written veterinary certificate, based on examination by the certifying veterinarian, that such a condition exists, and the same existed at time of sale, such times being of the essence. All warranties terminate seven days from date of sale, after which buyer shall have no right of return.' "

He set down the catalogue. "We haven't brought up the calendar, have we? It's been seven days and then some. Seems to me that all this is pretty moot."

Showers felt as though he were thrashing around in a jungle, in the middle of the night.

"Ned, you and I have done business for years. Our fathers did, and their fathers. I'm not bringing all this up just to be frivolous, or because I've lost my mind. Something is damned wrong."

Haney stood up as well. "If you're convinced of that, David, that's good enough for me. I'm not about to let any Dandytown Bloodstock transaction pass under a cloud. All I've been doing here is try to make clear all the procedural difficulties you face. Believe me, please. If there's anything I can do to help you with this, I will."

"Just tell me what action there is that I *can* take."

"The most logical thing is to go to the courts. You can file suit over most anything. But you'd have to sue Alixe, and she'd have to sue that Moody woman, and she'd have to sue the people in New Jersey. It could take years, though. And you'd need a lot more proof than the suspicions you've brought up to me."

Showers nodded. "What else?"

"Well, you could file a complaint with the Thoroughbred Association, challenging the pedigree. A notarized letter will do. Or you can write a letter to me, and I'll pass it on to those New Jersey people with one of my own."

Showers reached and shook Haney's hand. "Thank you. Thank you very much."

"What are you going to do?"

"Everything you suggested."

Showers stopped at Alixe's farm before going on to his own. She was still out, and had not said when she would return. The firemen and sheriff's party had gone, but her stablehands and several of her house servants were out in the yard, still working to clean up the mess. A number of the recaptured horses had been put back into the surviving stable building, but many were still in the fenced front yard.

"Put them in my barn," Showers said. "Most of the stalls are vacant. You'll have to bring over some feed."

"Yes sir, Captain Showers. Miss Percy will sure appreciate that."

"Tell her she's welcome to anything she needs."

Becky's Toyota was parked outside her cottage. He left her undisturbed and went directly to the main house. He'd attend immediately to the letters Haney had suggested.

The pain in his injured leg had returned. His lower back ached as well. Ignoring this, he went to his closet and retrieved his typewriter, setting it up on his desk and inserting a piece of stationery with his farm's letterhead on it.

The words wouldn't come. An overwhelming grogginess did. And then sleep.

He was awakened by the phone. It was Alixe.

"You all right, Captain?" she said. "You sound like you've just crawled out of the grave."

"I dozed off in my chair. I should have just gone to bed."

"Wish I could have joined you, love. Been all over Dandytown. We found the two bays. They were in an orchard on the Berryville road. Must have been five fucking miles from my place."

"A lot of fences between here and there."

"Yes. Very interesting, that. I've done some detective work, too.

Found out how Billy Bonning spent the night, or at least how he says he spent the night. The son of a bitch was fucking that new Charlottesville woman of his at the Raiders Motel."

"He told you that?"

"No, but a bartender did. The owner of that filthy place says he saw them go in and saw them come out this morning. But, who knows, maybe he fucked her to sleep and then slipped out to burn my barn. Maybe she's just covering for him."

"Alixe. Ned Haney had some ideas. There's not a lot we can do, but there's something. We should talk about it."

"Not tonight, m'dear. Thanks for taking in my homeless orphans. They were grazing my lawn down to the nubs."

"It's the very least I could do."

"You're a hell of a man. The best in the county. I curse the day you ever laid eyes on Lenore."

"Good night, Alixe. See you in the morning."

"In the morning. I've got an idea where we can hide that bay stallion. You won't like it, but it's a good idea."

"What's that?"

"There's a girl jockey up in Charles Town in West Virginia. She used to ride for me during my brief career in flat-track racing. She's got a little barn on her place. She'd take really good care of the bay—and it would be the last place in the world anyone would look for a horse of yours or mine."

"You're quite certain that's necessary?"

"David. You want your barn burned down, too? You want to see Becky lying in the ashes like that groom?"

"Good night, Alixe. Pleasant dreams."

Making himself a cup of coffee, he tackled the letter to the Thoroughbred Association first, managing somehow to make it comprehensible. The other took longer. When he'd finished, it was nearly midnight.

He stepped outside. Alixe's stable hands had moved her horses into his barn, but were still working on them. He could hear them talking, to each other and to the horses, sometimes loudly and profanely.

Showers went over to join them. They'd been feeding and rubbing down the stock, and were almost done. They declined his offer to help, so he went down to the big stall at the end, where they'd put the Queen Tashamore bay.

He seemed glad of so much equine company. One of Showers'

barn cats sat perched on a shelf on the stall wall—a visiting friend.

Showers entered the stall. The horse backed up at the intrusion, but then stood still, allowing him to approach. Speaking to it gently, he patted its neck, wishing he had a name to call it.

He looked into the bay's eye. His father would have kept this horse—or sold it quickly for the money it was worth to buy others, and fuel his country gentleman lifestyle. His father, after all, had sold Queen Tashamore. Showers could imagine the man on the phone right now, ringing up Bernie Bloch, saying, "If you want this stallion, you'll pay its true value. That's how we do things in Banastre County."

What was this splendid animal's true value? Was there some defect that neither he nor Alixe nor Kerry Donahue had detected? Was it sterile? Was it balky? Where had it come from? What had it been through in its young life? It knew so many secrets.

"David."

Becky was standing in the open stall door. She was wearing a nightdress, her large breasts much revealed by the open neckline, and a pair of unlaced L.L. Bean outdoor shoes.

"You've slept the day away," he said. "Now you'll be up all night."

"David, I think Billy was here last night."

"That's what Alixe thought. She was sure he was responsible for the barn fire. But it appears he was somewhere else. With a woman."

"He was here. Do you remember that videotape he left behind? The one marked VICKY?"

He looked down at the stall door. "I thought you were going to return that."

"I had it in my tape machine. And now it's gone. It had to be him. I mean, you didn't take it, did you?"

"No, I didn't take it."

"That goddamned Billy. He must have gone into the cottage when we were all over at Alixe's."

"No one saw him."

"Who could have? We were all out chasing after horses."

"Becky. It was his tape. You should have returned it."

"It belonged to Vicky. I was going to burn it."

"What was on that tape?" The question was dishonest. The few seconds he'd spent watching it now made him feel very guilty.

140

"You knew Vicky. Some awful and degrading things—things her family wouldn't want anyone to see."

"You're sure you haven't just misplaced it?" he asked.

"No. It was in the machine. And now he has it."

"We have more important problems. If it's gone, it's gone. It had nothing to do with you."

She said nothing.

"Becky, will you be all right out here? I have to go back to Washington tomorrow."

"I know. You always do."

# Eight

obert Moody had never before missed a cabinet meeting, but he had the best reason imaginable for skipping the one scheduled for this morning. After three false starts, the Senate Foreign Relations Committee was at last going to vote on the Earth Treaty, and Moody didn't want to be more than a few feet away from those who would be casting the votes. He wanted every one of them to be looking into his eyes when the count came.

The committee room was in the Dirksen Senate Office Building. Moody, accompanied by Wolfenson and two other aides, had the limo pull up at a rear entrance, sent one of the aides ahead to hold an elevator, made a quick call to the White House on the car phone to be certain the president had received his message explaining his absence, then swept inside, security guards and bystanders moving quickly out of the way.

"What's the last nose count?" he said to Wolfenson, as the elevator doors closed.

"Three wobblies. Including Sorenson. He had Japanese visitors out to his house over the weekend. Some people from that auto plant they're building in his state."

"I'll take care of him," Moody said.

Upstairs, a number of lobbyists were hanging about in the corridor, along with a large contingent of press and television reporters. Moody moved past them, nodding but ignoring questions, until he came to a correspondent whose paper was friendly to the administration. Halting at the man's greeting, he began chatting with him. The others quickly gathered around, and he was shortly caught up in a full-fledged if impromptu news conference.

Most of the questions followed the line that the treaty was in trouble and the president was facing serious embarrassment. Would he try again if the treaty failed? Did the president have only himself to blame because he was too aloof and standoffish to work the lawmakers in person? Would the newest report on the greenhouse effect make a difference?

Moody dealt with them noncommittally but at considerable length, surprising the news people with his friendliness. The exercise was all to a different purpose. He had positioned himself near the hearing room doorway without looking as though he intended to be there, visible to every committee member as he or she came along the corridor. When he caught a glimpse of Sorenson hurrying down the hall, Moody quickly concluded his answer to the last question posed him and waved off all others. Pausing to gather his assistants about him, he started for the committee room just as Sorenson drew near.

"Good morning, Senator," he said, almost cheerily.

"Good morning." Sorenson looked unhappy.

With a deft movement, Moody drew him aside.

"I just wanted to tell you that I put your wife's name through this morning for the Kennedy Center."

"You did?" Now the senator seemed impatient.

"Yes." Moody glanced at his watch. "My secretary should be calling her with the news right now. I expect she'll be real happy to see you when you get home tonight."

Moody's point hit home. He ground it into the wound.

"It'll require approval by the trustees, but I don't expect any problem. Do you, senator? No problems, right?"

"Thanks," said Sorenson. He pushed ahead.

Moody and his people took VIP seats set aside for them in the front of the spectator section. The room was very crowded. Moody noticed David Showers sitting among other State Department staff over to the side, and was reminded that he had three messages from the Japanese ambassador on his desk. He had no intention of returning the man's calls until after this vote.

The chairman held off long enough to allow one of the members to ask some last-minute questions of a staffer from the Environmental Protection Agency. That done, he asked for a call of the roll. As each cast their vote, most of the senators made statements that amounted to short speeches, carefully worded highly political

*143*

expressions of concern for both the environment and constituents' jobs. Sorenson merely said "aye."

The vote was unanimous.

The cabinet meeting, as usual, had started late, and was still in progress when Moody returned to the White House. As he entered the room, heading for his usual seat just behind the president, he sensed they had been waiting for him. The president was beaming. He'd obviously received the news.

The treasury secretary was droning on about the money supply, reading from a report. Taking note of the president's ebullient reaction to Moody's entrance, the secretary quickly wound up his presentation, then sat back. All eyes turned to the boss.

"Thank you, Mr. Secretary," the president said. "Thank you very much. Uh, ladies and gentlemen, as most of you know, this administration faced its first major test on the Earth Treaty this morning. The note that was handed to me a few minutes ago brings good tidings. We have prevailed. There was not a single dissenting vote."

The cabinet broke into applause, led by the vice president.

As it subsided, the president turned to look back at Moody. "There wasn't a hitch of any kind, was there, Robert?"

"None whatsoever, sir."

"I am not only pleased, I am deeply moved," the president said. "This success was the result of tireless effort and a refusal to compromise an awesomely important principle. Each and every one of you did your part, but I am particularly grateful to the late secretary of state—to my friend Skip Hollis—and his staff, who worked day and night making this possible. Skip gave his heart and soul to his effort. In a sense, he gave his life. A major reason for his going to Geneva was to use the opportunity to press the issue with the foreign ministers gathered there. And with great effect. I've also been informed that the British House of Commons approved a bill of ratification a few hours ago."

He halted, staring down at the polished tabletop. Moody worked hard to keep his expression utterly blank.

The president cleared his throat, regathering his composure.

"We also owe a great debt to a man I consider my right hand. Governor Moody was in the trenches fighting for this to the last round. I couldn't have done without him."

More applause followed, this time led by Waldemar Sadinauskas. The vice president's hands came together softly. He allowed himself a quick, dark glance at Moody, who returned it.

The vice president was no fool. A senator from Ohio who had been the first to enter the last presidential race, he'd been clever enough to drop out and declare for the eventual victor on the eve of the Pennsylvania primary, which the president had won in a close vote. It had been clear to Moody that the man had stood no chance even in his home state, but the president had credited him with making the victory possible, and rewarded him accordingly. Moody knew the vice president to be a treacherous sonofabitch, and had worked hard to keep the man from gaining any real influence.

He'd done this very carefully, however. The vice president was not oblivious to Moody's ambitions. Any attempt to dislodge him would involve a serious fight. But it could be done. Moody was laying plans and gathering ammunition. Among other things, he had learned that the vice president's holdings—though placed in an inaccessible trust—included stock in a number of public utilities that still used dirty midwestern coal as well as nuclear power, both of which would be severely limited by the domestic legislation that was to follow ratification of the Earth Treaty, presuming the legislation was enacted.

The vice president had also been a good friend of Majority Leader Reidy. He'd turned on Reidy in the primaries, but they could find common cause again, especially if Reidy saw the vice president as an instrument of revenge. Many in the press were already writing that a challenge to the president was possible from within his own Democratic party if the new environmental laws proved as unpopular as some expected. The country was still recovering from a very long and deep recession.

And then there was the matter of the vice president's girlfriend—a sweet little blonde from Cleveland who worked as social secretary to the vice president's wife. The president, in his pained way, might countenance an indiscretion or two, but not a full-time mistress—especially one on the public payroll.

Moody had engaged in more than one or two indiscretions, but had been damned careful about them. He'd never kept a mistress, except for a few months with Deena when he was still married to his ex-wife. He'd never ever messed with any of the women on his staff.

His biggest problem, he knew, was his friendship with Bernie Bloch, but he'd severed all his business ties with the man long before he'd joined the president's team. His money now was all in government bonds and real estate—housing developments, hotels, and office buildings. He was probably the cleanest person in the administration, except for Sadinauskas and the former nun who was secretary of education.

As a man from the hollows, Moody knew a lot about the creatures of the wild. He knew about rattlesnakes, and their practice of coiling together in a heap for warmth as they hibernated through the winter. It was one of nature's more diabolical methods of keeping down the population of these predators. The first one or two snakes to awaken in the spring ate all the others.

The president might run for a second term, or not; replace his running mate, or not. Choose an eventual successor, or not. Whatever happened, Moody was going to be one wide-awake rattlesnake.

"Well, then," said the president. "A most inspiring and promising morning. Thank you all, and God bless."

Returning to his office, Moody wasted no time getting the Japanese embassy on the line. Despite the urgency of his earlier calls, the ambassador was now "unavailable." Moody settled for the deputy chief of mission, who spoke English so inscrutably that Moody wondered if the man quite realized who he was. He made that blisteringly clear, and left the fellow with a short, terse message. If the ambassador wished to speak to him, he would make himself available, in his office at the White House, in one hour. If the ambassador could not make that appointment, well, it might be weeks before he would be available again. These were very busy times for the United States of America.

Hanging up, he sat back and stared at the phone, feeling like.a man who had just lighted a fuse. It detonated. The ambassador's office called back within three minutes. He would meet with Moody when and where instructed.

Moody ignored the rest of the messages on his desk, but decided to place one more call. He hadn't lingered to talk to Senate Majority Leader Reidy at the Capitol, but phoned him now—on his private line. Reidy answered cheerfully enough, but, with a quick apology, put Moody on hold. Moody presumed he was being yanked around, but he didn't care. He'd play the game. His secretary appeared in the doorway, mouthing that the president wanted to see him. Moody nodded, then waved her off. Finally, Reidy came back on.

"Hello, Bobby. Having a nice day?"

"I just wanted to offer my congratulations. It was a hell of a victory."

"Well, my congratulations to you, Governor. You boys sure knocked yourself out on this one. You deserve a nice long vacation."

"The hell we do. We've got to keep moving. How soon can we get a vote on the floor?"

"I was just thinking about that." Moody could hear him riff through some papers. "I don't see any reason why we can't call a vote the first week after Labor Day."

"Labor Day? The president wants to move now. Certainly by June 30. It was your idea to split up the package and move on the treaty fast. So move."

"Bobby, this is the United States Senate, not the Maryland legislature. Everyone's going to be looking for a way to vote both sides of this one. The Republicans'll dream up every kind of weird amendment you ever heard of. Besides, we've got the budget resolution and the new arms control treaty to deal with. June 30. That's crazy."

"All right, we'll compromise. Take care of the budget. Take care of the ICBMs. Then keep them in their seats until they vote on the Earth Treaty."

"No recess?"

"Not until there's a vote. Maybe you could turn off the air conditioning."

"Ho, ho, ho."

"Move on it, Senator. We're not fooling around."

"I can see that, Governor. All right. I'll get it on the calendar. I don't expect I'm going to be a very popular fellow."

"You'll be popular with me. And the president."

"I just hope you get a whole heap of those Kennedy Center appointments to hand around."

Moody hadn't yet told Deena he'd given hers to Senator Sorenson's wife. One of the many messages on his desk was from Deena.

"We've got whatever it's going to take."

"Okay, Bobby. Nice talking to you."

"Always a pleasure, Senator."

Moody closed the door to the Oval Office behind him gently, then went to stand in front of his boss's desk. The president was toying with a ship's model he kept on his desk, a replica of a square-rigged brigantine that had done duty in the War of 1812. He flicked the tiny anchor with his finger, watching it swing to and fro on its little chain.

"Sorry for the delay, sir," Moody said. "I was talking to Reidy about the Earth Treaty. Keep them hustling up there."

"Indeed, indeed. I just wanted to ask you to join me at the press briefing. Help me deal with the questions."

"I've been thinking about that, sir. I think you ought to cancel the briefing."

"Cancel it? We've just won a great victory."

"I know, sir. And you're guaranteed two, three minutes on the evening news. Easy. But I don't think a standup in the press room is what you need. You know what the press corps is like. A lot of those newsies are nothing more than professional cynics. You'll get some softies, but there are some real hardasses out there, too. They'll just whack away at you, try to diminish the success we had today, cast doubt on our chances before the full Senate. It won't matter what answers you give them, not if they get enough nasty questions into their sound bites."

"But this hardly seems the time to hide from the press."

"I'm not suggesting that, sir. We're on a roll here. We've made a big score. We ought to get the maximum out of it. I think we should ask the networks for some prime time tonight. Fifteen minutes ought to do it. A quick setup here in the Oval Office. You sitting beside your desk, maybe. Informal. Get that globe in, and maybe that model ship."

The president gave the anchor another flick, then turned the miniature brig around with bow facing forth.

"Fifteen minutes? What do I have to say, aside from being very pleased about the Foreign Relations Committee vote?"

"You've got a lot to say. You can seize upon this as a major expression of the public will, treat the full Senate vote as a mere formality, keep the momentum going. Your pitch can be a call to the world leaders who've been dragging their feet to get behind the treaty now. You can lace it with some more horror stories. I've got a guy on the intergovernmental council from the State Department who has come up with some beauts. Did you know that it's now expected that ninety percent of the population of Australia will get some form of skin cancer because of ozone depletion?"

"Gosh, no? Is it as bad as that?"

"I wasn't sure how you'd feel about going on television tonight,

**148**

sir, but just in case, I got the speechwriters going on this yesterday."

"You were that confident?"

"Yes sir."

The president smiled. "Well, I think it's a fine idea, Bob. By all means."

"Very good, sir. I'll have the press office get on to the networks right now."

He started toward the door, then halted, lingering. The presidential eyebrows went up. The anchor flicked again.

"Something else, Bob?"

"I was wondering, sir, if you've given any thought to a replacement for Secretary Hollis yet." Moody was taking a chance here. The man had only just been laid in his grave.

"As a matter of fact, I have. What do you think about Acting Secretary Richmond?"

Moody swore to himself. He should have been moving on this a hell of a lot sooner.

"He's a fine man, sir. An excellent career officer. I'm sure Secretary Hollis found him indispensable. But he's a follow-through guy, an implementer, not an initiator. You need someone who will seize the initiative wherever possible, press the issue at every opportunity. Not just carry out instructions. And there's something else, sir. Richmond is a longtime career man. He's served five presidents and I don't know how many secretaries of state. Given what's at stake here, I think you need someone who's devoted fully to you, fully committed to the cause. Someone, well, like Secretary Hollis. I mean, as devoted and committed as Secretary Hollis was."

The tiny anchor swung up hard and got caught in the ship model's rigging. The president pushed the boat away.

"Well, I do want to attend to this soon. Any other suggestions you may have would be appreciated."

"Yes sir. In the meantime, I wondered if you'd mind if I took a few initiatives of my own. Lean on a few ambassadors now that we've won the committee vote. As a matter of fact, I've got the Japanese ambassador coming by this afternoon. I'm sure he would have gone to Secretary Hollis, if it hadn't been for the tragedy, but in the, er, interim, he sought me out. I think they may finally be open to some negotiation. What I was wondering, sir, is whether you'd mind if I was a little firm?"

"Firm? With the Japanese? By all means."

"Thank you, sir. I'll give you a full report."

He reached the door, but this time the president halted him.

"Uh, Bob? I'd rather it didn't get bandied about that we refer to the ladies and gentlemen of the news media as hardasses around here."

He smiled. So did Moody.

Moody had his secretary bring him fresh coffee. While sipping it, he decided he'd best attend to the call from Deena.

She was still in their apartment at the Watergate. Normally, she'd be out on her social rounds at this time of day. He wondered if she was ill. She'd still been in bed when he'd left that morning.

"Hi, honey," he said. "What's up? We've got a pretty full plate here today."

"I heard. It's all over the radio about the vote. Did he say anything about secretary of state?"

"Please, Deena. Not now."

"Sorry, darlin'. That's not why I called. I just wanted to tell you I've invited Bernie and Sherrie Bloch over for dinner tonight."

"Denna, the president's going on television tonight. I've got to be with him. I won't be able to get out of here until at least nine thirty. Why didn't you ask me about it this morning?"

"You left at six thirty, Bobby. I'll make it a late supper. Bernie wants to talk to you. He knows you don't like him to call you at your office."

"He could call me at home."

"Bobby, you haven't been home before eleven all week. Come on, darlin'. We haven't seen them since we all went out to the races. It'll be fun."

Moody sighed. He needed to unwind, charge his batteries. He owed himself a few belts with his best friend. He was a big winner that day. Winners did what they wanted. "All right."

"Thank you, darlin'. You're the best husband I ever had."

As he hung up, an excellent idea occurred to him. He had been neglecting Bernie. Whatever it was his friend had in mind to say to him, there was something he could do to put him in a good mood. Bloch had never been to the White House. Moody hadn't thought it wise to have him call on him during business hours, but on a social occasion, as part of a big mob of guests, it ought to do no harm at all. He flicked through his calendar, then had his secretary ring up the first lady's social secretary—in this administration, a man.

"Robert, dear boy." There were rumors about social secretary

Toby Kevin's sexual preference, but Moody didn't let that bother him. You had to deal with the players, and the fellow was certainly that. He was another of the administration figures who had been to school with the president. His job wasn't as lowly as it seemed. People were almost willing to kill for White House invitations.

"We've got the president of Mexico coming this month," Moody said. "Is that going to include a state dinner?"

"Why, of course."

"Well, I was just thinking. The guy's a big horse nut, isn't he? Raises Arabians or something?"

"He has one of the biggest stables in Mexico."

"Well, why don't we invite some local horsemen? I was thinking particularly of Bernard Bloch."

"Bernard Bloch?"

"Sure. Not because he's a friend of mine. He's about as major a horseman as we have around here nowadays, and he's gone into this steeplechasing in a big way. Won a big race recently, what was it, the Valley Dragoon Chase? Out in Dandytown. I was there."

The other man was silent. Another bright idea occurred to Moody. His mind was firing on all burners that day.

"Not just Bloch. I was thinking maybe the Fairbrothers, too. Lynwood Fairbrother? And his lovely wife. Keep the Republicans happy. We're going to need them on that treaty business."

"That, Robert, is an excellent idea. I'll have them put on the guest list."

"And the Blochs."

"And the Blochs. If you insist."

"Just a suggestion. After all, he is a big campaign contributor."

"There's a place for those people, I suppose."

"Thanks, Toby. You're a prince."

After the receiver was safely in its place, Moody allowed himself a loud profanity. The social secretary's disdain for Bloch infuriated him. For crying out loud, they had had some sleazy rock star at the last state dinner, and some prime-time television soap opera queen who must have slept with every producer in Hollywood twice.

The Japanese ambassador was exactly on time. Moody made him wait. He was about to have the envoy ushered in when he realized there was one more call he had to make—one he should have made days before.

The chairman of the Democratic National Committee was in a meeting. Moody got him out of it immediately, on pain of a job transfer to something dreadful in the Health and Human Services Department.

"You've got a man named Peter Napier working for you," Moody said, once hurried and pointless pleasantries were dispensed with. "Where is he?"

"Beats the hell out of me," the chairman said. "He didn't come in today. He doesn't come in a lot of days. He's always off doing stuff for Reidy or somebody."

"Well, I need him to do some stuff for us. I need him out of town instanter."

"Out of town where?"

"I don't care."

There was a pause. "What's going on, Bob?"

The man was a straight shooter—rare for his line of work. Moody knew he had to reply in kind if he was going to get his cooperation.

"Someone signed his name to something that could cause us a problem. It's my job to take care of problems. It's your job to help."

"What was it he was supposed to have signed?"

"You don't need to know. No one knows about it. Napier doesn't know much about it. I don't want him to. I want him out of town. Far. You have a committee put together yet on site selection for the next convention?"

"I've got a few guys in mind, but Bobby, the convention's not for nearly three years."

"I know exactly when the convention is. Assign Napier to committee staff right now and get him off to do some advance work. I don't care what. You have San Francisco or New Orleans on the list? I hear he's the kind of guy who'd be happy in either place."

"San Francisco and New Orleans are always on the list. Let the good times roll. It's a hell of a municipal slogan."

"Give him his choice, but get him on a plane. This afternoon. Tell him to check out hotel accommodations. And recreational opportunities. Tell him to take his time."

"I'll have to find him first. Honest, I don't know where he is."

"I'll bet you probably have a pretty good idea. I can think of a bachelor congressman or two who can give you a tip, if you'll pardon the expression."

"We'll find him. But seriously, what's up? Is this a problem that could affect the National Committee?"

"It never happened. Neither did this call. Okay?"

"Okay. You great statesmen sure move in mysterious ways."

*152*

"You ain't seen nothing yet. Thanks. I owe you."

He buzzed his secretary. "All right, Anne. I'll see Mr. Aomori now."

The ambassador was tall, balding, thin, except for the slight diplomatic paunch to be expected of those who spent so many working hours at embassy receptions, and very formal. He even bowed. Moody took him to the comfortable armchairs he had carefully arranged in the corner, giving the ambassador the one with the best view out the windows of the Ellipse. He was going to be firm, but also friendly. He had Anne bring tea. He hated tea.

"I'm really sorry to keep you waiting," Moody said. "The fur has really been flying around here today."

"Please?"

"I mean, we've been very busy. I know you've been wanting to see me, so I thought I'd give you the very first opportunity. I won't have many until we get this treaty ratified."

"Yes. I am most grateful. Uh, we would like to congratulate you on your success today."

Moody shrugged. "It was a foregone conclusion. So's the full Senate vote. Politicians read the polls, Mr. Ambassador. There's not a lobbyist in town as persuasive as a poll. The American people want this treaty. They're afraid of what could happen to them without it. They don't want to put this off any longer."

"You have helped to make them afraid."

Moody put some sternness in his voice. "The president has made his concern very clear."

The ambassador took a sip of his tea. His hands were very graceful. He held his cup as though it were a precious work of art.

"Mr. Chief . . ."

Mr. Chief? Where the hell did he get that? "The official title is assistant to the president. Most people call me Governor, or Colonel."

"Colonel? You were in the military? In . . . ?"

"In Vietnam. I'm not old enough to have been in World War Two." He laughed. The ambassador did not. "Why don't you just call me Bob? The president does."

"Mr. Moody," the ambassador began again. He struck Moody as a fellow who had probably never called anyone by his first name in all his life. "We are informed that you are not confining your efforts on behalf of the so-called Earth Treaty to the United States Congress."

"Of course not, Mr. Ambassador. The treaty is the centerpiece of the president's foreign policy. We want to get everybody aboard. It won't work otherwise."

"We are informed that you are now intending to focus these international attentions on Japan."

"We'd sure like to have you with us, if that's what you mean."

"We are informed that you may be contemplating certain, uh, inducements to Japanese cooperation, inducements involving trade, import restrictions, government regulation, limitations on foreign investment—all very serious matters."

Moody decided his best response would be to say nothing, to sit there impassively. Inscrutable.

"We are informed there is an internal White House memorandum to this effect."

"Internal memoranda are for internal consumption, Mr. Ambassador. But I know of no such memo. And believe me, I see all the paper that moves through here."

"There was a communication from a Mr. Napier. He is on your staff?"

"I don't know who your sources are, but there's no Napier who works for the White House. I think there's a guy by that name with the National Committee, but they don't have any official status. They're strictly political. And they represent the entire party. They don't speak for the administration." He paused. "Not necessarily."

The ambassador studied him a moment, then smiled. "Would it be possible, do you think, to arrange a meeting with your president?"

Moody shook his head. "I'm afraid I'm as high as you're going to get, at least until a new secretary of state is appointed. You know the protocol."

"I have already spoken with Acting Secretary Richmond. He suggested I talk with you."

Moody appreciated Richmond's deference, but not his failure to tell the White House he'd been approached by the Japanese. He made a mental note to give the guy a good kick in the ass about it, at some future and appropriate occasion.

"Your prime minister could meet with the president," Moody said, "if he'd like to make an official visit. I can ask the president if he'd be willing to meet with your foreign minister, should he visit the United States, but the president's awfully busy these days, as I'm sure you can understand."

"Mr. Moody. This matter is of some urgency. Legislation is to be introduced next week in both the House of Councillors and the

**154**

House of Representatives of our Diet. It is legislation for the consideration of the so-called Earth Treaty. Do you understand what I am saying? My government is interested in giving this treaty very serious consideration, to see what is possible."

"I understand, Mr. Ambassador. I think it's terrific news."

"It is not *news* yet, Mr. Moody. I have come to speak with you so to make certain that you understand that the very serious matters I spoke of before—threats of trade restrictions and all such—these could have very serious repercussions in Japanese domestic politics. These could be very disruptive if they became public. Most regrettable."

Moody took a sip of his own tea. It was weak and lukewarm. Letting Aomori wait a little longer, he took another sip, then set down his cup with finality.

"Mr. Ambassador, I understand you perfectly. And I'll make sure the president does, too. And let me tell you, I'm sure you have nothing to worry about. Nothing whatsoever."

He stood up. The ambassador, taken aback by Moody's abruptness, finally did so also. Moody shook his hand.

"I'm really glad you came by," Moody said. "What you've told me is very encouraging. I'm sure the president will be delighted. He considers Japan one of America's closest friends, as I'm sure you know."

"Thank you, Mr. Moody." The ambassador gave another slight bow.

"If anything," said Moody, putting his hand on Aomori's shoulder to urge him toward the door, "if what you say about the Diet continues to be encouraging, why, I think new trade restrictions and all that would be the last thing you'd have to worry about. In fact, I think some new understandings might be reached. In time."

"This is very good to hear, Mr. Moody."

Moody accompanied the ambassador all the way out to the lobby. He felt so good, he would have gladly opened the man's car door for him.

Returning, he went directly to the Oval Office, walking right in.

"Mr. President, I've got some terrific news. The Japanese are beginning to move on the treaty."

ABC declined to clear time for the presidential address, preferring to run its scheduled Diane Sawyer interview with Madonna, but CBS, NBC, CNN, and Fox made fifteen minutes available. The president was as stilted and uncomfortable-looking as always, but his stiffness at least went well with the gravity of his message. The instant analysis by news commentators that followed was all favorable. The president was pleased, and Moody was ecstatic. He hummed to himself in the car on the way home. He couldn't recall when he had last done that. Probably not since the first night he had gone to bed with Deena.

She had whipped up a buffet straight out of the recipes of *Southern Living* magazine, heavy on olives, dips, and minced salad. Moody had grown used to such food, but Bernie Bloch, a steak, potatoes, and matzo ball soup man, showed little appetite for it. Sherrie was more than halfway toward drunk and, after spilling her plate onto the carpet, ate nothing more at all.

While Deena and the Moodys' maid attended to cleaning up the mess, Bloch used the occasion to suggest that he and Moody step out onto the balcony for a cigar. Moody didn't smoke, but got the message. Bloch had the incurable habit of lighting up his Dominican Imperiales wherever and whenever he wanted. Now he wanted something else.

A jetliner roared by close overhead as they stepped outside. The warm wind was from the south, requiring planes landing at National Airport to use a Potomac River approach that took them by the Watergate and the adjoining Kennedy Center just above rooftop level.

Bloch, leaning on the railing, cupped his hands to light his cigar, waiting for the jet and its noise to pass by.

"Bobby," he said finally. "I still have a problem with that horse."

"I've already told you. I don't want you messing with May over it. I'd like to get back on her good side one of these days. Friend that you are, Bernie, you're just going to fuck that up for me."

"May? You just said it, Bobby. We're friends. Friends for life. I'd never do anything to get her riled up. The thing is, she sold the horse. From what I've been able to find out, the same goddamn night she bought it. She took it away from me, and then got rid of it, just like that."

"Like I told you, Bernie. I'm sure she didn't have the faintest idea you wanted that horse."

Another jet was approaching, its landing lights making it look like a circus floating in the sky.

"Yeah, well, maybe not. Take your word for it. Anyway, she

**156**

sold it to a horsewoman out there named Percy, and guess what she did with it?"

Moody let him answer his own question.

"She sold it to that gray-haired jockey. David Showers. *Captain* David Showers. The guy in the State Department."

Moody was beginning to feel haunted by the man. "You're sure of that?"

"You bet your ass I'm sure. The sonofabitch has filed a complaint with the Thoroughbred Association, and another one with the auctioneer. He's asking for an inquiry. There was some minor error in the veterinarian's certificate, and the guy's making a federal case of it. The vet was one I use sometimes. Used to use. Vicky Clay's husband, the dead guy. He was as big a junkie as she was, and he fucked up the certificate. So now this Sir Lancelot is causing me a problem."

The jetliner careened slowly by, lower than the first one, its engines screaming.

Moody waited. "How is he causing you a problem if you weren't involved in the transaction?" he said finally.

"I'm involved, because I've got to have that horse."

"Look, Bernie. This has nothing to do with me. And if May sold it, like you say, it has nothing to do with her. It's a horse, for God's sake. You've got dozens of horses."

"I wasn't buying the horse for myself, Bobby. It was for a second party. I gave my word, to some very important people. They don't care anything about anything except that they get the horse. Like I promised. I don't know how well you know the racing business, but . . ."

"I don't want to know anything about it."

"All you need to know is I've got a real serious obligation here. I promised somebody that horse. And thanks to you, it got away from me. I've got to deliver. This is as important to me as any deal I ever made. I've got to have that horse."

"Why don't you just go to Showers and make him an offer? I don't think he's got a lot of money. Make him a decent offer. Whatever the horse is worth to you."

"I intend to make him an offer. Only I'd like you to make it to him for me."

"Me? Look, Bernie. The man's a career foreign service officer. They're like the Vatican over there. A priesthood. An outsider can't screw around with them. I can't lean on him because of some horse deal of yours. He could start some official proceeding. Anyway, I owe him. He came through for us on the treaty in a really big way."

"Bobby, *I* came through for you on that fucking treaty. And in a very big way. You know how generous I was to the party in the election? Well, I kept on being generous. I laid down a lot of money on that treaty. A hell of a lot."

"What are you talking about?"

"Just campaign contributions, Mr. Straight Arrow. All on the up and up. Didn't ask for nothing. They know where my sympathies lie. What you ought to keep in mind here, Bobby, is that I intend to keep on being generous. I've got a lot of friends on that Senate floor now and you're going to need every one of them."

"I don't want to hear this."

"Maybe you don't, but listen good. I really, really need your help. You've gotten my help when you needed it, don't forget. You asked for it, and you got it. And not just when we were starting out. I got that TV time for you and your president when you needed it before the Illinois primary. I took care of those guys who were going to sell your man out for Reidy. Hell, I took care of Reidy. I'm just asking for a little giveback. Only I'm going to count it as a really big favor, the biggest of my life. And I'll pay you back in a big way, a way that'll really count."

"What do you want me to do, Bernie?"

"I want you to talk to this guy Showers. Tell him you don't want your daughter caught up in this trouble he's stirring up. Tell him it was all a big mix-up. Tell him the truth, that you were supposed to bid on this horse for me, and you fucked it up because you had to get back to Washington for God and country. Tell him I'm real sorry it happened and that I want to make it up to him. I'll pay him whatever he wants for the horse. Offer him fifty thousand. He might think it funny if you offer much more, but if he presses, make it whatever he wants. Everybody's got their price, right? Everybody. Even those snooty bastards out in horse country."

"Can't you do this yourself?"

"No. I'm not the one to talk to him about your daughter getting mixed up in this. And I'm not the one to bring up something else. You say you owe him one on the treaty? So offer him a little something extra, a sweetener. He's in the State Department, right? All those guys live for is to become an ambassador. So make him one. Or offer to make him one. Hell, you've been handing out those plums to fucking car dealers. The *Washington Post* was screaming at you the other day about that. Here's a chance to make a first-rate career appointment. Just make it to some country far away, one where he won't have any use for horses."

Bloch relighted his cigar. The lights of yet another airplane appeared in the murk to the northwest.

"There's nothing illegal about this, Bobby. You could get in more trouble for the logrolling you've been doing on the treaty."

"I don't know, Bernie."

Bloch puffed, causing a large cloud of smoke to gather about his face. He let the breeze slowly disperse it, then took the cigar from his mouth.

"If I told you my life depended on it," he said, "would you help me out?"

The jet's approach was high, but its noise was even louder than the others. Moody looked hard at his friend but the man kept his eyes on the river.

"Okay, Bernie. Let's go inside."

The spilled food had been cleaned up. The two women were seated in opposite chairs, Sherrie holding a refilled drink, babbling on; Deena staring at her coldly. The stereo was playing some very saccharine "beautiful music." It seemed starkly inappropriate.

"I forgot to tell you," Moody said to his guests. "I've got you on the list for the next state dinner."

In bed that night, Deena gave him another very good time. Afterward, they lay on their backs, her head on his outstretched arm.

"Are you going to help Bernie?" she said softly.

"Do you know what he wanted?"

"No. Just that he needed an important favor."

He gazed at the ceiling's empty darkness.

"I'm going to do what I can for him." He prepared himself. "Deena. About the Kennedy Center board. I had to give the next spot to Sorenson's wife. It sewed up his vote."

He felt her shoulder muscles tense, then relax. She rolled over and kissed him on the cheek.

"That's all right, darlin'. There'll be another. First things first."

# Nine

howers had come to the office wearing what, by the dress code of a foreign service establishment, were unpardonably casual clothes—a lightweight sport coat, frayed white button-down shirt, old striped tie, khaki trousers, a dusty old pair of loafers. His boss had given him a few days off as a reward for his contribution to the successful vote, and he planned to drive over to West Virginia that morning to meet Alixe, after spending a few minutes in his office going through his mail and clearing up some neglected paperwork. Before he could escape, he received two telephone calls.

One was from his cousin, Jack Spencer, who sounded a little husky from drink but otherwise alert and cheerful.

"So, hurray for our side," Spencer said. "How does it feel, finding out you actually made a right decision once in your life?"

"What are you talking about, Jack?"

"The triumph of the Forces of Good," he said melodramatically, "and all thinks to you."

"All I did was work up a few reports, and testify before the committee a few times—along with several hundred other people."

"I'm not talking about the U.S. Congress, old sport. I'm talking about the Japanese. I thought you'd have gotten the news through official channels by now. It's on the wires. The Japanese Diet has taken up a ratification bill. Our Tokyo correspondent is calling it 'a surprising turn of events.' Needless to say, I wasn't surprised. First thing your side of the family has done without consulting your ancestors. Unless you count our little chat at the Willard."

"A ratification bill? You're sure?"

"We make up a lot of our copy, but this is a statement of fact. Made me proud to be an American. At least, proud to be related to the Showerses."

"I'd rather we weren't having this conversation."

"I'm the soul of discretion, mate."

"I doubt what I did made any difference at all," Showers said. "The Japanese ambassador went to the White House. No one knows what they said there, but I'm sure that's what got the Diet going. Nothing to do with me."

"Much too modest, cousin, as always. You and I will always know otherwise. That piece of paperwork you showed me . . . ?"

"No such paper. It doesn't exist. At least, not anymore."

"That was wise. I thought you bureaucrats always made endless file copies of everything."

"Jack, I really wish you'd change the subject."

"Righto. Anyway, are you clear of this now?"

"My work from now on should be extremely dull and routine. They're even giving me some time off to go out to the country. You ought to come out this weekend. Give your liver a rest."

"Dandytown is the last place I'd go to rest the old liver. Not to speak of the old libido."

"Well, you're welcome anytime."

"It'll be a while. In any event, well played, cousin. You surprised me."

"Goodbye, Jack. Take care."

"You, too."

The next call, coming almost immediately after, was from the White House—a summons, unexplained and imperative. He was to report to the West Wing lobby at once. The woman calling did not say to whom he was to report. The directness, lack of courtesy, and air of mystery gave him a fair idea as to who wanted to see him.

There were some new environmental reports on fishing-catch depletion in his hell box. He put them in a briefcase to take along.

That and the suitcase he had brought with him went into the back of his Jeep Cherokee. It had rained that morning and the traffic was backed up and moving slowly. Preoccupied by his thoughts, he nearly had a minor accident weaving among the numerous double-parked vehicles along F Street near the Old Executive Office Building. He found an empty space in a "government vehicles only" stretch of 17th to which the State Department sticker on his bumper entitled him. The Jeep would not be molested.

He presented his department identification badge to the guard at the White House northwest gate. His name had already been given clearance and the uniformed security officer behind the bulletproof glass buzzed him in immediately, delaying him only to look through the briefcase. A television crew preparing to do a standup alongside the driveway beyond stopped their work to take a careful look at him, but apparently dismissed him as no one important. As with all visitors, the marine sentry at the West Wing's double entrance doors came stiffly to attention and gave him a crisp "Welcome to the White House, sir." The receptionist inside checked his name against a list on her desk, then asked him rather brusquely to take a seat. He did so on a couch beneath an early nineteenth-century landscape.

A pretty young woman dressed conservatively in a long-skirted suit appeared before him almost immediately, saying "Please come with me, Mr. Showers" before he could even rise. No one else in the lobby paid him any attention.

He wasn't at all surprised that she took him to the office of Chief of Staff Robert Moody, but he was surprised at the enormous size of it, calculating it must be larger even than the president's. Moody, wearing a dark, pinstriped summer suit, came around the desk and greeted him politely, leading him to the group of large comfortable chairs in the corner. Hot coffee was brought at once.

"Maybe you're getting tired of running into me," Moody said, after coffee was poured and his secretary had left.

Showers was struck by how quintessentially American the man's ruddy, bony face looked—a face out of a frontier painting by George Caleb Bingham.

"Not at all."

"I've an official and an unofficial reason for asking you here this morning," Moody said, sitting back a little stiffly, his dark eyes fixed measuringly on Showers'. "The official one is that we're pleased around here with the way you've performed on the treaty. Real damned pleased."

"I heard about the Japanese this morning." Showers wondered if he should be addressing the man as 'sir' in this circumstance.

Moody's back stiffened further. "Yeah. Well, let's not go into that. I don't anticipate you'll be dealing much with the Japanese again. Ever again. If you get my drift."

"I believe I do."

"Good. You're a smart guy, Showers. There's a lot of education over there in State, but not a lot of smarts."

That Showers let pass.

"Anyway, we feel you're being wasted over there in what amounts to a staff job. We also feel we ought to be making more career ambassadorial appointments than we have. The president is very concerned about this, but he's also made it clear he wants the very best. What I'm trying to tell you is that we've put your name at the top of the list—for a vacancy that's just opened up."

"For ambassador?" Showers couldn't restrain the thrill that ran through him. His father had disdainfully predicted that such a thing would never happen, that he'd end his career as an obscure civil servant laboring in some dusty bin.

"U.S. ambassador to the Republic of Iceland. I believe that's a country where you have some background, and a few friends. None of them Japanese." He smiled, but not genuinely. The expression seemed misplaced on his dour face.

"Yes."

"Well, then. Do you accept?"

"Accept?" There was a worrisome doubt nagging at him, but he couldn't stop his words. "Of course, sir."

Moody's smile softened and became more natural. He leaned forward to take a drink of his coffee, then sat back, much more relaxed now. Showers sensed he was being sold something.

"Now for the unofficial part. You've met my daughter May?"

"Yes sir. Briefly. Out at the steeplechase in Dandytown, the weekend you were there."

"In fact, you bought a horse from her."

The thrill became a chill. "I bought a horse from a friend who bought it from your daughter. It was a little irregular, I'm afraid."

"In fact, you're raising a stink over it, right? An official stink?"

"Mr. Moody. The horse's papers were not in order. I've asked for an investigation. Your daughter's not really involved."

"The hell she isn't. This amounts to a charge of fraud."

"Not at all, sir. Not as far as she's concerned."

"Look, Showers. We're both busy men. I shouldn't be taking up our time with this. But it's got me a little . . . steamed. I love my daughter, very much. We've had some differences. But I love her. She's my only child. She's had some troubles recently, and I don't want her to get involved in any more."

"Mr. Moody—"

The other man cut him short with a commanding chop of the hand. "Listen to me. This whole thing is my fault and I feel really bad about it. May used to ride when she was a girl, and she's owned a couple of horses. But she doesn't know a hell of a lot about the horse-trading business and I don't think she was really aware of what she was doing at that auction. *I* was supposed to buy that horse that night, for a friend."

"You mean Mr. Bloch."

The dark eyes began to burn. Moody's voice became quieter. "I was the only one who was allowed to leave the inn that night because the sheriff was questioning people about what happened to . . . to those two unfortunate people. He let me go because, well, you don't detain the chief of staff of the president of the United States. As a favor, I promised to stop by the auction and bid on that horse for Bernie. But, like you, I always put my job first. We had that trouble down in Belize that night and I skipped the goddamned auction because I wanted to get back to the White House as soon as possible. You understand why I had to do that? The country first, right?"

"Yes sir."

"Otherwise I would have been there and all this never would have come up. I don't want it to go any further. I don't want May to be making depositions or whatever out there in Virginia when she's supposed to be rehearsing for a play. A Shakespeare play, for crying out loud. Tough stuff."

"Have you talked to her?"

"Will you just listen to me, Mr. Showers? I want to get this horse thing behind us, in a way that will make everybody happy." He drank more of his coffee. Showers left his untouched. "Now I don't have any business dealings with Mr. Bloch. Haven't for years. I don't have business dealings with anyone. But he's still my friend and I've talked to him about this. He's still interested in owning that horse. He's a man of some means, Mr. Showers, and he's willing to be very generous. He mentioned a figure of fifty, no, a hundred thousand dollars."

"A hundred thousand?"

"That's not unusual, is it? I'm told show horses out your way go for a lot more than that, horses that little ten-year-old kids ride. Hell, I paid more than forty thousand for the last one May had."

"It's nothing to do with money . . ."

"Just listen. He'll pay you a hundred thousand for the horse. You drop this inquiry you started, and May won't have to trouble her pretty head about anything. And you can go on serving your country—as ambassador. A hundred thousand ought to be enough for you to keep that farm of yours going while you're overseas, don't you think?"

Showers took a deep breath, working to keep complete control of himself. He felt terribly trapped, as much as if he were locked up in a cell in the basement of the FBI Building. But there was a way to escape. His only way. The truth.

"Mr. Moody. My interest in that animal has to do with its pedigree. According to its papers, it's descended from a line my family used to breed, out of a mare named Queen Tashamore. I bought it to restore the line to our stable. But if the pedigree's not right, and I have reason to believe that it's probably fraudulent, then—"

"What difference does that make if you sell the horse?"

"It makes a difference no matter what. My name is now involved with the legal history of that horse. I can't erase that. What I can do is everything in my power to have the matter cleared up."

"That Queen Tashamore of yours must have had a lot of descendants. We'll find another one for you."

"There's something else, sir. The woman I bought the horse from had her barn burned down under some very questionable circumstances. A groom was killed and she lost a horse. I have reason to believe that there's a connection with Mr. Bloch's interest in my horse."

"That's bullshit, Showers! Bernie Bloch is one of this country's leading financiers. He's a big contributor to a lot of important charities and to my political party. He's a civic leader. How the hell can you say this?"

"He has an employee, Billy Bonning. He used to work for me. He's caused us a lot of trouble and there's reason to believe he was at the scene the night of the fire."

"I know about that kid. You're right, he's a lot of trouble. So was that sister of his. Bernie should never have hired him. If it's true what you say about his giving you a hard time, I'm sure Bernie will fire him instanter. But you can't hold Bernie Bloch responsible for something this bad-ass kid may or may not have done. You can't fuck around with the reputation of a man of his stature this way. And that goes for my daughter's as well. You're supposed to be an honorable man. Isn't that what you people live by out there, honor? What right have you to screw around with these people this way?"

Showers said nothing. The two men stared at each other.

"I've said what I have to say—officially and unofficially," Moody said, looking at his watch. "In a few minutes, I have to see the president. I want you to think about this, very seriously. Take some time off. I'll arrange it with the department."

"I've already been given a few days off."

"Take a week. But no more than that. I'm not sure when May's coming to town but I don't want any of this waiting for her when she does. Take some time, but give me a decision, on all the particulars. All right? Do we have an understanding here?"

"I understand you, Mr. Moody."

The chief of staff did not get up. Showers hesitated, then did so himself.

"It doesn't have to be Iceland, Showers. It can be anyplace you like."

"Thank you, sir," Showers said, then went out the door.

Nervous, his hands trembling on the wheel, Showers drove up 17th Street to where it joined Connecticut Avenue. On impulse, he pulled suddenly to the curb into a bus loading zone, next to a sidewalk pay phone.

He wanted to talk to his cousin, but realized he had no idea where to find him. He had only one quarter. He called his secretary, and had her connect him, after a brief search, with a friend of his on the State Department's Northern European desk.

"A quick question, Bill. Has our ambassador to Iceland resigned, or been recalled?"

"He's being transferred. No one knows where to yet, or why, but he's been told to pack his bags. It just came through an hour or so ago. How did you find out about it? The Icelanders don't even know."

"I heard about it when I was at the White House."

"Does this have something to do with the Earth Treaty?"

"I hope not. Thanks, Bill."

A traffic citation officer, a young black woman a little too large for her uniform, was giving him a ticket. There were trucks double-parked all over the avenue, but she was writing him up for stopping two minutes in a bus zone. He didn't argue with her. He was reflexively courteous with black people. No one in his family belonged to the Sons or the Daughters of the Confederacy.

"Sorry, sir," said the woman. "But the law's the law."

She smiled as she tucked the ticket in his windshield wiper.

"I understand," he said.

The ticket was for fifty dollars.

Thus admonished, he kept his speed well within the limit as he drove out of town, though he felt a great urgency. Once on the Capital Beltway, heading toward the interstate that led upriver to western Maryland, he let the Cherokee creep up to sixty-five, keeping pace with traffic. He didn't want to do anything to attract attention to himself. Moody had not only infuriated him, he scared the hell out of him. As the struggle over the treaty demonstrated, the United States government wasn't very efficient at carrying out great enterprises, or even carrying out its normal duties. But it could reach anywhere, interfering with the lives of ordinary people whenever or wherever it wished. A White House telephone could be a terrible weapon. Showers thought of the ambassador in Iceland. The man's life was being dramatically changed, for reasons he knew nothing about, for no good reason at all, just because of an obscure horse auction in Virginia.

Showers followed Interstate 70 to its junction with 81 at Hagerstown, then turned south and crossed the Potomac into West Virginia. Reaching Highway 9 just south of Martinsburg, Showers exited and headed east to Charles Town. He was to meet Alixe in a rundown bar near the racetrack. He was very late, but she didn't seem to mind. He found her at the bar, joking with some other customers.

"You care for a stirrup cup, m'dear?" she said, treating his arrival casually.

He shook his head. "I'm sorry to be late. Moody called me over to the White House."

Her eyebrows went up. So did her glass. Emptying it, she slid a twenty-dollar bill across the bar, watching carefully as the bartender counted out her change. She was worth several million dollars, but kept a mind to where every penny went.

"I brought my pickup," she said, as they went out into the parking lot. "We'll take it. Aren't many Jeeps up here with State Department stickers on them."

As they drove over to the Charles Town racecourse, he told her about Moody's offer of a hundred thousand dollars. He left out the matter of the ambassadorial appointment. That still preyed on his mind.

"A hundred thousand," she said. "Now we know something's wrong."

"How is he?"

"The bay stallion? Selma says he's doing just fine."

"Selma?"

"That's her name—the girl jockey I told you about. She says the bay is the finest bloodstock she's ever been aboard."

"She's been riding him?"

"Exercising him. On her place. Don't worry. No one will notice anything out of the ordinary. I've boarded some flat-track mounts with her before. Never any trouble. Fine girl, Selma. Common origins, don't you know. A woodsy. But a fine girl."

"Why are we meeting her at the track?"

"It's where she works."

With the bay hidden safely away, they'd have time to pursue their investigation with the Thoroughbred Association—and prepare a lawsuit, if they could persuade May Moody to take their side. That was the part that worried Showers the most. He didn't know what the actress's relationship was with her father. He had no idea what he was going to say to her. He'd left a message for her at the Shakespeare Theatre in case she called in, but she hadn't responded.

He told Alixe about that.

"I think she'll go along," Alixe said. "Didn't get to talk with her that much, but I like that girl. I think she'll do whatever makes you the happiest."

"Why do you say that?"

"She meant for you to have that horse, from the very beginning. That's why she bought it."

"You mean it's a gift?"

"Something like that, because of what you did for Jimmy Kipp. Only I daresay I've fucked everything up."

"For God's sake, Alixe. Why didn't you tell me?"

"Wasn't supposed to, m'dear. Now I've fucked that up, too."

"We shouldn't be doing this."

"Of course we should. She meant the bay for you, not Bernie Bloch."

They entered the track through the horsemen's gate, parking alongside a big barn. There were a number of horses in the yard, some being tacked up for exercise, others returning from their workouts. A short-legged, ungainly-looking chestnut ambled by them as they got out of the truck, the girl rider in the saddle one of the most striking creatures Showers had ever seen. She was very small, with an English upturned nose, but her skin was quite dusky, almost the brown of the horse. Her sleek black hair was pulled back in a tight ponytail beneath her riding helmet. She wore a close-fitting T-shirt and faded jeans, and boots whose original color had long before disappeared beneath layers of mud and dust. Though tiny, she seemed entirely made of muscle, her body moving in unison with the horse's, as though part of it. There was something almost Asian about her, making Showers think of the ancient Mongols who had virtually lived on their ponies, sweeping inexorably westward across the steppes.

She caught Showers' stare and returned it with a flicker of a glance. She noticed Alixe, and turned her head full face to nod hello, her eyes briefly on Showers again, then darting away. She let the horse keep moving, turning forward again as though to resume some deep contemplation. She sat the animal with extraordinary, effortless poise, completely relaxed, utterly calm. He guessed she was one of those riders who'd taken to horses from the time they were able to walk. He wondered if she might be a better rider than any of the moneyed folk in Dandytown, condemned to perform her skill at this back-country track simply by accident of birth.

"Selma?" Showers said.

"Yes indeed."

"You trust her?"

"Yes sir. She's probably got more things going than Vicky Clay ever dreamed of, but she keeps them to herself. Keeps everything to herself. Most closemouthed girl I ever knew. Don't worry. I'm paying her well. So well, she's probably wondering if she has to sleep with you."

"I hope you mean I'm paying her."

"Fear not, Captain. It's all going on the bill."

The girl finished with the horse she was on, dismounted in a graceful, catlike leap, then handed the bridle to a groom. She glanced around her, then started for the truck. Showers opened the door and stepped out. Without a word, she climbed into the seat, making room for Showers to get back in again. Their arms touched briefly as he closed the door. The muscles of her forearm were like a piece of hardwood.

"Hot day, Miss Percy," she said.

"Is it safe to go up to your place?" Alixe said, turning the pickup out of the yard.

"Yes ma'am. I don't get many callers, 'cept my ex-boyfriend lookin' for drinking money. And he ain't been around much since I fired a twelve-gauge in his direction one night a couple weeks ago."

"Has he seen the horse?" Showers asked.

*169*

"No sir. Last I heard he was working over at Laurel. He's a jockey, like me. Not much damn good, though."

Alixe knew the way. She drove north up Highway 9 toward Kearneysville, then turned left onto a gravel road, following it for a mile or two, pulling up finally into the scrubby yard of a farm gone to weed. The small house was wooden frame, in need of paint. The barn behind it looked as though it had never been painted.

"You live here?" Showers asked politely.

"When I'm not livin' somewhere else. Was my granny's place, but then she died."

The barn's shadowy interior looked cool, but was nearly as hot as the muggy outdoors. There were only three stalls. The bay's was in a dark corner, out of view from the open door.

"This is a bit close to the road," Showers said.

"Stop worrying, David," said Alixe. "They'll be tearing through every steeplechase barn from South Carolina to the Philadelphia Main Line before they think of looking in this place. We're aristocrats, mind. Mr. Bloch thinks he knows our ways."

The bay seemed glad to see Showers and came forward to have his neck rubbed. He seemed as comfortable in his new surroundings as he had been in Showers' stable. He was probably getting used to being moved around.

Showers stroked his nose gently, then carefully curled back the horse's lip. The tattooed number, of course, was still the same. He looked down at the horse's white stockings. He'd imagined nothing. Trying to get to sleep, in the middle of the night, he'd worried that he'd made an awful mistake.

"Alixe, there's something we should have thought of. We should have contacted the owners of the sire and dam, the ones that were listed in the catalogue."

"All right. Let's do that. When we get back."

They returned to Dandytown via a long, circuitous route, going up to Harper's Ferry, crossing into Virginia over the Shenandoah, then following country roads that led down along the eastern slopes of the Blue Ridge, so they'd approach Dandytown from the east.

Alixe drove the pickup truck very fast. Showers, trailing her in the Jeep, had to make an effort to keep up.

This rolling, luxuriantly verdant countryside was usually a solace to him, a solitary drive through it providing more comfort and serenity than Alixe could ever hope to enjoy from her whiskey.

But now the hills and sprawling pastures only served to make him feel desolate, a man alone. All he'd asked was to own a part of this beauty, this simple but soul-enriching life. His friends and family had long ago warned him that he couldn't have both, that his government career could cost him this. But his life and work in Washington had nothing to do with his troubles. His problems had been brought upon him here in Dandytown by intruders—by invaders.

One choice before him was simple. He could not now in good conscience accept the ambassadorship—not knowing how and why it was offered. The lifelong guilt he'd feel taking a promotion dishonestly would be far worse a fate than never receiving one at all, even if it meant remaining in his dusty bin the rest of his working days.

But what penalty would he incur if he let Bloch have his horse? Certainly not for any hundred thousand dollars, though he could hear his cousin Jack render an opinion on that point: "Anybody who can screw Bernie Bloch out of a hundred thousand in a horse deal deserves the thanks of a grateful nation."

What, though, if he took merely ten thousand—the price May Moody paid for it? He could return the sum to her, and she could repay whatever small amount Alixe had paid her—what was it, a thousand? Every account would be balanced, and he'd be back where he'd been when all this had started. Ahead, actually, because now he had Moonsugar.

If it hadn't been for the sheriff's clumsy attempt at a homicide investigation, Bloch would now be in possession of the stallion free and clear, in a perfectly legal transaction. Meade Clay had done the bad Coggins before the bay had come to Dandytown Bloodstock for auction. If it was fraudulent, that would be Bloch's concern. There was no compelling reason for the horse to be in Showers' stable. He'd convinced himself there wasn't a drop of Tashamore blood in those equine veins. He'd be guilty of fraud himself if he kept the horse on the terms of its pedigree, especially if he brought it to stud.

By selling the horse to Bloch for a fair price, he'd have both the billionaire and his friend Moody obligated to him. Not that he wanted anything from them, except of course to be left alone.

He'd seen how quickly Moody could arrange the transfer of an ambassador. What might the man be able to do to a minor staff deputy like himself? He could find himself posted in a trice to vice consul in Tirana, Albania. At the very least, he could be taken off the treaty. Moody could do it with a single phone call, a single nod to a subordinate. Showers had worked for the treaty like a priest serving God. Moody could deny him the sacrament, excommunicate him.

The overcast sky had become dark and lowering to the southwest. Showers' eye caught the flash of lightning. Alixe's pickup was drawing ahead, disappearing behind a rise of ground.

He pressed harder against the accelerator. He'd been deceiving himself with this mental soliloquy, tempting himself with the worst sort of evil. He couldn't give up the horse to them now. He owed it to Moody's daughter, to Alixe, to the dead groom. He owed it to himself. To give Bloch and Moody what they wanted would be a pitiful surrender.

His title of "Captain" doubtless sounded like a silly honorific to some, but Showers took it seriously. His father had volunteered for military service in World War II, had volunteered for combat and been decorated for singular performance in it. Showers' family had been represented on both sides of the Civil War, and at least two of those who had fought for the Confederacy had died of horrible wounds incurred in terrible battles here on the soil of Virginia.

He hadn't deluded himself about some of his motives for entering the ROTC program in college. The two years' active duty that were required of him after graduation meant two more years in which he could keep away from his father, two more years to defer taking any responsibility for his family's deteriorating affairs. But his army time had been of more consequence to him than that. It was also with his grandfather in mind—all his forebears—that he had first put on a uniform. England's Prince Edward, dropping out of the Royal Marines to become a theatrical stagehand, could not have experienced more shame than Showers would have felt avoiding military service.

Unfortunately, the army had not indulged him completely in his wishes to follow in the family footsteps. He'd twice requested duty with infantry units, only to be denied by a computer-programmed assignment system that had sent him to Germany for a year to serve as an administrative officer with an intelligence unit, and then for another year running the army riding stables at Fort Bragg. To compensate for this, he'd maintained his reserve commission long after he needed to, and then joined a local National Guard unit, remaining as active as his foreign service career would permit.

The unit had been activated only once, during the Persian Gulf war, but his State Department assignment had taken precedence, and he'd been involuntarily excused from active duty. He'd regretted that deeply. He never wanted to regret such a failure to meet a challenge again.

It was raining by the time he reached his farm, a steady, pounding rain that had turned the waning day instantly to night. In the bouncing flair of his headlights as he turned into his yard, he saw Becky standing out in the midst of it, her head wet and bowed, her arms hanging limply. Alixe, pulling up first, ran to her. Showers slewed the Jeep to a halt nearby, leaving the engine running.

Becky looked up at them, her eyes wild. One seemed oddly misshapen. Her whole face did. Her lips were swollen. There was clotted blood on her chin. She was whimpering.

"For God's sake, child, what happened?" Alixe shouted.

"They're after Billy. The sheriff's after Billy."

"Billy was here?"

"The sheriff's going to put him in jail."

Showers put his arm around her and began to pull her toward his house, but she wouldn't budge. "Get her some dry clothes!" he shouted to Alixe. "Hurry!"

As Alixe lunged away toward the cottage, Showers picked Becky up in his arms, surprised at how heavy she was. With great effort, he got them up the slippery porch stairs and into his house, laying the girl down on his living room couch. She had begun to cry, staring up at him helplessly. She had three good-sized bruises on her face, the nastiest alongside her eye. Her lip was badly cut at the corner.

"Billy did this to you?" he said.

"Yes."

"And the sheriff has him?"

"He's after him. It's my fault."

"How did the sheriff get here?"

"I called him."

She began sobbing in earnest, lifting herself to bury her injured face in his arms. The door slammed as Alixe came in, a large bundle of clothes and towels in her arms.

"Get your first aid kit," she said. "And then get scarce for a few minutes. This girl needs to get dry in a hurry!"

By the time Showers returned from the kitchen with his medicine box, Alixe had removed Becky's blouse.

"Don't stand there ogling her, man!" Alixe said. "Go make some coffee. And bring back some bourbon with it."

He came back this time to find Becky sitting up, snug in a terry

*173*

cloth robe, her hair all frizzled from Alixe's efforts with a towel. She winced as the older woman dabbed at her lip with antiseptic. She had stopped crying.

"You're sure you don't feel dizzy?" Alixe asked. "You can see my face clearly?"

"Yes. I'm all right."

"You're sure you don't want a doctor? Why didn't the sheriff take you to a doctor?"

"I wouldn't let him. And he went after Billy. He said he was going to throw him in jail."

Showers set down his tray. It bore three steaming cups of coffee, and a nearly full bottle of bourbon.

"Pour out half of one of those and fill it with whiskey for her," Alixe said over her shoulder. Becky was shivering.

Showers did as bidden. The girl took the cup greedily, swallowing and then coughing. Her shoulders heaved, then stilled.

"I'll have one of those, too, David," said Alixe. She reached to touch Becky's cheek. "There's no fracture. I hope there's no concussion."

Becky drank again. There was still a slightly crazed look in her eyes. "I'm all right. I was afraid he was going to do worse. I ran and called the sheriff. I don't think he believed I'd do it. He left. The sheriff came and then turned around and went after him."

"What were you doing standing out there in the rain?" Alixe said.

"I was afraid. I didn't want to go back inside."

"You should have run to my place. Where were my boys? They're supposed to be looking after the horses over here."

"They went back to your stable for something. I guess they were waiting for the rain to stop before they came back."

"This'll be the last time that happens. I'll make sure there's at least one man over here twenty-four hours a day."

Showers sat down. "What did Billy want, Becky? Did he come here just to hurt you, or was he after the stallion?"

"No. Not that."

"What then?"

"Never mind. It doesn't matter! Just keep him away from me! Please!"

"Becky," Showers said. "It might be best if you went back to your parents for a while. Just until we clear up this problem with the horse."

"No."

**174**

"Becky, please."

"No! If I go back there, that'll be the end of everything."

"You'll be safe there. I don't know why we should have to be worrying about that, but under the circumstances—"

"I don't want to go! I want to be here. I want you to be here! I want the horse to be here! Why is all this happening? It's like I'm cursed or something. Shit!"

"You just picked the wrong man for a husband," Alixe said. "You're sure as hell not the first one to do that."

"I'll take care of Billy," Showers said quietly. He rose. "If he's not at the sheriff's office, I'll find him."

"You just be careful, David," Alixe said. "There are a lot more Bonnings in this town than there are Showerses."

"I'm not worried about Bonnings."

"You sure are having a lot of trouble out your way, Captain Showers."

Sheriff Cooke ushered Showers into his office, leaving a sleepy-looking deputy to man the front desk. It seemed a quiet night. The two-way radio was silent. No phones rang.

"You have Billy Bonning here?"

"Sit down, Captain. Please. Coffee?"

Showers did so, shaking his head at the offer of refreshment.

"Yeah, I've got Billy," the sheriff said. "Got him in one of the detention cells in back. My only customer tonight."

"A frequent customer."

The sheriff grinned. "Bad Boy Billy has graced us with his presence more than once. I think the first time we had him for the night he was all of sixteen. Drunk and disorderly. When he got old enough, he started doing his drinking at the inn, where you can get away with that."

"Is that where you found him?"

"No. He was at the Raiders Motel. His new lady friend keeps a room there. It was the first place I looked."

"Did she tell you he was with her all evening?"

"No, not this time. Hell, he was soaking wet."

"He attacked Becky. He hurt her quite badly."

"I know. I hate these domestic quarrels. We get more calls on those than anything else."

"This wasn't a domestic dispute, Sheriff. The man trespassed on my property, broke into the cottage, and attacked Becky."

"Maybe so, maybe not. She won't press charges, you know. I

asked her to file a complaint, but she just stood there screaming at me. I called your place a few minutes ago, and she wouldn't even come to the phone. Miss Percy gave me a hard time about it. Wouldn't let Becky talk to me."

"So bloody what?"

"Do you know how many of these domestic hassles we get? I'd have to ask for an annex to the county jail if I charged every husband who took a whack at his wife, or vice versa."

"They're no longer married."

"Well, technically they are. The divorce won't be final for a year. I tell you, Captain, we get these things all the time, especially when there's a divorce involved."

"You said 'if I charged every husband.' Haven't you charged Bonning?"

"Like I told you, Captain. Becky wouldn't file a complaint. There were no witnesses or anything. We don't know what the hell happened. I locked him up for the night. It's the least I could do. But it's also the most. Unless he's charged, I've got to let him out in the morning."

"Sheriff, this man is a danger to Becky, a danger to my horses, a danger to the town. He tried to steal a horse from someone at the auction. He was on my property the night of the barn fire. It's more than probable he started it."

"You and Miss Percy have already given me an earful of that. But the investigator from her insurance company found no suspicious cause. I couldn't find anything! The fire started in some hay. You know barn fires. That can happen spontaneously in weather like this. And nobody filed any kind of complaint about horse theft. As I understand it, Miss Percy came home with that horse and sold him to you."

"That doesn't change what happened."

"Get someone to sign a complaint. I'll charge him and we'll bring him to trial. Gather up your witnesses. But in the meantime, all I've got down on the log is a domestic. You can hardly blame the guy for going out of control. Look at what's happened to him in the last few weeks. You fired him. His wife threw him out. And his sister got murdered by her husband. What would you do?"

Showers glowered at the sheriff. His father would have dealt with the man decisively. He would have told Cooke that he'd be out of office after the next election. And he and his fellow horsemen would have made that stick.

"I want to talk to him, Sheriff."

"I don't think that's a good idea."

"You let me talk to him, now, or I'll go to Judge Merrick and get a court order to do so."

Judge Merrick had been a friend of his father's. The judge did not like Sheriff Cooke. Horsemen of the stature of Lynwood Fairbrother and Showers could get whatever they wanted from the judge, though Showers had never before abused this peculiar privilege. To his mind, using it in any way was abusing it.

"Judge Merrick can't write you any paper that'll make me overturn proper procedure," the sheriff said. "But, all right. I'll give you a few minutes with him. Just don't get him riled up again, and don't get near the bars."

Bonning was sitting on the floor in the rear of his cell, smoking a cigarette.

"Fuck you, Showers," he said, by way of greeting.

Showers stood without speaking until the sheriff, understanding Showers' mind, turned and walked away down the corridor.

"Why did you come to my farm tonight, Billy?" He kept his voice very low. "Did you come for the stallion?"

"I don't give a shit about any horse of yours, Captain. You've got nothing but nags and hacks."

"Why did you come?"

"I wanted to talk to Becky."

"Were you there the night of the fire?"

"Fuck you."

"What did you want from Becky? Money? Information about my horse?"

Bonning flicked his cigarette out between the bars, narrowly missing Showers. He lighted another.

"I came to get something that belongs to me. Something I left behind."

"You've taken everything that belongs to you, and a few things that were mine."

"This wasn't yours. It was a videotape. One of mine. I've got a right to my property."

"You took that tape. The night of the fire."

"No I didn't."

"Why are you lying? Becky told me about it the next day."

Bonning's blue eyes fixed on Showers. He had known the youth since he was a small boy, had had him living in his house. But he knew him not at all.

"Yeah, so I was there the night of the fire. Half the town was out there. With everyone running around, it gave me a chance to . . . well, I went into the cottage and looked for the tape."

"You took it!"

"I couldn't find it. She's stashed it somewhere. But it's mine, damn it."

"What's on that tape?"

"Vicky's on it. It's not something she'd want left around. Vicky was a funny girl, you know? I mean, we just put her in her grave. She doesn't need any shit like that around to remember her by. I want it back. It's mine. I went to Becky tonight but she wouldn't give it to me."

Showers stepped up to the bars, gripping them tightly. His voice came out unnaturally deep, startling him as much as it did Bonning.

"Billy, if you come anywhere near Becky again, if you put one foot on my property, if you even drive by slowly, I'll kill you."

Bonning leapt to his feet. "Sheriff! This man just threatened to kill me! He said he'd kill me! Get him out of here!"

Cooke appeared in the corridor. He'd been standing not far away.

"I'm afraid I heard that, Captain. I think we'd better call it a night."

Showers dropped his arms to his sides, clenching his fists. He stared down at the floor a long moment, then started walking away.

"Fuck you, Showers!" Bonning shouted after him. "I'm going to get what's mine, you asshole!"

In the outer office, the sheriff took Showers by the arm.

"Look, Captain. I'll take care of all this. But let's not have any more trouble, all right?"

The rain had stopped. Alixe was waiting for him in the darkness of the porch, sitting in a chair. She had a bottle and glass on the table beside her, and something metallic in her lap.

"She's asleep," Alixe said. "It didn't take too much hooch. You want some?"

"Yes."

She slid him the bottle. He drank from it, like someone in a western movie.

"You've got a lot of antique firearms in your house, David. Do you have a permit to go with them?"

"Yes."

She took the object from her lap and set it on the table. It was a large revolver.

"Take it," she said. "I have a pile of them. My father left me a bloody arsenal. I gave the boys in the stable a couple of shotguns and I have one of these in the truck."

"I don't need it," Showers said. "I have my army automatic in my Jeep. I've had it there ever since the fire."

"Your father would be proud of you, David. He'd probably be laughing his head off over all this, but he'd be proud of you."

# Ten

At breakfast the next morning, Becky was very quiet, eating little and rising quickly to clear her place. In the kitchen, helping her with the dishes, Showers tried talking to her about Billy and all that had happened, but she would have none of it, saying simply she never wanted to hear about her estranged husband again. She seemed not so much sad or frightened as embarrassed—even ashamed. There was no point in asking her about the videotape. The bruises on her face now looked quite ugly, but she refused to go to the doctor and insisted she was suffering no pain.

When they had finished the chores, he let her go off to the stables without another word. He wanted to check on Moonsugar, but decided to wait until later, allowing the girl to deal with her torments, if that's what they were, unmolested.

It wasn't as though he lacked anything to do. His first concern was Robert Moody and his "official" and "unofficial" propositions. Showers would deal with both in straightforward manner. He got his old typewriter down again, deciding it would be just as well to leave it on his desk indefinitely. Only God and the devil knew what words he'd be required to bring forth from it in the next few weeks. The letter he wrote to Moody was very formal and official, but its body contained only one sentence: "Upon consideration of your offer, I find I must decline."

He read it over, then penned in a small correction, changing "offer" to "offers." He put the letter in an express mail envelope, then drove into Dandytown to post it immediately, stopping afterward at the offices of Dandytown Bloodstock to look up the names of those listed as the owners of the stallion's sire and dam. The sire's was a breeder in Potomac, Maryland, whom he recalled having met once at the polo club there. The dam's was a woman with a farm in Pennsylvania. Ned Haney told Showers he'd forwarded a copy of his letter to the outfit in New Jersey, but had heard nothing back. Indeed. The barn fire was reply enough.

The day was very bright and sunny, cooler and drier than muggy yesterday. If the pastures were not too muddy, he thought he might take his hunter out for a ride. Perhaps Becky would be willing to accompany him. Or Alixe. Another name occurred to him. Lenore.

Repeating a pattern that had recurred frequently over the long years of their relationship, Lenore had been all over him during race week, when he'd been at the center of attention and activity, but then she had drifted away when he'd resumed his dull, routine existence. She was a woman with a compulsive need for constant stimulation and amusement. He'd long before realized that his inability to provide that was at the heart of the failure of their long-ago marriage.

He knew no remedy. Joining her in her sporadic sprees and binges, as he had attempted in their youth, had provided no solution. Neither had indulging her persistent efforts to resume what he had once cherished as an idyllic romance, but which had turned into a long, degrading, and much-interrupted affair. The invariable result had been oppressive guilt for him and eventual boredom for her. Showers was no bluenose, but those few things he did hold as sins—disloyalty, infidelity, selfishness, cruelty, inconsideration— repelled him. Lenore sought out the sinful in everything, so that she might wallow in it. He was most attractive to her when she could not have him.

She came breezing out the screen door and down the front steps of the big Fairbrother mansion just as Showers pulled to a stop in the well-groomed gravel drive. She was in a dash for her car, and barely halted as he came up the walk.

"David, darling," she said, mouthing a kiss as she brushed by. "No time to say hello, goodbye, I'm late, I'm late, I'm late."

"For what?" He stopped and turned, facing her receding back.

"For a party, dear boy. The duchess of something or another is accepting curtsies at a garden thing of Muffie Brandauer's in Middleburg." She paused, finally, at the door of her Jaguar, and looked back at him. "Do you want to come?"

"I thought we might go riding today."

"Riding?" she said, snapping open the door. "Wouldn't think of it. I'm having my period, darling. Hate that in the saddle."

She got into the driver's seat, then stuck her head out the car window. "Why don't you ask poor Lynwood? The man is so stricken with ennui he's wandering around fondling his trophies."

Showers hadn't seen Lynwood on a horse in more than a year.

The big engine exploded into life. Roaring off, she left deep furrows in the neatly raked gravel.

He knocked at the door, a needless formality, then stepped inside. Fairbrother was in his enormous study, standing at the windowless wall that was lined with bookshelves, nearly all the expensively bound volumes they contained having to do with horses and steeplechasing. He was rubbing at a large silver cup with his handkerchief, attacking some minute spot of tarnish.

"David," he said, looking troubled. "You just missed Lenore."

"Not quite. She spared me a few seconds."

"Sit down. Sit down. Spot of whiskey?"

It wasn't quite eleven A.M. "No thank you."

"I hear Moonsugar's recovering nicely. Pity he won't ever be able to race again."

Showers didn't want to pursue that point. "I've acquired another horse."

Fairbrother glanced at Showers' dusty riding boots. He was wearing old brown oxfords with his gray flannels and sport coat.

"Heard about that. Fine-looking animal, I'm told."

"I've had a bit of trouble about it. The papers are bad. I've asked for an investigation."

"Heard about that, too. I understand Mr. Bloch is involved. If he causes you any difficulty, I want you to tell me at once. We'll back you to the hilt. Can't have that sort of thing in Banastre County. Common as mud, that man."

Showers had thought of asking Fairbrother for advice, but something far more useful suddenly occurred to him. A number of magazines were scattered on the long reading table beside them— *Country Life* and other upscale English and American periodicals, most of them devoted to horses.

"Lynwood, you know quite a number of horsemen overseas, don't you?"

"Oh yes. Lord Molgran. Dickie Chattersworth. In England. I know a few people in Ireland as well. No Germans, though. Can't stand to do business with them. They're all business, don't you

*182*

know. A few French fellows, but not many. Don't like them very much."

"But you do know people in England."

"My boy, I've sold horses to the queen." His eyes twinkled as he spoke, as though it were a marvelous revelation. He had told Showers about this point of pride at least a hundred times.

"Have you heard about any recent theft of a horse over there, a valuable horse?"

"Nothing that comes to mind, though it happens all the time, don't you know. The finest horse in Ireland was stolen by those damned thugs in the IRA. Never heard from again. It would help if they'd adopt the American system and tattoo the lips. But they won't do it. It invites thievery."

"Lynwood, I'm talking about a very particular horse. A bay stallion, with three white stockings."

The twinkle vanished. "Oh, yes. I see."

"Could you ask your friends—in England, wherever?"

"Well, I can't very well ask the queen. But yes. Certainly I'll get some letters off today. As it happens, my afternoon is quite free."

Showers would have preferred that he use the telephone, but he was imposing on the man enough.

"I'd be very grateful."

"Not at all."

Showers rose. Fairbrother did not.

"There's something I wanted to ask you, David. This Earth Treaty. I gather from the *Washington Post* that it's rather harsh in its coal-burning restrictions."

"Yes, it is."

"That's a bit troubling. A lot of people in West Virginia and Pennsylvania depend on coal mining for their livelihood."

As, to a significant extent, did Fairbrother. "The dead trees and lakes in the Adirondacks are a bit troubling, too," Showers said.

"Suppose so. Suppose so. You, uh, wouldn't have a copy of that treaty at your disposal, one I might borrow for a while? I am rather curious."

"I can get hold of a draft. But it's all very preliminary. There will likely be a number of changes before it gets out of Congress."

"I understand. If it's no breach of regulations or propriety, I'd appreciate having a look at it. Just to educate myself. Rather keen on learning more about it, don't you know."

"I'll see if it's possible, Lynwood. I gather the press has already seen part of it, especially the *Post*. I don't suppose it would hurt—if it gave you a better understanding of the problem."

"Exactly. I'd appreciate it very much." He looked at Showers darkly. David supposed it was just his bad mood.

Though she'd finished with her work, Becky was not interested in a ride. Alixe, however, was more than game for some time in the saddle, complaining she'd been too much out of it in recent days. She tacked up her own favorite hunter and had him in Showers' yard before he had even cinched the girth of his own horse.

They followed the fence line of his back pasture up to the gate at the top of the hill, then, fastening it closed behind them, moved on into the meadow beyond. The ground was soft but not mushy, and they confidently moved their mounts into a trot. A grassy slope led farther upward. Passing through a scattering of trees and up a following rise, they emerged on a grassy plateau and urged the horses into a canter, dancing them along the perimeter of the flat until they came to a few clumpy boulders that marked the brim of a bluff. Alixe's horse needed only a grunted word to come to a halt. Showers', too little exercised, was more ornery, and required a hard pull of the reins. Showers felt some painful stiffness in his legs, but it came from his lack of riding, not his much diminished racing injury.

"Glorious fucking day," said Alixe, gazing down at the rolling valley below.

"Better than some."

"It's funny," she said. "Both our places look like a single spread from up here. You don't realize how close together our houses are."

"I realized it the night of the fire."

"You know, your father once tried to screw me up on this hill. Did I ever tell you that?"

She had, but she'd been seriously in her cups at the time, and he hadn't known whether to believe her. He certainly hadn't wanted to.

"My father had some regrettable traits."

"Scared me to death. I was awfully young then. Almost fell off this little cliff getting away from him. But afterward, I think I was perhaps a little sorry it didn't happen. Had the most ridiculous notion, don't you know, that he wanted to leave your mother and marry me. Foolish girl. Hell of a handsome man, your father. I think he was terribly jealous when you married Lenore."

"He never got near her." Showers relaxed his hold on his horse's reins, letting him graze.

"Oh, she let him get near, all right. But never near enough. Enjoyed making him miserable."

"Sometimes I think that's her mission in life. She seems to think that, anyway."

"Tell me something honestly, David. Do you really believe, deep down believe, that one day she's actually going to come back to you?"

"Probably not."

"Do you really want that? After what she's become?"

"That's a question I never try to answer."

"I think she'll stay with Lynwood to the end. He's pretty old now. Drinks as much as she does when no one's looking. The end could be fairly soon, like it was with your father. Then again, he's the kind of proud, stubborn son of a bitch who could outlive us all, like old Judge Merrick seems bent on doing. One way or the other, I see Lenore sticking with him. Her flirty-flirty days are beginning to slip away."

"Lenore will be flirting with her undertaker."

Alixe leaned forward, hands on her pommel, stretching her back.

"You and I have got ourselves into a fair piece of trouble with that bay stallion, David." She straightened, brushing a few pieces of bramble from her breeches. "You've got a problem with Lenore that's going to keep you tangled up the rest of your days, unless you cut loose from all your sentimental notions about her. But the biggest trouble you've got on your hands right now is that unhappy girl living in your cottage."

"Becky's all right. She's just going through a bad time."

"It's going to get worse, and it's going to get worse for you. It's not just that you and that farm are all she has in her life. It's all she damn well *wants* in her life."

"She'll grow out of it."

"To employ a phrase, horseshit. Do you like her?"

"Of course."

"She's not that bad-looking, you know. If she lost some weight, she'd be damned pretty. No siren like Lenore, to be sure. But a damned handsome woman."

"Alixe, please. I'm a generation older than she is."

"You two are a lot closer in age than Lenore is to old Lynwood—hell, than I am to some of those fine young gentlemen I sometimes bring home from Winchester with me."

"Alixe . . ."

"We have a wonderful way of making arrangements out here,

David. It's our great gift, the secret of our keeping our way of life going for so long. You could do right by Becky and still have Lenore—or anyone else—in the only way that matters."

"That's about the worst thing you could possibly suggest."

"I'll put it this way, Captain. You're a man who faces up to things. I just want you to face up to this. With Becky, it counts *now*. You can't wait. If you want to find a way to cut loose from her, you have to do it now. The longer you wait, the worse it will be. If you want to do the noble thing, what you're so famous for, you should marry her. And damned soon."

She gathered up her reins, turning her horse.

Showers said nothing. They rode back as swiftly as the terrain would permit, but, once back in the pasture, slowed their horses to a walk to cool them off. Nearing their houses, Alixe waved farewell and turned her horse toward her place. Showers, thoughtful, plodded on. Dismounting in the stable yard, he glanced over at his house. His day suddenly changed. Parked next to his Jeep Cherokee was a yellow Volkswagen Beetle convertible with a slightly damaged rear fender. Squinting, he saw what looked to be a California license.

She was seated in a wicker chair on his porch, staring off at the nearby foothills. She seemed a much smaller woman than he remembered, but, surprisingly, even more beautiful, perhaps because she was so simply dressed—a thin white blouse, a khaki skirt, her legs bare, her slender feet in sandals. Her thick black hair was combed long and loose, falling over her shoulders, carelessly arranged but not unkempt. She seemed less a movie star than a country girl. She could have posed for an illustration for *Wuthering Heights*.

"Miss Moody."

She rose quickly to greet him, treating him to a happy smile, skipping down the steps and reaching to shake his hand.

"Hello, Captain Showers. I hope you don't mind my dropping in on you out of nowhere like this. I just got back to Washington and I had an impulse to drive out to the country. The farther out I got the more I loved it, and finally I decided to keep going until I got here."

"Didn't anyone ask you inside?"

"The woman who answered the door asked me to wait out here. She doesn't know who I am. I mean . . ."

Showers cursed Becky. Her discontent was no excuse for bad manners. "I'm terribly sorry."

"No. I've been fine. It's such a wonderful day. I've enjoyed myself immensely just sitting here and taking it all in."

"I have to get the tack off my horse and get him into the barn. I'll just be a minute."

"May I come with you?"

"Of course."

He'd forgotten that she was experienced with horses. She held the hunter while he fetched a rope halter, then removed the bridle for him as he pulled off the saddle. Their arms brushed in the process. The touch of her smooth, warm flesh was innocent, but not a little electrifying. He feared he was becoming star struck.

"He's very pretty," she said. "I had a horse this color once."

Showers patted the animal's shoulder. "He's a trusty old trooper. I've had him eleven years."

Depositing the saddle gear in the tack room, he returned to lead the hunter into the shadowy dankness of the barn. She walked along behind him, glancing into the stalls they passed, now filled with Alixe's homeless horses.

"I love this smell," she said. "Always have. It reminds me of where I lived when I was little."

"In Maryland?"

"Western Maryland. Out near Cumberland, in the mountains."

"I hadn't realized you were country folk like us."

"A long time ago."

She kept looking into the stalls, at last confronting him with the question. "Where is he?"

Showers stopped. He wasn't ready for this. "You mean the bay stallion."

"Yes. You haven't turned around and sold him on me, have you? You told me you liked him."

He continued on, slipping off the halter as the hunter proceeded docilely into his stall.

"No I haven't, but I'm afraid he's not here," Showers said, closing the stall door. He wondered if he should be telling her this. He wanted to trust her, as much as he wanted her to trust him. But her father was now his enemy. "I have him at a stable west of here."

"Why is that?"

"For safekeeping."

"I don't understand."

"Let's go to the house."

He tried to think of something casual and friendly to say as they walked back across the yard. Idle conversation was supposed to be a talent of gentry—not to speak of diplomats. He had grown up among people who had chattered their way all through life without ever saying anything significant. But nothing useful came to mind. She walked along at some distance from him, looking uncomfortable, her dark eyes a little troubled. Finally, he said something he needed to say.

"It was very kind of you, to make that horse available to me. I appreciate that, very much. I had planned to bid on him, but as it turned out, I just didn't have the kind of money I thought it would take."

"All I did was sell him to that nice woman, Alice Percy."

"Alixe Percy. But you didn't need to buy him in the first place. And you sold him at quite a loss. I intend to make that up to you."

"Mr. Showers. That's not necessary."

"I'm just trying to tell you that I'm . . . well, you're a very generous person."

She bit her lip, making no response, stepping uncertainly into the house as he opened the door for her.

"Would you like a drink?"

"Something soft. Coca-Cola. Anything like that."

He caught sight of Becky running up the stairs. He called after her, but she ignored him.

"Becky is part of our little family here," he said. "She's been going through a rough time lately. A divorce."

"You don't have to discuss my personal life with strangers!" Becky bellowed from the landing. Showers heard her ascend the rest of the steps and stomp along the upstairs hall.

"I'm sorry. She's really quite friendly. As I say, a bad time."

He took May into the kitchen, offering her the most comfortable of the several antique chairs in the room. She lighted a cigarette.

"I don't think there's a kitchen this charming anywhere in Los Angeles," she said, glancing around. "Though some people spend thousands trying."

He smiled to encourage her friendliness, found a small dish for her to use as an ashtray, then took a plastic liter bottle of Coke from the antique refrigerator. "The house is more or less the way my mother left it," he said. "I haven't changed anything much since she died."

"I'm sorry. That she died."

"It was many years ago."

He seated himself across the table from her. She was getting a little nervous.

"Mr. Showers. Captain. Is there a problem with the horse?"

"Yes. I'm afraid there is."

He decided to tell her at least as much as her father already knew. He explained that the Coggins and veterinarian's certificate that came with the bay were for a different horse, that the bay was much younger than the age given in the auction catalogue—in sum, that the bay was an impostor. He told her about the fire, and his suspicions about Bernie Bloch, how Bloch wanted the horse very badly, and was now offering him a large amount of money for it.

"I hate the man," she said quietly. "He's my father's oldest friend and he's a slimy sonofabitch. He introduced my father to the . . . to the woman who's now my stepmother." She studied her cigarette. "Excuse me. I shouldn't be saying such things. I hardly know you."

"I work for your father, in a sense. I'm with the State Department. I've been reporting to him on this environmental treaty we're working on. I'm afraid your father has involved himself in the matter of the horse. It was he who made the offer to me—on Bloch's behalf. It's put me in rather a difficult position."

"You mean he's leaning on you, as he would put it?"

"It's an apt word."

"And a man was killed in that fire?"

"It was very bad. We were lucky to save the horses."

"Oh God." The words came out in a stream of smoke. She shook her head, then wiped at the corner of an eye, smudging her mascara slightly. The floorboards above them creaked. Then stopped.

"The young man who bothered you the night of the auction," Showers said. "His name's Billy Bonning. He used to work for me. He's . . . he was Becky's husband. He works for Bloch now. He's caused us some trouble here. Last night he gave Becky a beating. The sheriff put him in jail for the night, but he had to let him go when Becky wouldn't press charges. I've warned him to stay away—I made a rather serious threat—but I'm worried. Bloch seems to want that horse very badly indeed."

She covered her eyes with her hands, keeping them there until she had recovered her composure. Finally, pushing her hair back from her face, she took them away, staring sadly at the tabletop.

"Every goddamned thing I try to do . . ." Her words embarrassed her. She turned away, looking out the window.

"I'm really sorry to be intruding on you with all this," he said. "I just wanted to explain why I felt it necessary to move the horse.

It's in hiding, really. It's a terrible shame. I don't mean to cause any problems with your father."

"There's nothing you could do that would make that any worse." She put out her cigarette and started to take out another. Hesitating, she put it back.

"I'd rather you didn't discuss this with him," Showers said.

"We don't talk."

"I've declined his offer. In writing."

"Can he do anything to you? In your job? He's got a terrible temper."

"No. Of course not." It was a necessary lie. "I'm protected under civil service laws. There's nothing for you to worry about. But I'm going to keep the horse hidden away for a while. I've started an investigation into its papers. When I get enough information, I'm going to take legal action. A lawsuit, to clear up the title. If you don't mind, Miss Percy and I would like to make you a party to the suit. I mean on our side of things. It would help enormously. You're the biggest victim in this, in a sense. You're out a lot of money."

"Money?"

"The only legal alternative would be for Alixe and me to sue you, and that's a dreadful idea. This is an awful muddle. If you'd join us in this, just sign a court brief, we'd take care of everything. You wouldn't be bothered any further."

She sighed, then turned back to him. "No, Captain Showers. I don't want this to go any further. I'll take back the horse." She reached into her purse and took out a checkbook. "Just tell me how much you want."

"Want? I don't want anything. My intention is to pay you back, for all your trouble."

"I've caused all the trouble." She began writing. "Just sign the papers over to me and tell me where I can send someone for the horse."

"But Miss Moody. Where would you keep it? You're staying in Washington?"

"I'm in one of the little apartments on Capitol Hill the theater keeps for actors. I moved my things in yesterday morning. I was looking forward to a lovely little vacation before I start rehearsals. Another plan gone to hell." She tore the check from the pad. "Here's five thousand dollars. Will that cover what you've spent?"

"Miss Moody, please!"

May stood up, staring at the check, her eyes blurring with the beginning of tears. She barely knew this good man, but was dead certain that he'd never accept her money, that he'd insist on working his way out of this mess she'd visited upon him on his own, that she was only getting in his way.

Money. Always money. It had haunted her life like some dread inherited disease. She'd tried to escape her father's money by making her own, but it had caused just as many problems. Maybe more. Her mother had never cared for money, never depended on it. She'd confronted the miseries that came her way without recourse to it, and so had survived them, ably. She was even happy, out there in West Virginia. May wondered what it must feel like, being that happy.

"Very well," May said, taking back the check. She gathered her things up and put them in her purse. "I have to go back now. I'm sorry."

"Please stay. I know Alixe would like to see you. If you like, I'll take you to see the stallion."

"No point in that. I'll find some way to get my father off your back. I have a friend in Washington. He's with a bank. I'll have him work things out with you about the horse." She started toward the door.

"Will we see you again?"

"Goodbye, Captain Showers."

He hesitated, then followed her outside. She got into her little car and started the engine. He got there in time to put his hand on the door before she could drive away.

"Miss Moody . . ."

"You're a nice man," she said. "Sorry you were unlucky enough to have someone like me cross your path."

She stared at his hand. Realizing his discourtesy, he removed it. May ground the car into gear and sped away, fleeing to no place she wanted to go.

# $\mathcal{E}leven$

U S. Postal Service express mail had no special priority in a White House where communications marked SECRET and TOP SECRET sometimes languished unread for days unless they were marked with special priority codes. Showers' letter, delivered before ten A.M. to the White House mail room in the New Executive Office Building on 17th Street, did not reach Chief of Staff Moody's desk until late that afternoon. Because it was not in any official envelope, it was almost routed to the general correspondence section, where "Dear Mr. President" letters arrived in the hundreds every day. But one of the White House secretaries remembered Showers' name from the clearance sheets for the intergovernmental council meetings on the treaty and saw to its expeditious delivery.

Moody, returning from a National Security Council conference chaired by the president, glanced at it, pushed it aside to attend to his phone messages, then snatched it back, deciding he wanted to get this little extracurricular problem behind him as soon as possible.

He read the one-line message, leaned back in his chair, and swore. At least the sonofabitch had gotten directly to the point, instead of meandering around it with the long, mealy-mouthed, cautious obfuscation that might be expected from most of his State Department colleagues.

But Showers wouldn't play. He had sent Moody a "Fuck you." Moody didn't like those. Not from deputy assistant secretaries.

He reached for his phone, prepared to raise hell with every

minion at State until Showers was brought onto the line, then recalled that the man was out in Virginia, taking days off. It occurred to him that he really didn't want to talk to Showers anyway. He had done what Bernie had asked—a little more than he'd asked, actually—and now he'd get out of it. Some things, to paraphrase Bogie in *Casablanca,* didn't amount to a hill of beans. Moody had a country to run.

He called Bloch's private office number, but got his secretary. She said Bernie was in his Rolls, headed for Baltimore, and gave Moody the number of his car phone. Moody swore again. The only thing less secure than a car phone was fucking skywriting.

"Good to hear from you, Bobby," said Bloch, his voice surprisingly loud and clear. "Sooner than I thought, or don't you have anything to tell me?"

"Nothing good. The 'captain' won't go for it. His answer amounts to what McAuliffe said to the Germans at Bastogne."

"Did you . . . ?"

"Everything we discussed. No dice."

He could imagine Bernie chewing furiously on his cigar at this moment.

"Can you talk to him again?" Bloch said. "You know, no more Mr. Nice Guy?"

Bernie was asking too much. It was one thing to yank the string of some obscure political appointee ambassador off in Iceland without explanation. It was something else to mess with a veteran government official with connections when he was expecting trouble, no matter how far down the ladder he was. There were a lot of diabolical things Moody could arrange to do to Showers— he'd done a lot worse to much higher-ranking people who'd crossed him—but he'd have to be damned careful about it. And it would take time. He had no more time for this.

"No can do. Not now."

"Bobby, your daughter's been talking to him."

"May's in Washington? How do you know that?"

"I've got friends in Dandytown. They saw her out at his place. Old yellow Volkswagen, right?"

She'd had that car five years. No movie star Lamborghinis for a Cumberland, Maryland, girl. Or maybe junk wheels had become Hollywood chic.

"I want you to leave May out of this, Bernie. This is the last time I'm going to tell you." Moody wondered how much of this his secretary might be catching. He should have sent her on some errand before placing the call.

"I understand. But it would sure be appreciated, you know, if she could help us out a little here."

Us? "No go, Bernie. The way things stand, I doubt she'd help me out of the pits of hell."

Bloch didn't respond. Moody drummed his fingers on the phone base. This was taking too long.

"Tell you what," Bloch said finally. "Why don't you and Deena come out to my beach place this weekend?"

"Negative. I'll be with the president at Camp David. I'll see you at the state dinner, remember? It's not that far off."

"Yeah, right. My big night at the White House." He didn't sound happy about it.

"Big night. You can talk horses with all the Mexicans."

"You know, Bobby. If you can't do anything for me, I'm going to have to take care of this myself."

"Whatever. I'm in kind of a hurry now."

"Okay, my friend."

"Just remember what I said. Leave May alone."

"Not a hair of her head, Bobby. We'll see you."

Moody sat quietly for a moment after hanging up. He didn't want to think about this anymore. There was too much else going on. On top of everything, the bastards in Belize were shooting off guns again. With the president's permission, he and St. Angelo had asked the chairman of the Joint Chiefs of Staff to send in more marines.

He clicked on his intercom.

"Where's General St. Angelo, damn it? I need him now!"

Showers came back to Washington much sooner than he had planned. Becky had fallen into a sullen funk from which she refused to emerge, and Showers had found it impossible to stay around her. It didn't matter that she spent most of her time in the cottage or stable. The threat of another explosion became oppressive. She'd come to remind him of a very dangerous horse he'd once owned. It would be compliant, if irritable, for weeks on end, and then of a sudden turn violent and try to throw him. He'd kept it, uselessly, for nearly a year. Alixe had urged him to have it destroyed or sold to a slaughterhouse, but he'd resisted, only to have it kill itself by throwing a tantrum in the stable yard and running out into the road in front of a car.

He wanted desperately to help Becky, but simply didn't know how. While in Washington, he thought he'd have a talk with her parents. He'd have to work himself up for that, just as he would to pay a call on May Moody at the theater.

There was a small surprise waiting for him at his apartment. In the pile of gathering mail was a letter from his National Guard unit. He'd had to skip his last two monthly meetings because of work on the treaty, and he feared this might be some official notice that he'd gotten himself in trouble. Instead, it was merely a reminder that his two weeks of summer camp was coming up at the end of the month. He'd be spending July Fourth at Fort A. P. Hill north of Richmond, where the support company he ostensibly commanded was to take part in a field exercise.

It might be a godsend. He could get away from everything there. But first he had a lot of business to attend to, most of it to do with that beautiful bay.

He reached the owners of the stallion's sire and dam. The Pennsylvania woman was rude and difficult at first, but both told him exactly what he'd expected to hear. The foal of that breeding had indeed had only two white stockings, unlike the bay, and it would now be a five-year-old. They knew nothing at all about the purchaser. The colt had been sold at auction as a yearling. They'd heard nothing of the New Jersey outfit before or since.

Moody had let his letter go unremarked. Showers' superiors at State said nothing out of the ordinary. Showers continued to go up to Capitol Hill when summoned by senatorial staff. He participated in his intergovernmental council meetings, including one held in the Roosevelt Room in the White House. Moody had dropped in at one, sitting quietly in a corner for a few minutes, glancing at Showers only once. Then he'd left, leaving no summons or message for Showers when the meeting concluded.

Sheriff Cooke made a promise over the phone to keep an eye on his and Alixe's farms, and Alixe said he'd made good on it. No one in Dandytown had seen any sign of Bloch. Billy Bonning, according to reports, had moved into his girlfriend's place in Charlottesville, apparently tiring of the housekeeping at the Raiders Motel. Lenore had gone off to spend a few days with friends— doubtless at least one of them male—in Saratoga. Lynwood was anxious to see a copy of the treaty, which Showers was not yet able to provide, but had not heard anything back from his horse friends in England. Showers considered having the embassy in London check through British newspaper files for stories of horse theft, but that would be an unpardonably personal use of official channels.

In time, settling into an uninterrupted routine of long, dull hours at work and an occasional movie or drop-by at an embassy reception, he began to let his worries diminish.

Then, on a Sunday morning, this lulling interlude came abruptly to a halt. He picked up his *Washington Post* and *New York Times* from the hallway and brought them out onto his small balcony overlooking a corner of the harbor. Filling his coffee cup, he began his ritual weekend read. There was not a lot of interest in the *Post*'s main news and world news sections, but when he turned to "Outlook" and its op-ed page, a column headlined TRADE WAR WITH JAPAN? jumped to his eye.

He froze. It was a guest column, run as outside opinion. The author was Jack Spencer.

It mentioned no names, but noted disapprovingly that reports were circulating in the capital about secret White House attempts to threaten Japan with trade embargoes and punitive restrictions and regulations if it didn't support the world environmental pact. It alleged that the administration was even passing around an internal memo outlining the punitive measures to be taken.

In Washington, this would go off like a bomb. The Japanese would read it. Moody would read it. Showers felt just as he had the moment Moonsugar had lost control going over that last jump. The ground was rushing toward him.

# Twelve

o you have any idea what all this is about?" the president asked
Moody.

They were seated on the screened porch of his Camp David
lodge. Moody had come over to join his boss for breakfast
and a discussion of what might be accomplished at the
routine conference that had been scheduled after the president's
morning tennis game. He accepted the folded newspaper page
with a courteous nod, looking at the op-ed column that the president had circled with his fountain pen, causing a slight tear in the
paper.

Moody gave a start. He knew the columnist Jack Spencer as one
of the Washington press corps' burned-out gang, a man who lived
from day to day and drink to drink, not caring what he turned out
anymore, as long as it filled the space. He hadn't attended a White
House daily press briefing in weeks. Moody had feared from
the beginning that reports about the "Napier memo" might get into
the press. Spencer was the very last person he'd expect to end up
with a scoop.

"Beats the hell out of me, sir," he said, setting down the paper.
"Somebody's blowing smoke."

"How in heaven's name could they print something like that?"

"It's an opinion page, sir. They run all kinds of crazy things
there."

"I've never heard of this columnist. Do you suppose he could be
related to the New York Spencers?"

The monumental inconsequence of that particular almost made

Moody laugh. "He's one of the minor newsies. Not a major player. Shows up sometimes for the briefings. He works for one of the smaller supplemental wires. I think most of their clients are in the Midwest."

"The Midwest." The president spoke the word as though it were some foreign, exotic place. "Do you suppose he talked to someone in the administration? Or is this just rumor-mongering?"

"I don't know, sir, but I'm going to find out."

"Well, you take care of it, then." He glanced at Moody's clothing—another dark business suit. "Now, will you be able to join us for tennis today? I'm told you've been taking lessons."

To the president, a person who didn't play tennis was almost as alien a being as someone who didn't sail. Moody's inexperience as concerned the latter hadn't been that much of a problem. When he went out with the president on his boat, all he really had to do was sit there, and occasionally yank on a rope—which the president insisted on calling a "sheet." Moody's inability to play tennis, however, had been a surprisingly embarrassing deficiency. He'd enrolled in a course of lessons, but found them so time-consuming he'd dropped out early on.

"Still working on it, sir, but I think I'd better concentrate on this. I don't believe there's any threat to the treaty here, but I don't want to take that for granted. Someone's going to have to deal with the Japanese, and I think it better be me."

The president smiled. He seemed so happy these days. "Whatever you think best, Bob."

Moody walked briskly along the asphalt path that led back to his own quarters, unmindful of the sweat that had begun to soak his shirt. He was certain the Spencer column was Showers' doing—a hand grenade lobbed back into the enemy's position. He had to admit the guy had balls. Leaking information to the press had been considered a felony in the Bush administration. In this one, it was practically a capital crime. Gentlemen, as the president liked to put it, don't do such a thing. Maybe Showers was no gentleman. Moody wondered about that, and why he would have gone to a third-rater like Spencer.

Maybe the leak had actually come from the Japanese, a ploy to give them an out if they meant to back away from the treaty.

It didn't matter. He was going to shut this story down in a big way.

Once inside his cabin, Moody went directly to his phone. His first call was to the party national chairman, who had been reading his Sunday paper, too.

"This is what somebody signed Napier's name to, right?"

"No one in the White House knows anything about this," Moody snapped back. "Especially the president. The thing in the *Post* is the first he's heard about it—and that's exactly what we're going to tell the world at the press briefing tomorrow. But I want you to get Napier on the next plane back here. I don't care if you have to call every fern bar in San Francisco till you find the one he's sipping his daiquiris in, but I want him in Washington tonight. I'll get him a room at the Four Seasons Hotel in Georgetown. He's to go there directly and stay there until he hears from me."

"You must miss him a lot."

"Ha ha. Just take care of it."

His next call was to Wolfenson, who was off duty that weekend. Moody searched his memory for the name of the White House secretary the man was screwing that month, and had her roust him out of bed in a hurry. His orders were to find out everything he could about the columnist Spencer, especially everything negative. Most particularly he wanted to know who the man's regular sources were, and if they included David Showers.

The *Washington Post* he reserved for himself. He knew he'd get nowhere with the opinion page editors. Opinion was opinion. The First Amendment, riding tall. But he needed to start a backfire lest the news side decide to take Spencer's assertions seriously. So Moody called a high-ranking editor he knew on the paper's national desk. Speaking calmly, he told him the president was extremely upset about the Spencer column because it was dead wrong and, because it had appeared in the *Post*, the Japanese could take it seriously—with unpleasant consequences. As though tipping the edition to advance information, he told him the entire matter would be cleared up at a special news briefing the next morning.

The conversation wouldn't put out the fire, but it should help make the editor a little skeptical about the Spencer column, and skepticism that began in the *Post* newsroom usually spread through the entire town.

With Spencer's wire service, Moody was less conciliatory. He called the bureau chief names, and charged him with disseminating lies and fraud. He called Spencer the most unreliable and irresponsible journalist ever to be allowed in the White House, and said that was coming to an end. He warned the bureau chief that unless the service retracted and apologized for the column it could expect to be last in line for pool slots and seats on presidential planes for as long as the administration was in office. The bureau chief sputtered a protest. The man would sure as hell change that line after the morning briefing.

Moody would not contact the Japanese. He'd wait until they came to him. Whether they were involved in the leak or not, he didn't want them thinking the White House was running scared.

Maybe there was serendipity in all this. Now he could deal with Showers. He'd already decided exactly what to do.

Showers waited a long time before trying to call his cousin. He didn't know what to say. The piece in the *Post* had left him as dumbfounded as it did furious, as curious as he was deeply hurt.

His fraudulent conversation with Mr. Kurosawa of the Japanese embassy had been the only time in his entire career when he'd violated his own personal code of honor and ethics. He hadn't realized punishment would come so swiftly.

He read through the column one more time. Jack had used the phrase "reports circulating in Washington" as a cover. It was an old, time-honored device. Moody would see through it. The "leak" police would be sent into action, but Moody would know exactly where to go.

Showers punched the buttons of Spencer's home phone number slowly, and was almost relieved when the ringing gave way to an answering machine's recorded greeting. He left an anxious message for his cousin to call him at once, and then was at a loss at what next to do. On impulse, he tried to reach Sadinauskas, but discovered his residence phone had been changed to an unlisted number.

Staring at the phone, at the fine layer of dust that covered it, he felt a desperate need for a friendly human voice. Alixe had gone up to West Virginia. He'd talked to her the night before. Becky would be of no help to him. Lenore, he knew, was still in Saratoga.

He waited an hour or so in the diminishing hope that his cousin would return his call soon, then went for a walk along the harborfront to try to calm himself. He had never before realized how laden with menace this prettified, monumental city was—even on such a sunny and cheerful day.

Reaching the fish market at the end of the quay, he wandered among the malodorous stalls for a few minutes, then retraced his steps. Returning home, he called Spencer again, with the same result. He waited. He slept. Awakening, he read more of the newspapers, unable to concentrate his mind on much.

Finally, he made himself a sort of meal. Once it was safely in his stomach, he mixed himself a drink, taking it out onto his balcony. He was squandering the day. As darkness gathered, he felt the need to escape his apartment again, this time to take a drive. The evening was relatively cool, and he drove the Jeep slowly along the parkway by the river, the air conditioning off and his window rolled down. The tourist season was fully under way, and there was considerable traffic. One car followed his all the way to the Memorial Bridge, and turned with him onto Independence Avenue, as though on the same perambulation. Annoyed by it, he pulled over to the side by the Education Department and let it pass—a nondescript white sedan with no one he could recognize inside, and a commonplace District of Columbia license plate. The automobile sped on down the avenue, turning at the next corner. Showers continued on, toward Capitol Hill. He'd finally decided on a destination.

A security guard answered the bell at the Shakespeare Theatre. He was surprisingly friendly, saying he didn't know if rehearsals for the new play had begun, but that if any work was being done by the director or cast, it would be over at a rented hall a few blocks distant at Eastern Market that the theater company used.

It was an old and somewhat shabby-looking building. Its entrance door stood ajar. Showers stepped inside, finding himself in a long vestibule with two sets of double doors along its rear wall. He opened one, and peered in. The hall was mostly dark, but a number of people were seated in a circle of folding chairs at the far end, starkly illuminated by two standing floodlights. Their voices were very clear. They held scripts in their laps and were reciting lines. May Moody was sitting sideways to him, wearing shorts and a blouse.

A nearer voice, just behind him, startled him.

"Excuse me, sir. But the hall is closed."

He looked to see a young man wearing jeans and a Shakespeare Theatre T-shirt carrying a cardboard box full of coffee containers.

"I wanted to speak to Miss Moody."

"Miss Moody? Well, you can't. I'm sorry. We're doing a read-through. They're still casting some parts."

Showers stepped out of the man's way, but didn't want to accept defeat.

"Please," he said, taking a State Department business card from his wallet. "If you don't mind. Could you take her this?"

He scrawled a quick message on the back of the card: "I need to talk to you. It's important."

The young man let him drop the card into the cardboard box, then went on into the hall. The group paused in its proceedings to allow the man to distribute the coffee. Showers, moving back into the doorway, watched him lean over May and hand her the card. She studied it, then looked toward the entrance. He couldn't make out her expression, but sought her eyes. She turned away, whispering something to the young man and shaking her head.

He came quickly back to Showers. "Sorry, sir. But she doesn't want to see you." He closed the door.

Peter Napier, weary from his long, hurried trip, sat in his hotel room in stocking feet and with shirt pulled out and unbuttoned. He'd endured a pay TV Mel Gibson movie without hearing any word from Moody, and now was watching an old British comedy series on one of the public channels. He needed sleep, but was too excited to even consider it.

It was after midnight when the knock came at his door. He'd expected a telephone call first, and the visitor's sudden arrival took him a little scarily by surprise.

At least it was the person he'd been expecting. He stepped back quickly to let Robert Moody into the room.

"I don't have a lot of time," Moody said. "My wife expected me home an hour ago and she's in a bad mood."

"Yes sir."

Moody went to the television set and snapped it off. Seating himself in a chair, he motioned to Napier to do the same. It made Moody uncomfortable that the young man's bare chest was exposed.

"I got back as soon as I could, Mr. Moody. I'm afraid I don't understand what's going on."

Moody stared at him for a long moment. The fate of the world always ended up in the most ridiculous hands.

"I've got a job for you," he said. "It's important."

"Yes sir."

"We've run into some trouble on the treaty. I won't go into all the details. You don't need to know. But there's a phony story going

*202*

around that we're threatening Japan with a trade war if they don't ratify—"

"I know. There was something about it on the news tonight."

"Shut up and listen. The story's bullshit but it could piss off Tokyo and we've got to shut it down fast. You're the man I need. You're discreet, right? You do what you're told. And you know a lot about politics."

"Thank you, Mr. Moody."

"I want you to tell a lie. It's nothing illegal. It's nothing like another Watergate, but it's damn important. It's a lie to help your party, your president, and your country."

Napier's mouth was gaping open. Moody took a folded sheet of paper from his pocket, and handed it to him.

"Read this."

It was a neatly typed, official-looking memo on National Committee stationery, addressed to the party chairman. It said that the party's candidates faced a serious problem in the next election because of fears that the treaty's conditions might impact negatively on American jobs. The treaty would be particularly hard to defend if Japan were allowed to continue its domination of world trade and the American consumer market while refusing to go along with the same environmental restrictions the United States was imposing on itself. The memo urged the party's National Committee to consider adopting a policy of calling for sanctions against Japan and its exports if it rejected the treaty.

"This sounds fine to me, Mr. Moody, but you've got my name on the bottom. It's dated more than a month ago. I never wrote this. Somebody at the committee said they were putting my name on a campaign letter about the treaty or something, but it wasn't this."

"I want you to say it is. I want you to lie. This will get us off the hook. It's a perfectly reasonable memo. And it'll explain everything—put an end to all the crap. It'll get this story off the president's back so we can go on about our business."

"Who do you want me to lie to?"

"To the whole fucking world. There's a press briefing tomorrow and I want you to be there. We'll distribute copies of this memo and have you take the podium and say you wrote it and this is all the whole damn thing amounts to. You won't have to testify before anybody. You won't have to say anything under oath. There's no danger of perjury. It's just politics. Political damage control."

Napier saw himself standing before the reporters, the presidential seal on the podium in front of him. He might be on the news that night—if not the network, probably the local.

"This is all?" he asked.

"Probably. But you might get pressed on how this whole thing got out into the press, how it turned into this bullshit story. If that happens, I want you to tell another lie. I want you to say you showed this memo to a man in the State Department named David Showers."

"Who's he?"

"He's the sonofabitch who leaked the bullshit story to the reporter who broke it. The guy's his cousin. I just found that out today. I want you to say you showed it to him in a bar—a bar up around DuPont Circle. It's called Wilde Thing."

Napier's eyes widened. The establishment was a noted hangout for gays. "But I don't even know this man."

"Yes you do. You met in the Wilde Thing."

"But what will that say about me?"

"Have you ever been in that bar before?"

"Yes. A few times."

"Then it won't say anything unusual."

Napier set the memo down on the table in front of him. "This is really important, you say."

Moody was not going to repeat himself. "If you'll do this for us, we'll take care of you. You once asked me for a White House job. I can't get you that—not on the president's staff. I can't get you anything until after we get the treaty through. But I can get you a spot on the staff of one of the presidential advisory commissions. You'll get an office in one of those buildings next to Blair House, a White House pass and—after a while—maybe we can even extend White House mess privileges."

Napier took a deep breath, exhaling with much satisfaction.

"If you can't do this for us, then the hell with you. We'll have no more use for you on the National Committee. I'll see to it you never work in politics again, at least with our party. Your next job will be as a waiter in the Wilde Thing. You get my drift?"

"Yes."

"You'll do it?"

"Sure."

"Okay. Sign it." He handed the man a pen.

"I want you to stay here tonight," Moody said, as Napier carefully wrote his name. "Don't take any phone calls and don't make any. Someone will come by in the morning to get you over to the White House."

Napier stood up. Moody pocketed both pen and memo, then did the same.

"I'm always happy to serve the president," Napier said.

"Yeah, right. Good night."

# Thirteen

**M**oody, Senator Reidy, and Waldemar Sadinauskas met for a very early breakfast at the Hay-Adams Hotel, across Lafayette Park from the White House. Each had logged the rendezvous on his schedule as a strategy meeting on the treaty—though in the Washington vernacular it might be more properly termed a CYO session—as in "cover your ass." None of them was very hungry. Thanks to the column in the Sunday *Post*, mention of the mysterious Japan memo had found its way into a number of the morning papers, including the *Wall Street Journal*.

"You're sure this is going to work, Bobby?" Reidy said, picking at his scrambled eggs. "Napier is about as big a flake as you'll find in this town."

"So why have you had him working for you?" Moody said. "May I remind you, Senator, this whole fucking thing was your bright idea."

Sadinauskas looked troubled. "If you're going to blame anyone, pick on me. I was the one who suggested using David Showers."

Moody liked Sadinauskas. He considered him his guy. "It made sense at the time, Wally," he said. "If we were going to plant something as goddamned outrageous as the memo Senator Reidy here dreamed up, we needed a real straight arrow to look convincing to the Japanese. Showers was perfect. Though after today, he's going to look a little bent."

"Does his name have to come up?"

"I hope it doesn't, but it probably will. Especially if the president wants to know 'everything.'"

"What'll happen to him—Showers?"

"You know how the president feels about leakers."

"You're not going to fire him?" Sadinauskas said.

"You can't do that," Reidy said. "Not over this. He's not some staff assistant with a political plum job. He's career foreign service. There are official procedures. If he appealed, there'd be a hearing. You wouldn't want our friend Napier dancing out for a chat at one of those."

"I've no intention of trying to fire Showers," Moody said. "Hell, the man has a first-rate record. But if push comes to shove—and today looks like it could turn into a hell of a football game—I'm just going to see to it he gets an offer he *can* refuse."

Sadinauskas glanced around the dining room. Most of the other breakfasters looked to be lawyers and lobbyists, busily engaged in their own murky matters.

"I wish you'd leave Showers alone, Bob."

"Look. He's a casualty. They happen. Let me remind you guys that we're not a bunch of crooks. We're not stealing money here. We're not breaking into somebody's campaign headquarters or trying to subvert the government. We're trying to get our big ally Japan to go along on the biggest goodness issue since the Emancipation Proclamation. This is the fate of the earth. What's a guy like Showers compared to that?"

Sadinauskas bleakly sipped his coffee.

"What if there are more casualties?" Reidy asked. "What if worse comes to worst and things get beyond your little charade with Napier?"

"You mean if Showers kept a copy of the original memo, or gave one to the Japanese? And he decides to jump up on a soapbox?"

"It's something to ponder."

"Won't happen. He's a straight arrow, right? Never lies. He told me he destroyed it. I believe him. You know him, Wally. Is he the kind of guy who would fuck up something like the treaty just to save his ass?"

"He's a rare bird—for Washington."

"But what if?" Reidy persisted.

"In a worst-case scenario, Senator, someone'll have to take a fall. Like Admiral Poindexter in Iran-Contra."

"Got anyone in mind?"

"You thought it up, I approved it, Wally set it up. Any volunteers?"

Sadinauskas sighed. "I'll take the fall. I'm the most logical. It would do the least damage if the buck stopped with me."

"You're a knight in shining armor, Wally. A credit to all Lithuanian-Americans. But don't worry. It's not going to happen. Look, Napier and Showers are fucking nobodies. Way the hell down the food chain. And this guy Spencer is no Peter Zenger, either. We can get hold of his bar tabs to prove it."

"Things like this never happened to Thomas Jefferson," Reidy said.

"The hell they didn't," Moody said. "Go look up how he fucked around with John Marshall and Aaron Burr, and the mess that caused. Like the guy said in Chicago, politics ain't bean bag."

Reidy looked at his watch. "Anything else on today's happy agenda?"

"Yes, and it ain't bean bag, either. Do you still have the treaty on the Senate calendar for after the Fourth of July?"

Reidy smiled the smile of an exasperated saint. "After all this?"

"I'll say it again. I think 'all this' is going to disappear by tomorrow."

"Even so, Bobby. I've got a lot of skittish guys on my hands. I think we ought to wait for the dust to settle. I don't want anyone seizing on the memo flap as an excuse to go south. Let's let things quiet down."

"How long?"

"I think everybody needs a nice summer vacation. I'd like to call the treaty first thing after Labor Day. The new arms control thing is going to push us well into July as it is."

"Labor Day? Shit! The president will blow his top. You told me you'd keep the Senate in till they ratify."

"Tell him we need the time to work on some guys. It's the truth. You'd win if there was a vote today, but it wouldn't be a walkover like the committee action. The lobbying has been heavy against us, and I think there's some big money down. Here and there, anyway. If we wait a little, I think we can get some more guys aboard. Tell the president that all I want is to make the vote for the treaty as big as possible. Give me the summer. Who knows, maybe something wonderful will happen to give us a boost. Maybe an oil tanker will go belly up off Alaska again, or the Russians will hand us another Chernobyl."

"I've seen reports that say that's not exactly implausible," said Sadinauskas.

"I've more or less promised the president I'm going to deliver the

Japanese," Moody said. "If we sit on our hands, they'll sit on theirs."

"So slice open an oil tanker in Tokyo Bay."

Moody toyed with his orange juice glass a moment, then looked up. "There's an easier way to do it."

"There's always an easier way," Reidy said.

"Okay, let's wrap this up," Moody said. "It's showtime."

The press briefing went perfectly. The president's press secretary, who'd been told nothing more about the Japan memo than the president had, began the session routinely. The memo came up about five questions in, after a long back-and-forth about the budget and some queries about the troubles in Belize, to which the press secretary responded with the same vague answers he'd used with similar queries the week before.

On the memo matter, he deferred to Moody, who came out to the press room a few minutes later, as though interrupted from some far more important business. He brought Napier with him, however, and an aide who distributed copies of the reworded memo Napier had signed the night before.

"We've gone to all this trouble," he said, "because we take anything that might affect the president's environmental initiative very seriously, even a bunch of nonsense like this. There is no secret White House memo. There are no plans for a trade war against Japan. This is all there is. You can ask Mr. Napier here. He wrote it."

They didn't ask Napier. His reputation in Washington—what little he had—was as a minor political gofer and gadfly gate crasher who liked to get his picture in the party page section of *Washingtonian* magazine.

One reporter asked, "What was the president's response to this memo?"

"He never saw it," Moody said. "The same way your publisher never sees the memos you write asking for more paper towels in the men's room."

"Is the president considering taking sanctions against countries who don't ratify the treaty?"

"Not that he's told me about. The treaty's a collegial effort, a world partnership. If there's any talk of sanctions, you're more likely to hear it at the United Nations. And I haven't heard any. I might remind you that the United States hasn't ratified the accord, either."

A woman from one of the networks had been trying to get his attention. She stood up to improve her chances.

"Yes dear?" Moody said. It caused titters. And grumbles.

"Would you characterize the Japanese as the world's worst polluters?"

Hadn't this woman ever been in Eastern Europe? "Hell, no. Let me remind you that both houses of the Japanese Diet are advancing ratification legislation as we stand here. Japan is our ally, our economic partner, one of our best friends. We have every confidence they'll do the right thing. Now, if you don't mind, I'd like to get back to work. If you still want to chit chat, that's what this guy's for." He pulled the press secretary to the podium, and turned to leave.

"Why did we send troops to Belize?" a reporter shouted.

"They needed some R and R," Moody said, over his shoulder. He hustled Napier out of the briefing room with him.

"Was it all right?" Napier asked, when they were back in Moody's office. He was all flushed and sweaty.

"It couldn't have gone better. Thanks."

"But I didn't get to say anything."

"You'll have your chance in a few minutes. We're going in to see the president."

"The president?"

"I want you to go through the whole routine, from writing the memo to showing it to Showers in that bar. And then I want you to apologize for the difficulties this caused."

"Apologize? To the president? Am I in trouble?"

"Not at all. He appreciates little scenes like that. Probably reminds him of his school days. All I want is for him to feel he knows everything there is to know about all this. Just tell him you wrote that thing out of excessive zeal. You feel that strongly about the need for the treaty. He'll probably pat you on the head."

Napier's anxiety vanished.

"And afterwards," Moody continued, "I want you to get lost— for a long time and far away. You can draw on the National Committee contingency fund for money. Just let us know where you are."

"Yes sir."

"I don't want you surfacing here until I give you the all clear. I mean it. If you turn up on the party circuit here I'm going to have you sent to Belize with the marines."

Acting Secretary Richmond called Showers to his office late in the day. Given that they didn't know each other well, he seemed excessively friendly and solicitous, yet very serious.

"I've had a communication from the president," Richmond said, when they were both seated. "It concerns you."

Showers sat calmly. He'd been preparing himself for what was to come from the moment he'd read Jack's column in the *Post*.

"He's upset about some reports that appeared in the papers this morning and over the weekend about Japan and the Earth Treaty. Are you familiar with them?"

"Yes."

"He's been given to understand that the source of these reports is you. That you picked up some unsubstantiated information from someone with the Democratic National Committee named Napier and that you passed it on to a journalist, who happens to be your cousin."

"The latter part of that assertion is true."

"You're admitting that."

"Of course. It's the truth. But I've had no dealings with this Mr. Napier."

"You weren't with him one recent evening in an establishment called the Wilde Thing?"

"No. I've never heard of the place. Is that what they're saying?"

"That's what someone told the president."

"It's nonsense. I showed my cousin a memorandum that I understood was written by Mr. Napier, but I don't know him, except to see his picture in the magazines occasionally. I've never met him. He was just a name on the memo."

"And how did you come into possession of that?"

Showers did not want to say anything that might sink his friend Sadinauskas. Certainly not until he'd had a chance to talk with him. He would do nothing that might jeopardize the outcome of the treaty vote. He'd sworn that to himself in the very beginning.

"I'd rather not say, sir."

"Honor among thieves?"

"No. It's just irrelevant to the issue at hand. I talked to my cousin. I should not have. It was a very serious mistake."

Richmond pursed his lips, rocking back and forth gently in his big leather swivel chair. He was a good man. Showers hoped he would be named secretary of state.

"There were no extenuating circumstances, David?"

Showers hesitated. "To be truthful about it, there were. But I don't want to go into them. Not until such time . . ." He averted his eyes. "Not until the treaty is an accomplished fact."

"You're quite sure? That could take a very long time."

Now Showers looked directly at his superior. "They involve a matter of contention between me and an official in the administration. But it's a private matter, and has nothing to do with the treaty. I don't ever want it to. I just want you to understand, sir, that through all of this I thought I was acting in the best interests of the president's initiative and this department."

"Except for talking to your cousin."

"Yes."

Richmond had a file folder on his desk. He opened it, and flipped through a few pages.

"You have an exemplary record, David. You should be working at a much higher level than you are. I note you've recently turned down two rather decent overseas assignments, just so you could continue working on the Earth Treaty."

"In fairness, I should tell you that there was also a personal consideration in that. I have a horse farm in Virginia that's required a lot of my attention lately."

"I know. I've watched you race." Richmond studied a few other entries in Showers' file, then carefully closed it, folding his hands in front of him. The time had come.

"I have to tell you that I share the president's concern," he began, speaking more formally now. "I'm afraid my choices are limited. Let me say first that there is absolutely no question of dismissal or disciplinary proceedings. As I told the president, I don't think there's a need for anything more than a letter of admonition to be placed in your record. You've been a valued foreign service officer. I see no reason why you can't continue your career to retirement. But some action is going to have to be taken. Obviously, you can't continue serving on the intergovernmental council, or have anything more to do with the treaty. I'm afraid you're going to have to accept reassignment."

Showers had seen that coming. "To what, sir?"

"An overseas posting. What has been suggested is the consular affairs section of the embassy in Khartoum. The Sudan continues to be of great concern to us."

The Sudan. The land of dervishes and Fuzzy Wuzzies and Chinese Gordon's severed head. How apt. He might as well be sent to the North Pole, except that would be too close to Washington.

*212*

"I'm afraid, sir, that I must respectfully decline."

Richmond stared at him. "David, you can't refuse this assignment. Not under any circumstance. You've already declined two other postings. You know regulations. You know what this means."

"Perfectly well, sir. I've no choice but to submit my resignation. You'll have it today."

"I'm awfully sorry about this, David."

Showers rose. "I understand, sir. Fully." They shook hands.

Showers paused. "I've one favor to ask you, sir. I understand our ambassador to Iceland has been given notice of reassignment. I think that, if you were to consult with the White House chief of staff, you might find that there's really no need of that. You might tell Mr. Moody that's all I had to say."

When he returned to his office, his secretary read something in his face and gave him a sadly questioning look. He merely smiled in return—an expression of lips, not eyes. She'd been with him nearly two years, and should have an explanation. He'd write her a long letter. For now, he merely let her go home early.

He slumped wearily at his desk, gazing at his upside down globe in the corner. The world—treaties, presidents, governments, and great events—was moving on without him. Like hundreds of thousands of minor figures in the footnotes of history, he had fallen into the ditch.

Taking out the Mont Blanc pen Lenore had once given him as a birthday present, he wrote out his resignation by hand, adding no embellishing comments. When the ink had dried, he put it in an envelope marked Departmental Mail.

He had a few framed photographs on his desk. One was of him and Lenore on horseback, taken many years before. In the beginning, it had served as a sort of talisman of hope. He put it in his briefcase along with the others, and a few other personal items from his desk drawers. He'd leave all the official papers—and the globe. It was their world now.

There were some messages, none that need interest him anymore, except one. It was from Waldemar Sadinauskas. The call had come in while he was talking to Richmond.

The energy secretary answered the phone himself. "I just heard."

"Probably before I did."

"Probably."

"I've resigned, Waldemar. They offered me Khartoum."

Sadinauskas excused himself to talk to someone in his office, then got back on the line. "Sometimes, at this time of day, when I'm going to be working late, I like to take a little walk. Why don't you join me?"

The secretary was waiting on the corner outside his office building as promised, standing by a street vendor who had just sold him a hot dog. Sadinauskas munched on it as they walked.

"Did you put it in writing, your resignation?" he said.

"It's in the mail."

"You don't have to do it."

"Yes I do. You've known me long enough to know that."

"I've been in this town a hell of a long time, Dave. A lot longer than I've known you. I think the most important thing I've learned is that these people come and go. They take over the town like conquerors, never stopping to realize that they're going to have to give it all up someday. That they're going to end up as nobodies like everyone else. Who's scared of Mike Deaver or Ed Meese now? Or John Sununu?"

"I'm not scared of Moody."

"I know that. What I'm suggesting is that you could wait them out. Who knows who's going to win the next election? The State Department takes care of its own. You could come back."

"Just to collect a pension? No thanks, Waldemar. I'm not that kind of lifer. In any event, I need to be here now. At least I need to be in Virginia."

The traffic rumbling by them was heavy—evening commuters mixing with the tourists.

"Well, you're not without friends, and I hope you still include me in that. I can get you a job. I don't mean anywhere in the administration, or up on the Hill—unless you want to work for the Republicans. But there are a lot of think tanks who'd love to have you. They don't pay all that much, but you could still have a hand in working for the treaty. I wouldn't recommend any of the professional lobbyist outfits. I think every one of those hired guns is working against the treaty. But hell, we'll get you something."

"I suppose I could end up having to take you up on that, but not now. Thanks anyway."

Sadinauskas finished his hot dog and crumpled up the paper wrapper, tossing it in a sidewalk trash basket. He wiped his mouth on his handkerchief.

"You probably think I set you up for this," he said.

"I have a fair idea of what's happened, but I don't blame you. I'm

*214*

sure you were just doing what they asked of you, just as I did when I agreed to show that memo to the Japanese."

"You should blame me. I was the one who thought of you for this. I let you get caught in the squeeze."

"I could have said no. I almost did. And you certainly didn't tell me to talk to my cousin."

"I don't feel very good about you being hung up to dry all on your lonesome. If you want—and I mean this, Dave—I'll come out and join you. Moody's cover story includes some unpleasantly suggestive stuff about you and Napier. I can spare you that. I'm willing to come out and say the memo came from me. That I thought it up and asked you to do it. *Ordered* you to do it, if you like."

"It would end your career. They wouldn't even bother sending you to Khartoum."

"My pension's guaranteed. Maybe, at long last, it's time for me to get out of here. The Constitution doesn't guarantee any of us a job for life." He stopped, and put his hand on Showers' shoulder. "I'll do it, Dave. Just say the word."

"I hope you realize how much I appreciate that, but no thank you. It wouldn't change things, really. It would only make matters worse for the treaty."

They moved on.

"The hell of it is—I mean, I've never liked Reidy," said Sadinauskas. "And Bob Moody's no Santa Claus, either. They play rough and they play by their own rules, and no one even knows what they are. But the fact is, they're on the side of the good guys. I don't think Reidy likes this treaty very much, but he's a party man, and he seems to be working his ass off for it. And Moody is as much a president's man as I've ever seen in this town. A lot of chiefs of staff—Don Regan, Jim Baker, who was that guy Ike had, Sherman Adams?—they had their own private agendas. I swear Moody would take a bullet for the president."

They had walked nearly completely around the block. Showers' Jeep Cherokee was at the curb. He halted.

"I appreciate this, Waldemar. I count you as a friend."

"Anything I can do, Dave. Absolutely anything." He reached into his pocket, looking suddenly embarrassed. "I forgot. Moody gave me a message for you. I don't know what it says."

He handed Showers a small sealed envelope. It bore no markings of any kind. Showers tore it open. Inside was a single sheet of paper. It bore the words "You lose."

"Well?" said Sadinauskas.

"It says I'm doing the right thing," Showers said. He crumpled it up and dropped it in his pocket.

Returning to his apartment, he found he had a visitor waiting for him—a tall, aging, good-looking man in an expensive but rumpled suit, sitting on the low concrete wall outside the apartment building entrance and looking like hell.

"Hello, cousin," said Jack Spencer. "Let me buy you a drink."

Showers studied the man's bleary face. "Are you sure you need another one?"

"Don't you? After today?"

"All right. But save your money. I have some gin."

Upstairs, Spencer glanced around the small apartment, and at the harbor view from the balcony. "Not bad."

"I'm going to have to give it up. After today, I won't be able to afford the rent, not if I'm going to keep up the farm. I'm not sure I can even do that."

"They gave you the sack?"

"Not quite. They were going to send me to the Sudan, so I quit."

"You wouldn't have liked the cuisine. My reward was a newsroom ass-chewing of the undignified sort that Stalin used to give editors at *Pravda*. I also have a new job. Politics, adieu. No more column. From now on I cover capital arts and culture. Also social life. The only way I'll see the White House again is covering guest arrivals at state dinners."

Showers made simple drinks of gin and ice. "What you wrote was the truth."

"The truth is whatever gets on the evening news, old sport. This didn't make it."

They took chairs on the balcony. Neither spoke for a while. A large sailing cruiser chattered along the channel on its auxiliary motor, the dying sun glinting on its metalwork. Spencer stared at it as he might at an unusually beautiful woman.

"Why did you do it to me, Jack?"

Spencer drank. "Why'd I do it? Because I'm a rotten sonofabitch, that's why. And a damned fool. Never thought of myself as that. I always thought that I might be a little like you. But I'm not at all. I did it, David, because my masters had been leaning on me hard, complaining my columns were too 'insubstantial,' that I never had anything to say. I needed a big score. I thought you were in the clear. I didn't think the White House would do anything more than

*216*

issue a denial. I assumed people would think I got it from the Japanese, or one of the usual 'reliable sources' I occasionally drink with. Moody's quite the smart fellow." He stared after the boat until it had disappeared behind some others. "I screwed you, David. It's the worst thing I've ever done in my life. And that's saying something."

"What did you tell your editors?"

"That I couldn't reveal my sources. I said they should stand by the story anyway. They didn't. Our morning line lovingly embraces Mr. Moody's little show-and-tell press briefing this morning."

"It's all right. I think the treaty's safe. There's been no protest from the Japanese. Moody's cover-up will probably work."

"Maybe so. But that doesn't help you." Spencer drained his glass, and got up to pour another drink.

"I want to help you," he said from the kitchen. "That's why I've come by. I'm dead serious. God knows I'll never make this up to you completely, but I want to give it the old prep school try. I'll have a lot of time on my hands in this wonderful new assignment. As long as I turn out enough words about the pretty pictures in the National Gallery, no one's going to worry about where I am. In fact, they'll likely be happy to have me away from the newsroom as much as possible for a while."

He returned, leaning against the doorway. "I mean it, David. Anything. I still have a lot of resources in this town. Contacts, even friends. I know my way around. If you want to get back at the White House, I'll find a way."

"That's the last thing I want. Right now at least."

"Well, you name it. Blood is blood."

Showers watched the sun slip behind the trees of Potomac Park across the channel. It occurred to him that the day had not been entirely ruinous.

"I don't want you to feel obligated to me because of what's happened," he said. "I never put you to your word not to say anything."

He turned in his chair to look at his cousin more directly. "If I ask your help, I don't want it to be as penance of sin. I want you to do it for the family."

Spencer lifted his glass. "To the family. The holy family. What do you need done?"

"Are you well acquainted with a man named Bernard Bloch?"

"Only by reputation, and I can smell it from here."

"Let me tell you about a horse I just bought . . ."

# *Fourteen*

For a week, Moody had the daily White House news summary brought to him as his first order of business every morning. He went through the thick compilation of Xeroxed news clips with great diligence. The Japan memo story disappeared after the first day. It became as dead an issue as Senator Everett Dirksen's bill to make the marigold the national flower—a tiny little blip on the seismograph, come and gone, soon to be utterly forgotten. He'd seen Spencer at the Kennedy Center a couple of nights later, covering the opening of a bad play. Showers had completely vanished. Bernie Bloch had even stopped bothering him about the man. And that damned horse.

Now came the hard part.

The Japanese had not come to him. There'd been no word from them whatsoever. The White House congressional affairs office reported they'd gone to ground on Capitol Hill as well. At the same time, the Japanese Diet had not even scheduled ratification for debate. The president was getting curious as to why they had applied the brakes.

Moody had learned a little about the Orient during his service in the military, enough to know that silence could be a loud message. He would have to go to them.

He picked an odd piece of neutral ground for a meeting—a one-flight-up Asian restaurant on Wisconsin Avenue not far from the British embassy called Germaine's, a place much favored by old China hands among Washington diplomats for its authentic and varied cuisine. It was favored most by secondary-level dips, however—sherpas, not summiteers—and Ambassador Aomori seemed a little uncomfortable to find himself in surroundings of such modest stature.

But, what the hell, a White House chief of staff far outranked a mere ambassador, and Moody didn't mind.

The food was very good, and mollified the ambassador somewhat.

"Let's get down to business, Mr. Ambassador," Moody said. "Are you satisfied now about that White House memo business, that it was all something carved out of a walnut shell?"

Aomoro smiled politely. "We have taken note that press interest in the subject has become negligible."

"There isn't any."

"Negligible. Yes."

"And?"

"We find no interest in the subject among members of your Congress."

"Well, there you are. I've already explained to you the White House position on this."

The ambassador took a bite of stir-fried pork. He used a fork, not chopsticks.

"Perhaps some clarification is still in order," he said, wiping his mouth neatly but with great fuss.

"What's in order is a little Japanese action on ratification. Last report I had, your Diet has gone to sleep."

"Democracy is not an efficient process, Mr. Moody. Something of this magnitude requires much study."

"There have been draft copies of the treaty floating around the UN for more than a year. We've got sixty-two signatories. Your lobbyists on the Hill know more about its provisions than most of our congressmen."

Aomori shrugged, then took another bite. Once again he carefully wiped his lips, almost a ceremony.

"My foreign minister would like to talk to your president. The prime minister is interested as well. Perhaps a visit in late summer."

"Save your yen. I can tell you exactly what he'll say. I know the man as well as my own father." (He knew him much better, actually. His father had deserted the family when Moody was a small boy. If his mother hadn't moved in with the manager of the local coal mine, the family would have sunk into hopeless poverty, and Moody would not be sitting here now.)

"He'll tell you that the treaty isn't negotiable. That there's no linkage with anything else that might interest you, not as far as he's concerned. It's already been thrashed out in the United Nations and approved by a consensus committee vote—with your country among the notable abstentions. You have to vote it up or down. The president favors up. He won't want to hear about anything else."

Another bite. The napkin again.

"Let me put it this way, Mr. Ambassador. The president is one of those politicians who isn't a politician. He sees himself as the country's number-one public servant, noblesse oblige. A man of principle. He doesn't bend. He's not the kind of man you enjoy negotiating with."

"We have observed what you say."

"Your foreign minister, prime minister, emperor, whatever. They're all welcome. But if you want to bring him around on anything, you're going to have to deal with the people who know how to do it, the people who are close to him. His most trusted advisers."

"Yes?"

"And, as one of his most trusted advisers, I can tell you you're not going to bring him around on this treaty. He won't give an inch." He paused for emphasis, taking a sip of his Japanese beer. "However, there are some ancillary matters that you might find it useful to discuss—with the president's close advisers."

"Linkage?"

"It's not that bad a word."

"In our earlier meeting, you mentioned the possibility of a more relaxed and generous trade climate."

"Yes I did. One that would encourage greater Japanese investment. We need more jobs in this country, Mr. Ambassador. We're going to need more after this treaty goes into effect. I can sure as hell tell you I wouldn't mind seeing an auto plant or two in West Virginia. That's something I'd work like crazy for, if all the environmental standards are met."

"That would require the assistance of your Congress."

"You have a lot of friends there, as I'm sure you know. Majority Leader Reidy is certainly one."

"A very practical man."

"Look, Mr. Ambassador. There are few things that mean more to me right now than Japanese ratification of the treaty. I'd give my right arm, if you know what I mean."

"The treaty infringes on our sovereignty."

"Mr. Ambassador, this is just a vote. If you want to put it another way, a promise. It'll take years to get all the machinery in gear to enforce the treaty. Who knows what'll happen? Things change. The United States worked for more than twenty years to get the Law of the Sea Treaty on the books, and then Ronald Reagan came along and put it on the shelf."

"The Law of the Sea. It is a most neglected document."

"All you're worried about is being told what to do, right? Foreign interference? Well, if you sit down with the president, he's going to tell you what to do."

"What are you suggesting, Mr. Moody?"

"I'm suggesting your foreign minister would find it a hell of a lot more productive to talk with one of the president's close advisers—especially if there's a chance you really will give us a yes vote on the treaty. And you know which adviser I have in mind."

"The foreign minister cannot make a formal visit to the United States merely to hold discussions with a presidential assistant."

"Of course not. But there's always Tokyo. Nice big private hotel rooms. We're all going to be going on vacation in a little while. The president loves his vacations. I'd welcome an opportunity to visit the Far East again. Of course, if I ended up having a lousy vacation, who knows? Maybe this Jack Spencer is a pretty sharp newsman after all. Maybe he's got some good sources—maybe one close to the president. Maybe he was right after all, about the trade sanctions. Am I overcoming the language barrier, Mr. Ambassador?"

Aomori finished his meal. After using his napkin, he folded it carefully into a neat square.

"You are a very interesting man, Mr. Moody."

The president was posing for pictures with two more "blades of grass"—a retired couple from Cape Hatteras who had launched a successful campaign to ban dune buggies from a fifty-mile stretch of the Outer Banks. When the photo session was over, Moody went in for his regular afternoon one-on-one. He broached the subject of a Far East trip at once.

"Send you, Bob? Just you?"

"I've been over there before, sir—the hard way, if you'll recall."

"I'm familiar with your war record. But that was Vietnam."

"I've been in on most of your meetings with those people, sir, and I've dealt with some of them on my own. Acting Secretary Richmond would go along as well, of course—as head of the delegation. We'd hit all the economic powers on the Pacific Rim, those that haven't ratified yet—Taiwan, Korea, Japan, maybe China. Got to go to China if we're going to talk pollution."

"But isn't this something I should do?"

"I don't think so, sir. Some would interpret it as a sign of weakness, that you're going begging. Others might resent it, look on it as bullying—especially Japan. General MacArthur revisited. Anyway, sir, you deserve a good long rest after all you've done this year. I'd much rather see you charging up your batteries on your boat. Remember what happened to James K. Polk, sir. Died three months after leaving office. From exhaustion."

"Few presidents have mastered the ability of delegating authority."

"And none so well as you, sir. The big target of the trip would be Japan, of course. But with a tour like this, it wouldn't be so obvious. In fact, I'd like to start with Korea. If we can get ratification out of them, it might get the Japanese moving. They've been sitting on their asses."

"They have been a disappointment. I thought we had a promising start."

"The Koreans could be moved pretty easily, but I'd need your permission to bring up a national security matter. They've been getting enough carrots out of us with all the aid we're still sending. This would be a stick."

"What stick?"

"The possibility of an American troop withdrawal."

"But you were the one who talked me out of that."

During the campaign, the president had called for a pullout of American forces on the Korean peninsula if Seoul didn't behave more liberally toward its domestic political opposition. Moody had convinced him that the Korean government would only become more oppressive if that threat was carried out.

"Yes sir. I'm not suggesting a reversal. Just a reminder that troop withdrawal remains a possibility. Get their attention."

The president looked at his watch. He had a tennis session on his schedule next. "It all sounds very sensible, Bob. What troubles me is the idea of your being gone for so long. I need you to deal with Congress. I'm still disturbed that the treaty vote has been put off until September."

"Senator Reidy seems to be doing everything that needs to be done. And a lot of the members are going to be home in their districts, or traveling. Anyway, getting some more countries signed up is probably the most useful thing I can do to get our own lawmakers moving. Especially if one of those countries is Japan. I'm sure Secretary Hollis would agree if he were here. You know how he felt about the Japanese."

"Poor Skip. The day doesn't go by that I don't think of him."

"Me too, sir."

"I don't know, Bob. I want to think about it some more. We have the Mexicans coming and all. I'll decide after they've gone."

"All right, sir."

"Something you should know, though. I've decided upon reflection that perhaps Richmond isn't the right man for Skip's job. I just don't know him well enough."

"Yes sir. Have you chosen someone else?"

The president glanced up. "I'm getting closer," he said carefully. "I can tell you this, though. If I do let you go on this Far East trip, I'd certainly make no decision on replacing Skip until I'd seen the results of that."

"Is there anything I can do to help you—make up your mind, that is?"

"Just wait, Bob. Just wait. You must learn to control your impatience."

Showers experienced an odd feeling of metamorphosis as he put on his army fatigues. Not that he was changing into another person. Captain Showers was the same in or out of uniform, in the saddle, or at his bureaucratic desk. Rather, it was a feeling of anonymity, of invisibility. For two weeks, he would be just another line officer in just another National Guard company on just another summer maneuver—a serial number among hundreds of thousands of others in Pentagon computers, a tiny figure beyond the notice of the mighty powers in Washington, powers who supposedly kept their gaze on far horizons, with no concern for the little bugs beneath their feet. He was comfortable with that—for the time being.

He tugged his web belt into place, adjusting the highly polished brass buckle into proper line, and checking the shine of his combat boots. As a civilian in the horse country, he dressed casually and a little carelessly, as was the mode. On active duty, he was a spit and polish officer—not a martinet, but very correct.

Placing his neatly folded dress uniforms atop the gear already in his duffel, he closed the bag, snapping the carrying strap in place. He was bringing no civilian clothes on this sojourn. He had no intention of leaving military jurisdiction—unless there was an emergency.

Shouldering the bag, he went downstairs. Alixe was on his porch, about to come inside. She'd been over in Middleburg and he hadn't talked to her in more than a day. He stepped outside to join her, setting down his bag.

"I was afraid I was going to miss you."

"So was I."

"All packed?" she asked.

"Yes. I don't bring much."

"Would you like to stop over for a stirrup cup?"

He smiled. "No thanks. I think that's an infraction of regulations. I'm on active duty the minute I get in my car."

"Well, David, we'll be glad to see you back."

"I'm worried about leaving you here alone."

"It won't be any different than when you're away in Washington. But, hell, don't worry. I have my boys here. The horse is safe. You'll be gone. Nothing here really to interest anyone. Cooke sends a sheriff's car around every night. And Billy's still down in Charlottesville, last I heard. If anything happens, you can rush back home with all your soldier boys, just like Jeb Stuart."

"I left numbers in the kitchen where I can be reached, even if I'm out in the field."

"Just don't tarry down there after your two weeks are done."

"You've talked to Selma?"

"Every day. She's a weird one, but she's doing her job. Says everything's fine. Lynwood's friends in England have nothing useful to report yet?"

He shook his head. "There've been a few notable thefts over there, but no bay stallion. No horse of enough value to merit all this."

"Any word from those interesting New Jersey folks?"

"I talked to Ned Haney this morning. They sent him a rather stiff letter, saying they'll look into the matter, but it may take some time. They have a busy race schedule this summer."

"The bastards. Shouldn't we go ahead and file suit now? We have the horse and the bad Coggins. What more do we need?"

"We need May Moody."

"Not if we name her in the suit."

"Let's talk about it when I get back." He had set down his bag. He reached to pick it up again. "I'd better saddle up."

She followed him to the Cherokee. "Have you given any thought to what you want to do after you get back? You don't have a job, David."

"I mean to keep the farm."

"Do you mean to work it? Full time?"

"I don't know. I haven't thought that far ahead."

She leaned back against the hood of his Jeep, scuffing at the dirt with the heel of her boot.

"Well, think hard, Captain. We count you as one of us out here, but you're not really, not completely. You know, I've been mucking around in horse shit and foaling mares and schooling hot-tempered colts since I was a little girl. Even Lynwood Fairbrother spends time in his barn every day. It takes that. We're not here just to enjoy the fine country air. We're trying to maintain something, the way our daddies and granddaddies did before us. I know you've spent every free minute you've had out here. But you've given a hell of a lot more time to the goddamn government, for all the thanks it's gotten you. A lot of people are amazed you've kept the farm going as long as you have."

She took a sip of her drink, then gestured with her glass.

"What do you have here? The house, a few outbuildings. A stable with only three of your own horses in it. What the hell would your granddaddy say? I mean it, David. If you had put your mind to it, if you'd really worked this place, it would be one of the finest in the county. That's what your grandfather would have wanted. That's what your father wanted when he made you promise not to let the farm go."

"It's still here."

"As what? The Showers family museum? And how long will you be able to keep it up without some money coming in? You won't take a penny from me or anyone else in Banastre County. What would happen if you had to put this place up for auction? How would you like it if Bernie Bloch put in the high bid?"

"I'd never let that happen."

"The bastard probably cost you your job, David. All sorts of things are possible for a man with that much money. We've seen some of them. Why God lets people like that become rich is beyond me."

"It's going to end, Alixe. You know why I'm doing this. It's not simply because any of us might have been cheated, or because a horse may or may not have been stolen. I'm doing it because they're trying to use the Queen Tashamore name. They're involving our breed in a counterfeit. I'm not going to let them. I swear it."

"Do you suppose Vicky knew what was going on?"

"She knew something."

"David, do you think that's why she's dead?"

"I hope not. But we're going to try to find out."

"We?"

"If my cousin, Jack Spencer, comes around, help him out—whatever he needs. He's not a stranger."

"I'm familiar with his lineage, Captain. Better than yours, except he's not from Virginia. But he's a reporter. There are things that go on around here that perhaps ought not ever appear in a newspaper."

"He understands that. He's family. Treat him accordingly."

Showers put his duffel in the back seat of the Jeep. "About the farm, Alixe, I think about it all the time. I'll do some more thinking while I'm down at Fort Hill." He looked around. "I should say goodbye to Becky. I don't know where she went."

"She's in the cottage. She doesn't want to talk to you. She doesn't want you to go."

He glanced down at his fatigue uniform. "She knows I have no choice."

"She's not exactly herself." Alixe took another sip. "I didn't want to bring this up, with you having to go off and soldier, but I'm afraid that girl's giving us something else to worry about. I know I'm a hell of a person to talk, but I think she's been taking more than the occasional nip. And I fear she might be into something else, some of that fun stuff that Vicky used to make life so interesting."

"She wouldn't do that."

"I'll send her on some errand, and take a look around the cottage."

"Let me know."

"Call me in a day or two."

"I will. I've got to go."

She gave him a kiss on the cheek, then a manly slap on the shoulder.

"Give 'em hell, Captain."

The Shakespeare company had finished casting, down to the last understudy, and May was free until rehearsals began in earnest a few weeks later. The respite was not entirely welcome. She had come to Washington earlier than was really necessary in an almost frantic desire to escape California, without stopping to think long upon what might await her. Now she felt a desire to escape the capital, to go anywhere—perhaps to New York to visit with theater friends, or take some time by herself at the seashore in Rehoboth, Delaware, where she had vacationed as a child. She loved the Washington area. She had drawn up a long list of remembered places she wanted to revisit, and new ones she'd like to explore, but, except for her unfortunate foray out to Dandytown, she had seldom ventured far from her apartment, except to go to the rehearsal hall over by Eastern Market, or to a nearby restaurant to eat. A Washington with her father in it was too small a place.

Her banker friend had promised to do what he could to buy the horse back from David Showers, but had made little progress. He'd called the night before to report that Showers had gone out of town for two weeks. She was on the brink of saying to hell with the entire business, and let these stubborn men settle their own quarrel. She was perplexed and not a little angered by Showers' intractability. But, for all her lovely good intentions, she had brought this trouble upon him. She owed it to her guilty conscience, if not to him, to try to prevent things from getting any worse. Damn her father and his greedy friends anyway.

This morning, her destination was less than a block away—the Folger Shakespeare Library building that housed the replicated Shakespearean theater where her acting company had performed until its recent move to a larger auditorium. The library staff had offered her a tour of the facility and its world-famous collection, including a visit to the underground vaults, with their treasure of original Shakespeare folios and such rare books as the Bible Queen Elizabeth I kept in her private chapel at the time she was anguishing over the fate she would ultimately bestow upon her unfortunate kinswoman, Mary Queen of Scots.

May was looking forward to it. The library was air conditioned, as her apartment was not. It was charming enough, one of four dividing up an old Victorian townhouse, but quite small—a bedroom, living room, kitchenette, and tiny bath. Kelly McGillis, among other major actors and actresses who had played the theater, had endured such quarters for two months or more, and so would May. But during the long, hot days it became oppressive.

She put on a light summer dress and sandals, breakfasting quickly on three Oreo cookies and a cup of instant coffee. The morning paper was uninteresting, filled with government news about some obscure crisis in a Central American country she knew nothing about, as well as endless columns of reportage and commentary on the federal budget and some arms control and environmental treaties before the Congress. Her father was doubtless fascinated by every word, but May found it all very boring. In

227

California, she had read *Variety* far more religiously than the *Los Angeles Times*.

May had gone only a short ways down the shady street when she was halted by insistent soundings of a nearby automobile horn.

She looked about uncertainly, then saw the long Mercedes-Benz—and the bright blond hair. She would have preferred giving everything up and going back to California to facing this.

She stood her ground. She didn't approach the car, despite the urgings of the woman behind the steering wheel to do so. Finally, the woman got out and came up to her.

"Hello, May," she said, with Southern softness.

"Hello, Mrs. Atkinson," she said, using Deena's previous married name. "Why are you bothering me on the public streets?"

"I was going to ring your bell, but I wasn't sure you were home—or if I'd be welcome."

"You wouldn't be. How long have you been lurking out here?"

"I just want to talk to you, May. It's important."

"No thank you." She turned to walk away.

"It's about your friend, Captain Showers."

May halted. "What about him? And he's not my friend. I hardly know him."

Deena smiled. "You have seen him, haven't you? Out at his farm?"

"How do you know that?"

"Can we sit in the car?"

"No!"

"Well, May, darlin', this is really important. You know what's happened to him."

"I don't."

"Why, he's lost his job."

"What? My father fired him?"

"Oh no. Certainly not. Your friend made some kind of mistake. It was so bad he had to resign."

May simply stared.

"But I'm afraid," Deena continued, "that he may try to get back at your father for what happened to him, even though your father had nothing to do with it. He's already gone after your father's best friend—Mr. Bloch. Stirring up all that ruckus about that stupid horse you bought for him. Your father's a very important man now, May. He's involved in very important matters. He shouldn't have to put up with this childish nonsense. And he won't. If your friend

228

keeps this up, he's only going to get himself into some really big trouble."

"What the hell does that horse have to do with my father or Bernie Bloch? I bought it at an open auction. I decided I made a mistake and I sold it. Showers ended up with it. So what? Why in hell should my father give a damn? Especially if he's so busy running the world?"

"You made a mistake. That's just it. A little mistake, in the beginning. But now it could grow into a great big mistake. You have to understand that."

She took a step closer. The lapels of the red suit she was wearing were cut very low. May could see sweat gathering in her cleavage.

"That doesn't have to happen, darlin'. You've come here to do a play, and I'm sure you're going to be just wonderful. You don't want to be caught up in some investigation or lawsuit way out in Virginia. Your friend Captain Showers wants a horse. He can have one. I understand Mr. Bloch is willing to pay him a great deal of money for the one he got from you—enough to buy a dozen horses. If he'll do that, and stop this foolishness, I'm sure your father would do everything in his power to get your friend reinstated. Your father can make a lot of things happen in this town."

"Did he send you to tell me this?"

"Oh no, May. You know he respects your privacy. I came to see you all on my own—because I want to help. I don't want this nasty little business to interfere with the big work he's doing, not in any way."

"If my father had the slightest shred of respect for me—I won't bring up love—he would have turned on his heel the minute he first laid eyes on you."

Deena's face flushed. "I've always hoped that you and I might become friends someday," she said, moving even closer. "And I still hope that. But you seem bent on making an awful mess of everything. And it will be awful, May, I promise you that."

"What do you mean?"

"For your sake, May, for our sake, for everyone's sake, talk to Showers. Get some sense into him. You're a very charming and very beautiful girl—a great star. I'm sure he has some fondness for you. I'm sure, if you put your mind to it, you could be very persuasive."

Inside, May was boiling. She clenched her fists.

"You could solve everything right now, honey," Deena said, "if you'd just tell me where that handsome 'captain' of yours has taken that horse."

May hit her as hard as she could, hurting her wrist, her hand stinging afterward.

"You little shit," said Deena. Her cheek was a violent crimson.

May walked quickly away, hurrying across the street. When at last in the coolness of the Folger Library, the great brass-fronted doors closed behind her like protective castle gates.

Her hand was still bothering her when, a good half hour later, she was taken to the underground room where the Queen Elizabeth Bible was kept. She declined the invitation to look through the chemically preserved, four-century-old pages, for fear of somehow injuring them, but she did press her hand against its cover, touching the finely crafted surface as the queen herself must have done.

She now understood perfectly how that troubled woman could have brought herself to having her kinswoman beheaded.

Bernie Bloch sat in his huge leather chair, staring out the window at a coal ship that had left the docks and was steaming slowly out toward Chesapeake Bay. He wished he were on it.

He was in his office in a shiny new building he owned, which overlooked Baltimore Harbor. He had kept to it and his upstairs apartment suite the better part of several days, staying out of the Virginia and Maryland horse country, staying away from Washington, lying low while his lawyers and hired men worked at finding him a way out of his jam. They'd come up with nothing. The hired men had only made things worse.

And now the source of the worst of his worries had once again hunted him down.

"Mr. Bloch," said his secretary, from the small intercom speaker in his telephone console. "He's still on the line."

"Yeah, all right." Taking a deep breath, he picked up the receiver. "This is Bloch," he said quietly.

The other party paused, as though for effect.

"You said you'd call me," the man said, finally.

"Yeah, I know. I'm sorry. Got a lot going on. And this is taking a little longer than I thought. But don't worry. Everything's under control."

"Bullshit." Another pause. "We don't understand why there's a problem."

"There's no real problem. Honest. I just want to be a little careful about how I do this."

"You haven't been careful enough. We don't like the kind of mail we've been getting."

"I'm sorry about that. It's just paperwork. I've got lawyers dealing with it. We can tie it up for months."

"We don't want it tied up. We want it in the shitcan. We don't want no more mail. What we want is our merchandise."

"I understand. I—"

"If we don't get our merchandise, we're going to want a refund. Not just a refund, but a return on our investment. You know how much we figured the merchandise is worth. We may want twice that much. Maybe three times. Just for our trouble."

"That's no problem. If it's just money—"

"It's not just money. We had a little talk up here. We decided something. If we can't get our merchandise back, we don't want anybody else to have it. We don't want it on the market anymore. We don't want it around. We want it to disappear. We don't want more mail. We don't want any chitchat with the racing commission. We're sportsmen, outdoor guys. We don't like it inside, not in places like Virginia courtrooms."

"What're you saying?"

"What am I saying? I'm saying, they shoot horses, don't they? I'm saying dogs gotta eat, and you know what goes into dog food. I'm saying that, with things so far out of hand, maybe that's the best place for our merchandise—if you can't get it back for us."

"That may not be so easy. I mean, it'll take a little more time."

"You've got a lot of money, Mr. Bloch, but you don't have a lot of time. Or a lot of smarts. If you can't take care of this, then we will. We don't want to, but that's what we'll do. We've got to protect our investment."

"Okay, okay."

"Not okay. I think our partnership's going to have to be dissolved. That's too bad, but it isn't working out, is it? Maybe you're not cut out for this kind of business. For the world of sport. Not this sport, anyway. Maybe you should have bought yourself a ball team."

Bloch suddenly felt as though his office had been turned into a freezer. He couldn't bring himself to speak.

"It would be best, you know," said the voice on the other end, "all the way around, if we dissolved the partnership on friendly terms. You agree?"

"I agree."

"Good. You see to it."

# Fifteen

pencer's bureau chief, surprised and pleased to see his de-frocked columnist adapting to his lowly new status well enough to be showing some initiative, readily agreed to his idea for a feature story on the Virginia horse country, provided Spencer work in something about Elizabeth Taylor's time there as mistress of then husband Senator John Warner's big Middleburg horse farm. The editor even suggested a sidebar for the sports wire on steeplechasing, and another for travel sections on country inns in the area.

Spencer devoted his first day to Middleburg and Upperville, where he dug up a few colorful anecdotes about Warner and Liz and established himself as nothing more suspicious than a writer after a feature story. The next day he went to Dandytown. Alixe Percy was as helpful as Showers had promised, especially after Spencer happily joined her in a couple of glasses of Virginia Gentleman. She put him in touch with several of the more notable horse people in the community, and they were all genuinely hospitable to him when he came to call on them. Spencer had long experience at eliciting information in the process of idle conversation—a skill he'd used effectively with IRA Provos and El Salvadoran military officers alike.

The horse folk were most garrulous on the subject of Vicky Clay. She seemed as much a topic of gossip dead as she had been alive. He learned that she was widely considered to have been at least the part-time mistress of her employer, Bernard Bloch, but had slept around with a large number of other men, concentrating her attentions in recent weeks on the rich and famous who gathered in

Dandytown for the steeplechase and horse show season. He was also told that she had talked to friends about divorcing her husband, Meade, and seemed to be looking for a way to get herself out of Dandytown and into a more comfortable situation—though no one Spencer talked to could imagine what civilized person, however sex crazed, could long abide the girl.

The person who knew the most about Vicky Clay, Spencer was told, was the young woman who had long been her closest friend, her sister-in-law Becky Gibbons Bonning, but Showers had asked him to stay away from her.

After lunch in the Dandytown Inn, where his waitress was more than happy to describe the murder-suicide scene as the maid and desk clerk had discovered it, Spencer stopped by the offices of the local weekly newspaper. They let him look through their files of back copies, ostensibly to review their stories on the Valley Dragoon Chase weekend, but he managed also to take ample notes from their accounts of Vicky's death and the subsequent investigation and inquest proceedings.

His next stop was the sheriff's office adjoining the county courthouse, where he received a much less warm welcome. Spencer kept to his cover story—just doing a feature on the horse country— but said the murder-suicide and the community's reaction to it was a damned interesting episode, and certainly something he couldn't leave out.

"It's old news," the sheriff said. "The case is closed, mister. The papers out here wrote it all up anyway. We don't have anything new to add."

"Couldn't I look through the case file? It wouldn't take but a few minutes."

"Hell, no, you can't look through it. I don't know how you people do things back in Washington but you can't come out here and start rummaging through our files. I don't even know who you are?"

Spencer showed him his U.S. Capitol press pass.

"This isn't the Congress."

"That doesn't matter. I'm an accredited journalist and your files are public record."

"They're official law enforcement records. If you want to get a writ, go ahead and try, but I don't think you'll get very far. I thought you were writing about horses?"

"Horses. Drugs. Dead bodies. All part of the local color, it seems."

"Good day to you, Mr. Spencer. We've got police work to do here."

He went to the door, holding it open.

Spencer didn't want to waste time. His bureau chief had assigned him to cover the state dinner for the president of Mexico at the White House that night, and it was a long drive back. But he lingered in town long enough to pay one more visit, one Showers had suggested, to the assistant commonwealth attorney who'd worked on the case, a man named Wayne Bensinger. Showers had said he was young and inexperienced, but honest. A rich horse-woman he knew—Lenore Fairbrother—had once tried to get the man to fix a drunk-driving citation for her. The sheriff had agreed to try to get the charge dropped, but the case had already gotten onto the county court docket, so young Bensinger went ahead and prosecuted her. She was eventually acquitted for lack of evidence. The sheriff claimed he had misplaced the blood alcohol test results. But Showers had been impressed with the young man's principles, and had interceded with Lynwood Fairbrother to prevent him from giving Bensinger any kind of hard time.

It seemed worth the risk to drop some of the pretense about a feature story on horses and tell Bensinger his chief interest was the Vicky Clay murder. Spencer supposed the sheriff had already figured that much out. There was more plus than minus in revealing that he was Showers' cousin as well. Word of that would get around sooner or later—the way these people loved to gossip, probably sooner.

"No, the sheriff's wrong," Bensinger said, as they sat in his hot little office in the courthouse. "The case isn't officially closed. It's just inactive. The coroner's jury finding was on the cause of death, which was by injection of etorphine. Murder-suicide was put down as the probable circumstance. Nothing else was indicated by the evidence. But Meade Clay wasn't tried and found guilty. The law just made an assumption. If the sheriff turns up some new evidence, we'd open it up again."

"The sheriff doesn't exactly seem disposed to do that."

Bensinger shrugged. "We don't get many homicide cases out here. The sheriff did everything he could—he must have talked to half the people in the county—but I guess he's just as happy not to have to mess with it anymore."

The prosecutor was sitting at his desk in shirtsleeves, his tan jacket hanging on the back of his chair looking wrinkled beyond hope of pressing. Spencer wondered if the man owned more than two suits.

"The state police have looked into all this?"

"Oh sure. I mean, they were on the scene during the investigation, and they have all the reports. My boss sent copies of everything to Richmond. But the principal jurisdiction is here."

"Why settle on murder-suicide?"

"There were no witnesses to anything else. The hotel room door was locked. There was no access through the windows on that floor and no sign of a break-in. The victims' prints were the only ones found on the two syringes that were used. Meade Clay had about every motive you could think of. And the means used—well, it would be unique to a veterinarian. Knowing the fatal dosage and everything."

"But in her case the dosage wasn't immediately fatal. She died a couple hours after he did, right?"

"Yes. It must have been horrible. Lying there completely paralyzed, with him dead beside her."

"Not completely paralyzed. She made a lot of scratches on his back. That's what the papers said."

"We weren't sure about those. The coroner said that happened while he was still alive. She had a reputation for being, I guess you could say, sexually active. They'd made love. Apparently just before he'd administered the drug."

Bensinger blinked amiably at him behind his thick glasses. Spencer had the odd feeling the young man was glad he was there.

"My cousin David said you and the sheriff asked him whether Meade Clay was right-handed or left-handed. He said Clay was left-handed. Where did he inject himself, if that's what he did?"

"In the left shoulder. With his right hand. But that doesn't necessarily mean anything. Junkies inject themselves in all kinds of places. He was a cocaine addict. So was she."

"But that's not how you take cocaine."

"No, it's not."

Spencer was tired. He wanted a drink. He had a long drive back to Washington and would have to make it a fast one if he was going to get into black tie in time to be at the White House for the guest arrivals. He was planning to come back to Dandytown in a few days anyway.

But many things could change in a few days, including the prosecutor's friendly, helpful mood.

"You say there's been no new evidence. Have you gone over the old evidence again?"

"As a matter of fact, I have. At least the transcript from the inquest. Nothing jumped out at me."

"Would you mind if I had a look?"

Bensinger frowned. "I can't let you do that. Regulations. You'd have to get permission from the court."

"You mean a judge?"

"A judge. Or the court clerk."

"My cousin said there's a judge here who's an old friend of the family. Judge Merrick? Well, I'm family."

"He'll be happy to see you, then."

Spencer looked at his watch. "I don't have a lot of time. I have to be at the White House tonight." He paused to let those two words work their magic. "Couldn't we dispense with all the formalities, since all I want to do is look, and it's public record anyway?"

Bensinger bit his lip. "You're going to do a story on this?"

"If I do, our conversation today won't be in it. You might say you have Captain Showers' word on that."

More magic. "All right. Since you're in a hurry, and Judge Merrick would probably let you do it anyway, I guess it's okay. I've got the whole file right here. I've kept it."

He went to an old cabinet next to his desk. The drawer gave a raspy squeak when he pulled it out.

"To tell you the truth, Mr. Spencer, I've had a few doubts about this myself. Just couldn't figure out why. Maybe you might have some ideas." He sat the file down in front of Spencer.

As Spencer moved the file to his lap and opened it, a sheaf of photographs fell out—some pictures of the Clays; nude bodies, both in the hotel bedroom and on a medical examining table. Spencer had seen a fair number of corpses in his time on the police beat as a young reporter. The expression on Vicky Clay's face made hers seem more grisly than those of a lot of mutilation victims.

One photo was a close-up of the scratches on Meade Clay's back.

"I thought you were going to read the transcript."

"I am, Mr. Bensinger. These somehow caught my eye."

"They're pretty horrible. I think about them sometimes, late at night. This is my first murder case."

"Where did you go to law school?"

"UVA."

Spencer had had prep school friends who had gone to that estimable institution. "Why aren't you in Washington making some

236

money with a big firm? You could get a job like this with a mail order degree."

"I plan to go into private practice out here, maybe over in Winchester or Leesburg," Bensinger said defensively. "My family's from here. My wife's from Warrenton."

Spencer set the picture of the scratches in front of the man. "You may have lived a cloistered existence at UVA, Mr. Bensinger, but I've been around a little and, let me tell you, any woman who did this to a man would bring his amorous feelings to a halt in a hell of a hurry."

"I thought about that."

"There's a pattern to them. Did you notice that? A kind of circular pattern. Almost like writing."

"I guess there is."

"I'd like to have someone take a look at this, someone with an expert eye."

Bensinger bit down on his lip again. He stared closely at the photograph, then looked up, still squinting. He reminded Spencer of Showers, trying to decide what would be the right thing to do.

"You're part of the Showers family?" Bensinger said.

"Our mothers were sisters."

"All right. For the captain's sake. But get it back to me fast."

"I'd like to look through this transcript, but I'm running a little behind."

"I'm not going to let you take that, Mr. Spencer."

"Well, I'll be back. And don't worry. No one will know about this—except my cousin."

Bensinger rose, handing the photograph back to Spencer.

"One more thing," Spencer said. "Do you handle cases of fraudulent livestock transactions?"

"If there was a big swindle or something, I guess we would. If it was just a dispute over a horse sale, those are usually handled in a civil suit. There aren't many cases like that, not here in Dandytown."

"But if a crime were involved?"

"Sure."

"I may have some business for you."

When he left, he found a parking ticket in the windshield of his car.

State dinners were very much a formalized ritual, following the same time-tested script of pomp and circumstance no matter who was president and who was the honored guest—the president of Togo accorded the same treatment as the prime minister of Britain or the chancellor of Germany, the same red carpet, marine band, elaborate menu, and glittering array of famous names on the guest list. An invitation to dine at the White House was prized no matter what the occasion.

The first lady's social office was ostensibly in charge of these affairs, and social secretary Toby Kevin, a man with an irrepressible flair and fondness for getting his name and picture into the newspapers and social magazines, fluttered everywhere. Early on in the administration, he'd proposed that state dinners be elevated from black tie to white tie events. He'd become the object of some ridicule when it was learned that his suggestion was motivated solely by a desire to wear some of the outlandish foreign decorations he'd acquired over the years. He had one from Brunei that rivaled anything worn by British royals.

He was hanging around the scene this evening more like a head butler than a royal, but was causing no less worry to the first lady. The United States was particularly sensitive to the feelings of its increasingly important neighbor to the south, and, with the Belize crisis still bubbling, the White House wanted no repetition of the kind of gaffes that had occurred in the past, such as President Jimmy Carter's telling a "Montezuma's Revenge" joke at a state banquet in Mexico City in 1979, or an affront that had been narrowly averted in the Bush administration. A not-so-clever chef of the time had decorated the "Mexican surprise" dessert for a state dinner with miniature Mexican huts complete with frosting figures of sleeping Mexican peasants in sombreros slumbering against the hut walls. Mrs. Bush's social secretary had hastily knocked these offensive niceties off all one hundred dessert plates, but only minutes before the dinner had been about to commence.

This evening, Kevin was contenting himself merely with ordering functionaries of both countries about on pointless errands. Finally, the president's wife herself issued him a direct request to get out of the way and join those preparing for the official welcome of the Mexican president on the steps of the North Portico.

It was extremely hot and muggy out there, with lowering storm clouds threatening a downpour. The Mexican president was overdue, and if he didn't show up soon, Kevin, the military honor guard, and the others on the steps could find themselves thoroughly soaked. By the time the motorcade approached, the great, ancient trees on the White House lawn were beginning to sway with gusts of forbidding wind.

Spencer, arriving at the last minute, joined the other newspeople in rather raffish evening dress gathered in a noisy crowd behind a velvet rope in the east entrance hall on the White House ground floor, which guests had to pass through on their way upstairs to the Executive Mansion's main level. The top-ranking American and Mexican officials entered elsewhere, of course, but most of the invitees had to run this gamut. The drab and frumpy corporate CEOs and their wives attracted little interest, but the movie stars, members of Congress, and military officers who came through the hall were greeted with sudden flares of television and news camera lights and small barrages of trivial questions.

"Is this your first time at the White House, Miss Shields?"

"General, are you concerned about the situation in Belize?"

"Are you happy with the budget compromise, Senator?"

"Mrs. Moody, is that a Bob Mackie gown?"

Deena, unaccompanied by her husband, had arrived with Bernie Bloch and his wife. The Blochs stood uncomfortably by while Deena posed for the cameras and chattered with the reporters, holding up other guests in line behind them. None of the newspeople seemed to recognize the billionaire, or care about his presence.

Spencer recognized him. He couldn't resist the opportunity to fire a couple of shafts.

"Mr. Bloch," he asked, leaning out over the rope, "are you concerned about the effect the Earth Treaty's going to have on your coal mines and chemical companies?"

Bloch, startled, eyed Spencer sharply. He looked quite dumpy in his tuxedo, which reminded Spencer of something a Las Vegas nightclub emcee might sport at a mafioso wedding—or funeral. A couple of women reporters pressed up against Spencer, their notebooks at the ready, hopeful that something significant was being said.

"I'm a big supporter of the president," Bloch said. "He's my man."

"Are you working with your friends in the business community to get them behind the treaty?" Spencer smiled, as though this were all perfectly innocent.

"I'm not a politician. I tend to my affairs."

"I suppose you're spending a lot of time with your horses. I understand you've become quite the sportsman."

Bloch glared at him. If he were describing it in a column,

Spencer would have called the look "murderous." Spencer just kept smiling.

"Who are you?" Bloch asked.

"I'm the eyes and ears of the American people."

Bloch grabbed his wife's arm and marched off down the hall, leaving Deena on her own with the reporters. His wife caught her foot on the hem of her gown, nearly tripping.

"Who was that?" said one of the newswomen at Spencer's elbow.

"That's Bernard Bloch, the Baltimore billionaire," said another woman. "Donald Trump without hair."

"Does he have some connection with Mexico?"

"None at all," Spencer said. "He's here because the president's his man."

There is no head table at state dinners. The ten or eleven round tables set up in the state dining room, each seating up to ten, were arranged without precedence, although the president's table was at the center, near the huge portrait of Abraham Lincoln above the room's huge fireplace.

Normally, Moody sat with the president's party, but this night had taken pains to be seated next to Bloch's wife at a table over to the side. As he feared, Sherrie had arrived more than half in the bag, and he didn't want to trust any of his aides to see to her good behavior. As it was, it was all he could do to get her through the meal. She talked very loudly, and scattered pieces of lettuce from her salad onto the table-cloth around her plate. Thunder rattled the windows, adding to her nervousness. Soon they could hear the thud of heavy rain.

As it turned out, Bloch was the only horseman they'd been able to get at the dinner, despite the honor of the invitation. Two had declined immediately; Lynwood Fairbrother had called late in the afternoon to say that only his wife would be attending. Lenore was at a table toward the center of the room. She ignored Moody completely through the evening.

After dinner, the custom was for the guests to stroll about the White House's long Cross Hall and other public rooms, as waiters served demitasse and liqueurs, before proceeding into the East Room for the evening's entertainment, which this night would be an operatic soprano singing numbers from *Carmen*. The president and first lady in the meantime received the official Mexican party in the Blue Oval Room, posing for pictures with the Mexican president, Pablo Marantes, and his very beautiful wife.

240

Usually, that was where Moody stationed himself, but now he instead went searching through the crowd for Lenore Fairbrother, finding her finally in the Red Room beneath the oil portrait of Angelica Singleton, Martin Van Buren's coquettish daughter-in-law.

Lenore was with General St. Angelo, and was being very charming. She wore a long, midnight blue, off-the-shoulder gown easily as expensive as Deena's low-cut sequined Arnold Scaasi dress, and far more elegant. Lenore wore little jewelry, in contrast to the Tiffany window displayed on Deena's ample chest. She had her hair swept back and up, exposing her long and regal neck. To Moody's surprise, she greeted him effusively, complete with a kiss on the cheek.

"Hello, Chiefy darling," she said. "I've just been learning what a terribly important man you are around here."

St. Angelo gave Moody an embarrassed smile, then slipped away.

"I've never been here before," Lenore continued. "Isn't that amazing? Of course, I've been to the palace simply zillions of times."

"The palace?"

"Buckingham Palace, dear boy. And a weekend at Balmoral. My previous husband was knighted, though of course he did absolutely nothing to earn it. Simply slept around with the wives of the right members of the cabinet, and when it came time to draw up the honors' list, there he was." She looked around the room. "This is all very nice, of course. Very American."

"You're American."

"Not really, darling. I'm a Virginian."

"Where's your husband tonight? He stood up the president."

"No he didn't, Chiefy. He stood up you. He wouldn't think of coming. Not for a moment. Not after what you did to poor Captain Showers."

"What are you talking about?"

"We *all* know what happened, Mr. Moody. Everyone in Dandytown thinks it's just despicable that you'd punish our local hero that dreadful way just because he wouldn't sell your slimy little Baltimore friend a horse. That sort of thing just isn't done, you know. It's considered very low. If these were olden times, Captain Showers probably would have called you out by now, with Lynwood glad to be his second."

"Called me out?"

"A duel, dear boy. Wouldn't that be fun? Far more fun than this dull, dull dinner. Thank heavens I'm going to something far more amusing afterwards. Would you like to come, Chiefy? It would be fun to have you there. I don't think anyone there will have ever met anyone like you."

"Mrs. Fairbrother. David Showers resigned. He was given a transfer. He refused to accept it. That was his decision, not mine. I had nothing to do with it. And I've nothing to do with that horse. That's all between Showers and Bernie Bloch."

"Not true, Chiefy."

"Excuse me, Mrs. Fairbrother, but just how the hell would you know?"

"You'd be simply amazed, Mr. Moody, at how much I know. How much we all know. Just because we own a few pickup trucks doesn't make us rednecks. My father was an ambassador, y'know. He's the one who got David into the State Department. My husband owns a rather large bank just up the street from here. The place next door to ours is the country retreat of a United States senator. That girl over there, who works in your press office? Her aunt and I came out together."

"Came out?"

"Debutantes, dear boy. Don't they have them where you come from?"

He could feel the red in his face. "If you'll excuse me, Mrs. Fairbrother."

She took his arm, pulling him close.

"Have I upset you, Chiefy? I didn't mean to. I'm just teasing. Really. I'm sure that when you're not being so important, you're actually a very nice man. The same way that David is a very nice man, when he isn't being so insufferably noble."

She looked up at him, staring into his face as though deeply fascinated. He couldn't ignore the wicked curl to her smile, however.

"We really ought to be friends, don't you think?" she said, then kissed him on the cheek and swept away. He heard her shout "Darling!" to a tall man in glasses, someone from the U.S. trade office.

The military ushers were encouraging people to move into the East Room for the entertainment. Moody started down the hall, but was caught up from behind by Deena. She looked angry, a mood with which he'd become very familiar in recent days.

"You've got to do something about Sherrie Bloch," she said. "She can barely stand up."

Moody glanced among the crowd for Bernie. He was by one of the marble pillars, talking with a congressman.

"I'll get Bernie," he said.

"Don't bother him."

"Don't bother him? She's his wife!"

"She might start yellin' at him. Cause a terrible scene. Do you want that? They were quarreling on the way over."

"I shouldn't have invited them."

"He shouldn't have married her. God, what an awful woman."

"Look, I've got to join the president. You deal with her."

The entertainment segment of the evening proceeded without too much untoward incident, except for Deena and Sherrie Bloch taking their seats late, and Sherrie giving out a loud belch in a quiet moment before the soprano began singing. A Secret Service man or someone also managed to knock a candlestick off a table in the rear during the president's brief remarks at the conclusion. The president showed no irritation, however. On the contrary, he seemed quite ebullient. He and Marantes—a well-educated gentleman with perfect manners—had hit it off nicely. During their afternoon meeting, which Moody had attended along with acting Secretary of State Richmond, the Mexican had agreed to support American policy in Belize fully.

Moody wasn't cheerful. On top of everything else, he'd noticed Jack Spencer standing among all the women reporters in the press pool allowed to attend the "mix and mingle" that followed the dinner. Moody had thought he'd deep-sixed the man for good.

He would talk to the first lady's press office to make sure this didn't happen again. Press pools shouldn't be open to everyone, certainly not enemies of the administration.

The last scheduled event of the evening was the dancing in the Grand Foyer, begun by ritual with the marine band playing "Shall We Dance?" and the president and first lady taking a few turns around the floor before inviting the others to join in. Not aware of the protocol—or much of anything else—Sherrie Bloch tried to drag her husband onto the floor at the same time. One of the military ushers discreetly held them back.

Finally, the president nodded to the vice president and his wife. As they swept out onto the floor, the other guests did the same. As was expected of them, so did Moody and Deena. Her eyes were fixed on Sherrie Bloch.

"You've got to get her out of here, Robert. She's going to fall down."

"You do it," he said. "Get them both out of here. You're all so goddamn inseparable."

The Mexicans were leaving. Moody hurried to join the president as he escorted them out the door and down the front steps to their waiting motorcade. Marantes made a point of shaking Moody's hand among all the others. The violent thunderstorms had passed and the warm night air was drying, though lingering puddles glistened on the pavement.

As the cars sped away, the president paused on the steps.

"This went splendidly, Bob," he said. "Quite splendidly indeed. You were very helpful this afternoon."

"I've just kept abreast of things down there."

"Much better than Richmond." He put his hand on Moody's shoulder. "I've decided you should make this Far East trip. I'd like you to leave as soon as you can. If I know you, you've already made preparations."

"Yes sir."

They returned inside. The president took his wife by the arm, waved to the guests, then started up the grand staircase to the family quarters. They seldom lingered longer than the first dance.

Moody looked for Deena to tell her the president's decision. He was relieved when he couldn't find her. He'd sprung the news that they might be traveling to Asia on her a few days before, and she'd not received it happily.

"I don't want to spend my vacation eating rice and bowing to a lot of women in kimonos," she had said.

"It's important, damn it. If he lets me go, it's because he wants to see how I'll perform. I could damn well use your help."

"I'm not a geisha girl."

"You want to be Mrs. Secretary of State, don't you? Well, this is a big part of the job."

"You don't have the job yet. The way you've fumbled around getting Bernie back his horse, I'm surprised you have the job you have now."

"If the president says yes, we go. We both go."

They hadn't spoken much since.

Looking vainly among the dancers, Moody supposed Deena had gone off with the Blochs. The last time she'd done that, she'd stayed with them for the night in Baltimore.

Moody felt an arm in his.

"Shouldn't we be going, Chiefy?" said Lenore Fairbrother.

"What do you mean?"

"To the party I told you about?"

"You can't be serious."

"Dance with me."

"I thought you were mad at me."

"I am, darling, but that shouldn't interfere with our having a good time."

He hesitated, then took her into his arms. He was a clumsy dancer, capable only of a minimal sort of two-step, but she managed to follow with considerable grace. She looked up at him seductively.

"You were in the military, Chiefy?"

"Yes. In Vietnam."

"An officer?"

"Of course. I'm a lieutenant colonel in the reserves."

"That's simply marvelous, Chiefy. I'll introduce you as 'Colonel.' "

"Introduce me to whom?"

"To the people at the party. You'll love them. There's a royal French princess, though I'm not sure whether she's House of Orléans or one of the Bourbons. And Lady Sansome. And Harold Cooper, the press lord. And Jeffrey Esterhazy the painter. And just scads of divinely decadent people."

"Here in Washington?"

"Yes, right here in deadly dull Washington."

General St. Angelo was watching them. So was Jack Spencer, leaning against a pillar, a notebook in his hand.

"You're joking," Moody said.

"I never joke about parties, Colonel darling. And anyway, I need a ride. It's at an ambassador's house, so it would be in the line of duty. You're quite the diplomat, I hear."

Spencer was grinning at them.

"It would be a crazy thing to do."

"It's good to do something a little crazy once in a while."

"My wife . . ."

"She left with your dear friend Mr. Bloch, and his loving wife."

"I can't."

"The president's gone to bed, darling. Are you a stuffy old early-to-bed bureaucrat, or a man who does what he wants?"

She pulled herself snugly close to him. He could feel her breasts against his chest.

"I'll drop you off," he said, "on my way home."

He dismissed his driver for the night and, locking his White House briefcase in the trunk of his black official car, took the wheel himself. She was fascinated by the glowing array of communications equipment beneath the dashboard and amused herself by pushing buttons until he insisted she stop.

"Dear boy," she said. "Are you afraid I might start a war?"

The Northwest quadrant of the capital had taken a pounding from the storm. West of Rock Creek Park, a number of traffic lights along Massachusetts Avenue were darkened and still swaying in the wind. Tumbles of small branches and swaths of blown and rain-pressed green leaves covered large areas of the pavement. When, following her directions, he turned off into the dark, curving lanes that were the streets of the expensive residential district on the far side of the park, he found the going increasingly difficult. Huge old trees, felled by the winds, had fallen over the roadway in several places—at one point dragging down a menacing tangle of power lines. He had to back up several times, probing ever westward in search of an open thoroughfare.

Moody became more and more uneasy about continuing with this adventure, and fought a compulsion to take Lenore back to Georgetown, where she said she was staying with friends, and then proceed directly home. But he was intrigued by everything about her, the expensive scent of her perfume, the mystical beauty of her classic profile glimpsed in the soft, faint light from the dashboard, the amazing fact of her sitting there beside him. He was excited. His experience with infidelity, begun in the last years of his first marriage, had been unexceptional enough—a couple of government secretaries in Annapolis thrilled to do it with the governor, a few frustrated wives of friends (including the then Mrs. Deena Atkinson), the occasional loose piece of ass like Vicky Clay. This woman was different. She had "special" stamped all over her. Hell, she'd been in the picture spreads of *Town & Country* magazine, and here she was playing seduction games with Bobby Mack Moody, born in a collection of shacks called Shivers Springs in Jade County, West Virginia.

Her directions led them to a narrow road that, with all the bordering house lights out, seemed to take them into a deep forest. At length they came to two large stone gateposts and she announced they had arrived.

The driveway was blocked by a fallen tree some one hundred

246

yards within, and the guests' cars were parked in a disorderly jumble to either side of the asphalt paving, a few chauffeurs standing in a group, talking and smoking. Moody found an opening behind a long Cadillac and, with considerable difficulty, parked. He hit the button locking all the doors as soon as they were out of the car. It would take a safecracker to get into the trunk.

A short, swarthy man who looked to be a servant guided them to the beginning of a path. Candles set in little plates had been placed along it, tiny beacons leading in zigzag fashion uphill through the trees and brush.

"It's rather like a fairy tale, isn't it, Colonel?" she said, stepping lightly along the trail ahead of him. "A Grimm Brothers fairy tale. I love the Grimm Brothers, don't you? So deliciously grim. Children eaten by witches. Ballerinas with their feet cut off."

One of the candles had gone out, and for a long stretch, they were completely in darkness, except for a glimmer of light falling between the treetops from a small sliver of moon. Tripping over a log, she lost her balance and fell against him. He caught her, his hand slipping to her breast.

"Naughty, Colonel," she said. "Naughty, naughty boy." She lingered a moment tantalizingly in his arms, then slipped away, plunging on ahead. When she reached the light of the next candle, she ran in little leaps and bounds the rest of the way to the house, Moody stumbling along far behind.

The house was huge. Their ambassadorial host represented a minor island nation in the Caribbean. Moody guessed he must be the wealthiest man in that country.

He was standing at the front door, flashlight in hand. Lenore greeted him with a warm embrace, then turned to introduce her companion.

"Sebastian, this is Colonel Moody. He runs the White House, I think, or possibly the world."

"Oh yes," said the ambassador, his smile almost maniacal in the weird light. "I believe we have met before."

Moody couldn't recall the man at all. He'd probably been part of some milling swarm at a State Department reception, accorded a fleeting "Hi, how're ya" from Moody as he'd worked the crowd.

Lenore skipped on inside, abandoning Moody to their host. He prattled on about how honored he was to have the White House chief of staff at his residence, and then, pressing a glass of champagne into Moody's hand from a butler's tray, led him into the darkened house, the walls of its shadowy corridors and rooms flickering with the candlelight.

There were paintings everywhere—native art, the ambassador said, dancing his flashlight over them. They seemed mostly jungle and mountain scenes, all very primitive, reminding Moody a little of voodoo, though the ambassador was quite light-skinned, and spoke with a French accent.

Finally, Moody escaped him, but to no great purpose. Lenore had disappeared. He stepped into a large, richly furnished room filled with strangers, standing awkwardly a moment, then shrinking back against a wall. He hated being on his own at parties. One of the reasons he'd been so attracted to the idea of marrying Deena was that she was so much at ease at them. His first wife hated formal parties. She was far more comfortable sitting around friends' kitchen tables.

A very buxom, blond woman with a German accent pounced on him. She obviously had no idea who he was, but began talking to him with great familiarity, snatching him up another drink when he finished his champagne and then tugging him out through large French doors onto a terrace, its flagstones limned by the frail moonlight.

"I want you to meet Albert-Philippe," she said. "He needs help in finding a country."

She confronted him with a very thin, almost femininely handsome young man with dark curly hair and light blue eyes. He seemed nervous, on the verge of anger.

"Albert-Philippe drives racing cars," said the German woman.

"Once I drove racing cars," he protested. "Now I can do nothing. I cannot stay in Europe. It's impossible, impossible. I don't know where to turn." He studied Moody carefully. "I am thinking of South America. But it is so boring. So lower class. Peasants everywhere. Indians. Disgusting."

Moody recognized no one else at this gathering, but oddly, he knew about this man. He'd seen his picture in *People* magazine, copies of which Deena kept in a rack by the toilet of their bathroom. The youth was less a racing driver than a Riviera beach bum. He'd made a pass at Monaco's Princess Stephanie, getting a richly deserved bum's rush, and later had hired on as paid companion to a notorious American-born Spanish countess-by-marriage, who'd been rendered a near invalid by her drug habits. She'd died shortly afterward, and more than a million dollars had turned up missing. According to the article, charges had been lodged against the young man in France. Moody began to feel very uneasy in his presence, in this house.

He mentioned the heiress's name. "You worked for her?"

"Worked?" said the youth, throwing up his hands. "I slaved for her. I got her up. I cleaned her up. I got her dressed. I made her eat. I put her to bed. I do this, day after day, and what is my reward? I am hounded out of my own country!"

"Whatever you took, Albert-Philippe," said the blond woman sweetly, "you earned it."

Moody backed away, into some prickly bushes. The youth stalked away, but the German woman moved closer, driving Moody farther into the bush.

"I have big bazooms," she said, smiling. "They intimidate some men. Like you, I see."

Leaves scratching his face, Moody pushed his way clear and fled inside. He found Lenore over by the fireplace, beneath a painting depicting what looked to be some hellish crime, or ritual execution.

"Are you having a wonderful time, Colonel?" She gave the last word a French pronunciation.

"I can't believe I'm in Washington."

"Ah! Here's the princess. You must meet the princess." She thrust him in front of a small, dark, sharp-nosed woman who eyed him disdainfully.

"Your Highness, may I present Colonel Moody. Colonel, darling, this is Marie-Claire of France."

The woman impatiently offered her hand. It occurred to Moody he was supposed to kiss it, but he'd never done that before. He shook it instead. "How do you do," she growled, then turned away from him, talking to Lenore in French.

There were refreshments on a sideboard, none of the offerings any kind of food Moody recognized. He made a small plate of what looked to be dessert and went to a couch, sitting down next to a very dignified-looking older woman, who introduced herself as Lady Sansome. She seemed to recognize him, and began a pleasant conversation about the changing Washington diplomatic scene. The buxom blonde had taken a seat on the other side of the room. Eyes glistening in the candlelight, she watched Moody as might a lioness pondering a nearby zebra.

"Who is that woman?" Moody whispered to the Englishwoman.

"Oh, that's Ilsa. Do you fancy her?"

"Do I what?"

"In English country houses, it's customary to slip upstairs before the coffee. It's rather late, but you ought to manage it."

"I don't, I don't fancy her."

"Brilliant." She yawned. "Well, then, do you fancy me?"

All of Moody's alarm bells went off. Excusing himself clumsily, he stood up. He wanted to rush out the door, but decided to make a last stab at getting Lenore out of there.

She was sitting now in a winged chair by the fireplace.

"I have to go," Moody said, leaning close. "Do you need a ride home?"

"Go? Dear boy." She got up, presumably to say good night, but once she was clear of the chair, she thrust Moody down into it and thumped herself down on his lap.

He grimaced. She had a bony bottom, and her awkward perch pained his thighs.

"Are you all right, Colonel darling?"

"No."

"Well, it's not as though I was sitting on your thingie, or am I?"

"I've got to go." He rose, nearly spilling her on the floor. "Good night. My regards to your husband."

He fled the house as he once might have a Vietcong ambush, but she came after him, calling out his name, keeping up with him all the way down the hill.

They stared at each other across his car. "Open the doors, dear boy. I want to go for a drive."

He hadn't gone half a mile down the narrow road when she asked him to pull over. He almost struck a tree.

"What a zoo," he said.

She made no reply. Instead, she crept over toward him, placing her knee carefully to avoid the phone console between their seats. She kissed him, her loosened hair falling over him, her lips tasting of champagne. He reached to her back, then slipped his hand down beneath her skirt and up again, pulling down the elastic of her panties. Her bottom didn't seem so bony now.

"Mmmmmmmmmmm," she said.

"You're really something, Mrs. Fairbrother."

"Yes, I am. Yes, I am."

She leaned back now, he thought to remove her dress, but instead she then scrunched down, opening the fly of his trousers.

"My," she said. "Your thingie's most impressive."

She caressed him. He closed his eyes, waiting.

"Would you like me to kiss you there?"

"Yes."

"Really?"

"Yes!"

She sat up. "Then promise me you'll give David Showers back his job."

"What?"

"His bloody job. Promise me you'll reinstate him. Then I'll kiss you wherever you like." Her wicked eyes were full of purpose. She touched him once again. "Come on, Colonel. Promise."

"Is that why you brought me here?"

"Horse country people are very loyal, Colonel. Didn't you know?"

"You and your goddamn Showers can go to hell!"

He snapped open his door, then sat feeling very foolish. He had nowhere to go. This was his car. Furiously, he zipped up his pants.

Lenore got out on her side, leaving the door open.

"I suppose you'd prefer to go home to your wife," she said, standing in the road. "She knows how to kiss you, doesn't she? I know that very well. I saw her in the Dandytown Inn kissing a man just where you wanted to be kissed, only it wasn't you, was it, Colonel darling?"

"What are you talking about?"

"Come by sometime and I'll tell you who it was—after David has his job back."

Restarting his car, he saw her skipping back up the road in the red glow of his taillights.

# Sixteen

pencer found he was enjoying himself. A newsman's most useful trait is not his intellect or writing ability but his curiosity, and Spencer's was flaming along on all burners. He was having such a good time that he even put aside booze for a while.

He kept diligently at his "research" for his horse country feature, pausing only to turn out a few party pieces and art exhibition reviews to satisfy his bureau chief that he was remaining productive. He returned to Dandytown, spending more time with the increasingly helpful prosecutor, Wayne Bensinger, who surprised him by handing over a copy of the inquest transcript.

It wasn't that useful. After going over all the statements and depositions taken by the sheriff the day after the murder, it seemed that the better part of Dandytown had been in the inn around the time of the homicides, and that, with all the milling about and socializing that night, a sizable number of people had absented themselves long enough to have paid a visit to the Clays' hotel room. The list included the Blochs, the Moodys, the Fairbrothers, Billy Bonning, Becky Gibbons Bonning, Alixe Percy, and even his cousin David.

All good newsmen possess another quality—the ability to acquire and keep contacts. In a long career, a journalist will traverse virtually every walk of American life, and gather friends and acquaintances all along the way—beat cops and scientists, society grandes dames and grubby politicians, movie stars and mafiosi.

Spencer's circle was wider than most, and included sports writers. After returning from Dandytown, he'd called a track writer he knew from his old paper in New York, a man who, with the exception of the *Chicago Tribune*'s Neil Milbert, was probably the best in his field.

The man had to go scrounging in his files, but he did manage to come up with a recent theft of a valuable bay stallion with two white stockings.

"It was an Irish horse. Worth a couple of million dollars. Some of us had expected to see him in the Derby."

"A colt?"

"A two-year-old. Bloodlines like a rare old wine."

"We had someone check in both England and Ireland, but they came up with zip," Spencer said.

"It didn't happen in England or Ireland. The horse was sold at a colt sale in the West of Ireland this spring. A Canadian bought him. Ted Ryan. He'd hardly gotten it home to British Columbia when someone lifted the horse from his barn. Thought it was a ransom job at first, but there hasn't been a peep. At least none we've heard about. The even-money bet is that the horse is dead. You can kill an animal like that pretty easy if you don't know what you're doing."

"Would anybody have a picture of this horse?"

"You can try the *Irish Times*. They run horse pictures the way the London papers run nudies. Or the *Vancouver Sun*."

Spencer made a note to do so. He then asked his friend about the racing outfit in New Jersey.

"Have I ever heard of them?" the man said. "Jack, you know how people complain about the way New Jersey smells? I think most of the stink comes from these guys."

"Have they ever been in trouble with the racing commission? The law? Anything?"

"Nothing that stuck, but, don't worry, their time will come. What's this all about?"

"I'm writing a story about horses, and as usual I don't know what I'm doing."

"You're writing a story about two-million-dollar Irish horses that got hijacked in Canada?"

"One of the horse people I talked to said they had seen such a horse and wondered where it came from."

"Saw it where?"

"I forgot."

"Yeah, right. What're you on to, Jack?"

"When I find out, you'll be the first to know."

It occurred to Spencer that might not be a bad idea. His track writer friend would be a lot more responsive to this particular subject than Sheriff Cooke had shown any indication of being.

Spencer did some checking in his own bureau's files on Bernard H. Bloch, financier, industrialist, real estate developer, and sportsman. Most of what he found was ridiculous—drooly in-awe-of-the-very-rich pieces of the sort that had been turned out by the ton about Donald Trump, John Kluge, and Henry Kravis. Unlike these estimable gentlemen, Bloch had had some brushes with the authorities, however. One of his chemical plants in Delaware had been shut down by the EPA for pollution control violations. He'd also been not a little smudged by the big savings and loan scandal in the 1980s, and, many years before that, had been tried for attempting to bribe a zoning official in Maryland. He'd been acquitted. The attorney who successfully defended him had been one of his business partners.

His name was Robert M. Moody, later governor of the state of Maryland. Bernard Bloch had been his campaign chairman.

Spencer's acquaintances also included a number of useful sources in the Pentagon and its attendant civilian defense-oriented think tanks. It was to the latter he now turned. The Defense Department had the best computers in the world, but the machines used by the Beltway Bandits, as the civilian consultants around Washington were known, were no slouches.

A friend with a big consulting firm in Arlington owed him a remembered favor—a story Spencer had held back on a big mistake the company had made on an Air Force project. Spencer could think of no better time to collect.

The man was happy to pay up. It was a story that could always be resurrected. He took Spencer to the most elaborate computer setup the company possessed and got quickly to work, first taking videotape footage of the photo of the mysterious scratches—magnifying and refining the image considerably. Then he fed the tape into his computer's disc memory, and projected the image on his monitor. Using his display generator, he was able to twist and contort the scratch lines in all manner of ways—causing them to turn dimensionally in the manner of a hologram, expanding them, compressing them, elongating them, superimposing one upon another.

"It's quite a tangle," he said. "What the hell is this?"

"They're scratches on the back of a dead man."

"I wish you hadn't told me."

"Do you see any pattern?"

"Too many patterns. Like a kid drawing the same thing over and over on the same piece of paper."

"A woman did it. She was dying at the time. Probably paralyzed. Drugs. I have a feeling she may have been trying to use the fellow's back for a blackboard, trying to say something."

"Fascinating." Spencer's friend fiddled with the computer's controls a moment more, with no discernible result.

"Don't give up," he said. "Let me try something."

Most of the scratches abruptly vanished from the screen.

"I've eliminated all but the deepest impressions. Now I'll extend all the lines in the directions they were following."

The screen abruptly filled with what looked like an overturned bowl of spaghetti.

"Terrific," said Spencer unhappily.

"Patience, Jack. Patience." He fiddled again. The computer moved in for a tight close-up. "Observe. I'll now eliminate the sections of the lines that extended beyond the original impressions."

There was another transformation.

"Good Lord," Spencer said.

"Science, Jack."

"Whatever. There, anyway, is the letter *B*."

"*B* it is. Now let me work on the rest of it."

The magic became harder to produce. Spencer's friend labored like someone programming a space mission, his fingers moving as gently as if a wrong move might detonate the screen.

Finally, wiping perspiration from his forehead, he sat back.

"Best I can do, old buddy. We've got a *B,* what may be an *e* or an *a* or an *o,* and what I think is a small *r*—though I can't be sure. The rest is indecipherable."

"It's more than I hoped for."

"I don't know what this is about, but none of this would be of any use in a court of law. It's all electronic speculation. It might give you some ideas, though."

"It has. Can you give me a printout of all this?"

The man pushed a button. "As we speak. And I can also record the whole process we went through on another videotape for you. Just don't let anyone know where it came from. My boss thinks I'm working on missile trajectories."

Alixe had tried all manner of entreaties to get Becky out of her cottage and off Showers' farm for a while, only to be rebuffed with sullen silences or temper tantrums. The girl did not want to stir from her redoubt against the outside world until Showers came home, though she had had little enough to say to him when he'd been hanging about the place before his national guard maneuvers.

She had been staying in bed, or near it, coming to the door in her robe or nightgown, her hair uncombed, her eyes reddened, as though from crying. At length, she stopped coming to the door. Alixe tried the telephone, but Becky never answered. She used it, though. Alixe heard her talking on it one morning when she'd crept up to a back window.

Perhaps the girl's problem was simply disappointment—dreams suddenly realized with Showers finally leaving the State Department, then just as abruptly dashed when he'd showed no inclination toward settling down to the life Becky had envisioned for him—for them both. All he had on his mind was the bay stallion, and righting the wrong the animal represented. Many in Dandytown thought of Showers as a softy, because of his reflexive kindness, but Alixe knew better. He was a hard man, as hard as she'd ever encountered—the sort of man who'd pursue what he'd set his mind to as resolutely as a barn-crazy horse galloping hell-bent for home without regard for whip or bit or obstacle. Alixe had been grievously in error in suggesting Becky as a wife for him. She was as ill suited for a man like that as she had been for Billy. Lenore wasn't much up to him, either. Lenore didn't like to keep weak men for long, but she could never abide a man she couldn't control.

As the days passed, and Becky seemed if anything to grow worse, Alixe thought of telephoning Showers down at Fort Hill, but rejected the idea. He wouldn't abandon his duty post unless there was a genuine emergency—the U.S. Army regulation kind. Even if she could persuade him that was the case, his return might not accomplish any good at all. What Becky probably needed was a big kick in the behind, and Showers was not that kind of hard man.

Alixe did telephone Becky's psychiatrist father, but he was no help whatsoever. In his wimpy, unhappy way, he proved as unyielding on a point of principle as Showers. Rebecca had run off at a legal age and of her own volition. He would assist her in any way he could, but only if she asked him. She would always be welcome, but he and his wife were not going to reach out for her, not anymore. He suggested that Alixe give her a sedative.

Becky probably had sedatives of assorted kinds enough.

In the end, it was hunger that drove Becky out. Alixe had noted the diminishing food supplies in Showers' larder. When milk, bread, spaghetti, and peanut butter were gone, Becky was up the next morning and into her Toyota, heading for town.

Alixe figured she had at least an hour to search the cottage. Banging and rummaging through cabinets and drawers, she found nothing. Then, sitting on Becky's disheveled bed, she gave some hard thought to her problem. If the girl was hiding anything, it was from Showers or Billy. There were some things a man would instinctively avoid.

Going back into the bathroom, Alixe reopened the cabinet beneath the washbasin, pulling out a large and nearly full box of sanitary napkins. It was quite dusty, and, as she suspected, not nearly full at all. Removing the wrapped packets on top, she found something altogether different from what she was looking for.

There was no cocaine, no pills, no pint bottles. There was a diary, which Alixe could not bring herself to look through, and a small stack of Polaroid photographs, which she could not resist examining. They were all of Becky, and she was naked in all of them—in two, posed rather obscenely. Alixe supposed they had been Billy's idea. His fondness for any kind of pornography was not a well-kept secret.

At the bottom of the box was a videotape cassette, bearing a piece of tape with the word VICKY on it. Alixe stood holding it a long moment, uncertain what to do. Like many people with the traditional views of her class, she considered television a vulgar, middle-class amusement, and had no TV set in her own house. Neither did Showers. Her stablehands had a set in their quarters, but no VCR.

Becky had one in her living room.

Though it couldn't be long before Becky returned, Alixe went to it. The controls were simple enough to figure out, and shortly the screen glowed with the image of Vicky Clay's naked back and behind, positioned above the face of another woman, reclining nude on a bed.

Alixe stared raptly, fascinated to see years of what had been mere gossip come to life in the flesh. As the VCR whirred on, Vicky reached some point of satisfaction and stiffened, arching her back. Relaxing slowly, she rolled over to the side, allowing the other woman to sit up. Alixe was stunned to see who it was.

It was not Becky, who entered the picture from the side, naked. She climbed upon the bed and sat there, the three women seemingly unaware of the camera, which might well have been positioned in some hiding place by the wretched Billy, who was fully capable of such a mean and devious trick.

Alixe moved closer to the screen, watching as Becky lay down, urging the third woman to make love to her. Somewhat reluctantly, she began to do so, but was interrupted by Vicky, who began to harangue Becky. Alixe heard her mention Showers' name, and saw Becky sit up again, angry. Alixe turned up the volume, but after a moment, hastily clicked off the set and ejected the cassette.

If she didn't hurry, she was going to be caught here by Becky, and then all hell truly would break loose. She had heard and seen enough. It was imperative that Showers see the tape, but she didn't dare just walk off with it, for Becky would surely notice its absence. After an agonizing minute or so of indecision, it occurred to her that Becky had probably viewed the tape several times and might not be much interested in doing so again—at least not soon.

There were a number of cassettes in disorderly stacks on the shelf beneath the VCR—from the look of them, mostly copies of rental movies. Alixe picked one at random, removed it from its box, and peeled off the hand-printed label, exchanging it for the one marked VICKY. Sticking the cassette with the bedroom scene in the belt of her breeches underneath her jacket, she put the disguised tape in the bottom of the sanitary napkin box, piling its other contents on top of it and returning the box to the place where she had found it.

Then she got out fast, gunning her pickup out of Showers' yard and onto the road. She had just turned into her own drive when Becky's Toyota came whizzing by.

Alixe braked. She had a lock box in her study and there were dozens of other places in her house where she might hide the tape, but after a barn fire and Billy's break-in to Becky's cottage, none of them seemed altogether safe. She looked at her watch. She had almost an hour before the bank in Dandytown closed. She kept several safe deposit boxes there. It would be the best place for the tape. She wanted no one else to see it but Showers, at least for the time being. If Becky did discover it missing, Alixe didn't want it anywhere the girl could lay hands on it.

Backing out of her drive, she headed for town, wondering how much food Becky had brought home with her.

Showers drove his National Guard Jeep at the head of the little convoy, the company first sergeant beside him. They had finished their maneuvers, their battalion losing the training exercise to an infantry outfit from Fort Bragg, but doing so honorably. His support unit had been in the rear, but had acquitted itself well, beating off raiders twice and surviving an ambush. As they'd been up against regular army troops, Showers felt rather proud.

They were returning from the sprawling, pine-forested bivouac area to a dispersal point in the fort's headquarters compound. After their borrowed equipment was returned and their blank ammunition and fuel accounted for, his company would be free to leave for home. He was looking forward to that. The soldiering had invigorated him, and he needed to get busy with all the things he had decided to do. The military maneuvers had been conducive to productive thought and had put him in a very decisive frame of mind.

He'd called his cousin Jack, who had informed him he was making progress and said he expected to make a lot more in the next few days. That he had discovered the probable owner of the bay was welcome news. That Vicky Clay had apparently scratched the first three letters of Bernie Bloch's name into her husband's back came as no shock to Showers, not after he'd looked at that dead groom's face.

He'd tried to reach Alixe, but she'd been out both times he'd called.

Pulling into the headquarters compound, he parked the Jeep and stood watching as his following three-quarter- and two-and-a-half-ton trucks formed up side by side for unloading. A young second lieutenant rushed up from one of the vehicles, but Showers gave his instructions to the first sergeant, a large, mellow-voiced black man named McKinley Williams, who, like Showers, had served in the regular army. He'd won the bronze star in Vietnam.

Dismissing him with a friendly salute, Showers turned to check in with his colonel, then halted in stunned surprise. In the front row of a nearby parking area reserved for civilian vehicles was the dented yellow Volkswagen convertible with California plates. Leaning against its door was May Moody, wearing jeans and a blue blouse.

She smiled in friendly fashion at his approach, as though the dreadful scene at his farm had never occurred. "So, you really are a captain."

"You never call," he said. "You just appear."

"Oh, I called," she said. "I got an earful of abuse from that girl on your farm. She told me your whereabouts were none of my bloody business and that I was the last person in the world you'd want to see."

"That's not true. I'm sorry she was rude to you."

"I've had worse from directors—not to speak of fellow actors. I called your office. Your former office, I was sorry to hear. They told me you were down here. It took forever to get through to the right military person, but I finally managed to learn that you'd be returning from the field this morning, so here I am. What's 'the field'?"

"Some farmland southeast of here. We defended it, and lost."

"Well, welcome home, soldier."

Their eyes took each other in for a moment. "I'm glad to see you," he said. "Very glad. I was going to call on you tomorrow."

She became more serious. "I want to help you, Mr. Showers."

"David."

"David. I've decided to be a party to your lawsuit. I want to help you any way I can. I'm not going to let Bernie Bloch and my father get away with what they've done to you."

He had left the Cherokee at his National Guard company's small compound near Dandytown, and had planned to ride back in one of the military vehicles, but she offered to drive him out in her Volkswagen, and, when he demurred, she insisted on it.

They stopped first at her apartment on Capitol Hill. She wanted to see the horse, and thought she'd stay the night at the Dandytown Inn.

He sat in his fatigues on the couch in her tiny living room while she went to pack a small bag. She left the door to her bedroom partially opened while she gathered her belongings, pausing afterward to brush her hair. Showers could see her moving shadow cast by reflected sunlight on the opposite wall, the dancing strokes of her arm and brush magnified in silhouette. It gave him an embarrassing feeling of intimacy, as though he were sitting next to her, sharing a private moment.

May went into her bathroom. Showers turned his attention to the books on her coffee table—Katharine Hepburn's autobiography, a volume of Shakespeare's plays, a compendium of famous Hollywood murders, and, surprisingly, Antoine de Saint-Exupéry's *Night Flight*—in French: *Vol de nuit*. Except for a few Dick Francis novels he noticed on a nearby bookshelf, there was no book that had to do with horses.

The bathroom door clicked open, and she stepped into the room, the scent of perfume accompanying her.

"Just about ready," she said. "You've been very patient."

"Not at all."

She returned to the bedroom. In silhouette on the wall, he watched her finish up her packing. They'd be together much of the day into the evening and likely the next day, but he wished he weren't taking her to Dandytown.

He glanced down at his olive-drab military duffel, set by the door. Before leaving Fort A. P. Hill, he'd signed himself out a box of pistol ammunition. He'd stopped to replace the blanks in his clip.

She rejoined him, carrying her bag.

"Okay." She gave him something more genuine than a movie star smile. "This time I may be able to enjoy myself."

They stopped for a late lunch at the Red Fox Inn in Middleburg. Conversation had been difficult in her noisy little open car while on the interstate, and when they had talked, it had been casually. As they ate their meal—salad and iced tea for both of them—they got down to serious business.

"Tell me everything," she said.

He collected himself. "I suspect—I believe very strongly—that the horse you bought was stolen from a man in Canada. His name's Ted Ryan. He's a very important racing figure up there and I think the bay is quite valuable. They gave the horse the papers of a very similar animal, one descended from a mare my father owned, and tried to pass him off as one and the same. The stolen bay had no registration number on its lip, so they were able to give him the other horse's tattoo. All very convincing."

"Who are 'they'?"

"I presume they're business associates of Mr. Bloch. In New Jersey. I'm informed he does a lot of business up there."

"But if the horse is so valuable, why did they put it up for auction?"

"It was a way of laundering the whole business. Bloch would pick him up at the sale, for such a small amount no one would pay any attention. The title would be legitimate. He'd be free to race him, syndicate him for stud, whatever. Bloch and his friends could have made an enormous amount of money."

"But that swine is already filthy rich. Why would he go through all that just to make a little more?"

"People like that always want more. Till the day they die. And he likes winning horse races. A sleeper like the bay would take a lot of people by surprise. I don't think Bloch really knows much about horseflesh, but his friends in New Jersey do."

"And I messed it all up for them."

"Not just you," he said. "The sheriff kept everyone at the inn, because of the murder. Bloch couldn't get to the auction. He asked your father to go in his place, but there was a crisis in Washington and he went to his duty post instead. I admire him for that, at least."

"You probably think my father's an evil, despicable man," she said, finishing her salad. "After he left my mother, that's what I thought, too. He can be a real bastard—ruthless, arrogant, as inconsiderate as they come. He lies a lot, too, and I hate lies. In L.A., everybody lies. That's one of the reasons I had to get away from there. But he's not evil. I've thought about that lately. He's just weak—weak in all the wrong places. Weak about women, weak about his friends, weak about his ego. He has a powerful lot of resentments—about all he had to overcome, about people like you."

"There's nothing special about people like me."

"If that were true, Captain Showers, you wouldn't be here at this moment, and neither would I." She sipped her iced tea. "I know this sounds like Richard Nixon or something, but my father is not a crook. I hate him for what he did to my mother, but to the best of my knowledge, he's never cheated anyone, not even when he was making all that money. I truly don't believe he knows that horse might have been stolen. I don't think he cares who gets the horse. It's just—please don't misunderstand—but, in a way, he reminds me of you. He feels deeply obligated to Bernie Bloch, about a lot of things. He stands by his friends. He's loyal to people who have been good to him—and there haven't been many. The newspapers like to call him an opportunist, but I think he really believes in that pompous old fool of a president." She paused. "He's ruined your career, hasn't he?"

"No, I did that all by myself. He tried to bribe me with a promotion, if I'd sell the horse back to Bloch. But he didn't fire me when I refused. I resigned because I had to. I broke department regulations."

"How?"

"It doesn't matter. I trusted someone I shouldn't have. He's trying to make it up to me, and doing a pretty good job of it. Thanks to him, we've learned a lot about this."

"Who is he?"

"My cousin. He's a newspaperman. His career wasn't helped by this, either."

"I'm sorry."

**262**

"He'll do all right. He's quite a survivor."

"My father grew up with different rules than you did, David. Maybe fewer rules than you, but a lot more than most of the men he's had to deal with in his life. Bernie Bloch doesn't have any rules. He just does what he wants." She lighted a cigarette. "You won't have to worry about my father for a while. He's out of the country now. My stepmother, thank God, is with him. She scares the hell out of me. She came over to my apartment a few days ago. She threatened me. About the horse."

"Threatened you in what way?"

"She didn't make that clear. The scariest thing is that I don't think my father knew anything about it. I think she did it for Bernie."

"Why?"

"Because he's worth more than a billion dollars." She exhaled a long stream of smoke from her cigarette, then tapped its ash. She had long, slender hands, very much like Lenore's. She wore no nail polish—Lenore never wore it, either. Something about Lenore's hands nibbled at his memory, but he couldn't quite catch hold of it.

"We'd better be going," she said. "Do you have the horse in Dandytown? You promised me I could see him."

He stared at the table, saying nothing.

"You don't trust me, do you?"

"I trust you, May. I'm just worried about taking you out there. This could get a little dangerous."

"I can take care of myself. You don't know the things I've been through."

"May, my cousin thinks that the dead girl, Vicky Clay, tried to scratch a message on her husband's back. A name. According to my cousin, the first three letters appear to be *B-e-r*."

"As in Bernie. God."

"He thinks they were both murdered. And there's something else. Someone burned down one of Alixe's barns and ran her horses off. We're sure they were after the bay. A man was killed, May. One of her grooms."

"Have you gone to the police?"

"The police is Sheriff Cooke. And we don't have proof of anything. The insurance company ruled the fire an accident. All we have is enough evidence to show that the horse is a fraud. That's why I want to press a civil suit. Those New Jersey people will have to testify. My cousin's called the man in Canada. He wants to see some pictures. If he's satisfied it's the horse, he'll come right down. We can clear everything up."

"I said I'd help you."

"I'd like you to sign some papers. Then I think you should go back home, where you'll be safe."

"I'm all alone there." She reached and took his hand. "And—please don't think I'm coming on to you, Captain Showers—but I feel a hell of a lot safer with you."

They stopped to pick up his Cherokee where he had left it at his National Guard company's assembly point, then, with May following in her Volkswagen, went on to the farm. Becky's Toyota was parked by the cottage, but he was of no mind to deal with her now. That would have to wait until May had returned to Washington.

They went into his house, proceeding directly to his study. She read over the papers, then signed them, smiling as she set down the pen.

"There," she said. "Now let's go see the stallion. Are you going to wear that uniform? Show off your captain's bars?"

"No."

"I'll wait in the car."

Hurrying upstairs, he changed into khakis, loafers, a white button-down shirt, and his old blue blazer. He loaded two more clips for his automatic with ammunition, slipped them into the side pockets of his jacket, then put the pistol in his belt at his back. He had just fetched his camera from his study when his phone rang.

It was Alixe. She was in the bar of the Dandytown Inn.

"My stable manager said he saw a green Cherokee drive by a few minutes ago, so I guessed it was you coming back from the wars."

"I'm about to leave again. I'm going up to Charles Town."

"I need to talk to you, David. I went through the cottage. I found a videotape."

She paused.

"I know about the tape," he said quietly.

"Do you know what's on it?"

"I watched a little of it."

"Well, I watched a lot. The Dandytown Chamber of Commerce wouldn't like it. We have to talk about this. I'll be over as soon as I can."

"I can't, Alixe. I have somebody with me."

"Lenore?"

"No, not Lenore. It's May Moody. She's helping us with the lawsuit. I need to take some pictures of the bay. It's the first thing we should have done."

"You'll be back tonight?"

He hesitated. "Yes, I should think so."

"Call me from up there when you're done. I'll be at home, waiting."

"I will. If you hear from my cousin, tell him I need to talk to him."

He heard shouting outside. Becky in full temper was unmistakable.

"I have to go, Alixe. Becky's out in the yard. I think she's screaming at May."

"I'll be right over, as soon as I call Selma and tell her you're coming. Don't take Becky with you."

"There's not much chance of that. See you soon."

He hurried out the door, fearing that May Moody had driven off, but she was still in her car. Becky was standing by the door, holding a riding crop.

"Leave her alone, Becky! Go back in the house."

The girl's face was mottled. She seemed on the edge of violence.

"She says she's going off with you, David!"

"That's right," Showers said. "I'll be back tonight."

"But you just got home!"

May started the car.

"I'll be back tonight," he repeated.

Becky thrust herself against his chest, clinging to him. Her hair smelled as though it had been long unwashed. "Please, David. Stay! Please!"

He took her shoulders, and set her back. "Calm down, for God's sake. Everything's all right. We're just going up to look at the horse. I'll be back tonight."

She began crying hysterically. He looked at her eyes, wondering what else Alixe might have found.

May put the Volkswagen in reverse, spinning backward in a half circle until the passenger side was facing him. She opened the door.

"I won't be long," he said, separating himself from Becky. "Alixe is coming over. Please, calm down."

May started moving the car as soon as he got into the seat, not waiting for him to shut the door. Becky began shouting obscenities, then threw the crop. It hit May on the back of the head.

"Damn!" she said, and ground the gearshift into second, speeding away. Showers looked back. Becky was standing with legs apart, her fists clenched at her side.

As they wound on down the road, Showers turned to examine

**265**

May's head, probing gently through the rich, dark hair. The crop had fallen into the rear seat.

"You've a small bump," he said. "Does it hurt?"

"Of course it hurts. Is she like that all the time?"

"No. It's recent. We don't know what it's about."

"Well, I have a pretty good idea."

He directed her to a turning. Soon they were on the Berryville Road.

Selma was waiting for them, her dusky face as impassive as before, though Showers sensed she was glad he had come.

He worked quickly—a close-up of the stallion's head, a full-length frontal view, a three-quarter shot. He had Selma curl back the upper lip for a picture that clearly showed the tattooed registration number.

"Give me the camera, Captain," Selma said. "I'll get the two of you."

Showers and May went to the horse's side. She put her arm around his waist. He did the same. He reminded himself that movie stars posed for pictures with people like this all the time.

May turned back to the horse, stroking his neck. "I'd forgotten what a beauty he is. I almost wish I'd kept him."

"There were times when I've wished that, too," he said.

Selma took the lead in hand, and started walking the bay away.

"Take good care, Selma."

"I won't let harm come to a hair of his tail," she said, over her shoulder.

"I don't mean him. I mean you. Would you like me to stay up here with you?"

"Don't you worry, Captain Showers. I'll be fine. You learn a few things, growin' up in West Virginia."

May decided she didn't want to spend the night in Dandytown, even—perhaps especially—in the Dandytown Inn. She was in no mood for a long drive back to Washington, either. After an awkward moment, an idea occurred to him.

"There's a place in Shepherdstown, just up the Potomac from Harper's Ferry."

"The Bavarian Inn."

"You know it?"

"When I was a little girl, we lived in Cumberland. I know all the river towns. We'd stop for dinner sometimes at the Bavarian Inn, on

*266*

the way back from Annapolis, when my father was in the legislature. I used to love the potato pancakes."

"I'll buy you all the potato pancakes you can eat."

She patted her very flat stomach, and grinned. "That won't be very many."

As it turned out, she ate everything on her plate, and had German chocolate cake for dessert.

"I won't do this again for a year," she said. "I'm very addictive. Start me on anything, and I want all I can get. It got me in a lot of trouble, a few years ago."

The waiter poured more coffee. May lighted a cigarette, waiting for him to leave.

"I'm an alcoholic, David," she said, exhaling. "Does that bother you?"

"Half the people I know are. My father was. My cousin is, I think. He's trying to do something about it, but . . . well, it must be hard."

"I did something about it. I went to one of those places. It was damn hard. They had me scrubbing floors, like my mother had to do, when she was young. I never, ever want to go through that again. It was like being a slave."

She smoked for a moment. He sat, watching the tiny changes in her expression. She reminded him of an ever changing painting. Every few minutes, a new and different portrait.

"I was also a drug user," she said, her voice a little leaden. "All the Malibu fun stuff—cocaine, hash, uppers, downers. Anything my friends were into was great with me."

Her eyes turned full upon him. She waited for his disapproval. He merely waited.

"I did something about that, too," she said. "Much too late. I don't think there was a director or a producer I didn't tell to fuck off." She looked away. "Sorry. I also used to swear a lot. I got fired from a couple of pictures. I had trouble getting work. I had to beg for my last role, and it was in a dog of a picture that I don't think played ten theaters."

"I'd love to see all of your films."

"No you wouldn't. That's why this play at the Shakespeare Theatre is so important to me. That's why I took the risk of coming to Washington—my father's city. The chance to work with Michael Kahn. He runs the theater. He's the greatest teacher Juilliard ever had. If I can make a success of this . . . It's my best hope of getting back to where I was. Not to what I was. But where."

"Do you mean Los Angeles?"

"L.A. New York." She shrugged. "Back."

"When does your play close?"

"In October. You'll have to come see me in it."

"I'd like that."

She stubbed out her cigarette, and reached for her purse. He quickly slapped a credit card of his own down on the table.

"David, you've just lost your job."

"I'll worry about that later. We have to get you a room."

"Are you going to go back home?"

"I thought I would. I'll be back in the morning."

"Please stay with me." She colored. "I mean, in a separate room. Could you?"

It would be cowardly of him, staying up here, but he didn't want to face Becky. Not that night. Alixe wanted to talk to him. He'd call her. "Yes. Certainly."

She lingered in her chair after he had signed the check.

"I've a favor to ask of you," she said. "Tomorrow, can we go riding?"

"Sure."

"Could I ride the bay? Just once?"

He frowned. "I don't want to take him off Selma's little farm."

"That doesn't matter. I'll just ride him around the farm."


After they checked in, he walked her to her room. She unlocked the door, pushing it open, then turned to face him.

"I'll be just down the hall," he said.

She lifted her face, stepping close. He didn't know if she was saying good night, or if this was an invitation for more. He didn't know what she expected of him, what he expected of himself.

He kissed her. That much he knew they both wanted. She held him tightly, breasts pushing against him, the flesh of her back warm against his hand through the thin material of her blouse. He felt himself swaying. He knew he had only to touch her, somewhere intimate. But he was unsure. Perhaps she would resent it. They had only just met, really. She might not want that at all. It might just ruin everything. Lenore's mocking face came unwanted to his mind.

May stepped back, looking at him, curious, even a little amused.

"Where are you going, Captain?"

He pulled her to him again, kissing her with a parting of the lips, then holding her tightly, her dark hair against his cheek.

"I used to be married," he said. "To a woman from here. She's still here. We've been divorced for years, but sometimes it seems we're still married."

May stepped back, looking up into his eyes.

"I was married once, too. For a little while. I hardly remember him. That's one of the things I went through. Do you still love her—at all?"

"Sometimes I try to pretend that I do, but it doesn't work."

"Marriage isn't love, Captain. Love comes first."

She took his hands in hers and led him across the threshold.

He'd call Alixe in the morning.


The phone rang—a harsh, disturbing summons in the darkness. He had no idea of the time. They'd been sleeping deeply.

He answered, though it was May's room—not caring who discovered that fact.

"Captain Showers, it's Selma. We got big trouble. Billy Bonning's got the horse. I'm with him. Up in Pennsylvania. Near Chambersburg." She spoke in a monotone, her voice very leaden.

"What? Billy Bonning?"

"He showed up with a friend. They had guns. They must have followed that little yellow VW of yours. He didn't give me much chance to do anythin', Captain. I figured I'd live a little longer if I pretended to help him—for money. He gave me a hundred fucking bucks, the dumb bastard."

"Where is he? Where are you?"

"He's in a motel up Interstate 81. He and his buddy. I had to do them both, you know? Make 'em happy. They're sleeping. I seen to that. Whacked 'em both a good couple times in the head with the butt of a gun. I got their guns. And Billy's rig. And the horse. I'm in a gas station."

"Is the horse all right?"

"Yeah, he's okay. Not very happy. But he's okay. You better get up here, Captain. I don't know what to do."

"I'll be right there. You said a gas station?"

"At the Marion exit. I got the rig pulled around in back, but you can still see it from the road. A Chevy Blazer, with a green horse trailer."

Whatever Alixe was paying her, she was certainly earning it.

"Captain?"

He thought of calling the Pennsylvania State Police, but didn't know what that might bring on. Selma might have killed Bonning with her "couple of whacks."

"I'll be right there, Selma. If anyone shows up, just get out of there. Just run."

"Don't waste no time, Captain."

Showers wanted to avoid waking May, but she was sitting up, turning on a lamp, as he hung up the phone.

"I heard some of that," she said. "What's wrong?"

"I told you about Billy Bonning?"

"Yes?"

"He took the bay. At gunpoint. Selma got it back from him but I have to get up there and help her."

"Where is she?"

"Not far. Just across the Pennsylvania line. You stay here."

She bolted out of bed and ran to her bag, pulling on her clothes.

"May, I said stay here."

"It's my car. I'm going with you."

"May!"

"I got you into this, David. I'm going with you."

The traffic on the interstate at this predawn hour was mostly trailer trucks, bound for everywhere, whining and thumping over the pavement, red and yellow top lights passing into the night. Showers followed one off the exit and into the service station, gliding past it as the driver turned off its chugging engine, the truck's air brakes releasing pressure with a sigh.

Selma was standing by a soft-drink machine, a dark, slender figure in the garish light. Showers pulled the Volkswagen up next to her and got out.

"You're all right, Selma?"

"Tired. Scared. But, yeah, all right."

He gave her a hug. Her hard little body didn't yield.

"You're a hell of a girl."

"Save that shit, Captain. We gotta get out of here."

Showers followed her to the horse trailer, lifting the lock bar at the back. The stallion moved nervously as he opened the door, lunging back and hitting Showers with his haunch, knocking him back. He quickly shut the door again, heaving himself against it.

"We gotta get the rig off the road," Selma said. "I didn't know where to go."

May was standing uncertainly by. Two trailer trucks passed, and then another from the opposite direction. Two youths were in the

270

cashier's booth of the service station, talking and laughing, sneaking leering looks at the two women.

"I'll think of a place," Showers said. "I want you and May to go back to Shepherdstown. Call Alixe. Have her meet you there. Have her bring a trailer."

"You going to take the horse down there, Captain? They'll be looking for this rig up and down eighty-one. I didn't whack Billy that hard. Wished I did."

"I'll head west into the mountains. Find some back road to hide in for the rest of the night. I'll call you in Shepherdstown in the morning, and we'll arrange a safe place to meet. I'm going to take care of this horse if I end up having to lock him in the National Guard armory."

A passenger car came whizzing along the highway, headlights on bright, the glare flaring on the pavement. It slowed as it went by the service station, then resumed its high speed.

"You two get going. I'll call you tomorrow."

"You got a gun, Captain?"

"Yes. Why?"

"Then I'll keep this one." She opened her jacket, revealing a pistol stuck in her belt. "There's another one in the Blazer."

"You just get on to Shepherdstown. Stay in May's room and don't budge until I call you or Alixe shows up."

"Take care of yourself, Captain."

He got behind the wheel of the Blazer, hesitating before turning on the engine. He opened the glove compartment. Beneath a pint bottle of cheap whiskey, an opened cigarette pack, and a small tin of snuff, he found some soiled and tattered highway maps. On top was one for Virginia/West Virginia, but it also showed the western panhandle of Maryland, and a sliver of Pennsylvania just above the Mason-Dixon Line.

As he unfolded it fully, he heard the Volkswagen driving away. The women would be safe in the Bavarian Inn within an hour. Leaning forward, he studied the tiny lines of road in the dim glow of the overhead light. Except for his postings abroad, he had lived very near here all of his life, but knew little about this outlying territory. It was beyond the horse country. It was where a different kind of people lived.

He had some friends in the Shenandoah Valley, including one who had a farm near New Market along the western edge of the valley. But the only direct route there was Interstate 81.

Peering more closely, he noted some secondary roads that would take him through a gap by Dickey's Mountain and thence to Hancock, Maryland, on the Potomac. From there, he could go through Berkeley Springs, in West Virginia, and follow 522 down into Virginia. The sun would be well up by the time he got to New Market, but he could stick to the back country all the way.

He wished he knew how badly Billy Bonning had been injured, whether he was conscious and moving about—whether he had just the one man at his disposal, or many such friends.

It angered him that he should be so frightened, that he should feel such a fugitive less than a hundred miles from his family's two-century-old home. Common sense dictated a call to the police, but it seemed absurd to imagine telling this horribly complicated story to a bored sergeant in some state police barracks. The only crime he had evidence of in his possession was their theft of Billy's rig. What if Bonning had gone to the police—playing it straight, pressing charges of assault and robbery?

The door on the passenger side swung open. Showers looked up, startled.

"Let's go, David," May said.

"You're supposed to be with Selma!"

"It's better I go with you. I used to live in Cumberland, remember? I know this country. There's a place where I used to ride when I was a little girl, north of Highway Forty. It was there a few years ago. They have a big barn. If the owner's still alive, he'll remember me. I'll show you how to get there."

"May, if something were to happen to you . . ."

"If you don't get us out of here, David, something may happen to us both."

He turned on the engine. Driving slowly, mindful of the unhappy horse, he turned onto the Marion road, heading west.

In Bernie Bloch's penthouse apartment in Baltimore, the phone rang nine times. After the tenth time, he answered it. There had been one other call late on this night, and it had brought good news. He didn't think this one would bring good news. He was right.

"I was going to call you," Bernie said. "In the morning. We got the horse back."

"We already know about that."

"How in the hell could you? We just got it back a few hours ago. That dumb son of a bitch Showers led us right to it."

Sherrie was snoring loudly. Bloch pushed her over onto her face.

"We know about it. The hayhead you have working for you is

also working for us. As of tonight. He called us when he got the horse, after he called you. He just called us again, only now he doesn't have the horse anymore. Some fucking broad rolled him in a motel and took off with it."

"Shit," said Bloch. "Are you serious?"

"Yeah. Real serious. Listen up, Bernie. We're gonna take over now. The whole deal. We want you to stay out of it now before you fuck everything up for good."

"What do you mean?"

"We don't want you to go near no horses. Not your horses, not nobody's horses. You just stay there in Baltimore with wifey and tend to business, okay? We'll take care of things. Every fucking thing."

"Sure. Whatever you say."

"This prick Showers. The broad is probably taking the horse back to him. He's not at his farm in Virginia. You got any bright ideas where he might be?"

"No. I hardly know the guy."

"He was with that movie actress. The one who screwed up our deal."

"May Moody."

"Right. May Moody. He must have a shack job going. Does she have some place out there he might head to? Some nice little love nest?"

"I don't think so, but you'd better not mess with her."

"What are you telling me, Bernie?"

"You know who her father is. If anything happens to her . . . He's my friend."

"We're your friends, Bernie."

"Look—"

"We've been looking. But we don't like what we see. She turns up again, you let us know real fucking quick."

"Wait a minute. The Moodys used to live in Cumberland—Cumberland, Maryland. That's where I met her old man. We got into a deal out there. I don't know. There's a chance they went that way."

"We'll take a look. You just lay low."

"Don't worry."

"I worry. This is costin' us, Bernie. We expect to get paid for our trouble. The more trouble, the more we expect."

"Like I said, anything."

"You're a fucking chump, Bernie. I don't know how you ever got to play with the big boys."

He hung up.

Bloch turned on the light. Sherrie was sitting up, squinting at him, her face a wreck—as usual.

"What's wrong, Bernie?"

"He called me a chump," he said sadly. He was seated on the edge of the bed, looking down at his feet. "Nobody's ever called me a chump!"

"Who? What's happened?"

"Nothing. A little business deal gone wrong, that's all."

She squinted at the clock. "At five in the morning?"

"Never mind, Sherrie. Go back to sleep."

"Are you in trouble again? Are the tax people on to you?"

Bloch got up and went into the bathroom, seating himself with a grunt. He'd take his time, hoping she'd be asleep again by the time he came out.

Deena couldn't understand why he was still married to Sherrie. Deena was that dumb. If Sherrie got mad enough—and people tended to get a little pissed off in divorce proceedings—she could have him in jail in five minutes.

"I'm not sure you ought to come with me, young lady," Alixe said.

"David's in trouble," said Becky. "I'm coming."

Selma had called from a pay phone in Pennsylvania, telling Alixe what had happened, and urging her to meet her at the Bavarian Inn in Shepherdstown as soon as possible, and to bring a horse trailer, as Showers would need to change rigs. Alixe had pressed her for more details, but Selma had only muttered something about Billy Bonning and guns.

Alixe was lingering just long enough for a quick cup of coffee in Showers' kitchen. The first rays of sunshine were coming through the window, crimson in the hazy sky. It was going to be hot.

"Yes, he's in trouble, but he has that actress with him, and he sure as hell doesn't need you coming up there and throwing another tantrum."

"I'm over that, Alixe. I told you."

"And what occasioned this miracle?"

"I've been thinking a lot, thinking all night sometimes. I guess I've decided to give up."

"Give up?"

"Lenore is one thing, but I can't compete with a movie star."

"David's not star struck, Becky."

"He spent the night with her, didn't he?"

"See? I don't think you should come."

"I've got to, Alixe. I'm his friend. I'm the one who got him mixed up in this. I want to help. I've got to."

"You'll leave that woman alone?"

Becky stared into her cup. "Yes."

"I don't know." Alixe poured some whiskey into her coffee. She had a murderous hangover. Selma's call had come like a summons from hell.

"I not only think I should come," Becky said, sounding very grown-up now. "I think I should drive. Don't get mad, but I don't think you're in shape to handle a trailer rig right now."

"You're right, damn it all," Alixe said. "Very well. You drive."

"We'll take David's Jeep. That'll be fastest."

The whiskey had cooled Alixe's coffee quickly. She gulped the tepid mixture down and put the cup in the sink, then picked up the large revolver she'd set on the table.

"You're sure that's necessary?"

"I hope not, but you know what Billy Bonning's like better than any of us."

They crossed the yard and got into the Jeep. Showers kept his trailer on the other side of the barn.

Becky turned the key.

The explosive charge was placed just to the left of the drive shaft, and drove it up through the floorboards when it went off, venting the full force of the blast on the driver's side. Becky, held by her seat belt, died from the snap of her neck as her head was flung backward, her arms twisting grotesquely. Alixe, minus her left foot, was hurled out the right side door.

For a few seconds afterward, there was only oily smoke and echoes, and the pings and clatter of falling metal debris. Then flames rolled back from the engine into the passenger compartment, spreading over fabric, and then flesh. With a whump, the fuel tank erupted, and the Jeep was rendered a skeleton, starkly outlined within a storm of flame.

A groom came running out of the barn, then stood helpless and dumbfounded, shaking his head. He heard Alixe, and hurried over to her. She was shouting David Showers' name.

# Seventeen

T he bedrooms are small," the real estate agent said. She was middle aged, with dyed red hair and far too much makeup. She reminded Napier of a female impersonator. "But there are four. You said you wanted this just for yourself?"

"Yes. But I expect to have lots of houseguests. There are two baths?"

"And the powder room downstairs. But it's quite a bargain. Two thousand for six weeks. You understand, now. You'll have to be out by Labor Day."

"Yes, yes. I've been living in hotels. This will be much better. Perfect."

It hadn't been clear from the newspapers just when Moody would be returning from the Orient, but even if it was soon, Napier was sure the man wouldn't linger long in Washington. No one did in August. He'd be off to his place on the Maryland shore or some vacation spot like that. Napier had himself thought of going to Rehoboth Beach on the Delaware coast, but this place would do just as well. This marvelously charming townhouse was in Georgetown, not far from Wisconsin Avenue. There were all sorts of lovely bars within a few minutes' walk. None of them were places a man like Moody would ever drop in.

"We can sign the lease at my office. When do you want to move in, tomorrow?"

"Tonight."

She glanced around. The furniture was quite dusty.

"I don't see why not. They've been trying to rent this place all summer."

"Let me take one more look around."

"Are you having second thoughts?"

"Oh no. Quite the contrary."

He was already making plans. He'd have a few friends over that night and then, in a few days, a big party. Endless parties. No one at the National Committee had questioned his checks. He'd damned well earned the money. He could have gotten in some very big trouble if the business with the phony memo had gone wrong. As the politicians would say, he'd carried water.

If they did cut him off—and he knew this happy situation couldn't last forever—there were other ways to make money, especially with a nice house like this.

He led the woman downstairs, murmuring approval of the paintings. The living room was small, and the formal dining room even smaller, crowded with furniture, but he could move a lot of it out of the way. The sideboard would make a perfect bar.

"Lovely," he said. "I can't wait to move in. Is there anything more you need from me—I mean aside from a check and my signature on the lease?"

"No. You certainly don't need any more references. The White House social secretary is quite good enough for us. You're sure he won't mind my calling on a Sunday?"

"Oh no. He won't mind at all."

Jack Spencer had put in a hard-working week on good behavior, and decided he owed himself a little Saturday night binge, starting at the Jockey Club in the Ritz Carlton Hotel and ending up in some wood-paneled yuppie joint on Capitol Hill. There'd been a girl—a tall, skinny congressional staffer who'd mistaken him for someone important—but she'd bored him and he'd gone back to his whiskey. He'd forgotten how he'd gotten home, except that he'd started out walking.

Sunday morning he devoted to sleep, and the early afternoon to curing his hangover. A little after two o'clock, his phone rang. It was his computer analyst friend from the defense think tank.

"I'm down at the office, Jack. Something about this thing has been chewing at me, and I think I've figured out what it is. I've been messing with it for a couple of hours—nobody here to bother me."

"Something's wrong?" Spencer took a healthy sip of his breakfast vodka and Coca-Cola.

"I ran some refinements, and got a clearer image of my line projections. I don't think the third letter's an *r* or an *n*. I think it's more likely a *c*. I also wonder if there might be two sets of impressions—of scratches."

"What the hell are you talking about?"

"There seems to be two patterns, one superimposed over the other. One pattern of scratches is very light. The other scratches are quite deep. I'm not sure what it means, yet. Anyway, that third letter is definitely a *c*. B-E-C. You ought to come down and take a look."

"I'm in no shape to stare at some goddamn computer screen. I'm having trouble looking at my wall."

The man was giving up part of his Sunday for this. Spencer owed him.

"Okay. Give me time to shave. It'll take longer today."

The farm near Cumberland May had mentioned was still there, just as she had remembered, but there was a large yellow bulldozer resting at a tilted angle on the periphery of a defaced pasture next to the barn. A contractor's sign had been planted in the lawn by the main driveway. May went up to the house and found it darkened and locked. When no one answered repeated ringings of the doorbell, she went to a window and peered inside. Except for some cardboard boxes, the room was empty.

May returned to the Blazer and shrugged sadly. On the other side of the road the frames of a dozen or so small houses were standing in various stages of completion.

"Developments," Showers said. "Even out here."

"I thought the recession had put a stop to that."

"It never stops."

She climbed into the seat. "So now what?" she said, lighting a cigarette. She placed her hand on top of his.

"I'll try calling Selma and Alixe again from Cumberland. Maybe they've reached the inn by now."

"And if they haven't?"

"I know a man with a farm down in the Shenandoah Valley. He's a friend."

The little city's downtown was already bustling with traffic. They pulled up in a huge gravel parking lot near the old railroad depot, which had been converted into a museum. It was closed, but there was a public phone outside.

The call to the Bavarian Inn took most of his change, though the distance was not all that far. The clerk at the front desk said no one had seen any such girl as Selma and that, no, he hadn't noticed a yellow Volkswagen convertible in the parking lot. The long distance operator came back on, asking for more change. Showers hung up.

He called his farm in Virginia collect, but there was no answer. Calls placed to Becky's cottage and Alixe's house produced the same result. His Shenandoah friend was away, but his wife, though awakened from her sleep, seemed glad to hear from him, and urged him to come. He recalled she had flirted with him a little during a weekend he'd once spent there. He had known her husband for many years.

They stopped at a 7-Eleven to get some doughnuts and coffee, as well as toothbrushes and a small bag of plastic, throwaway razors. Gassing up at a service station on the edge of town, they washed up a little in the grubby restrooms. The bay was hungry, but there was nothing they could do about that. They gave him water, refilling a plastic bucket. He was very unhappy.

Showers had asked the store clerk for several dollars in change, and he made his calls again. His own line was busy this time, and remained so in repeated attempts. The other numbers just rang and rang. He tried his cousin in Washington. No answer.

He climbed inside the Blazer, starting the engine. "If we stick to West Virginia roads, we ought to be all right. We'll have to take a main highway back over the mountains to get into the Shenandoah. There aren't many crossings."

"Maybe we should stay in West Virginia."

"What do you mean?"

"I have kinfolk down there. Some related to my mother, some to my father. Some to both." She smiled, but her weariness showed markedly.

"We'll be safe with my friend."

The mountains ran in long, lumpy ridges—northeast to south-west. The valley between them was narrow and crooked. There were many farms. May slept, her head against his shoulder. Fatigue began to weigh on him as well. Even with the windstream from the open windows, the heat was oppressive. The back of his shirt was soaked with sweat. He feared for the horse in the back.

Because of the bay, he drove well under the speed limit, to keep the swaying to a minimum going around the constant curves. A number of vehicles came up behind them, crowding close and then swinging out wide to pass, usually in dangerous places.

A pickup truck was now approaching, very fast. Another car behind it. Showers tried increasing his speed a little, but when the road straightened for a short stretch, the center line breaking into dashes, he slowed to let the truck get by. It glided forward, filling his side mirror, then pulled abreast. Something was sticking out of its window on the passenger side. A rifle barrel. Above it a hateful face. Blond hair.

Showers pressed the accelerator to the floor. The engine coughed, then caught again. He shifted down into third. With the motor roaring at full throttle, they began to pull away, the trailer swaying wildly behind them.

May sat up, startled. "What is it?"

"I can't believe it!" he said. "It's that goddamned Bonning."

"You're sure?"

"Yes. He's got a rifle."

She lunged for the glove compartment, where she had put the other pistol.

"There's a car behind him," Showers said. "He won't try anything."

She leaned out her window, so far he feared she might tumble out.

"It's a Mercedes. It's right behind him."

There was the sound of a backfire. But it wasn't that. It had to be a rifle shot. When they had passed through the town of Romney, West Virginia, many miles before, there'd been a narrow blacktop county road, leading south. He should have taken it. Instead, he'd decided to stay on route 220, to make better time. He'd been terribly stupid, and both of them were going to pay for it.

May pulled herself back inside. "What can we do?"

"Keep going. Make it to the next town. Find some police. Someone."

He saw the pickup beginning another run up alongside them. He twisted the wheel back and forth, causing the trailer to swing out to the side. The bay must be frantic.

"You're going to get us killed," May said.

He was afraid he'd made that inevitable.

Still holding the pistol, she clambered over into the rear seat, rolling down the back window on the driver's side.

"Let him come up next time!" she shouted.

"Are you going to shoot?"

"Yes!"

"Do you know how?"

"Yes!"

"Don't kill him."

"Why the hell not?"

The road was following the course of a small stream, the curves frequent. He was driving right at the edge of control.

There were two more shots. Showers prayed Bonning wasn't firing into the trailer. There was another shot, the bullet smacking into a front fender. Then the driver of the pickup gunned it into top speed.

"He's coming!" Showers shouted.

May held the pistol with both hands, aiming the barrel slightly down. He was overwhelmed by her. Lenore would be down on the floor, cowering, where May should be right now.

He'd put his army automatic under the seat, but there was no way of reaching it now without slowing.

Showers caught a glimpse of the pickup's dark fender in the corner of his eye. Then May fired; the noise, just behind his ears, nearly deafened him. She fired two times more, aiming at the pickup's right front wheel. Showers saw sparks, and then the hubcap spun off.

Another shot. There was a puff of dust and a loud bang. The tire exploded in tatters, and the pickup swerved violently, its side smashing against the back of the Blazer. The driver over-corrected, and suddenly the pickup went into a spin, sliding backward off the road. Showers saw a fencepost flying into the air. He fought to keep the Blazer under control.

In the side mirror, he saw the Mercedes skid around the pickup, sway back and forth a moment, then come on straight and true. It was very fast.

They flew over a small rise, then into a right-hand curve. At its end, the road switched to the left. Ahead was a narrow bridge. Just beyond it, a dirt side road cut off to the right. It was a turn he would have wanted to make from a near stop.

Showers had driven army Jeeps and Hummers at speed over open country enough to know the feel of what he was attempting. As they thumped over the rattling bridge, he hit the brakes sharply once, making the trailer shift out to the side, letting the skid make the turn for him. As soon as the front wheels hit the bumpy surface of the dirt road, he jerked the wheel to the left to get out of the skid, then straightened and gunned the engine, regaining stability. As they roared toward a sudden curve, he pulled on the Blazer's four-wheel drive.

There was a scraping sound, but the gears caught, the tires digging. The Mercedes was at a disadvantage now. He saw it bouncing wildly through his dust trail. The road began to climb. It hadn't been graded recently, and there were large potholes everywhere ahead, shallow gullies running among them, cutting across the rocky, dusty surface.

He was running between thirty and forty miles an hour over this roughness, bouncing crazily, but pulling ahead. At this rate, the Mercedes might break an axle, but the trouble was that Showers didn't know where the road went. It might just abruptly end in some hollow, or at a cliff.

The Blazer bounded from a pothole, skittering left and bouncing again. He saw May hit her head on the door frame. Through the dust cloud behind him, he also saw a glint of sunlight on metal. The Mercedes' driver was very good. Another gunshot sounded, but it went wild.

The road ahead seemed to disappear, but it was just another turning—a sharp switchback to the right. The trailer almost toppled over as Showers churned around it, but righted itself with the pull of his forward motion. The road led upward now in a long, straight incline. He got the Blazer up to near fifty before he saw the next curve ahead.

Something had happened to the Mercedes on the switchback. The cloud of following dust remained empty all the way up to the approaching turn. It was another sharp one, to the left, worse than the first. Showers jammed the Blazer back into second. It lurched, careening sideways uncontrollably. The steering wheel had no effect. Like some great beast, the rig shuddered and banged around the turn, then jackknifed, van and trailer folding into a V and digging into the dirt bank opposite. The engine abruptly died. He could hear the bay screaming.

Showers hurt in several places, but ignored the pain, snatching up his pistol. "May, get out! Get out!"

She all but fell from the Blazer. Catching her balance, she stood looking down the road. He jumped down beside her.

"Are you hurt?"

"No, not badly." She held up her pistol, her eyes wild and frantic, some blood on her forehead.

"The horse!"

Showers' leg injury from the steeplechase had come back with a vengeance. Limping, he went to the back of the trailer. One back door opened easily but the other was caught fast. He pulled on it with all his strength, May at his side, helping. They could hear a car engine.

With a sudden wrench, the door gave way, and the bay came suddenly backward, kicking. May leapt out of the way, but Showers caught a glancing blow to his shoulder.

The stallion backed all the way out, snorting and tossing his head. Showers had left its halter on and was able to snatch at it as it went by. May grabbed at it, too. The bay reared, pawing, almost pulling the lead out of their hands, but they kept their grip. The animal settled, trembling all over. There was blood on his foreleg, a wide scrape, perhaps worse.

"Up the bank!" Showers shouted. "We've got to get into the trees!"

Clambering, sliding, finally letting the bay go up ahead of them, they made it up over the lip of the bank, into old leaves, brush, and brambles.

Another shot, just above them. Twigs came ticking down around them. The ground was more level here. The bay plunged on ahead of them. They caught up with it when it stopped uncertainly before a large fallen tree. A fusillade of shots rang out behind them, but all went high.

Showers got the horse around the obstacle, then quickly handed the lead to May.

"Take him up to the top of the ridge! I'll catch up with you!"

"David!"

"Please, just go! I know what I'm doing!"

He loved her at that moment like life itself. More. He gave her a gentle pat and shove, then turned and dropped behind the fallen tree trunk, sliding a round into the automatic's chamber. He listened to May and the bay moving away through the brush, rejoicing in every second of the sound.

There was noise from below. The Blazer and trailer had blocked the road and their pursuers were coming on foot, climbing the slope with much clumsiness, shouting and swearing.

He caught sight of one man, and then another a few feet to the side. They were wearing ties and jackets and held pistols, awkwardly, striking with their arms against the branches. Whoever they were, they weren't used to rugged country.

Showers calmed himself, slowing his breathing. Holding the

pistol with both hands, he rested it carefully on the log, moving his head slightly for a better view. An automatic like this was a nearly useless weapon in combat. Showers was one of the best shots in his battalion, and the best he had ever done was hit a small soft-drink bottle at twenty-five yards—in three shots. But these men, crashing along the way they were, couldn't have hit a truck.

One of them, pushing through the branches of a small tree, was heading his way. In a few seconds, he would have to make a horrible decision. In all his years with the military—on active duty, in the reserves, and the National Guard—he had never once fired a weapon loaded with killing rounds at a human being. He had thought about it often, hard and painfully, especially when his unit had gone on the list for duty in the Persian Gulf. It was a decision, he had realized, that he could only make when the time came.

The time had come. The man made it easier for him. Reaching a spot where he could see farther forward, the fellow raised his gun, aiming up the hill, toward May and the horse. Showers took a deep breath, let it out halfway, then held it, as he gently evened the sights. Remembering his training, he aimed low.

The shot hit the man in the groin. Showers saw splashes of blood on his shirt as he flew backward, screaming, landing on his back in a coil of brambles. The man to his left froze, then fired several shots in Showers' direction. One thudded into the log.

Showers swiveled the automatic carefully, then squeezed off another round. The bullet missed the second man, but came close enough to send him running back for cover. The first man was howling.

Now. Move now. He couldn't wait a second longer. Backing up into a crouch, pistol to the fore, he slipped behind a tree, and then another. Finally, he turned and began a rapid climb up the hill. He was near collapse from exhaustion when he finally reached the top of the ridge. May and the horse were standing as still as statues. Her eyes were wide and her mouth hung open. Then, seeing it was Showers, she sank to the ground.

"You should have kept going," he said, helping her up.

"No, no," she said, clinging to him.

"I shot one of them."

"Good."

He squeezed her hard, then eased away, looking around them. A narrow trail ran along the ridge, heading northwest, away from the road.

*284*

"They'll be coming soon," he said. "They'll really mean business now."

May was looking at the bay. "His leg's cut, but he's not limping. He's standing hard on it."

"Pray he holds up."

Showers pulled the animal around until it was sideways to a large rock. Holding the halter lead tightly, he swung his leg up. This first attempt failed, but with an extra lunge the second time, he managed to get up on the stallion's bare back. He pulled May up after him, then turned the horse onto the trail.

# Eighteen

There were thundershowers over the Washington area as Moody's plane, a government 707 formerly used as Air Force One, approached Andrews. The veteran pilot maneuvered around them, taking a vector out over Chesapeake Bay and then, in a long slow turn, coming at the air base from the southeast.

A limousine and a Secret Service chase car were waiting on the ramp—as Moody discovered, sent by the president. He'd earned this nicety. He'd earned a lot more.

Deena insisted that they drop her first at the Watergate, ignoring Moody's protest that it was out of the way and that the president was waiting for him. As he had feared, she'd hated every minute of the Asian trip. Her good behavior had given out the second day in China.

"Robert, I'm about to lose my mind!"

Acting Secretary Richmond was seated in the jump seat in front of them. He looked quickly out the window, as though there was something fascinating about the sheets of water cascading down the glass.

Moody relented. It would be a relief to be rid of her.

The State Department was just a few blocks from the Watergate complex. Moody let Richmond out at the C Street entrance. The diplomat had wanted to join him in making a report to the president, but Moody had strongly suggested he not, saying he intended just to have a few private words with the boss and that Richmond's comments could wait for the next cabinet meeting. Richmond had reluctantly accepted this. It was almost as though he realized Moody would shortly become his immediate superior.

If and when the president did say the magic words that would make Moody's wish come true, he figured it would be wise to keep Richmond as number two. There would be resentment enough from the rank and file over the appointment, and keeping Richmond on his side would defuse a lot of that.

There were a number of ways to encourage Richmond's friendship—among them, dangling the possibility of eventual promotion to secretary of state should Moody ascend the next step to vice president. Professional diplomats were in their game for the long run. They had a special talent for waiting out people.

The president received him in a formal sitting room up in the second floor family quarters. He stood up to offer his hand and a warm greeting. "I read all the communiqués, Bob. Looks like you accomplished quite a lot."

"If I can believe the Japanese prime minister, ratification is a certainty. Maybe in a week. They want to get it on the record quickly. Get the world off their back."

"Celerity is not always a Japanese trait. Did you extend my invitation to the prime minister for a state visit in the fall?"

"Did indeed—making it clear it's contingent on ratification. He's quite eager. Wants to talk trade."

"They always want to talk trade, unless we're angry with them."

"If they ratify, they'll expect some generosity."

"An exchange of gifts. Very oriental. We shall see." He sat, inviting Moody to do the same.

"Would you like some coffee?" One of the white-jacketed waiters was hovering nearby.

"Thank you." Moody's mind was logy from jet lag and the long hours in the plane.

"So, Bob. There's still the matter of our own ratification of the treaty."

"Yes sir. I plan to get back to work on that immediately."

"Won't most of the members be off on vacation? The Congress is in recess."

"There are telephones, sir. And I thought it might be helpful if we had Wally Sadinauskas and some of the other cabinet secretaries hit some key states and districts. Point out pollution problems. Make assurances about jobs. The benefits of energy conservation. The full press."

"Good idea. If they wouldn't mind."

"They won't mind if you want it."

The president leaned back, crossing his legs, folding his hands on his knee.

"Before you get back to work, Bob, there's something I'm delighted to tell you."

Moody felt as his daughter must have the year she'd been nominated for an Oscar. He remembered her, sitting in the audience, a mercilessly prying television camera showing the nation her tense, beautiful, expectant face. He could only hope his dreams were not about to be crushed the way hers had been that night. With the president, you never knew. He waited. The president seemed to enjoy making him do it.

"If it's acceptable to you," the president said, "if you think it best, I'd like to send your name to the Senate as the next secretary of state."

An inexpressible happiness swept over Moody, like the night he'd been elected governor—only a thousand times better. Loginess had become giddiness.

"I'm honored, sir. And very, very grateful."

"Mr. Bush's Jim Baker, I daresay, established a most acceptable precedent."

"Yes he did, sir. A very able man, for a Republican."

"I intend to do it this fall, Bob. Just as soon as we achieve a favorable Senate vote on the treaty."

Moody's blood suddenly chilled. The fall seemed a century away.

He caught himself. "That's fine with me, sir. But I . . . I wonder if sooner might be better than later."

"How so, Bob? As secretary of state, you'd be subject to all manner of distractions. I need you right here, getting those votes."

"The confirmation process will likely take quite some time, Mr. President. I could be working on votes in the meantime. But if you made the nomination now, it would give me some extra muscle. Extra leverage."

"Do you really think so?"

"Yes sir. Show your full confidence. If I'm not being presumptuous."

"Hmmmm."

"I'd move as soon as the Japanese ratify." Moody wondered if this was beginning to sound as though he was begging.

"Who do you recommend to take over your job?"

"Wolfenson, sir. He's first rate. Went to Columbia."

Not Harvard, Yale, or Princeton, but Ivy League.

"Does he know the Hill?"

"As well as I do, sir." It was a lie. What counted was that Wolfenson was one hundred percent Moody's man. Maybe he was asking too much. The whole pie.

"I'll think a bit on that one, Bob. But if you think it best that we send the nomination through now, that's fine with me. Your advice has been quite sound thus far."

"I'm really very honored, sir."

The president smiled, in his Waspy way. He was preparing to be witty.

"One gathers you have great faith," he said, "that the Japanese were telling you the truth."

If there was anything that would improve Deena's mood, it was this news. Moody all but bounded into his office, snatching up the phone before he was quite in his chair.

The Watergate line was busy. He waited—not very long; he was very impatient—then tried again. Still busy. She was probably calling all her friends, catching up on gossip, venting her spleen about the horrors of the trip. He summoned his secretary.

"Anne. I need Mrs. Moody. Keep trying till you get her. Every five minutes."

"Yes sir." She handed him a computer printout—names and phone numbers. "Your messages, sir. I put them in order of priority. Do you want to start on them?"

He glanced over them quickly. What he wanted to do most was get the word out about his appointment, but he couldn't do that until the president made it official—probably with a press conference in the briefing room.

He could tell a few friends. Sadinauskas had called while he was up with the president. Moody could tell him.

"Wait a minute," he said. "Who's this Lieutenant Anderson? From the Pentagon?"

"No sir. He's a police lieutenant out in Maryland."

"Why the hell did you put him on the top of the list? What does he want, a tour of the White House?"

"He said it was urgent, Mr. Moody. He called three times. He said it was about your daughter."

Moody stared down at his desk. "Okay. Keep trying Mrs. Moody."

The lieutenant was in his car, but the dispatcher contacted him over the radio and he went to a land line.

"Mr. Moody!" There was a strong country accent in his voice. "Thank you for calling, sir. I'm sorry to disturb you—in the White House and everything."

"Get to the point! You said this was urgent."

"Yes sir. Mr. Moody, we recovered an abandoned vehicle out here registered to your daughter. May Moody? California tags. A 1979 Volkswagen. Yellow."

He'd heard that May had once driven a car into the Pacific Ocean after a wild party. Maybe she was back to her old ways.

"I've not been in touch with my daughter. I've been out of the country."

"Yes sir. The California Highway Patrol got us a residence address for her in Washington. The District police attempted to contact her, both at the residence and at her place of employment, the Shakespeare Theatre? They haven't seen her for several days."

"Isn't this a lot of trouble to go to over an abandoned car?"

"Yes sir, but I'm afraid that, well, the county police recovered a body in some woods a few miles away. Shallow grave. Hunters found her. It's a white female, in her late twenties. Dark hair. A homicide victim, sir."

Moody didn't know what to say. He was terrified by what he was beginning to think.

"Is it her?"

"We don't know, sir."

"You don't know? She's a movie star, goddamn it! Go get a copy of *People* magazine."

He was overdoing it. May hadn't been getting much press in recent years.

"It's been pretty hot, sir, and the body's in pretty bad shape. What we'd like you to do, Mr. Moody, is come out and see if you can identify her."

Moody calmed himself. It had to be a mistake. Someone must have stolen May's car. She had no reason to be out there in the boonies.

"I can't come this afternoon." A National Security Council directive on his desk said there had been more fighting in Belize. U.S. forces had not yet been engaged. "It'll have to be tonight."

"Whenever it's convenient, sir." The man sounded a little testy. "We'd sure appreciate it."

Spencer's bureau chief was vastly amused that the steeplechase feature had become a murder case, but unsure how a car bombing at some country horse farm could translate into anything of interest for the national wire. The bureau chief was one of those too-long-in-Washington veterans who thought that nothing could be news unless some politician's name was pinned on it. Spencer reminded him of the Jayne brothers saga back in the 1970s—two Illinois horsemen who'd tried for years to kill each other, and eventually succeeded. A young woman rider had been killed in the process, blown up by a car bomb intended for one of the Jaynes.

"That was Chicago," the bureau chief said. "This thing is out in the sticks. Maybe moonshiners or something."

Moonshiners. On some of the priciest real estate on the East Coast.

"The car belonged to my cousin," Spencer said. "He was my source for the Napier memo column."

Napier. Politics. The Japanese. News.

"Say no more, Jack. Get the hell out there. And keep in touch."

There were sheriff's deputies at Showers' farm, and they refused to let Spencer on the premises. At the small hospital near Dandytown, he was stopped at the front desk—told that Alixe Percy was still in intensive care and no visitors were permitted. Absolutely none. Spencer drove on into Dandytown, recalling how much he'd liked the woman, how much he had enjoyed their having a couple of drinks together, how refreshingly different her breezy, unaffected candor was after all the well-educated whores and hustlers he'd dealt with for so many years in the capital. He hoped his cousin could provide some understandable reason for what had happened.

Wayne Bensinger was in his little office, still wearing the same rumpled suit. He was much more guarded than before.

"You heard what's happened?" he asked, wiping his glasses on his tie.

"The *Washington Post* had a story. In its Metro section."

"Yeah. They called. Wouldn't even come out." He looked at Spencer somewhat dubiously. "Do you have any idea where we can find Captain Showers?"

"I've been trying to get hold of him myself."

"Sheriff Cooke has a warrant out for his arrest."

"What?"

"My boss went along with it. They're real serious."

*291*

"But it was his car."

"That's right. And he was the last one to drive it before the bomb went off. Also, he stopped off at a weapons shed at Fort A. P. Hill and drew pistol ammunition before coming home. They haven't found any explosives missing, but who knows?"

"This is ridiculous."

"He's got a woman with him. That actress who was out at the Dragoon Chase. May Moody? You know anything about her?"

Spencer shrugged. "Not what you'd call my cousin's type. A Hollywood brat turned has-been. Trying to make a comeback."

"Her father's a very important man. I'm surprised he hasn't called us."

"Busy man."

"The worst thing for your cousin is Miss Percy's will. A copy's on file in county records. She named him as her sole beneficiary. Seven million dollars and counting. The captain's money troubles are well known."

"How is she? Is she going to make it?"

Bensinger shrugged. "She lost part of a leg. Some burns. Lost a lot of blood. Concussion." He paused. "She's been conscious, though. She asked for you. She asked for Captain Showers, first. Then you."

"Can I see her?"

"No sir."

"The girl? Becky?"

"Died instantly. I didn't see the body. Didn't want to. I'm still getting over Vicky Clay."

"Did you get the computer analysis I sent you?"

"Yes. The letters *B-E-C*. Very interesting. I showed it to my boss. He wasn't interested. Doesn't see how anything like that can be introduced as evidence."

They sat a moment without speaking. A large fly buzzed against the grimy window, then settled on the edge of the bookcase, as if contemplating the titles.

"Mr. Bensinger, do you believe for a minute that my cousin had anything to do with this?"

The prosecutor looked pained. "No sir, I don't. I don't think my boss does, either. But the sheriff is hell-bent on it. A lot of the horsemen are upset about what's been going on. Lynwood Fairbrother has been raising all sorts of hell. Thinks this is very damaging to Dandytown and steeplechasing."

"What do you think?"

"I think this is a damned nightmare and I wish we'd get to the end of it. It's really beyond our competence, but the sheriff won't call the state police in. I wish a federal crime was involved, so we could turn it over to the FBI or somebody. That's why I hoped we'd hear from Mr. Moody."

He stood up, shoving his hands in his pockets. "Miss Percy mumbled something about her safety deposit box, about something in there she wants Showers to have."

"Can we take a look at it?"

Bensinger shook his head. "Only someone with her power of attorney. That's a pretty short list: a big law firm in Washington, and Captain David Spencer Showers. I tried the law firm. They want to talk to Miss Percy first, and the hospital won't allow that." He took out a handkerchief and blew his nose. "Excuse me. Hay fever."

"You live in the wrong place."

"That's sure enough the truth since all this started." He paused. "About the safety deposit box. There's a chance we could get a court order. There's a Judge Merrick. He'd help us, maybe. He'd do it for your cousin."

"Will you ask him?"

"I'd have to check with my boss."

"Will you?"

"Okay. But you can't be involved."

"I don't want to be involved, but I'd appreciate being informed."

Bensinger moved out from behind his desk, an indication he wanted Spencer to go.

"I wouldn't hang around here too long," he said. "The way things are going, Sheriff Cooke'll probably arrest you as an accomplice."

The Maryland county had no morgue. The body of the girl they'd found in the woods had been taken to a local hospital and put in a freezer in the pathology section. It was still in a body bag.

"I'm afraid this won't be very pleasant," the lieutenant said.

"I've seen it before," said Moody.

"What?"

"In Vietnam."

"Oh yes. Well, I was there, too, but I never saw anything like this."

The hospital attendant opened the bag, spreading apart the seam. Large dead dark eyes bulged out in a bloated face, the swollen tissue colored a greenish yellow, where it wasn't blackened. The darkest tissue was along a jagged cut that ran deep across the girl's throat. Her long dark hair was matted, here and there still containing little bits of dirt and leaves.

Moody had seen men die with their intestines strung out. He leaned closer, wanting to make absolutely sure—though he was almost dizzy with incipient sickness and relief.

"That's not May," he said. "It's not my daughter. I don't know who that is."

"You're sure, sir? With all the discoloration and—"

"I'm sure." He glanced along the length of the bag. "If nothing else, my daughter's much taller."

Outside, he stood a moment on the rain-moist pavement. His car and driver were waiting, engine running. Above him, the clouds were breaking, slivers of night sky with a star or two showing. The horizon was near, a bumpy line of hills, all black in the night. Just beyond them was West Virginia. Its nearness was troubling to him.

He got into the car wearily. Deena had seemed more startled than overjoyed by his news about the State Department appointment. She'd said no to going out for a celebratory dinner, pleading exhaustion from the trip. Of course she'd refused to come out with him to look at this body. He was at a loss to understand what had happened to his marriage, how it could so suddenly go swirling down the toilet. His first wife had never changed. She was the same person at their divorce hearing that she had been as a young girl in the hollows.

"Back to Washington, sir?" said the driver.

"No. I want to go to Baltimore. Make it fast."

The doorman was impressed by Moody's official car and rang up the Blochs' penthouse immediately. Bernie took a long time answering, and said something to the doorman that made the man uncomfortable.

"You can go right up, sir," he said finally, and buzzed Moody in.

Bloch admitted him wearing a bathrobe and slippers. For a fat man, he had very skinny legs.

"Come on in, Bobby. You know what time it is?"

Moody, teeth clenched, said nothing. He followed Bloch into the huge living room. The lights of Baltimore Harbor glittered outside the window.

"You want a drink, Bobby?"

"No."

**294**

"You sure? I'm gonna have one."

"All right. A little bourbon."

Bloch went to a bar set up in a corner. "Welcome back. I hear congratulations are in order. Secretary of state. That's something. Who would have thought it, back in the old days."

"How do you know about that?"

Bloch's back was to him. "I guess Sherrie was talking to Deena. A little while ago. You were out."

"I was out in western Maryland, looking at the body of a dead girl. Very dead. Throat cut. They were afraid it was May. Her car was found not far away."

Bernie's face was white when he turned around. "It wasn't May, though, right?" He set down their glasses.

"May's missing. Showers is missing. That goddamn horse of yours is missing. There's a dead girl with her head half cut off. Showers' car was blown up with a bomb—one woman dead and another in the hospital. What the fuck is going on, Bernie?"

"I don't know. I have nothing to do with it."

"Bullshit."

"Bobby, come on. We're friends, friends for life, remember?"

"Vicky Clay's dead. Her husband's dead. Four dead bodies, Bernie, and I don't know where my daughter is."

Bloch took a gulp of his drink, then sighed. "Okay, there's been some trouble, but I've got nothing to do with it."

"Keep talking. I want to hear everything you know. Tell me about your friends in New Jersey, Bernie. They're mixed up in this, right?"

"No, no. They're businessmen, like me. Like you. They do everything with lawyers."

"They want that horse."

"They want the horse. Showers wants the horse. Who knows who else wants the fucking horse? Only it's Showers who's got it. And from what I hear, he's got May."

"What are you trying to tell me, that the son of a bitch kidnapped her? That he's holding her hostage? That he killed all those people? What kind of fairy tale is that? The guy's a Boy Scout, remember?"

"Those people out there in Virginia are crazy. They live like it was two hundred years ago. Those are the people who started the Civil War, you know?" He took more of his drink, glancing nervously out the window, as though there was something threatening him out there in the dark sky. "Look, what I think it is, is this kid Billy Bonning. They've got some kind of blood feud going.

You know what that's like. You grew up in West Virginia. Showers threw him off his farm. Bonning's sister got whacked, maybe by her husband, maybe not. Bonning came back and beat up his ex-wife, and Showers threatened to kill him. That's what all this is about. I'm sorry I ever hired that kid. I canned him, though. Like I told you. I've got nothing to do with this."

He was sweating.

"I'm calling in the FBI, Bernie. I'm going to get the director out of bed and I'm going to have those hills out there crawling with agents by morning."

Bloch sat up, blinking. "No, no, Bobby. No need for that. God's sake. The feds? Shit."

"*I'm* a fucking fed, Bernie. And my daughter's missing. I want her back!"

"She hasn't talked to you in years. She could be anywhere. You know what's she's like. Didn't she walk off a movie once? Turned up in Mexico."

"You told me she was with Showers. How the hell do you know that? If you're not going to give me some answers, Bernie, I'm going to get them myself."

He stood up, starting for the door. Bloch leapt after him, grabbing his arm.

"Hold on, Bobby. Wait up. You got me out of a deep sleep. I'm not thinking straight. Sit down. Let's work this out."

"Work it out? What're you saying? This isn't some deal."

"Sit down, Bobby. I'll tell you what I know."

Reluctantly Moody waited, wondering what words were going to come out next. Bloch went to pour himself another drink. Moody stared at his own, then sipped some. His nerves were like a battery charge.

"Look, Bobby," said his "friend for life," seating himself again. "Showers and this Bonning kid are trying to kill each other, all right? The horse is just caught up in the middle. I guess May is caught in the middle, too. But Showers is a Boy Scout, right? I don't know what I was saying. I'm sure he wouldn't let anything happen to her. I'm sure he's trying to protect her. And if he can't, my friends will."

"What do you mean?"

"They're trying to get the horse back, okay? It's very, very important to them. I think I made that clear. But they're sure as hell not out to hurt anybody. They got their reputation. All right, something may happen to Billy Bonning. I hope to hell it does. But for God's sake, the daughter of the White House chief of staff? If anything, they'll be looking out for her. Deliver her safe and sound. Believe me. They know what they're doing."

"Every word you've said scares the hell out of me, Bernie. I'm getting help. I'm getting her back whatever it takes."

Bloch suddenly got very cold and serious. There was a look in his eyes Moody had never seen before—certainly not ever directed at him.

"You don't want to call in the FBI, Bobby. You don't want to talk to anyone about this."

Moody fought to control himself, then said, "I'm not going to pull any punches to protect you or any of your friends. I told you that the day I took this job."

"Just listen to me," Bloch said. "You go off crazy like this and you could pull the whole roof down."

"What roof?"

"The horse is stolen. It's hot. I don't know how my friends ended up with it, but they were stuck with a stolen horse. They couldn't race it unless they gave it a new identity."

"They could have returned it."

"What, and take a rap? No way. That's what all that screwing around with the auction was about. I've got connections with these guys, connections that could become public." He leaned back. He had Moody sitting perfectly still. "I've got connections with you, Bobby. I've carried a lot of water for you. You know the stuff I've done. I've got connections with the party. I'm one of the biggest fund-raisers. I'm chairman of a committee working for the Earth Treaty. I've got money down—campaign contributions—trying to get it ratified. How's it going to look if I end up taking a fall in this? What happens if this gets into the papers? What's it going to do to the treaty? You know what a prissy sonofabitch your president is. Do you think he's going to want you as secretary of state if there's a big scandal? Do you think he'll even want you around the White House?"

Moody leaned back in his chair. All the fatigue he'd been holding back had suddenly collapsed on him.

"Let me and my friends take care of this, Bobby. Things happen, you know. They get taken care of. Nobody ever hears anything about it. Happens all the time. Jack Kennedy was screwing Marilyn Monroe and nobody knew a thing about it. It would have stayed that way if someone hadn't blown his head off. That Vicki Morgan stuff with Alfred Bloomingdale. It never touched the Reagan administration. We all know there was a hell of a lot more to Watergate than that fucking crummy break-in. Millions of dollars worth. There are a lot of guys walking around Washington who ought to be in jail but never will be."

He sipped his drink, very confident now.

"All it takes is money, and knowing what you're doing. I've got a lot of money. My friends know what they're doing. We'll take care of this. We'll take care of Billy Bonning and we'll take care of Showers. We'll get your daughter back. No one will muss a hair of her pretty head."

Moody needed to sleep. He couldn't think.

"I'll give you twenty-four hours. If I don't hear from her by then—that she's okay—I'm going to the Director."

Bloch sensed a bluff. He shook his head. "They're out there in those hills. It's going to take some time. You gotta be reasonable, Bobby. Give it till the end of the week. I've seen you through a hell of a lot. You see me through this. Don't worry, I'll take care of you. I always have."

# Nineteen

A loose, rocky trail led down into the next valley, and the bay was pulling up limp by the time they got down it. After letting him graze a little in the wet scrub grass, Showers and May continued on foot, walking alongside the horse, following the edge of the woods and avoiding all roads, huddling at night beneath the trees, Showers sheltering May with his jacket and body.

The next afternoon, after hours in the rain, they decided to risk going to a farmhouse. The people they found were very poor—the farmer gaunt from overwork, his wife fat from cheap food. When May offered them money—a hundred-dollar bill—they became very cold and suspicious. For a moment, Showers feared they'd end up getting robbed by these hard folk, or worse. But the couple refused the money, gave them a meal and feed for the horse, and the farmer helped him make a crude poultice for the bay's injured leg. There was a town some twenty miles distant where the farmer thought Showers might be able to rent a truck. He drove him there in a creaking, chugging car that must have been ten years older than May's Volkswagen.

On the way back, the man drove slowly to make sure that Showers didn't lose his way. The rental outlet, little more than an ancient garage with a lot of rusting farm equipment around it, had had only one big open-stake truck available. It had seen many miles and had been used to carry pigs recently. Using some old boards, they managed to get the bay up into it. To Showers' dismay, he lay down.

"One of us had better stay back here with him," Showers said.

"I'll drive," said May.

He touched her forehead. She was very pale, and had been shivering. "You have a fever."

"I know the way. It's not an easy trip."

Not once did the farmer or his wife ask the nature of their trouble, or even their names. Before they left, May went up to the wife and thrust the hundred-dollar bill into her hand.

"It's honest money, ma'am," she said. "And it's worth every penny to us for what you've done. We won't be around when you might be in need, so you keep this. Please?"

The woman looked uncertainly at the currency, but held on to it. "We wish you safe journey, miss."

It was late into the night when May finally pulled to a stop and turned off the engine. The bay had been very still during the long, slow drive, but lifted his head at the sudden lack of motion. Showers patted the animal, and it went back to resting.

They were at another gas station, even more dilapidated than the one where he'd rented the truck. He sat up. The service station was closed. A dog was barking. The air was very cool. May was at a pay phone. After a brief conversation, she hung up.

"Is the horse all right?" she asked.

"It's hard to say. What about you?"

"I'll make it." She was leaning against the truck bed for support. "I just called my people. They'll be waiting for us. We'll be safe, David. Just a few more miles."

It was nearly an hour before they stopped again. Showers looked up to see not May but a large bearded man in overalls at the rear of the truck. Rising, he saw May standing nearby, a smaller, older woman next to her, her arm around May's waist. She had gray, well-combed hair, and was nicely but simply dressed. Though her cheekbones were wider, Showers saw much of May in her face.

"David," May said, "this is my mother."

Showers climbed stiffly from the truck bed, straightened his clothing, and then shook the woman's hand. They were in the driveway of a large stone house set on a steep slope. Down below, Showers could see a narrow road lined with houses and, farther along, some building fronts. There were few lights. High hills were all around them.

"May says you saved her life, Captain Showers," said the older woman. "That makes you a very welcome man hereabouts."

She had an old, proud, almost Scottish mountain accent, reminding Showers of a West Virginia man who had once worked for his father.

"If anything, I've put her in the way of a lot of harm. I mean to get her out of it."

"We'll talk about that in the morning. I've a shed in the back. We put some hay in. Tyrone and the boys will get your horse into it, if he can stand."

The bay had raised his head and was looking at them. The bearded man, apparently Tyrone, looked strong enough to lift the animal out by himself.

"I'll stay with him," Showers said.

"There's no need for that, David," May said. "These people know animals. The horse needs rest. So do we."

"Tyrone's going to take your truck back tonight to where you got it," May's mother said. "Best not to keep it around here."

"I don't know how to thank you."

"You brought May home. That's thanks enough. When you've eaten something, I'll have Bella make up your beds." A thin dark-haired girl peered around the side of the truck, then smiled.

He and May were led to separate bedrooms. Slipping into the blissful luxury of clean sheets, he found he badly missed the warmth of May's body next to him, and felt very lonely. But sadness quickly passed into sleep.

He awoke to brightness. Looking at his watch, he was surprised to discover it was past noon. Fresh clothes had been laid out for him—khaki pants, a cheap but sturdy white dress shirt, boxer shorts that looked a little too big, and white socks. A razor and toothbrush had been set on a fresh thick towel. The bathroom was spotless. It was a very sturdy and well-kept house.

May, wearing jeans and a white blouse, was looking better, and gave him a smile. The girl Bella brought him food. No one spoke much while he ate it.

"May has told me everything," her mother said, as Showers finished his coffee. "But there's something you don't know about, and I think you should. Come with me, please."

She took him into a study furnished with a rolltop desk and two overstuffed armchairs. There was a bookcase against one wall and two file cabinets next to it. A framed map of West Virginia hung over the fireplace. It seemed more a working office than a room in a house.

May's mother waited for him to sit down, and then went to the desk, bringing him a newspaper.

"The paper's a weekly," she said, "but they get the AP. This came out yesterday. I'm afraid it's got some bad news."

Showers studied her serious face for a moment, then looked down at the front page. He heard May come into the room.

Her mother pointed to a five- or six-paragraph story in the lower right-hand corner of the page. The headline read VA. WOMAN KILLED BY CAR BOMB.

The words hit him like hammer blows. Becky was dead. Alixe was near death in a hospital. He was wanted for murder.

He stood up, fists clenched, feeling utterly helpless. He looked to Mrs. Moody's desk.

"If you don't mind, I'd like to use your phone."

"David . . ."

He ignored May, picking up the receiver and dialing quickly—his own number. Someone had to be there. A groom. Perhaps even Jack.

It rang several times. It was answered by a voice Showers recognized—one of Cooke's deputies, a man named Haddleford.

"What are you doing there, Albert?" Showers asked.

"Is that you, Captain Showers?"

"Yes! What's happened? How is Miss Percy?"

"Still alive. Say, you'd better get back here, Captain. Sheriff Cooke wants to talk to you."

Could they trace the call? This was a rural line, but he'd been able to dial direct.

"Where are you, Captain?"

Showers hung up. May was at his side. Her hand went into his.

"There's another story further on," May's mother said. "They found May's car in Maryland. A dead girl turned up in the woods not far away. May thinks it was a girl who worked for you."

"Yes," Showers said slowly. "Selma."

"I don't think you should make any more calls," Mrs. Moody said. "Not until we know more about what's going on back there. May says you shot a man."

"Yes. I had no choice."

"I understand that. Those are very bad people after you. You're safe here. You don't have to worry about anyone in this town, in this valley. But we don't want to draw any strangers. I'm fearful for my daughter, Captain Showers, and I want to be very careful."

"Of course. So do I."

"My biggest worry is her father. I won't bring up our differences, but I know he loves May very much. He's a man of quick temper, a man quick to act. I suspect he's doing everything in his power to get May out of this, and he's got a lot of power."

She was looking at him very steadily, very much in command.

"He'll bring you harm, Captain Showers. May doesn't want that. I'll respect her wishes. What I have to do is find a way to let her father know that she's safe, without his knowing she's here. Will you leave that to me?"

"Yes. Of course."

"You just make yourself comfortable. I expect you'll be here for a while."

"I'll go check on the horse."

The bay was lying down, but the young man with him in the shed said he'd been standing earlier that morning and had taken some feed and a lot of water.

"The leg's still swelled up, but it ain't got any worse."

Showers examined the animal carefully. He supposed Moonsugar had been in greater danger after the racing accident, but there was no way of telling the bay's chances of survival. Few people realized what delicate creatures these big animals were. At least nothing more was going to happen to him.

Showers remembered something and stood up, searching in his pocket. He had thought to take the film out of his camera when they'd returned to Shepherdstown, but he hadn't had it processed.

"Is there someplace I can get this developed?" he asked.

"Mrs. Moody can take care of that."

May's mother left to drive over to a large town in the next valley, where she ran a settlement house and the small job training center she'd founded with part of her ex-husband's generous divorce arrangement and operated with a substantial part of his alimony payments. She'd not sought a federal grant because of the conflict of interest implicit in his White House position. She promised she'd have Showers' film processed as soon as possible and would be back in time for supper.

Tyrone had not returned. The bay's condition showed no change. May decided she'd take Showers on a walk.

It was hot in the afternoon sun, but Showers wore his jacket to cover the pistol in his belt. As they strolled along the blacktop, he took her hand.

"I feel a little bit at peace," she said.

"It's a peaceful place."

The road was bordered on both sides by ditches, with planks thrown across to provide access to the houses. They were mostly small, a few of ancient stucco or brick, the majority frame, badly in need of paint. Here and there, people sat on stoops or in porch gliders. Most were women, pausing in their day's labor to sip lemonade or a soft drink. On one set of steps, a large man wearing a camouflage fishing vest but no shirt lounged back with a can of beer in his hand, an open six-pack carton beside him. He nodded amiably as they passed. In one way or another, everyone greeted May and Showers. Because of May's mother, they'd been accepted overnight.

Leading downward, the road crossed an old steel and wooden bridge over a meandering stream low on water, then entered the town's little business section. On one side were two blocks of flat-roofed buildings, their storefronts largely vacant—a cafe, a grocery, and two-pump gas station apparently still engaged in commerce. On the other side was a single railroad track and a rusty coal-loading tower, its unused conveyor belt climbing the opposite hillside at a steep angle.

"Grim," Showers said.

"It's been like this for years. There are a lot worse places in the state."

"I like the people."

"They're not snobs like your friends in Virginia or greedy egomaniacs like my L.A. chums, but they have their bad sides, too. The man who was drinking beer likes to smack his wife around. That pretty girl who smiled at you is hell-bent on sleeping with every man she meets. A man from here was shot in a bar fight over in the next hollow. He almost died. There are a couple of families here who haven't spoken to one another for three generations. But they're certainly no worse here than anywhere else. They're very proud, and fiercely self-reliant. They'll share their last crust of bread or scrap of shoe leather."

A tan dog wandered up to them, sniffing, then returned to his doorstep and flopped in the dust. A few crows circled in the clear brilliant sky overhead.

"Do you come back often?"

"Every once in a while. I came out and stayed with my mother after getting out of that treatment center. It made it a lot easier."

"Does your father come from a place like this?"

"Worse, originally. A little place way back in the hills. No railroad. Barely a road."

"He never comes back?"

"No. I think it scares him."

"He was lucky to get out."

"Not lucky. His mother turned whore and managed to marry well—for West Virginia."

Showers thought of his own mother, an ancestor-worshiping upstate New York aristocrat who had been to Wellesley College and won a first at the Grand International Horse Show in New York City. He wondered how she would have survived in such a place, in such a circumstance.

"Do you feel like a little climb?" May asked.

"A slow one."

"Let's go up to the mine. The view there is spectacular."

The dirt road was as rough cut as the one where they'd wrecked the trailer rig. They paused to rest at one turning, then trudged on, Showers throwing his jacket over his shoulder and rolling up his sleeves. They reached the summit much later than he'd expected to.

The mine entrance was closed, a gate bearing a faded and loosely hung KEEP OUT sign held shut with a rusty chain. The lock looked as if it would fall apart with a sharp pull.

There was a miners' cart on the small track that led into the shaft. They sat down on its edge and Showers slipped his arm around her. She lighted a cigarette, then, exhaling, laid her head back on his shoulder.

"You see what I mean? It all looks like paradise from here."

There were many miles of hills and mountains in view, running north to south. Their forested sides were lush and darkly green. The prospect was as beautiful as any in Dandytown's rolling valley, but so different.

"It's hard to believe this and Virginia were once the same state," he said.

"Wasn't much taste for slavery up here."

"I've always wondered why these people stayed in these hills, why they didn't move on with the rest of the settlers."

"They were Scots, or Scots-Irish. It's wild here, like where they came from. Once they got here, they clung to it."

"Your father didn't."

"He wanted to be educated, then he wanted to be rich. Now he wants to be president. Someday he'll figure out what the hell it is he really wants. I hope it will have something to do with here." She sat up, leaning forward on her knees, looking back down the slope to the little town clinging to its creek below. "My mother's a Piney River girl. I don't mean the real Piney River. Hers was called something else. But there's a song about old West Virginia and a Piney River girl, and that's her. She goes by Jenny but she was born Geneva McDowell. My real name is Jenny Mae Moody. I changed it to May in high school. I might have been a Piney River girl myself."

Showers imagined May in a homespun cotton dress, her hair much like this, barefoot, dangling her legs in some mountain stream. He knew the question he wanted to ask her. He repeated it over and over again in his mind. But he couldn't speak the words. It wouldn't be fair to ask it in this distant, unreal place, so far from their worlds, where there were so many different answers than the one he wanted.

"Did you love her?" she asked. "Becky?"

"No."

"I mean ever."

"She wasn't the woman I was talking about. I tried to be a kind of father to her. Her own wasn't much good at it. He gave her everything she wanted, but never what she needed. Becky's the saddest part of everything."

"Has there been anyone else? For you?"

"Yes."

"Is she waiting for you?"

"No."

"I was married once. It was a romance that grew out of a nude scene in a movie. It lasted until his next film. Then he met another woman, an older more successful actress."

"I'm sorry."

"Not at all. It screwed me up for a while, but I got my revenge soon enough. She dumped him and moved on to someone else. She got a little bit of her youth back from him, and a lot of publicity out of it. She didn't give a damn about him otherwise. I wondered how he could stand it, being worth so little."

"I love you, May."

She came into his arms. He kissed her gently, but afterward, she looked away.

"What are you going to do, David?"

"Make sure the bay recovers, and turn him over to his owner. Then I'll settle everything else."

"I understand that. And I'll help you. They can't do anything with that ridiculous murder charge if I testify I was with you all that time. I'll help you get the horse business cleared up. I'll help you with Alixe. If you want to blow Bernie Bloch's head off, I'll find some way to help you do that. But when it's all over, what are you going to do? Run your farm? Look for another job? What?"

"I haven't given it much thought. I'll keep the farm. I have to do that."

"Why, David? Why do you have to do that?"

"Family. My father . . ."

"He's dead. You told me he almost lost the farm, with the way he spent money. What do you want to do? I'm not talking about your family, your father's ghost. I'm talking about you. What do *you* want, David?"

"I don't understand."

"David, by the time I was a teenager my father was a very wealthy man. All he wanted for me was respectability—the very best schools and the very best marriage I could get. Someone like you, perhaps, but with money, as much money as we had.

"That's not what I wanted. I tried to be something more than the highly marriageable daughter of this superachiever. I wanted to achieve something myself. I wanted my mother to be as proud of me as she was of my father. I had been in plays all through boarding school, and loved it. My father raised hell about it but I applied at Juilliard, and they took me. I was cast in my first Actors Equity New York play before I even graduated. David. Is there anything like that, that you really want? To look out over these hills, and dream on?"

"I forgot about your play," he said. "You're supposed to start rehearsals soon. And you're stuck here with me."

"To hell with the play. There'll be another. I've learned that much."

He was staring off at the eastern horizon, frowning.

"Let's go back," she said.

When they returned, the bay was standing up—and eating.

# Twenty

The news that the Japanese had at last ratified the Earth Treaty reached the White House by State Department communiqué some twenty minutes before it hit the news wires. Moody received it in his office, where he was waiting with a very edgy Deena. The president had scheduled a news conference on Moody's appointment as well as a following private luncheon in the White House family quarters. He'd never raised the possibility that he might cancel both events if the Japanese were not forthcoming, but Moody could only wonder. It would have been utterly humiliating for that to happen in front of Deena. It was humiliating enough watching her sit and fidget and seethe. The first lady was said to loathe Deena. The luncheon would be a uniquely hellish experience, however punctiliously correct. And here was Deena being made to squirm, waiting to find out whether she would be honored with the privilege of being allowed to endure it.

Deena would have to steel herself somehow. This was what life was going to be like, if he succeeded in joining the cabinet.

"Well, they did it," Moody said from behind his desk, waving the copy of the communiqué his secretary had just brought him.

"The Japanese?"

"Yes."

Deena stood up. "Hallelujah." She said it like a dirty word.

"Sit down, please, Deena. Now we have to wait for the president's call."

"Shit."

"Please."

"I don't know how you put up with this all the time, Robert."

"Right. You thought it was all inaugural balls."

He turned away. He was surprised by how cheerless he felt. He was still tormented by his conversation with Bloch—by his still having had no word from or about May.

Moody had trusted Bloch nearly all his adult life—trusted him with his money, with his political career, with carrying out special favors that could have gotten them both in important trouble if not carried out just right.

He'd never asked Bernie for anything to do with May before. Now he was trusting him with her life.

His secretary came in quite breathless with excitement. "Mr. Moody, sir. The president would like you to join him in the Oval Office."

The announcement press conference was anticlimactic. Reports of Moody's probable nomination had been leaking out of the State Department and the Capitol for days, and a piece predicting it had appeared on the *Post*'s federal page that morning—adding greatly to Moody's fears, as though its publication would cause the president to change his mind.

There were a few barbed questions from reporters, and the president pushed Moody forward to take them. At this, Moody was supremely competent. He turned his every answer into a polemic on behalf of the Earth Treaty.

The last question he took threw him for a moment. "Mr. Moody, there are reports some of your business friends back in Baltimore are working against the treaty. Is that going to hinder you in your new role?"

Who the hell was the man talking about? Moody stepped closer to the microphone. "Anyone who opposes this treaty is no friend of mine."

"No room for honest differences, Mr. Moody?"

"No sir. As the president says, it's the fate of the earth."

The president was pleased by his performance, and showed it at lunch by cutting his wife short when she began sniping at Deena about the need to maintain the dignity of the office while representing the United States abroad. For the rest of the meal, the first lady was mostly silent, letting her husband carry the burden of conversation. All were relieved when the ordeal came to an end with the last perfunctory sip of coffee.

When they were back in the sanctuary of Moody's office, Deena

**309**

headed for the wall cabinet where she knew he always kept a bottle of Jack Daniel's Black.

"I gotta have a drink, Robert. You want one?"

He shook his head. "You know damn well I never drink on duty. But you go ahead. I guess you earned it."

"Earned it? I just earned a hell of a lot more than a lousy goddamned glass of bourbon."

Moody, putting her out of his mind, went to his phone and his messages. The call he had his secretary return first was to Senate Leader Reidy.

"Mister Secretary," said Reidy, pronouncing the words as though he were the Senate doorkeeper. "Sounds good, doesn't it? You're going to be getting nothing but congratulations the rest of the day. Let me just say that I never had the slightest doubt you'd pull this off. You're a goddamn magician, Bobby. A winner."

"It's not a matter of magic now, Senator. It's down to grubby votes. What are my chances?"

"You haven't a worry, Bobby. You're as much a cinch as the treaty itself, and I've shown you my nose counts on that. It's just a matter of when you want the coronation. If you like, I can have the confirmation hearings set for this month."

"You're in recess until after Labor Day."

"Oh, I can always find a poor soul or two to show up for a committee hearing. Your friends on the committee will want to be there no matter what, I'm sure. In fact, I'd be surprised indeed if we couldn't get a floor vote on your nomination and on treaty ratification the same week."

"Treaty first."

"Naturally. How does the week of September ninth sound?"

"You're an optimist."

"No, Bobby, I'm a realist. I leave optimism to people like the president."

"September ninth? Really?"

"I'm not a kidder, Bobby."

"Well, your efforts are damn appreciated. You'll never know how much."

"Oh, I suppose that sometime in the future you might find a way to give me a little hint." He laughed.

"Thanks again, Senator." Moody hung up. One great joy of being secretary of state would be that he wouldn't have to deal with Reidy so much.

All manner of calls were coming in—from Richmond, Wally

Sadinauskas, General St. Angelo, the treasury secretary, the director of the FBI, the British ambassador, a producer at the "Today" show. Moody scanned the list impatiently. He couldn't call them all back. He wanted to get the hell out of there.

He sat up sharply, staring at one of the names, then quickly buzzed his secretary.

"Did this Mr. Kearny leave a number?"

"Yes sir."

"Get him."

"Yes sir."

Hal Kearny had been Moody's first law partner; his best man at his first wedding; for years, his best friend. They hadn't spoken since Moody's divorce. He wouldn't be calling now just because it seemed likely his old associate was about to become secretary of state.

Kearny was still living in Cumberland. Some people never changed.

"Bobby?"

"Sorry I missed your call, Hal. Busy day."

"I understand. It's quite an honor."

"Someday you good citizens of Cumberland can name a street after me. Maybe an alley."

Kearny did not joke back. "I told your secretary this was important, Bobby. It's about May."

Moody froze. Deena, pacing the room with her drink, noticed the change in his expression.

"What about her?"

"She doesn't want you to worry about her. She asked me to let you know that she's safe. She's fine. She'll get back to Washington as soon as she can. But you're not to worry. You're not to do anything about her. She wanted me to tell you that."

"Where the hell is she, Hal? In Cumberland? Where?" Moody was standing up behind his desk. Deena was watching him intently.

"She's not here, Bobby. She doesn't want it known where she is. She'll call you when she can. She's sorry she didn't talk to you before this. That's all she wanted me to tell you."

"Hal! For God's sake! We're friends. Where is she?"

"Sorry, Bobby. I promised."

"Damn it, Hal!"

"Sorry." He hung up.

Moody slumped back into his chair, his fingers drumming a staccato on his desk.

"What is it, Robert?" Deena asked. "Is it about May?"

Moody ignored her, thinking. It had to be Geneva's doing, Geneva's way of playing it safe. May would never have sought out Hal Kearny. Probably hadn't the faintest idea he was still in Cumberland. He'd been like a brother to Geneva. He probably still was.

May was with Geneva. Had to be. Best place she could go. Smart girl, May. You could hide a million horses in those hills in West Virginia.

He placed the call himself, the number returning to mind as though he dialed it every day.

It rang for the longest time. A man finally answered, his accent a shock to Moody—so familiar, yet from so long ago.

"Who is this?" Moody demanded.

"This is Tyrone. Is that you, Mr. Moody?"

"Yes, goddammit. Is my wife there? Geneva?"

"No sir. She's not here. She's away during the day, don't you know, Mr. Moody? Over in Wingo. If you want to wait a minute, I'll find the number for you."

"Never mind that, Tyrone! Put May on. Let me speak to my daughter."

"Jenny Mae? She's not here, Mr. Moody. The house is empty. That's why Mrs. Moody has me come by and check up on it."

May had to be there. She was just being really smart, not talking to anyone. He ought to just leave her be, at least until he could think this through. He still hadn't figured out what he was going to do about this. "All right, Tyrone. I get the picture. But if either one of them wants to call me—needs to call me—I can be reached at these numbers."

"Yes sir, Mr. Moody," he said, after Moody had rattled them off. "Now if you'll wait just a minute, I'll go see if I can find a pencil here and write them down."

"Who was that, Robert?" Deena asked, when he had finally finished with the call.

"Believe it or not, a town constable in West Virginia, the dumb sonofabitch."

"Have they found May? Is she all right?"

"What? No, it's nothing. Just someone I thought might know where she is. Come on, let's get out of here. I'm giving myself the rest of the day off. We'll go sit by the pool or something."

He thought of Deena in a bathing suit—and out of one. She could

312

do that much for him on this supposed day of days. She'd sure as hell been no geisha during their Asian trip. Not much of one since then, either. He needed a little interlude, a little time for his brain to work at a more natural speed, for his memory to serve up a little history and guidance. He'd been going through these last few weeks as frantically as if he were a company commander in Vietnam again. Hell, Napoleon used to take naps right in the middle of battles.

A couple of hours in the sun by the Watergate pool would be perfect. Just him and Deena. And his cellular phone.

Spencer's bureau chief was perplexed by his story on the horse country car bombing. True, Spencer hadn't exactly loaded it with information, but he'd stuck to all the basic rules of Journalism 101, and even managed to work in the fact that his own cousin was wanted for murder, though he'd left out his conviction that bomb victim Becky Bonning had herself murdered two human beings. His writing job, he thought, was worthy at least of Dick Francis, if not William Faulkner.

"But there's nothing in here about the Japanese, or that guy Napier," the chief said, glowering at his computer terminal screen.

"Sorry. They're not charged with anything. No one out there mentioned them even once."

"But there's got to be an angle like that. State Department heavy. Resigns under mysterious circumstances after pissing off the White House about the Japanese. His car gets blown up. Come on. Don't you know anyone at the Agency? Or the Bureau?"

The chief's first rule of journalism was, whenever in doubt, no matter what about, find someone to whisper with over at the CIA or the FBI.

"I don't have a source there who knows anything about horses. They don't spend a lot of time at the track, those fellows."

The bureau chief shook his head in exasperation. "Come on, Jack. They've got to be working this." He glanced over his desk in frustration. One of his favorite possessions had been a metal spike dating back to the eyeshade and sleeve garter days of newspapers. He'd kept it around long after they'd switched from teletypes to computers, going to great lengths to print out stories rather than simply electronically erasing them so he could enjoy the satisfaction of impaling paper on spike.

A few months before, someone had stolen it.

The chief pushed a button on the keyboard dumping Spencer's story into a computer storage queue.

"Do better," he said.

Spencer took that as a license for another trip to Dandytown, which he'd been planning on making anyway. Alixe Percy was improving, though the hospital still wasn't allowing visitors. Showers had managed to send Spencer an Express Mail package containing a lot of snapshots of the bay horse and a brief note that he was to forward them at once to the Canadian horseman Ryan, with a request that the man come out to Virginia as soon as possible if he was satisfied the animal in the pictures was his. Prosecutor Bensinger had called, suggesting that they meet late that afternoon at the Dandytown Inn—while urging Spencer to stay away from the courthouse and Dandytown proper.

Just before he left, Spencer's computer analyst friend called. He'd taken to this project like a kid with a new video game, and now had a new theory on the scratches he wanted Spencer to check out as soon as possible. And there'd been an anonymous note in Spencer's mailbox threatening him in vulgarly descriptive fashion with death and dismemberment. He'd received a number of letters in similar vein from lunatic readers over the years, but never one deposited directly in his mailbox without the apparent assistance of the Postal Service.

All part of the typical Washington correspondent's day.

Happily, his car did not explode when he started it. He was very pleased to be getting out of Washington. The August heat was beginning to build in with a vengeance, and it didn't go well with attempts at organized thought.

Among the horse pictures Showers had sent was one showing him and that knockout actress May Moody standing close together by the horse, with a ramshackle barn in the unfocused background. They all looked wonderfully content. Before sending the rest of the pictures on to the Canadian, Spencer stuck that photo in his pocket. He wanted to think of them like that—wherever they were.

He arrived at the Dandytown Inn shortly after three. Bensinger wasn't in the bar or the restaurant, and the bartender said he hadn't seen him at all that day.

A gin and tonic quickly quenched Spencer's thirst. A second provided a means of idling away a half hour or so, but by four o'clock, he began to get a little irritable. Finally, he shoved back his stool and went to the pay phone, calling Bensinger's office. A receptionist said he'd been away from the courthouse all afternoon. Spencer left no message.

Returning to the bar, he ordered a third drink, and immediately wished he hadn't. The room was largely empty, but a young man, walking with the aid of a crutch, had come in a few minutes before, taking a seat at the far end. Now he was coming toward Spencer's stool, clumpity thump, his glass in his free hand.

Spencer had been approached by enough people in enough bars all over the world to recognize each type in an instant—hookers, lonely housewives, party girls, junkies, lushes, traveling salesmen, confidence men, spies, bored businessmen, cops, barroom brawlers, weirdos, gays.

It appeared he'd just been caught by one of the latter. The man was young, with a tanned and rosy face; soft, delicate features; long eyelashes; and dark, curly hair worn overlong. Except for the crutch, he looked straight off the cover of a polo magazine—not that Spencer subscribed to many.

The young man eased himself clumsily onto the stool next to Spencer's, his injured leg brushing uncomfortably near.

"There are other places to sit, friend," Spencer growled.

"I'm sorry. I don't mean to intrude. Are you Mr. Spencer? Jack Spencer? The newspaperman who's writing a story about steeplechasing?"

"Who are you?" He'd heard there was a wide variety of sexual preference among some of the professional riders out here.

"You're Captain Showers' cousin? Is that correct?"

"Yes," Spencer said. "And you're who?"

"My name's Jimmy Kipp," he said, extending his hand. Spencer shook it limply. "I used to ride with the captain, until my accident. He saved my life."

Showers was always saving lives, rescuing damsels, healing injured animals, setting things right, saving the day. Even in his sailing days as a young man, Spencer had never once saved anyone's life—or given the possibility much thought.

"What can I do for you?" Spencer said, only slightly more friendly.

"It's what I can do for your cousin," Kipp said. "Everyone in town knows about the trouble he's in, the troubles he's had. I read that story that cost him his job with the State Department. About the memo, and the Japanese?"

"I wrote it."

"I know. That's why I've been coming around, hoping you'd show up again."

He paused to sip his drink. The bartender watched the two of them a moment, then moved down the bar to busy himself by the cash register.

"Some friends took me to Washington the other night," Kipp continued. "I was in the hospital a long time, and then recuperating at home. They thought I was ready for a good time. Anyway, we went to Georgetown, to a few bars. And we heard about this party, an after-hours party. You know, just for men."

Spencer sighed, wondering if he might have a better time if he just went home and reread the death threat he'd found in his mailbox.

"Well, it was a really fabulous party. And all kinds of famous people were there. People you read about in the magazines. I think two congressmen. And the first lady's social secretary. And some dancers and actors. I . . . I don't believe in 'outing.' I hate that. I'm not naming any names."

Of course not. The first lady had thousands of social secretaries.

"And I don't expect you to use any. Not in print. But, well, some of the people were going upstairs. To the bedrooms. One of my friends did. They charged him money."

"I'm shocked, shocked, that such a thing could be going on in the nation's capital."

"What?"

"Are we anywhere near the point?" Spencer asked.

"Yes. My friend had to borrow my credit card. They had a little machine. I still have the receipt. I'm going to let you have it." He dug it out of his wallet and set it on the bar. Spencer let it remain there.

"You're not trying to tell me that my cousin is in some way mixed up in this?"

"Oh no. Heavens no. Don't I only wish."

Spencer winced.

"Anyway," Kipp continued. "We found out later who owns the house, or rents it. It's Peter Napier. The man whose memo you wrote about? The one who lied about Captain Showers? Dreadful little man. Double chin and a little potbelly."

"You're sure about this? It's not just gossip?"

"It's not gossip. They say he's still with the government, or with the national committee, whatever that is. Anyway, he has this large

*316*

drawing account. And he uses it to finance these parties. And then he turns around and makes money off them."

"Do you remember the address of this place?"

"Yes," Kipp said. "I'll write it on the back of the receipt."

Spencer snatched it up the instant he was done.

"I'm really in your cousin's debt," Kipp said. "He not only saved my life. He helped pay my medical bills and he recommended me for a job over in Upperville when I'm fully recovered. So I, well, I thought that what I've just told you might help him get back at those people—straighten things out. I don't know. It could be something. I didn't like that Peter Napier at all."

"Oh, it'll help, all right." He fought to keep his utter glee from showing. If it checked out, the story he could write from this could blow people out of the saddle like a bloody bazooka, including perhaps even the almighty Robert Moody. "Right now, Mr. Kipp, I'd like to buy you a very large drink. You like brandy? I see they've got some five-star Courvoisier."

Kipp eyed him strangely, misunderstanding. The bartender, thankfully, intervened. "Are you Jack Spencer?"

"Yes?"

"Phone for you."

Spencer hurried to take it. The voice was Bensinger's.

"Sorry I didn't show," he said. "I had second thoughts about being seen with you. It's not been doing my local reputation any good, if you get my drift."

"That's all right. The trip wasn't a complete waste of time."

"It's in your car. Under the front seat."

"What is?"

"That little something Miss Percy wants your cousin to have. Can you get it to him?"

"I think so. Sooner or later."

"Hope it does some good. I can't do anything more for you for a while."

"Where are you?"

"Down the road. On my way home. I hope you'll come out again when things get back to normal out here. This is God's country, you know."

"Yeah, right."

Spencer didn't bother returning to the bar. He was out the inn's screen door and into his car before anyone else could even speak to him. There was a thick, sealed manila envelope under the seat on the passenger side. It bore only Showers' name. Spencer hesitated, then tore it open. All that was inside was a videotape cassette, with no labels.

He was stuffing it back in the envelope when he heard a woman's voice out his window, very near. Startled, he looked up into the lovely, fading, and very tense face of Lenore Fairbrother. The last time he'd seen her, she'd been dancing in the White House foyer with Robert Moody. She'd looked infinitely more happy then than she did now, though by no means more sober.

"I know you," she said. "You're David's wretched cousin, the newspaper spy."

"Describes me perfectly," he said. "You must have been reading my *Who's Who* listing." He turned on his car engine.

She gripped the top of his car door with both hands, as much for balance as in any hope of preventing his swift departure.

"Why are you here?" she asked, her eyes slightly unfocused.

"Nice day for a drive in the country." He gunned the motor once, in warning.

"Where is David? You must know. Tell me where he is."

"Out with a horse, I'd guess. Nice day for a ride, too."

"You bastard. Where is he? Where's David?"

Spencer reached and jerked one of her hands from the door by the wrist, causing her to stumble backward. Then he slammed the gearshift into drive and hit the accelerator. The car lurched forward, wheels spinning in the gravel, then catching, sped away, covering her in a cloud of dust.

In the rearview mirror, he saw her make an obscene gesture, then dart away. Spencer spun onto the highway and headed north toward the interstate. A few minutes later, to his amazement, he saw the tiny dot of a dark automobile appear far back on the road behind him. It gained rapidly, increasing in size until he was able to recognize it as a Jaguar. He saw that the driver was a woman, with long hair.

Both their engines were screaming. They were well over the speed limit. If Spencer wasn't careful, the good sheriff might soon be handing him something far more serious than a parking ticket.

A pickup truck was trundling along the road ahead of them. Though a car was approaching fast from the opposite direction, Spencer jammed the accelerator to the floor and whipped out to pass, completing the maneuver with just seconds to spare.

She was right behind him. She stayed there, close to his bumper, weaving slightly from side to side, her face almost maniacal. She was as good a driver as he—probably better—but drink and the heat combined against her.

He let the Jaguar sit there on his rear as they roared along toward the interstate, the sign announcing the entrance ramp approaching fast. Without slowing, giving no indication of his intention, he waited until the very last instant, then spun his car to the right—swerving and skidding, but staying on the ramp.

Lenore didn't quite make the turn. He saw her careen into the shoulder lane, then disappear beneath the overpass. He hoped she was uninjured, but he wasn't about to go back to make sure. He kept his car between eighty and ninety well into the next county, before slowing to keep pace with the other traffic. She didn't appear again.

Lenore Fairbrother entered her husband's house like a projectile, aiming herself fixedly down the great central hall toward her husband's study and bursting through the door without pause. Unfortunately for what was to have been her subsequent detonation, he was not there. Blinking, temporarily defused, she stood wavering a moment, then relaunched herself, tearing through the rooms of the house one by one, calling out the syllables *Lyn-wood* in the piercing shrieks of a harpy, the sound reverberating ahead of her.

Fairbrother was standing at the head of the stairs, wearing a dressing gown over his shirt and trousers despite the heat. Startled by the sight of him, she fell silent.

"What in hell are you caterwauling about, Lenore?" Fairbrother could thunder when he was up to it. She became even more subdued, collapsing on the staircase and sobbing.

"Lenore! What's wrong? Are you drunk?"

"Worse than that," she said, now in a little girl's voice. "I've been arrested."

He began descending the stairs. He was barefoot, having been disturbed from a nap.

"For what have you been arrested?" he said, coming to a halt just above her.

"For driving under the fucking influence, that's what," she said, a little defiantly. "By one of your vulgar little sheriff's deputies."

"They're not my sheriff's deputies."

"Well, he's your sheriff. You paid for him."

"I endorsed his candidacy and I made a campaign contribution. We all did. But that's not going to be of any help to you now. Not this time. Did you have an accident?"

"Yes."

"Was anyone hurt?"

"Only the Jaguar, and it's a bloody shambles."

"What did you hit?"

"I scraped it along the side of an embankment. Oh, never mind, Lynwood." She patted the top of a stair. "Sit down, Lynwood, and comfort me. I'm so fucking miserable."

He did so. She raised herself to kiss his foot, then crawled up to him, laying her head in his lap. She looked very woozy. Fairbrother felt stiff and uncomfortable. He had needed this nap.

"What do you want, Lenore?" It occurred to him he must utter these words twenty times a day. "Do you need a doctor?"

"I want David to come back."

"We've been through this."

She sat up. "Yes, and you promised you'd get him back."

"I didn't promise any such thing."

"You asked the sheriff to have him arrested."

"I most certainly did not! That was Cooke's own idea."

"Your idea, darling. You said that if charges were placed against David he'd hurry right back to clear his name."

"Cooke suggested it. I merely gave my approval."

"All the same, darling, in Dandytown. David's going to hate you forever and ever."

"I'm sorry, but I was outraged that he'd decamp like that and leave us with all this appalling disorder to contend with. Great God—murders, bombings, fires, bloodstock investigations, lurid stories in the *Post*. I'm not certain we'll be able to hold the Old Dominion Cup. I've had inquiries from horsemen in three states asking if they should come. It's monstrous."

"Poor Lynnie." She stroked his foot. He moved it away.

"David's at the center of this scandalous business, yet he hasn't raised a finger to put an end to it. He just vanishes. I have to answer all the damned questions. Ned Haney won't say anything to anyone. Alixe is in the hospital and can't talk. Everyone's coming to me! I don't understand how David could be so irresponsible. His father wasn't like that. Damn good man, his father."

He quieted a moment.

"And I'm not certain the murder charges are spurious," he said.

"That's rot, Lynnie."

"The courts will decide."

"You're just jealous, Lynwood. It's your only passion. You think David's been making love to me."

"The maid told me he'd dropped off your clothes. In a package.

After that night at the inn. All of your clothes, Lenore, including your underwear."

"Oh, for God's sake, Lynnie. I just took them off."

"You made love."

"Lynnie. Poor love-starved David hasn't touched me since I married you. Point of honor, don't you know. You're being a fool, *comme toujours.*"

"I don't believe you."

"I need a drink, darling."

"No you don't."

"I need a new car."

"It's a total wreck?"

"The right side is. Altogether gruesome."

"Did they take you to the police station?"

"No. The deputy just drove me home. But he gave me this ticket. I have to go to court. In the morning."

"Did they give you a blood alcohol test?"

"I would not submit to such an indignity. You wouldn't either if you had seen the man's awful manners. You'd think I drove into that wall on purpose."

"What on earth were you doing?"

"Just out for a drive." She put her hand over her eyes. "Lovely day for a drive in the country. It was, anyway."

"You'll lose your license for refusing the test. I can get you a new car, but not a new license. It's quite automatic. State law."

"Can't you do something about that?"

"Absolutely not."

"Not? Though you can have David charged with murder?"

"No!"

"Well, who needs a silly license anyhow."

Fairbrother started to rise. She pulled him down.

"I have to go, Lenore. Telephone calls to make. I have to meet some people in town."

"Are they calls to get David back?"

"No. Merely business."

"I know where he is. He's with that hillbilly movie star. Probably in some hillbilly motel. He likes white-trash women, trashy white women. He likes to fuck them."

Fairbrother stood up. She used him to get awkwardly to her own feet, clinging to his robe.

"Please, Lenore."

"I've just had a marvelous idea, Lynnie. You know the governor.

You could have David's National Guard company activated. He wouldn't refuse a call to active duty. You know how he is about the bloody military."

"I never know when you're serious anymore, Lenore."

He started back up the stairs. She followed, for a few steps.

"I know!" she said. "Moonsugar."

"What?"

"Your horse Moonsugar. You gave it to him but you never signed over the papers. David's not here to take care of it. You've every right to bring him back."

"Someone ought to look in on those horses. You can't trust Alixe's grooms with her away in the hospital. All right. I'll send a man over."

"I want Moonsugar brought back here, Lynwood."

"All right, all right."

"I'm very, very unhappy, Lynwood."

He continued on up the stairs without her. When he had dressed and come back down again, she was lying on the hall floor, snoring.

Hours later, when Fairbrother returned from Dandytown late in the evening, his stable manager was waiting for him.

"I've got some bad news, Mr. Fairbrother."

"What now?"

"We went over to the Showers place like you said. The stock all looked good. I guess Ned Haney's had a vet come over to check up on them. In top condition, all of them. Especially Moonsugar. You'd never know he took that fall."

"And?"

"We brought Moonsugar back with us. I put him in his old stall. He was fine when I left him, but when I came back after dinner, he was dead. Mrs. Fairbrother gave him an injection. Said it was because of his broken leg."

# Twenty-One

ike nearly all people who grow up in the country, Moody was a walker. All his life, every day, even when caught up in the pomp and power of the Maryland governorship and the White House, he had found time to steal away for solitary retreats on foot. On busy days, during breaks in the president's schedule, he'd often slip out for a quick walk on the White House grounds, following the perimeter of the security fence down to where the South Lawn ended at the roadway dividing it from the Ellipse.

In their presidency, on quiet evenings, the Bushes had liked to walk their dogs down to this spot, frequently startling the tourists who paused by the fence to stare at the White House or pose for pictures with its grand South Portico in the background.

There were a few tourists hanging about there now on this hot, sunny morning—an elderly couple, a young family with small children, a boy and girl of college age dressed in T-shirts and skimpy shorts. None of them seemed to recognize Moody, perhaps taking him for a Secret Service man. He waited for them to move on, then leaned back against the fence, folding his arms in a moment of solitary contemplation of the presidential mansion set so magnificently at the top of the long green rise.

Generations of political writers and historians had referred to this house as "the prize," but it wasn't that. Not a trophy or a piece of booty. No possession. Just a transitory honor, and one that all too often turned into disgrace.

As a state legislator, Moody had stood in bitter cold on the Capitol lawn at the inauguration of Jimmy Carter, had observed the

*323*

pious, posed humility of the man, his saintly image belied by the conquering swagger of aides like Hamilton Jordan and Bert Lance. They had come in thumping their feet up on priceless antique desks and barking crude orders and sneering at venerated old-timers like House Speaker Tip O'Neill, proclaiming their day was done, as though the Georgia peanut warehouse man had brought forth the millennium. O'Neill had still been there when they'd left, doubtless shaking his head.

Moody had also been in Washington for the grotesque, glittering pageant that was Ronald Reagan's inauguration. He remembered the endless limousines filled with fur-coated, bejeweled women and overdressed men, prowling the capital's streets the way curious Nazis had the boulevards of defeated Paris in May 1940. He recalled the contempt and arrogance displayed by Reagan major-domos Ed Meese, Mike Deaver, and Don Regan—and later, George Bush's John Sununu—as they went about wielding the all too temporal power of their office, as he had himself done, he supposed, far too often.

They were all gone now, all pathetic or forgotten figures, unable even to command a good table at a second-rate Washington restaurant. Carter had seen himself as a peacemaking messiah. He'd ended up a pariah at his own party's next national convention. Reagan had wrapped himself in the golden aura of a mythic American hero, yet within hours of leaving office, he had put on a silly hat for the benefit of television cameras in Los Angeles and instantly revealed himself the amiable dolt he'd been all along. Moody's president, like Bush before him, was still struggling with the crushing federal debt that had been Reagan's only real legacy.

Moody's president would be gone one day, leaving nothing behind but this visionary global treaty, if they were lucky enough to get it ratified and its provisions codified in American law, if they could avoid its becoming as tragically meaningless as Woodrow Wilson's Versailles Treaty.

What then? Who then?

"President Moody." He sometimes repeated the words to himself, indulging in the fantasy of the boy from the hollows rising to host kings and queens in great splendor. But fantasy it was, and probably always would be. The vice presidency, laughable worm of a role, was in prospect now, but all Robert Moody really held in his hands was this hard-won claim for inclusion in the history books as the president's chief diplomat, a place at the head of the cabinet table, which sooner or later he'd have to give up to another.

**324**

He had a couple of heroes. Few schoolchildren had ever heard of either of them. Moody had no real wish to become like them, though he admired them greatly. One was Charles Loeb, who'd served as Teddy Roosevelt's private secretary. A very intelligent fellow, but unassuming, self-effacing, totally his boss's man, like thousands of men and women laboring in the federal bureaucracy this very day. Loeb had been TR's principal confidant and adviser and the real author of some of his boldest reforms, especially the trust-busting assaults upon some of the nation's greediest robber baron empires. When Roosevelt had been off on his grand tours and lengthy sojourns in the wild, Loeb could always be found at a nearby telegraph, quietly running the United States of America. Yet, for all his contributions, Loeb had remained in obscurity, a footnote for Roosevelt's biographers. Better known was his irascible son William, who won fame for the outrageous irresponsibility of the editorials he wrote as publisher of New Hampshire's *Manchester Union-Leader*.

Moody's other hero was Dean Rusk, a onetime poor boy like himself who'd risen to serve at the right hand of the high and mighty at the grand conclusion of World War II. His had been the sanest voice raised in the councils that had conducted the disastrously long crusade in Vietnam. Ultimately, it had been a colossal failure, but Rusk had believed in its essential good purpose as strongly as Moody had leading his men against North Vietnamese machine gunners in the central highlands.

Rusk's entire career had been one of unselfish, dedicated, sacrificial, and uncomplaining public service, yet he'd ended up without much more respect or gratitude than Bert Lance or Ed Meese had been accorded—a weary, embittered, forgotten professor at some obscure Georgia college, writing memoirs few would read. Had he contemplated such an eventual fate the day he'd been sworn in as secretary of state?

"Excuse me, sir."

Moody turned to see two overweight, middle-aged women standing on the other side of the fence, one of them holding an Instamatic camera.

"Excuse me, sir," the woman repeated. "Would you mind moving to the side a little? We'd like to take a picture."

Moody grinned. "Sure," he said. "I was just about to go."

He started up the lawn. There was a National Security Council meeting in a few minutes. Hostilities had broken out for real in tiny, distant Belize, and the marine force he'd sent there and reinforced was definitely in harm's way. It would be a tricky business getting the United States out of this one without some nasty bloodshed and embarrassment. Rusk had gotten Lyndon Johnson out of the Dominican Republic in 1965. Who now remembered that?

Approaching the South Portico, Moody stopped to look up at the mansion, recalling the many times he had stood with the president on the Truman Balcony, hovering near with some official paper or listening patiently as the president lectured him on some point of international principle. He had a photograph of the two of them like that, hanging framed in his office. The president had no such picture, only traditional silver-framed photographs of family and friends.

Moody lingered a moment longer, thinking of his last day in the Maryland statehouse before he'd come to Washington, surrounded by so many friends and followers and well-wishers. If he had contented himself with a term or two as governor of his home if not native state, it would have been a satisfactory culmination of a political career—far more satisfactory than most. He'd have remained a respected figure anywhere he went, addressed honorably as "Governor" the rest of his days.

Now, it was far too late for that.

After the NSC meeting came the cabinet meeting. After that, Wally Sadinauskas followed Moody back to his office. The president had a series of appointments with several ambassadors that Moody wanted to sit in on, so he was probably a little curt, not inviting the energy secretary to a seat, keeping him standing on the carpet.

"What's up, Wally?"

"Senator Sorenson wants to meet with you, with both of us."

Moody went to his desk and glanced at his schedule. "Can't today. Why didn't he call for an appointment?"

"He doesn't want to make it an official meeting. Nothing on any logbook. He says it's important. Can you do it tonight?"

Deena had made no plans for the evening, but there were a number of diplomatic drop-bys Moody didn't want to neglect. He intended to make it very clear how serious he was about becoming secretary of state.

"Important how?"

"It's about the treaty."

"Shit. What does he want, another fucking highway?"

"He doesn't want anything, except for the three of us to talk. There's some trouble. Big trouble."

"Aw, come on, Wally. I don't have time for this."

"I'm afraid you'll have to find it. Trust me."

"All right. Seven o'clock. We'll make it at the Kennedy Center."

"The Kennedy Center?"

The huge performing arts complex next to the Watergate had a big underground garage where one could arrive without anyone noticing. Its many elevators were equally discreet. At that hour, it would be busy with tourists and early theatergoers—not anyone from officialdom. Moody had used it for several very private meetings in the past, usually with women.

"The rooftop restaurant," Moody said. "I'll get a table in the back."


The junior senator from Wisconsin seemed more than nervous when he sat down with Moody and Sadinauskas; he looked scared. His hair was even mussed, lying in sweaty lanks across his forehead. He ordered a brandy manhattan, a very serious drink.

"Wally says we have a problem," Moody said. "I thought you and I had taken care of all our problems."

Sorenson took a deep breath, and then a sip of his cocktail. "There's a lot of heavy money and muscle being applied against the treaty. Some of it's coming my way."

"And you want a little something from me for moral encouragement?"

"No. I want you to know what's going on. You've been straight with me. I want to keep it that way."

"Well, Senator, there's been heavy money and muscle working against us from the very beginning. This doesn't exactly come as a surprise."

"It's being directed from Senator Reidy's office."

Moody sat back, squinting against the direct rays of early evening sunlight. "What the hell are you talking about? Reidy just showed me a nose count giving us seventy-five votes. I've seen surveys from the Republican National Committee giving us more, and those guys are against us."

"That's on the ratification vote," Sorenson said. "That's a breeze. We're all going to vote for that. Get our support for motherhood down on the record. But you let Reidy split the package up, remember? Ratification now. Implementing legislation later. That's where the lie-down is supposed to come. When you try to enact all this stuff into law. The bad guys carpet bomb the thing with all kinds of killer amendments, and we're supposed to sit back

**327**

and let it happen. No skin off our teeth, right? We've already voted to rid the world of pollution."

"Who's 'we'?"

"Reidy's got a list of buyees. It's a long list."

"You'd be surprised to see who's on it," Sadinauskas said.

"I'm on it," Sorenson said. "I don't know why. What's bothering the hell out of me is that I'm being treated as a foregone conclusion, as though I'm already delivered. They're not trying to twist my arm with all this; they're acting as though my arm was already broken, and what they're offering me is just payoff."

"And what're they offering you?"

"It's all legal, in my case, anyway. PAC money. I've never seen so much PAC money. Industry groups. Labor unions. Law firms. The leadership is supposed to protect us from this kind of pressure. Normally, nobody would even try it. Reidy's not only permitting it, he's encouraging it. He's made it clear it's expected of them."

Sadinauskas leaned close. "Bob, Reidy's using the implementation legislation as a fetcher bill."

Anyone who had ever served in a state legislature knew what one of those was—a measure so painful and so odious it would draw money and favors like flies to raw meat, a measure introduced for no other purpose. In the end, such bills always died, but not before they'd done their remunerative work.

"This isn't the Maryland House of Delegates, or the Illinois legislature," Moody said. "This is the United States Senate. The big time. Things aren't done that way."

What was he talking about? A number of almighty U.S. senators had been accused of taking a fall in the Keating savings and loan scandal. House Speaker James Wright hadn't been run out of office for jaywalking.

"Like I say, it's mostly legal," Sorenson said. "PACs. There are a lot of logs rolling around, though. And I think some under-the-table stuff here and there. Not to speak of under the covers. I'm told they've brought in some top-dollar call girls from New York, should anyone be in the mood for a little consultation during the amendment process. Whatever anyone's brave enough to take, it's theirs for the asking."

"How do you know all this?" Moody asked, his arms folded.

"Ours is a collegial body. And, like I told you, for some reason, I'm on the list."

"More to the point, Senator, why are you telling me this?"

"I want to be straight with you."

"Be even straighter. What's your motivation here? What do you want from me?"

Sorenson finished his drink. He wiped his forehead with a handkerchief. "I already have it, Mr. Moody. I hope." He gestured at the room. "My wife is really looking forward to going on the Kennedy Center board. Being part of this year's Kennedy Center Honors means more to her than my getting reelected. She wants to meet Lauren Bacall and Katharine Hepburn and Jack Lemmon. All those people. Really. She's ordered a ball gown from a designer in New York, and her appointment hasn't even been voted on yet." His eyes sought Moody's. Complete candor. "I don't want to do anything—not the slightest little thing—to screw it up."

Sorenson was holding something back. He was still nervous, even scared. Moody waited, letting him hang there for a moment, then leaned in close himself.

"Is this all you came here to tell me?"

Sorenson looked down at the tabletop. "No. Some of the biggest money on this is coming from somebody you thought was on your side. I didn't believe it when I heard it, but I talked to the man himself."

"And who is that?"

"Your friend Bernie Bloch."

Moody felt his face redden with his anger. He fought to control himself, wondering what he must look like. A fool. A cuckold. A mark in a con game. A few weeks before, he would have had Sorenson thrown out of the place for even suggesting such a thing. But he was learning better, wasn't he? The most infuriating thing about this revelation was that it really didn't come as a surprise.

"You're very, very sure about this, Senator?"

"Yes sir. Absolutely. I know how tight he's supposed to be with the White House. It threw me for a hell of a loop at first. I wasn't sure where I was supposed to be; if I had read the signals wrong. Anyway, I thought you'd want to know."

He must be afraid Moody was going to shoot the messenger.

"I appreciate it," Moody said. He put his hand on Sorenson's shoulder. "I'll handle this. Don't talk to anyone else about it. Just go about your business and when the time comes, vote your conscience, if you know what I mean."

"I certainly do."

"All right, Senator. Thanks for coming by. You probably want to get home to your wife." He looked to Sandinauskas. "Can you spare me a couple more minutes, Wally?"

                                    *    *    *

They went out onto the broad terrace that ran along the outer edge
of the roof, pausing at a spot that looked west up the river toward
the setting sun. The twin spires of Georgetown University's
Dahlgren Chapel caught the gleam along their leading edges. A
large motor yacht chugged along on the deepening blue of the
water.

"So I'm the last fucking rattlesnake to wake up," Moody said.

"What?"

"A West Virginia expression. So tell me, Wally. Do I have this
figured right? Reidy's going to kill the treaty by letting all the
influence peddlers in town walk right in and stamp it out?"

"It'll get the job done."

"And when the president screams, Reidy can just stand there and
point to the special interests. Blame the White House for a failure
of leadership?"

"I can hear his words now."

"But what the hell for? The treaty's no big deal for him, no life
or death issue in his state. He didn't even take a position on it in the
campaign. What's his big fucking problem?"

"He loves to win and hates to lose, Bobby. This is a man who is
still denying decent Senate Office Building space to guys who
crossed him over some penny-ante bill ten years ago. You kicked
the shit out of him in the primaries. You kept him from being
president. He's a hater, Bobby, and he hates you and the president.
He's just been waiting for the right shot. He's going to make you
lose. Lose very, very big."

Moody watched the sky changing colors. The high trees on
Roosevelt Island made him think of home.

"We can still stop this, Wally. Thanks to your friend Sorenson. If
we go public, we can stop it cold. I can get the president to have ratification pulled off the calendar. We can combine it with the implementing legislation again and make the bastards vote the whole
package all at once, up or down. And if we get it out to the newsies that
there's all this money down against the treaty, damn few 'buyees' will
dare vote no."

"True enough, Bobby, except for one thing. You'd be kissing
your own ass goodbye. Bernie Bloch is your friend. You're as tied
up with him as anybody holding public office in the country today.
If he turns up as one of the bad guys, how is it going to look for
you? Do I have to remind you that your name is before the Senate
Foreign Relations Committee for appointment as secretary of
state?"

*330*

For the rest of the evening, Moody tried to reach Bloch, calling all his private numbers and even his boat moored in Baltimore Harbor. His calls were all answered by servants or recording machines or not at all. Moody couldn't understand it. For nearly thirty years, he had always been able to reach out to Bernie, and Bloch to him, no matter where or when or what. Bloch had even left numbers for him to call when he was off on weekend shack jobs in Atlantic City or the Bahamas. Now, nothing.

Moody's anger had not subsided. It continued to roil, like a pot of water left on simmer, a pot that would begin to scorch and burn once the water had all bubbled away.

Reidy was going to lose this one. Moody intended to stop him cold. But it had to start with Bernie.

Moody was in his living room, his air conditioning on but his sliding balcony doors open to the night, staring out the window at the lights of Rosslyn across the river. Deena, nervous and fidgety, sat with him, refusing to go to bed.

"Why do you need to talk to him so bad?" she asked.

"An emergency. A big, fat, very important emergency."

"But what's it about?"

He glowered at her. He had told her in the beginning that there would be many, many things he'd have to keep from her—that on these occasions it would be so obvious to her that she shouldn't even ask. But she continued to pester him.

"Does this have to do with the government? With your job?"

"Yes. And that's absolutely all you have to know."

"Do you want a drink?"

"No."

She continued to sit with him, not very still. She had changed into a light silk bathrobe, and was apparently not wearing much underneath. She kept crossing and uncrossing her legs, flashing thigh.

"Deena," he said, finally. "I want you to be honest with me. Do you know some way to reach Bernie? Some way I don't?"

His wife squirmed a little in her chair. The legs changed again, left over right.

"I think I do."

"You think you do."

"Don't get this wrong, Bobby. He and I have just been talking a lot lately. He's been a help to me. I've been going all to pieces over this new job you're going to get. I'm not sure I'm going to be able to handle it. Frankly, Bobby, I've been scared to death. I talk to Bernie sometimes. He helps me. A shoulder to cry on."

"You never said a word to me."

"I didn't want to bother you. I don't want to hold you back in any way."

Lenore Fairbrother's words had never left him. She'd said she'd seen Deena performing fellatio on another man. He hadn't been able to make up his mind whether the woman had just been playing mean-spirited games with him or whether there was something to it.

But he couldn't imagine Deena with Bernie. He could not imagine Bernie being that stupid.

He couldn't have imagined Bloch sticking the knife into him over the treaty, either.

"He's having a lot of problems with Sherrie," Deena said. "She's really around the bend. He talks to me about her. He's got no one else."

Moody stared.

"Anyway," Deena said. "He has this new number. It rings a beeper."

"And he calls you when it goes off?"

"I have to leave a message. On a machine."

"Call him. Now."

She did so. They sat in silence afterward. Within twenty minutes, the phone rang.

"Hold on, Bernie," she said, after answering. "It's Bobby. He really has to talk to you."

She stood, holding the phone. Her robe had fallen open.

"Go to bed," Moody said, taking the receiver. "I'll talk to you later."

Deena gave him a very worried look, then walked away, the robe shimmering. He sat down, stretching out his legs, making himself relax, thinking calm.

"Where are you, Bernie? Are you anywhere near Washington?"

"Yeah."

"Where?"

"I'm in Charlottesville. The Boar's Head Inn. A little business meeting."

"I want you to come back. Tonight. I have to talk to you. In person. In private."

"No can do, Bobby."

"Let me put it this way. It's official government business."

"Can't. Sorry."

Moody sat without speaking a moment, wondering as he always wondered if someone might have a tap on his phone. He had always conducted his conversations as though that were the case.

"Then listen to me now, Bernie. Listen carefully, because I don't want you to have any doubts about what I have to say." He paused, steadying himself again. "I know all about the money you've laid down against the treaty. I know what you're doing and what Reidy's doing and how you've been working together."

"What kind of bullshit is that, Bobby? Who've you been talking to?"

"I know everything. I've got it all down cold. I have enough to put you and Reidy at a table with microphones on it. Under oath. Do you hear what I'm saying?"

"I hear you, but it's bullshit. What the fuck have you turned into, Ralph Nader or something?"

"I work for the president of the United States, friend. And you have put this administration in big goddamned jeopardy."

"Knock off the civics crap, Bobby. It's nothing personal, all right? It's just politics. Hard ball. Kick bite scratch, dog eat dog. Name of the game."

"Why did you have to do it? Why can't you just count your goddamned millions and leave the government alone? Leave me alone?"

"You're not that naive, are you, Bobby? Where the hell do you think those millions come from? Did you ever stop to think for a minute what that fucking treaty would do to me? To a lot of us? It's not just me, pal. You've got all our backs up, across the board, both sides of the line. There's big Republican money down on this one. Respectable names. Social Register. You'd be amazed."

"This isn't how it's done."

"Fuck you, pal. It's how it's always been done, and always will be."

"Not this time."

"Oh yeah? Don't be a chump. Everything's set. It's all in motion. Nothing you can do about it. No reason for you to. You'll come out of this all right. You can stay square with your boss. You'll be secretary of state in a month. By the time he figures out the rug has been pulled, you'll probably be sitting in the vice president's chair."

Moody waited, as though giving this serious thought. "I'm not buying in, Bernie."

Bloch sighed. His voice took on a very hard edge when he spoke again. "I didn't want it to come to this, but you give me no goddamned choice. You're not going to do a thing to screw us up. You're going to drop it."

"Come to what?"

"You've got to make me say it, don't you? A lot of people have turned up dead, pal. Including two young broads, and nobody has the faintest fucking idea who did it. They never will. You want there to be another dead body, Bobby? Another young woman? A real looker, out of California? Turn up in a ditch, and nobody knows why?"

"Are you talking about May?"

"Yeah, May. You love her, you said. You want her back, you said. So why put her in jeopardy? You told me you looked at that girl's body out there, how she had her head half cut off. Think of May's head. Think of her pretty face. These friends of mine, it's been all I can do to hold them off. Why should I even bother if you're going to try to put the screws to me?"

"You can't touch her."

"Listen up, Bobby. I know exactly where she is. She's holed up at Geneva's place in the mountains. She's been there for days. I've told them they can't touch her, but you push me like this . . . I mean, I could make a call and in five minutes she's dead. Why would you make me do that?"

Moody remembered May as a little girl, sitting on Bernie's lap, playing with the gold chain he used to wear. "You wouldn't do that."

"Bobby, I do what I have to. You know me well enough to know that."

"I don't know you at all."

"So what's it going to be?"

Moody's breathing was so heavy he sounded like an asthmatic.

"I want May out of this. Alive. Untouched."

"Terrific. So are you going to play?"

"I don't know."

"We should have a meeting."

"A meeting?"

"With some guys who can help."

"Your friends?"

"No. Your friends, Bobby. You've got a lot at stake in this. You want to protect your interests the same way I do."

"My interest is May."

"We're still in a recession, Bobby. Your investments have been locked up in a trust since your first day as governor. I'm told you'll be lucky if you end up with half what you had. You've got a long way to go in public service. You don't want to retire on a government pension. I'd like to see you have a little something set aside."

"Why?"

"We've been laying all this money on every yo-yo in the Senate. We oughta be placing a bet on a number that'll really count. Reidy may be a smart son of a bitch, but this is going to take real finesse, especially if we're going to keep the president steered clear of what's really going on."

"You're offering me money?"

"I want everybody happy, including you. I want a meeting. Tomorrow morning. Cut a deal. You, me, and Reidy. Maybe one of those big Republicans I was talking about, so you can see that all the bets are down."

"Where?"

"We need neutral ground. Make it a hotel. We'll get a suite. A little prayer breakfast. The Hay-Adams. Reidy likes it. It overlooks the White House."

"The Hay-Adams."

"Nine A.M. If Reidy balks, I'll call you. But I don't think he will. This'll knock his fucking socks off."

"And if it's a done deal, tomorrow afternoon, I get May back. Not a scratch on her, you understand? I'm going to hold you responsible for anything your 'friends' do."

"Understood. What about Showers?"

"I'd leave him be if I were you. He has some high-placed friends."

"That may be out of my hands. And the horse?"

"Bernie, I do not give a good goddamn about that horse."

"Okay. Fucking terrific. Bobby, for the first time in years, you're talking like a winner again."

"Good night, Bernie. Don't double-cross me."

"It'll be a happy ending, Bobby. A happy ending."

Afterward, Moody sat motionless in his chair for a very long moment. It was going to be a long night.

But first things first.

He went into their bedroom. The lights were off, but he could tell that Deena was awake. She had probably been listening to every word.

He clicked on the wall switch. Caught unawares in the sudden glare, she didn't look so lovely.

"You told Bernie where May was, didn't you?" he said. "You overheard me in my office and you tipped him off."

"Bobby . . ."

"Yes or no?"

"I was worried about her. I thought Bernie—"

"I'm going out for a while. I've got some thinking to do. I won't be gone more than an hour. I want you out of here by the time I get back."

"What do you mean?"

"Out. Gone. Removed. Take your clothes. Take everything I ever bought you. Take the big car. I'm sure you've kept that divorce lawyer of yours on retainer. But go. Get out. We're through. As you've pointed out, Deena, you'd make a lousy first lady."

# Twenty-Two

May and Showers had thrown back the top sheet to enjoy the fullest freedom in their lovemaking, and now they lay naked in each other's arms, wrapped only in the heat of the night. They had been very circumspect all these days and nights in her mother's house, confining themselves to the touch of a hand or a brief, hasty kiss, keeping to separate bedrooms, remaining respectful of Mrs. Moody's presence and proprieties.

But this night she was spending with a church family over in Wingo, leaving only the girl Bella in the house and Tyrone and his friends to take turns watching over the stallion in the shed. Showers and May had sat talking quietly after dinner and then gone for a walk, but, upon returning, had cast all inhibitions aside, hurrying to Showers' room, not caring what Bella in her little bedroom down the hall over the kitchen might hear.

With a rough urgency the first time, more tenderly and gently the second, he'd twice brought her to joyful climax—the dreamy, teary look in her eyes giving him as much pleasure as the sexual release. They'd held and stroked each other in between times and long afterward, speaking to each other in caresses of both words and touch. Finally, she had slipped off into a blissful sleep, lying against him, her head on his chest, her leg thrown between his.

He'd found no such bliss. Like a boat pulled to and fro by successive swells, he'd drifted in and out of consciousness, from stark awareness of the dark room around them into fitful dreams and back again, over and over, the dreams fearful, the wakefulness just as bad. Somewhere in the trees, an owl called. A car groaned along a road at some distance. Myriad insects buzzed and ticked and peeped in nocturnal ritual. May's breathing was soft and slow. Showers looked at the objects in the room, barely limned in the faint light from the window. A few stars in the sky. A glimpse of moon, suffused in haze. He thought of Vicky Clay, in her last hours and minutes, lying stiffly on a bed, her universe reduced to what she could see around her.

His pistol, a dark lump, was on the bed table. He'd not been more than a few feet away from it in all the time he'd been in this little town.

With his mind's eye, he saw the man he'd shot leap backward again, heard his scream.

Showers sat up, perspiring. He snatched up his wristwatch, squinting at it.

"May. Wake up."

She stirred and murmured. Nothing more.

"May!" He shook her shoulder.

She shifted, opening her eyes.

"What is it? What's wrong?"

"I want to go. Now."

"What? Go where?"

"I'm going to take the horse back. I'm going to give it back to them."

"Give it back? The horse?" She rubbed her eyes.

"We'll take it to Ned Haney's, to the auction house. If they want to come after it, it's theirs. I want nothing more to do with it."

"But why, David?"

"Because it doesn't matter. What matters is that Becky's dead. Selma's dead. Alixe has been butchered. We're hiding out here for our lives. All because of this one damned horse. All because of me. I've finally come to my senses, May. Everything I want in life, everything I really want, is with me in this room, in this bed. I'm not going to risk losing you. I'm not going to throw anything more away."

"David . . ." She came into his arms, her hair against his cheek. "In the morning, David."

"No." He swung his legs over the side of the bed. "Now. I want to drive back tonight and get this over with. Get dressed. Call Tyrone, and see if he can find us some kind of truck."

They dressed without speaking further. While she phoned Tyrone, he brushed his teeth and shaved, fearful he was taking too much time.

*338*

"He has to go up the highway," May said. "He'll be back as soon as he can, though he thinks we're crazy."

"That's exactly what I've been. Crazy. A damned lunatic."

They didn't want to bother with breakfast, but May made some instant coffee while they waited in the kitchen.

"What about my mother?"

"Tyrone can tell her. You can call her later in the day."

Headlights flashed on tree trunks outside the window, and an engine roared as a vehicle climbed the steep drive, then died. A door slammed. Then two others.

"He didn't take much time at all," May said.

Three doors. It was no truck.

Showers set down his coffee and went for the wall switch, turning off the overhead light. He grabbed May's hand.

"Quick. Out the back."

"What is it?"

"Hurry."

He unfortunately let the screen door slam behind them. They heard footsteps on the driveway. Pulling May, Showers leapt for some bushes, dropping to the ground. They crouched there as a man came around the back of the house, a flitting shadow, thumping by. He ran up the back steps and the door swung on its spring.

"Now," Showers whispered.

The two of them hurried up the hill, sticking to shadows. Ahead of them, a light burned in the shed. They heard the bay moving on the wooden floor. Before they could reach it, the front door of the shed opened and a man in khaki work pants and a sleeveless T-shirt came out, holding a shotgun. It was one of Tyrone's men. Showers had forgotten his name.

"Get down!" Showers called to him.

Instead, the man came forward, intent on what was going on down at the house. Showers saw his eyes widen. He raised and began to turn the shotgun, but was far too tardy. A bullet struck him in the chest, lifting him, the shotgun flying into the air.

It landed stock first a good fifteen feet away. Showers rolled for it, flinging out his arm, pulling it to him. He saw a figure in the driveway running toward him, with another behind. He had time only to yank the weapon to his shoulder and fire, lying on his back. The recoil jerked the stock up against his face. In the smoke and ringing echo of the report, he heard cries of pain.

Seconds passed. He was still alive. He got to his feet and ran. No shots were fired. No bullets thudded into his back. Looking back as he hurried through the doorway into the shed, he saw more headlights turning into the drive, far below.

May was with the horse, throwing a halter over its head.

"Leave him, May! We have to get out of here!"

"No, David. They'll kill him. That's why they've come—to get rid of all of us."

There was a smaller wooden door at the back. Showers went to it and kicked it open. It seemed much too narrow for the horse, but they had no other chance.

"Hurry!" Showers shouted.

May pulled on the halter. The stallion, neighing, skittered backward a moment, then, at another tug, lunged after her into the doorway, sticking fast.

She was outside, pulling frantically on the lead. Two gunshots rang, one of them splintering the ceiling wood above. Showers picked up a rake handle from the floor and gave the bay a smart whack across the rump. It kicked out, bellowing, the wood of the doorjamb giving a great squeak. Showers hit him again twice, as hard as he could, hating himself for this.

The horse screamed again and thrust forward. Wood splintered and gave way. In the darkness beyond, the bay rose up on his hind legs, pawing the air. Showers saw May duck, then tug on the rope, pulling the animal back to earth again.

He ran back to the wide front doors. The shotgun was double-barreled. Leaping to the side, he aimed down the slope and pulled the other trigger. The blast broke glass in the distance.

There was shouting, and more gunshots. Showers dropped the weapon and pulled his pistol from his belt, hurrying out the back after May. He heard her moving in the brush, not farther up the hill, but to the left.

He caught up with her, moving past the horse, grabbing her arm.

"May! Where are you going?"

"There's a path," she said. "They won't know about it. It goes to the mine."

The path led along the face of the ridge, sometimes up, sometimes down, narrow, and crisscrossed with roots, studded with rocks. They stumbled along it in the darkness, Showers hanging back a little, listening for their pursuers.

They seemed to have lost them, though on the road below a car was moving slowly—too slowly to be going anywhere distant. Dogs were barking, and lights had gone on in many houses. But they could hear no voices.

**340**

"We should try to get to a telephone," Showers said.

May stopped, looking over her shoulder, shaking her head. "We'd only bring trouble down on someone else's home. We can hide in the mine until morning. It's the safest place for the horse. They'll be gone soon. They can't just take over the town."

Showers touched the bay's side. It was sticky with blood—scraped going through the doorway of the shed.

"All right," he said.

Beyond the center of town, the path crossed a wooden footbridge over the roadway, climbed the opposite slope, and finally joined the dirt cut they had ascended on their first day. The bay began wheezing a little as they reached the top.

May held the horse as Showers poked at the lock on the mine entrance gate. It was rusted over, but not decrepit, and held fast when he yanked on it. He picked up a large rock and bashed at it twice, with no effect but to make a lot of noise. He could hear the metallic echo coming back from the opposite slope.

"I'll have to shoot it off," he said. "There's no other way."

The shot would ring through the little valley, but the echoes might confuse them. He had to hope.

He fired once. The lock disintegrated in a shower of sparks. He pulled its remnant free from the latch, then swung open the gate. May led the animal into the shaft, then stopped, waiting for him to close the gate. She had a butane lighter in her jeans, and after he had pulled the gate shut again, she clicked it on. The tiny, wavering flame flickered a pale light on the grimy walls. The rails of the cart track were littered with piles of ancient coal dust. It was cool in this place. She coughed.

"Have you ever been in here before?" he asked.

"Years ago. But I don't remember much." The lighter went out. "Hot," she said.

"I'll take it," he said. "We'll use it sparingly."

"You have to be careful. There are side shafts cut through farther in. One of them is for the old elevator. It goes straight down."

"Give me your hand."

They moved on, a chain of man and woman and horse. He'd flick on the lighter for a glimpse of the way ahead, then grope forward a few feet in darkness, repeating the ritual until at last they came to the first side tunnel.

It opened on both the left and right.

"Do you know which might be the elevator shaft?"

"I think the one on the right. But I'm not sure. It may even be farther along."

Showers paused, thinking, then picked up a piece of old coal. He tossed it into the opening to the right. It struck a wall and fell with a thump. He started to move into it, his foot striking a mound of debris and sending some of it scattering forward. Something about the sound of its fall stayed him. He flicked on the lighter again—the flame now very, very weak. There seemed to be some wooden buttressing, and a wooden bar sagging across his path. Beyond it, the tunnel floor ahead was inky darkness. Taking up another piece of coal, he lofted it into the black patch. There was a long silence, and then a tiny splash, far below.

"It's the elevator shaft," he said. "We have to back up."

The horse protested, trying to turn around in the narrow space, but May, pushing, finally got him rear first into the main shaft. They crossed it, taking the side tunnel on the left.

"We'll follow this as far as it goes," he said. "At least until the next turning. I wouldn't expect them to try to search the entire mine."

"I don't think they'll even come up here," she said. "Tyrone will be back soon. They can't have a lot of time."

They moved ahead, feeling their way along the moist wall. The shaft seemed to be curving slightly, but it was difficult to tell for certain.

May began coughing again. "David, isn't this far enough?"

"Okay." He clicked on the lighter one more time, to look at her face. It was smudged with coal dust. He brushed it off a little, then leaned to kiss her. The lighter went out. Carefully, they sat down, leaning back against the wall. He could make out the phosphorescent dial of his watch. It was nearly dawn.

The bay moved edgily. May had let go of the rope. She took it back up again.

"You said you loved me."

"Yes."

"Did you mean it? I've had a million men tell me they loved me."

He put his arm around her and pulled her close. "It's a lovely thought, isn't it? Telling our grandchildren someday about the night we spent in a coal mine with a horse while gunmen ran through the hills trying to kill us."

"It sounds like a movie."

"I love you."

**342**

"Say it again."

"I love you."

"It's so dark. I think I'm getting claustrophobia."

"Think of it as castle walls, protecting us, warm and snug."

"Not warm."

He held her more tightly. His hand was touching her breast.

"Kiss me, David."

He did so, wrapping her in his arms. Afterward, she leaned her head against his shoulder, holding on to his hand with both of hers.

"I love you, David. I was never able to figure out what love was before. But it's got to be like this. There can't be anything like this."

"I think we'd better stop talking now."

Time seemed to stop. He glanced at his watch, depressed by how little of it went by. It was as though they'd been pulled out of their lives, their beings suspended in a place without dimension, without reality. Death could be like this. Certainly, eternity must.

May seemed to sleep. Showers felt himself begin to nod off. He caught himself. He had reason to.

There were voices, distant, but uncannily clear. He could make out three distinctly, none he'd ever heard before. Whoever they were, they were angry, out of breath, and in a hurry. He could hear them knocking wood about.

Gently extricating himself from May, easing her back against the wall, he took his pistol from his belt and crept forward, moving past the horse. The shaft did curve. As he came up to the main tunnel—regrettably not very far away at all—the glancing arcs of flashlights became visible on the ceiling and the opposite wall.

Inching his way, he came to the corner, moving his head beyond it very slowly.

Their pursuers were silhouettes at the mouth of the tunnel, a faint gray light of dawn sky behind them. Showers feared the flashlights would catch his face, but crouched there, frozen, riveted, the pistol now warm in his hand.

"They gotta be in there," said one of the men. "That lock was shot off. And look at that. Hoofprints!"

"They blew Frank's guts away."

"You want to go first?"

Silence.

"We'll all go in. Let's get this over with."

The horse had heard the voices. He was coming toward Showers, a clopping walk. He'd gotten away from May. Looking back into pitch darkness, Showers tried to discern the animal's shape, guess where the head and halter rope might be. As the bay came closer, Showers rose up and lunged, but caught only air. He fell on his shoulder. One of the horse's hooves thumped down just inches from his head. He reached again, but the action only frightened the animal. It whinnied, plunging on.

Showers stood up. He had to stop the horse, but it was seconds too late. He'd be caught in the open now. They'd kill him, kill the horse, come back here and kill May, gun her down in the dark and dust.

As the horse clattered on, Showers flattened himself against the wall, peering around the corner. The men at the entrance were shouting. The flashlights danced. The bay bolted forward, coming up the shaft at a trot.

The gunfire came in a sudden stuttering echoing roar. All three of them were firing, flashes going off like fireworks. The horse smashed against the wall, screaming, rising, pawing wildly, head back. Then it went over on its side with a great crash, still screaming. The bullets kept coming. Its huge body twitched and jerked, then went still.

All was suddenly quiet. The clammy air smelled of gunpowder. The three men stood motionless.

Showers felt a hand on his back, and almost jumped. May. He got his arm around her, putting his hand over her mouth. Holding her tightly against him, he slowly relaxed his fingers, feeling her breath. She was trembling all over.

He looked back up the shaft. The men were just standing there.

"It's not moving," one said.

"Maybe they just stashed him in here and kept on going."

"You want to go down there and make sure?"

"What I want to make sure of is we got the right horse. We don't want to go through all this shit for nothin'. Get Bonning up here."

With Billy, there'd be four of them. Showers couldn't remember how many rounds he had in this clip. It should be full, minus the one he'd fired at the lock, but he couldn't be certain.

He'd wait for them to come down to him, and then kill as many as he could. There was nothing else to do.

Minutes passed. While the one went back for Bonning, the other two came forward to the corpse of the horse, leaning close, playing their flashlights over it.

"Sure is dead."

"Looks like the right one. Gotta be. Black horse. White blaze."

*344*

"Anything'd look black in here."

Bonning appeared at the entrance, taller than the others. He walked with his usual swagger, but stumbled, barely catching himself. The three others stood with him by the horse, keeping their lights on it.

"Is that it?"

Billy knelt down. "Did you have to kill it?"

"That's the job, asshole. Get rid of the horse. Is it the right one?"

Showers watched Bonning lean over the head. He guessed he was peeling back the lip to examine the number tattoo.

"It's him," he said.

"You're sure?"

"Yeah. It's the horse."

The man who'd been talking the most moved his pistol and fired a quick shot into the back of Billy's head. As his body sprawled onto the horse's, the man fired two more times.

"Now we got that done, too."

"Let's get out of here."

"Not so fast. The man said 'not a trace.' "

"We don't have time to cut it up."

"You want to burn 'em?"

"Are you crazy? This shaft's full of coal dust."

"I've got a couple of charges in the car. We can blow the entrance."

"Hey, dumb nuts. These people are miners. They'd just dig right in."

"We can douse the bodies with gasoline and set the charges underneath. That'll take care of everything."

"What if the broad is down there, and that guy she's shacked up with?"

"If they're in here, they'll stay in here. Go get the stuff. Hurry up."

Showers' indecision and frustration was tearing at him. How good a shot could he be? Did he have any chance of hitting even one of them?

"May," he whispered. "Is there any other way out of here?"

"God, David, I don't know."

She was crying, too loudly. He peered around the corner again. For a moment, there'd be just two of the men. He could creep along the shaft, getting as close as he could, and drop, firing. Maybe he could get both. Maybe he'd die trying. There was nothing else to

**345**

do. Nothing. May might be able to get away, somehow survive. That small chance was all he could give her.

Showers stepped around the corner, keeping low, his foot crunching in the loose coal. He saw one of the men turning toward him. He backed up, making noise, then pressed himself back against the wall. The man kept coming, passing by, then stopped. He groped forward, and hesitated again. Showers picked up a small piece of coal, and tossed it into the opposite side shaft. The man plunged after it. There was a crunch of old wood, and then a scream.

His two companions started coming after him, but froze at the sound of a gunshot, outside. Then several more. Showers heard shouting. One of the men ran back to the entrance, greeted by gunfire that threw him around in a dance. As he fell, the last remaining man looked back in Showers' direction, then moved toward the entrance, sticking close to the tunnel wall.

"Come out of there, you sons of bitches!" The distant voice was Tyrone's.

"Fuck you, asshole!" The man at the entrance got off two quick shots, then hunkered down, reloading his pistol.

He must know he was through. He was going to wait—kill more in the act of dying. Or maybe just kill more before surrendering. Who knew what went through such a mind?

Tyrone seemed to have several people with him. They returned the lone gunman's fire with a long fusillade.

It gave Showers the time he needed. All rage now, he strode up to the man, firing. He kept pulling the trigger until the automatic was empty.

They rode down from the mine in Tyrone's truck—Tyrone driving, May and Showers in the cab beside him, exhausted, several men with rifles riding up on the truck bed, the stacked bodies in their midst. The sun was coming up and everything was tinged with red, faces, house fronts, the leaves on the trees.

There were several cars pulled up at odd angles in the road in front of May's mother's house, men in suits standing around them. At the approach of the truck, they dropped into crouches, aiming handguns. Showers saw that one had a small submachine gun.

Red lights were twirling in the back windows of two of the cars.

"Federal agents!" shouted a man from behind one of the cars. "Throw down your weapons!"

Tyrone lurched the truck to a stop, pulling the hand brake fast. Slowly, he opened the door and stepped down.

"My name is Tyrone McPhee," he said, slowly but loudly. "I'm the constable of this town. These people are deputized. What's your business here?"

One of the men in suits came forward, gun in his hand, but lowered.

"You're who?"

"Constable McPhee." With care, he took an old badge from his pocket, holding it up for the other man to clearly see. "And who might you be?"

"I'm Special Agent Anderson of the Federal Bureau of Investigation. We're looking for a Miss May Moody and a David Spencer Showers."

"Well, there they be," Tyrone said, gesturing at the cab. "But not by much. You boys sure got a case of the slows."

Moody sat in his car, watching across H Street as limousines and taxis pulled up into the short circular drive of the Hay-Adams Hotel. He'd seen Bernie and another man get out of Bloch's Rolls-Royce and hurry inside, but waited until the taxi arrived carrying Reidy. When the senator had entered the lobby, Moody waited a few minutes more, and then stepped out on the sidewalk.

The suite number Bernie had given him was on the top floor, in a corner with a view that included the White House and the Washington Monument beyond. Moody had been in the suite several times before, sometimes for meetings. Once with a woman.

He rang the buzzer, standing alone, in clear view of the peephole. Bloch opened the door.

"You're late," he said.

"Had to stop by the White House," Moody said. "We've got a little war on our hands."

"So I heard. This shouldn't take long. Right?"

He ushered Moody into the sitting room of the suite. Reidy was in an armchair, looking a little agitated, his customary affability discarded. On the couch opposite him, Lynwood Fairbrother sat very stiffly, as though painfully uncomfortable. On the table was a coffee service. No one else was in the room.

"You're sure this is a good place to do this?" Moody said. He sat down in an empty chair, ignoring the coffee.

"Like I said," Bloch said. "A little prayer breakfast. They have meetings here all the time."

"Is this for real, Bobby?" Reidy asked. His dark eyes were filled with meanness.

"If you have any doubts, Mr. Bloch here can be my character reference."

"We go back," Bernie said, "as you know."

"What's he doing here?" Moody said, nodding toward Fairbrother. The horseman looked as though he'd just been slapped in the face.

"You wanted to see a Republican," Bloch said. "You can't get any more Republican than this."

Moody turned in his chair. "Do you know what this is about, Mr. Fairbrother?"

"A discussion of the proposed environmental treaty," Fairbrother said. "That's what I was told." His voice almost squeaked.

"An informal discussion," Bloch said.

"I was told you wanted to know my position," Fairbrother said. "I have very grave reservations. I think it could do very serious harm, to the economy, to the country."

"You're part of Mr. Bloch's lobbying effort against the treaty?"

"What do you mean?"

"I'm just trying to determine how deep your feelings run, Mr. Fairbrother. How widespread this opposition is. Whether the treaty is really in this much trouble. I don't want to be bluffed into doing something I'd really rather not do. If it's just a handful of you guys, I'm not going to let myself be railroaded. Not if there's a chance the treaty still might pass."

Reidy was staring at him. Moody avoided his eyes, keeping his own on Fairbrother.

"I can assure you the opposition is widespread indeed. The entire business community."

"Lots of you Republican fat cats?"

"We think the president is making a very serious mistake. We've tried to communicate this to him from the beginning. If the proposal could be discreetly withdrawn, or forgotten, it would be best."

"And you've put some money where your mouth is? People on the Hill know where all you guys stand?"

"I have made some campaign contributions. It's customary."

Reidy was shifting in his seat.

"All right," said Moody, sitting back. "I get the idea. If a pillar of the community like you is putting himself out like this, I guess feelings run pretty deep, indeed."

"I've merely been expressing my opinion, sir. But there are

many, many who feel as I do. Your president is going to have to come to an understanding about this, one way or another."

"Okay, okay," said Bloch. "He gets the picture. Thanks for coming by, Mr. Fairbrother. It's appreciated."

Fairbrother stood. "That's all?"

"I just wanted to give you a chance to speak your piece, off the record, as it were. Mr. Moody understands. Thanks for coming by. We'll see you out at the racecourse."

Fairbrother frowned. "Very well." He walked out with great dignity, like someone who had mistakenly entered the wrong club, and was trying to keep his error from being noticed. The door clicked closed.

Reidy leaned forward. "All right, Bobby. What's the deal?"

"You tell me."

"Bernie says you—that you've become privy to our, uh, legislative strategy."

"Strategy? You're going to let ratification go through, and then shitcan the enabling bill. A good old one, two. The president ends up on the floor."

Reidy hunched forward, pouring himself some coffee. "The treaty never had a chance from the beginning, you must have known that."

"No, I didn't know that. But you begin to make that clear. The way you've opened up people's pockets, it's probably inevitable."

"So what do you want?"

"First off, I'd like to know just how inevitable it is. What's the real nose count? How many members of the honorable body do you own now? On this issue anyway?"

"We got seven," Bloch said. "Seven in the bag."

"Seven? Seven makes this inevitable?"

"That's seven on the buy. For the U.S. Senate, that's a hell of a lot. There's another couple dozen, say, who now clearly understand our point of view. And maybe another couple dozen who would have opposed you on the implementing legislation no matter what."

"It's a done deal, Bobby," Reidy said. "Are you going to live with it, or what?"

"I'll have some of that coffee, now," Moody said. Bernie went to pour it for him.

"I'll ask you again," Reidy said. "Are you going to make it hard for us, or are you going to grease the skids?"

"I guess that would depend."

"On what? I've guaranteed your confirmation. It wasn't easy.

The career types are raising holy hell. Think you're a bumpkin. Don't like your style at all. If you weren't so popular with the Japanese these days, I would have really had to break some arms."

"Are the Japanese in on this, on your buy?"

Bloch smiled. "Nobody asked them. But they have a few investments in this country. American corporations, right?"

"You ought to be happy, where you're sitting these days," Reidy said. "I could have made you very unhappy. I still can."

"I understand that," Moody said. The coffee was hot. He sipped it gingerly. "But secretaries of state come and go. We have an election coming up. I like to think in longer terms than that. This is a very serious matter, Senator. I'm shouldering an enormous burden for you, just by keeping my mouth shut. And my 'friend' Mr. Bloch here has made some very unpleasant threats concerning my daughter. I don't like that at all. Seems to me you've got a long way to go before you've earned my goodwill. A real long way."

"What do you want, Bobby?"

"What are you offering?"

Bloch lighted a cigar. "If the treaty implementing bill comes up DOA, a lot of stocks are going to take off for the roof. That chemical company of mine closed at fourteen and a quarter, yesterday—down nine points from the year high. If the vote's what we think it's going to be, I can see it doubling, in a hell of a hurry."

"I don't play the market, Bernie. I signed a conflict of interest agreement."

"You don't play the market, but the people handling your trust do. I can offer them a lot of guidance. Hell, I can make the purchase for them. No money down. We'll just postdate the papers. When you leave the government, you'll be fucking amazed at what a wealthy man you've become."

"Talk figures."

"Seven figures? Eight? It's possible."

"This is all right with you?" Moody asked Reidy.

"It'll be my pleasure, Bobby, to have you in my pocket."

"Well, that's very nice." He sipped more coffee. "What else?"

"What else?"

"I'm just asking."

"How fucking greedy a hillbilly are you?"

"I just want to know how far you're willing to go. How much putting the screws to the president means to you."

Reidy sighed. "I'm not doing this just to be a prick, Bobby. If the treaty goes belly up, so does your boss. He's got nothing else. He doesn't have a lot of friends, outside of the Harvard Club. The party will be looking for a new candidate to save its ass."

"You?"

"I finished second."

"A distant second."

"I'll need a non-Catholic running mate, an easterner, to balance the ticket. I don't much give a shit who it is, but I wouldn't mind carrying the West Virginia and Maryland primaries."

"Is that a promise?"

"You don't guarantee anything, not in presidential politics. But let me put it this way. Jim Baker didn't get a guarantee of anything from the Reagan guys, when he got George Bush out of the primaries in 1980. But he ended up with what he wanted, because Bush was the strongest guy. You're a strong guy, Bobby. I'll grant you that much."

Moody finished his coffee.

"So now are you happy?" Bloch asked.

"No, I'm not happy, Bernie. I'm not going to be happy until I see May. When's that going to happen?"

"It'll happen. I told you, nothing to worry about, now that we're all in agreement here."

"When is it going to happen? This afternoon? This morning? Make me happy, Bernie."

"I've got calls out. I haven't heard back yet."

"Make your calls again. I want an answer before I leave."

"All right, all right."

Moody stood up. "I've got to take a leak. Mind if I use the john?"

"It's through the bedroom," Reidy said.

"I know." Moody went to the door and turned the knob. It didn't yield. "Shit. The damn thing's locked."

"We only took the suite for an hour," Bloch said. "I guess they didn't think we'd need the bathroom. Not that kind of get-together."

"I'll go find a maid," Moody said.

"Can't you hold it?" Reidy said. "We're almost done."

"What do you want me to do, use a tree in LaFayette Park? I'll be right back." He left the door to the suite open behind him.

There was a maid in the hallway, taking towels from a cart. Several room doors nearby were standing ajar.

"Excuse me," Moody said loudly. "We can't get into our bathroom. The bedroom door's locked. Do you have a key?"

"Sorry, sir?" she said, in a thick Spanish accent. "What you say?"

"Bathroom. I need a bathroom. Can I use one of these?"

The maid shrugged.

Moody entered the nearest open room, closing the door behind him. There were more than a dozen men inside, several of them wearing vests with the letters "FBI" on them.

"You got it all?" Moody asked.

The agent in charge indicated a television monitor, set atop a video recording unit. On the screen, in black and white, he could see Bloch on the phone. Reidy was on his feet, pacing back and forth by a window. Superimposed numbers in the right-hand corner showed the elapsing time and date.

"And my daughter?"

"She's clear. Just got the word."

"Well, go get 'em, then."

The chief agent nodded to the others, and most of the men hurried from the room. Moody stood in front of the screen, watching as Bloch's expression went from one of surprise to horror, as Reidy turned and punched the wall. The agents had guns and handcuffs out. There'd be no dignity in this at all. It would make for wonderful television viewing, on the evening news, for weeks and months to come.

Moody hoped Bloch understood.

# Twenty-Three

An unlikely procession entered Dandytown that afternoon—a West Virginia State Police car, three U.S. government sedans, and a refrigerated beer truck with the name of a West Virginia distributorship printed on the side. Mars lights twirling, they proceeded up the main street to the county courthouse, where a small group of men was waiting for them on the steps—Jack Spencer, Wayne Bensinger, and several sheriff's deputies among them. Sheriff Cooke remained inside his office, though he'd been informed by radio that the FBI party was coming.

Spencer stood up, startled by Showers' and May's appearance when they got out of one of the sedans. Their clothes were covered with coal dust. Showers had bloodstains on his shirt and the girl's long, dark hair looked as though a hay rake had gone through it. She clung to Showers, looking uncertainly about her. He went up to them, gripping his cousin's hand.

"Damned close run thing," he said. "You're all right?"

"We're fine. There are some people back there I'm never going to forget. I don't ever want to hear an unkind word about West Virginia again."

"Your horseman friend from British Columbia will be here tomorrow. He said he's certain the horse in the pictures is his, but he wants to see for himself."

"He won't like what he finds," Showers said. He pointed to the beer truck. "The stallion's in there. Dead. Very badly shot up, I'm afraid. But identifiable. It was horrible, what they did to it."

"They ended up the same way."

"Yes."

"They said you killed one of them."

"I think it's three."

Neither of them spoke for a moment.

"I'm sorry, Captain Showers," Bensinger said. "I'm afraid there are some formalities to attend to."

"I know. I'm prepared for them."

The presiding judge's name was on a placard attached to the courtroom door: THE HON. THOMAS H. MERRICK. Bensinger showed Showers and May to seats in the courtroom, then went down the hall to the chief prosecutor's office. His boss was at his desk, his tie undone, looking tired.

"They're here," Bensinger said.

"I know."

"Do you still want to go through with this?"

"Gotta go through the motions. The sheriff won't drop the charges, not until he hears from Lynwood Fairbrother."

"And where is he?"

The prosecutor shrugged. "In Washington. Some kind of trouble."

"You want to handle this?"

"You do it, Wayne. You're familiar with the case. I'm sick of the whole thing. I think I'm going to take the rest of the day off."

The arraignment hearing, which had been scheduled on a rush basis immediately after the FBI had informed Banastre County authorities that Showers and the girl were returning, was the only matter on the docket. Showers went to stand calmly before the bench as a bailiff read the charge. When the man was done, Bensinger rose from behind his table.

"If it please the court," he said, "the commonwealth would like to introduce two documents into the record, both pertinent to the criminal charge."

"Proceed," said the judge. He was in his eighties, but his voice was sharp and full of vigor. He looked extremely displeased.

"The first is a sworn statement taken this morning from Miss May Moody. It concerns the particulars of the charge of murder against David Spencer Showers, to wit, the alleged defendant's whereabouts on the day of the crime. She states he was with her for all the time in question."

"Accepted for the record," the judge said. He took the transcript from Bensinger, but instead of passing it on to the clerk, began looking through it.

"The second document, Your Honor, is a statement from Special agent Charles Anderson of the Federal Bureau of Investigation. It concerns an explosive device recovered from third parties during a criminal investigation in West Virginia this morning, an explosive device that bears similarity to the one used in the murder of Rebecca Bonning, and the injuries caused to Miss Alixe Percy."

The judge snatched it up. "Accepted for the record." He glanced over its paragraphs, then set it aside. Sheriff Cooke was sitting in the front row of spectator seats, arms folded, staring down at his boots.

"Has the commonwealth anything further to add?" the judge asked.

"No, Your Honor."

"No recommendation in this case?"

"I've no instructions, your Honor."

"Good God." The judge looked at Showers. "Have you defense counsel?"

"No sir," Showers said.

"You don't need any. The court is prepared to rule." He slammed down his gavel. "Case dismissed! Insufficient evidence! Damned insufficient evidence! You're free to go. Sheriff Cooke, approach the bench."

Sheepishly, the sheriff got to his feet. He stood before the judge looking far more a defendant than Showers.

"Yes, Your Honor?"

"After examining this case, I have just one word for you. And for Mr. Lynwood Fairbrother. November!"

"November?"

"That, I believe, is when you stand for reelection. You have tried to dishonor this good man's name with unwarranted criminal charges, sir, and there is no more honorable name in Banastre County. I'm passing on the record of this case, with comment, to Richmond." He stood, his black robe billowing behind him. "Court is adjourned."

Outside, on the steps, May turned and kissed Showers as though there were no one around for a hundred miles to see. She felt very light in his arms, as though the experience had begun to diminish her physically.

"You know what I feel?" she said.

"Very tired."

"Yes, tired. Happy. Relieved. But you know what else? I feel the future is finally beginning to happen."

"Very soon, May. Very, very soon."

"We'd better get going, Miss Moody," said the FBI agent who had accompanied them. "I'm supposed to take you back to Washington."

"My father," May said. "You're going to take me to my father, aren't you."

"My instructions are to deliver you to the Director's office, safe and sound. That's all they told me."

May looked to Showers. "I can't face him, David. I just can't."

"You've no legal reason to keep her in custody," Showers said.

"No sir. We've got her statement and everything."

"Then why don't you just take her home and let her get some rest? I'm sure that would make her father much happier."

"All right, sir, if that's what she wants."

"That's what she wants."

Showers put his arm around her, and began to walk her to the car.

"You'll have to see your father sometime," he said. "He must be very worried."

"It's a little late for that."

"He tried to help us. Grant him that."

"I don't even want to think about him, David. Aren't you coming with me?"

"I can't. Not yet. I'm not done here."

"You just can't tear yourself away from this place, can you?"

There was a lot he had to tell her, but this was not the time.

"I have to meet with the man from Canada. I'll join you tomorrow night. You get some sleep."

"I'll be terribly lonely."

"So will I."

"When you come, bring some things."

"Things?"

"Clothes. Bring a lot of clothes. I want you to spend every minute you have with me."

She kissed him one more time.

"On second thought," she said, "maybe not so many clothes."

She tried to smile at him brightly, but her face was very pale and drawn. He could see that she'd be asleep before they reached the interstate.

"Tomorrow, May."

Spencer stood next to him as the FBI cars drove off.

356

"We have some business to attend to, cousin."

"That we do."

Becky's personal things had all been gathered up and sent on to her family, but the television set and video recorder were still in the cottage, along with the rest of the furniture. Spencer had brought a briefcase with him. He set it on the coffee table, snapping open the locks.

"Do you want a drink before we start, David? This is pretty rough stuff."

"No thanks. Let's just get it over with."

Spencer took two videocassettes from the briefcase, putting one of them in the machine. In a moment, Vicky Clay's nude, gyrating body appeared on the screen, another naked woman beneath her.

"I've seen this before," Showers said. "Some of it."

"Watch the rest."

Embarrassed, he stared at the television set as the sex act came to its conclusion, and Vicky rolled off to the side. The other woman sat up.

Showers was stunned. It was Lenore.

"I've seen enough," he said.

"No you haven't."

Becky entered the picture, as naked as the others, climbing onto the bed.

"For God's sake, Jack. Can't you spare me this? The girl's dead. Who recorded this thing?"

"No one knows. Possibly Vicky Clay's brother. Or Becky, and she forgot to shut it off. But see it out. Listen to them."

Becky's sexual play was cut short by Vicky's taunting. She began chiding Becky for being no good with men, for never having slept with Showers in all the time she was under his roof, for being far too unattractive to ever get him into her bed. She began bragging of her own sexual experiences with Showers, prompting Lenore to relate some of her own. Each tried to outdo the other.

Spencer hit the pause button.

"Is this true?"

"Please, Jack."

"I know about Lenore Fairbrother. Did you go to bed with Vicky Clay?"

"Yes. Once. A long time ago."

"It must be something, to be lusted after by women like that."

"It's just because I won a few races. You win a trophy, and you become one."

"Groupies."

"Please."

Spencer put the tape in motion again. Vicky, who seemed to be under the influence of drink or drugs or both, boasted she could get Showers to sleep with her that night, and challenged Lenore to try to beat her to him. Becky said nothing, looking quite miserable. Lenore responded contemptuously, making a bet of it, claiming she could have Showers anytime, anywhere, any way she wished, sneering that if he had ever made love to Vicky, it had been out of pity because she was such a pathetic creature, and that he'd not make the mistake again. Vicky began calling her vile names. Lenore got off the bed, and started getting dressed.

"Did she win this little contest?" Spencer asked.

Showers remembered Lenore kneeling before him on the lawn that evening—rebuffed, driving away stark naked, furious that he'd rejected her.

"No," he said.

On the screen, Vicky and Becky remained seated on the bed, less hostile now, united by Lenore's obnoxiousness. They waited as Lenore, now dressed, crossed in front of the camera and walked out of the room, her high heels clicking on the wooden floor.

An impish grin came over Vicky's face. She was going to win, she said. She had something Showers would want very badly— information, about a horse that was going to be auctioned. Showers would do anything for a horse, she said. She told Becky about Bernie Bloch's bay. She extracted a promise from Becky not to tell Lenore. Becky, looking troubled, agreed.

They got up, Becky going into the bathroom. The camera continued to record, nothing on the screen but the empty bed.

Spencer stopped the tape.

"Becky told me about the horse," Showers said. "That's how everything started."

"Did Vicky say anything to you that night?"

"She tried to. She asked to talk to me in private. She was very high on something, could barely keep her balance. I didn't want anything to do with her. I'm afraid I was a little rude."

"And sometime that night, Becky went up and shot her full of horse tranquilizer, perhaps to keep her from queering the horse deal?"

"You're crazy."

**358**

"There's evidence."

"Bloody nonsense. She wouldn't do a thing like that."

Spencer got up and ejected the tape, replacing it with the other cassette.

"I told you about the computer analysis I had a friend of mine do. Of the scratches on Meade Clay's back?"

"It didn't sound very conclusive to me."

"Well, I found it very impressive. After all, this is a fellow who works up projections of missile trajectories for strategic defense systems, such as we have anymore."

He started the tape, returning to his seat. A brutally clear photographic image of Meade Clay's skin filled the screen, complete with moles and freckles and the horrible crimson scratchings. A moment later, the picture was transformed into a computerized diagram, with electronic lines representing the scratches. Their form and patterns began to change, stretching and shrinking, tangling into bizarre contortions.

"What he did was isolate the deepest impressions on Clay's back and complete the most likely patterns Vicky was trying to make. The computer projected the lines a million different ways, and came up with three letters. Watch."

"You told me about this."

"Just watch."

They did. The computer became an artist, laboriously painting and repainting. Finally, satisfied with its product, it stopped, erasing everything on the screen except the forms of three letters, the last one somewhat indistinct.

"You see. A *B* and *e*, and a *c*," Spencer said. "The last letter might also be an *n*, or an *r*. But the computer thinks *c* is the most probable."

"As in 'Becky.' But it could be 'Bernie,' as in Bernie Bloch. Really, Jack, it could be anything."

"The prosecutor's office wasn't very convinced, either. And it's a good thing."

"What do you mean?"

"My friend kept playing with this. He was able to determine that there were two sets of impressions—one very deep, breaking the skin, the other fairly light, very superficial. The girl was almost completely paralyzed, David. It's astounding she was even able to move her fingers. He decided it was most likely she had made the light impressions, that someone else came along and made the deep ones. His hypothesis was that it was the killer. He or she gave the

Meades their fatal doses, then came back later to see if they were dead—and discovered the scratches. They couldn't be erased, so he or she—she—wrote over them. If the sheriff had checked people's fingernails the next day, he probably could have found some traces of Meade Clay's blood."

A broken nail. A smudge of red.

"Take a look at this now," Spencer continued. "My friend ran everything through again, this time isolating the lightest impressions."

Showers stared transfixed. The computer's unseen hand drew three letters on the screen, including an *e* and an *n*.

The first letter was an *L*.

"My God."

"It doesn't do Becky much good now, but there you are. Put this together with what you saw on the first tape, and it's damn interesting. I don't think we can get that lunkhead sheriff to do anything with this, but the state police might be able to run with it. Or the FBI, now that your ladyfriend's father has brought them in."

Showers sat motionless.

"Mrs. Fairbrother's husband owns the inn," Spencer said. "She has access to the keys. Probably has her own set, given her interesting idea of fun."

Showers swallowed, but could not speak.

"I could ask if you want me to draw you a picture, David, but I just did."

"I know."

"I talked to Mrs. Fairbrother while you were away, among a lot of other people Alixe Percy put me on to. She joked about all the women out here who had killed their husbands without anyone knowing, how murder was just part of the general depravity. All I thought at the time was that she had a peculiar sense of humor."

"Give me the tapes."

Spencer went to fetch them. "Bensinger knows about the bedroom scene," he said. "Alixe had put it in a safety deposit box. He retrieved it for me."

Showers took the cassettes and then went into the kitchen.

"Are you going to call the police?" Spencer asked.

"No. I'm looking for some charcoal lighter fluid."

"What the hell are you talking about, David? You need those tapes."

"No I don't. As you said, this won't do Becky any good. It won't do Vicky any good. It certainly won't do me any good."

"Look, I know Lenore Fairbrother was once the love of your life, but for God's sake, murder is murder. Hell, she had that horse you saved put down. What was its name? Moonsugar."

"I'm well aware of that. I'm not doing this out of any past love for Lenore. I just don't want what's on here played out in a public courtroom. I don't want to have to testify in a trial. It could go on for weeks, and I can't be stuck out here that long."

"You'd let her go free just because a trial would interfere with your plans?"

"Yes, I would, as things stand now." Showers started out the front door.

"At the very least, you ought to let her husband get a look at these," Spencer said, following. "Let him know what he's living with."

"She lets him know what he's living with every day. I'm not interested in handing him grounds for a divorce. The idea of their living out their days as husband and wife rather appeals to me. It's the meanest thing I can think of for them."

"She could end up giving him a shot of jump juice some time."

"That's Mr. Fairbrother's problem."

Out in the yard, Showers took some straw and made a small pyre, setting the tapes in the center and dousing them with lighter fluid. The flames engulfed them in an instant.

"So much for that front page story. I've got another. It's all written—just sitting in my computer back in the office."

"And what's that, Jack?" Showers sounded very weary.

"That Napier creep? Who lied about the memo you showed me? He's got a little men-only bordello going in Georgetown. He may be using money from the national committee to pay for the rent. Your friend Jimmy Kipp told me about it. He thought you'd be of a mind to get even. We can really put the screws to them, David. The first lady's social secretary is a regular there. Kipp said he'd go on the record about that. We could really ding the administration."

"To get back at May's father."

"He has it coming."

"No."

"You could discredit Napier completely. You could get your old job back."

"That doesn't matter to me anymore. None of this does. I don't care and I don't want to hear about it. You said you owed me an obligation for the trouble your column caused. All right, I'll collect. Don't run that piece."

"Mr. Moody?"

"He's going to be family."

Spencer kicked some straw into the fire.

"You're not helping my career in journalism."

"Stick to art exhibitions. They're a lot more edifying."

The cassettes were melting, the smell of burning plastic noxious and strong. They stepped back.

"What about the saga of the counterfeit horse? I have most of that in the computer, too. All I need is a lead, and you've certainly handed me a good one today."

"That I wouldn't mind seeing in the public print at all. I don't ever want anyone coming out here and trying something like that again."

"Thank you."

"Thank you, Jack. You've gone a lot further than the extra mile."

"I'll go call in my stuff. There are no menacing foreign powers involved, but maybe my bureau chief will run with it anyway." He started for Showers' house.

"Don't take too long. I want to go see Alixe."

"So do I. She's the first woman I've met in a long time that I think I really like."

Showers stood alone, staring at the diminishing flames. Purification. Becky and Vicky would be remembered solely by their graves.

Spencer was back sooner than expected.

"Scooped again," he said. "But I suppose it's justice."

"What are you talking about?"

"Someone—and I guess we'll never know who—just blew up Bernie Bloch. Bloody car bomb. In the garage of his building. There was some blonde with him. They haven't been able to identify her."

The last item on the Oval Office schedule was "President meets with the Chief of Staff." This was how the schedule routinely ended, but this meeting was not routine.

Moody placed the neatly typed, two-sentence letter on the president's desk, then stepped back. The president stared at it somberly.

"You needn't have been in such a rush about this, Bob," he said finally. "This says 'effective immediately.' Really, this could wait a few days. Weeks, if you want."

"I don't think so, sir. If it's going to be done, it should be done now. You have to get the whole mess behind you, and I'm sure as hell part of the mess."

"Sit down, Bob, please."

Moody did so. He had never before felt so uncomfortable in this room.

The president ticked the anchor of his model sailing ship, then looked at Moody's resignation again. He seemed genuinely saddened.

"You're absolutely certain this is necessary."

"Yes sir. My friendship with Bloch has been a long one. I've no idea what may turn up, what he may have done—what he may have done in my name. The same goes for Reidy. I'd only be a liability. You need a clean house."

"You knew you'd have to do this, when you agreed to that meeting?"

"Yes sir."

"Well, let me say, Robert Moody, that you are a very fine man, indeed. I can't think of a president who was ever better or more unselfishly served."

"Thank you, sir."

"But what will you do?"

"I haven't given that a lot of thought. I'll be all right. I'm not exactly a candidate for the poorhouse. I'll get out of Washington for a while. Travel. I don't know. Maybe go back home. Who knows, someday I may run for public office again. I might come back and haunt you as a congressman."

"I hope you do. I truly do."

"Thank you, sir. For everything."

The president was in no hurry to conclude the conversation.

"How do you think it looks for the treaty now?"

"This blowup today will delay a vote—possibly until next year," Moody said. "It won't be a cakewalk. It never was going to be that. But, on the whole, I'd say you stand the best chance now you ever did. Anyone casting a 'no' vote is going to have to explain his motives very carefully. Especially those guys who were close to Reidy."

"I daresay you're right." The president glanced at the resignation letter one more time, then slipped it into a leather-bound folder on his desk, closing the cover very gently, forever ending the White House career of Robert Moody. "If this Belize thing will quiet down for a while, I'm going to go up to Wellfleet for a week or two.

Would you . . ." He paused. "Would you and Mrs. Moody like to join us?"

"Mrs. Moody and I have separated."

"Oh. I'm sorry to hear that." He looked anything but.

Moody rose. "That's kind of you, sir. I'll see you again soon. If not on Cape Cod, somewhere."

"Good, good." They shook hands. "If you don't mind, Bob. I'd like to call on you if I could, for advice, on the treaty and . . ."

This would last only until he had someone else in Moody's job he could cling to. With luck, it might be Sadinauskas, or General St. Angelo.

"Anytime, sir." He started toward the door.

"Bob?"

Moody looked back. He had never seen the man look so alone before.

"Yes sir?"

"I really don't know what I'm going to do without you."

"Thank you, sir. I think you'll do just fine."

No one spoke to him as he walked down the carpeted corridor to his own office. He'd sent his secretary Anne home early. To his surprise, she had started crying. He'd seen to it that she and Wolfenson and the others would get jobs elsewhere in the administration. It was the first rule of working in the White House, just as it had been with the people he'd grown up with in West Virginia, the people who had saved May's life. You took care of your own.

His framed photograph of Deena was still on his desk. He dropped it noisily in his wastebasket. The one he'd kept of May he put in his briefcase, along with a few personal possessions. The picture of himself and the president on the Truman Balcony he left hanging on the wall. It might tell his successor something.

He still had a White House car at his disposal, but he'd sent his driver home, too. He'd take a cab home. He decided he'd leave all the trappings behind, cut loose, and not look back. But, walking down the driveway from the West Wing lobby, he paused as usual to take in the White House's floodlit North Portico, the great white pillars, the semicircular half-moon windows of the second floor family quarters, a brightly lit chandelier visible inside.

Before the president's election, he'd often gazed at those windows, wondering what it would be like to stand on the inside looking out. On inauguration night, he'd gone up there as soon as was seemly, feeling like a child at Christmas, looking down at the mere mortals on Pennsylvania Avenue.

Now he was on the outside again.

He turned in his White House pass at the guardhouse of the Northwest Gate. Word of his resignation had quickly spread through the entire Executive Mansion establishment, and the guard took the coded, laminated card without surprise.

"Goodnight, Mr. Moody. Hope we see you again soon."

"Thanks. Thanks for everything."

The guard buzzed the door lock open. Moody walked through briskly, listening to the click as it closed behind him. Then he stepped onto the sidewalk.

From the moment he'd first signed on, he'd continually reminded himself that this day would come. He'd seen so many onetime mighties and worthies walking the streets as ordinary citizens, waiting at traffic lights, hailing cabs—former CIA director Richard Helms, former defense secretary and World Bank president Robert McNamara, former everything Elliot Richardson. Now, for the first time, Moody realized what it meant.

He couldn't go back through that gate. Not like before.

Like his ancestors who had served in the Union Army during the Virginia campaigns of the Civil War, Moody had always been a man to march directly to his goals. Once deciding upon a course, he stuck to it, dodging dangers and skirting obstacles perhaps, cutting corners where he had to, but always keeping his ultimate destination firmly in mind. As the president's man, he'd hooked all his ambitions and aspirations to passage of the treaty, and driven relentlessly, with skill and stamina and raw goddamn guts, toward the prospect of its success.

Now it was a very real prospect, but his headlong push had left him here on the street.

Two men in suits came by, carrying briefcases, talking earnestly, paying him no mind. A pretty girl with a Smithsonian souvenir bag sauntered along after them. She glanced at him, then looked away. What was he, after all? Just another fifty-three-year-old man in a dark suit, one of thousands in Washington.

He'd not had any lunch. He thought for a moment of walking over to Maison Blanche, an expensive Gucci loafer joint of a restaurant on the other side of the Old Executive Office Building. It had long served as an unofficial White House mess for major figures in the administration and the glad-handing lawyers and lobbyists and consultants who fluttered like moths in their light. In the past, Moody's appearance at the door would bring the maître d' scurrying forward, summoning waiters and busboys to see to his every need.

How might he be greeted now? Whispers. Averted eyes. A table in the rear? It might take days for that to set in, but he didn't feel up to taking the risk. Even if the glad-handers came up and surrounded him with bonhomie in his hour of need, he felt too weary, too beaten down, to talk to any of them.

He raised his arm. The cab stopped and he got in, sitting there a moment after closing the door.

"Where to?" the driver said, impatiently.

Where indeed?

"The Watergate."

"The hotel?"

It might as well have been.

"No. The residential entrance."

His housekeeper was surprised to see him. He was home earlier than he had been in months.

"Would you like me to fix you some dinner, Mr. Moody?"

He set down his briefcase on the foyer's marble floor. Deena had taken all her clothes and jewelry, but not touched any of the garishly expensive furnishings, all of which she'd picked out. The apartment was depressingly empty, but she still seemed a presence. He'd have to move out of here as soon as possible. Maybe he'd go to his Ocean City place, and leave it to someone else to pack all this up.

"No thanks," he said. "I'll get a bite in the restaurant downstairs."

The housekeeper told May where she could find him. Ignoring the maître d', she strode on into the restaurant, standing awkwardly in the middle of the room until she noticed him at a table in the far corner, sitting alone, his eyes fixed on the dark Potomac visible outside the wide windows.

He'd hardly touched his food.

"Daddy?"

Startled, he turned toward her uncertainly, as full of apprehension as surprise. She'd never seen him look so vulnerable, so old.

She sat down before he could rise. It took a while, but he was the first to speak.

"They told me you didn't want to see me."

"I'm sorry," she said. "I needed sleep."

"I guess you went through hell up there. I'm afraid I'm at fault for some of it. I'm sorry, May. I had no idea about Bernie. None. I probably should have, but when someone's been such a help to you, for so long . . ." This sounded so futile and small. He regretted saying it. "I finally woke up. I did what I could. I wish it had been more."

"I know that, Daddy. It was on the news driving in from Virginia, about Bernie's being arrested, about how you and the FBI set it up."

"He made bond immediately. They should have set it at a billion dollars."

"He's dead, Daddy."

"How can he be dead?"

"Someone put a bomb in his car. There was a woman with him." She halted, then hurried with the next words. "It wasn't his wife."

Moody slumped in his chair. He put his hand over his eyes for a moment, then abruptly took it away. Staring at his plate, he picked up his fork idly, as though to give himself something to do. Then he set it down again, clumsily, causing it to fall onto the tablecloth.

"God."

"I called your office at the White House. They said you weren't there. That you had left for good."

"Yeah. For good."

"Did they . . . ?"

"I resigned, May. The same way your friend Showers resigned his job. I guess for pretty much the same reason."

"It meant a lot to you, that job."

"Not today."

She had an impulse to touch him. When she was a little girl, and he'd come home from work looking sad and troubled, she used to climb into his lap and hug him. She could still remember the scratchy feel of his chin.

She put her hand on his. During her childhood, his hands had been rough and calloused. Now they were soft and well-manicured. A gentleman's hands.

"Are you in any danger?" she asked.

This produced a grin. "Not from those New Jersey bastards. They don't want the kind of trouble that would bring down on them. There's not much I can testify to, anyway—about that goddamn horse."

She kept her hand where it was.

"I'm going to be married, Daddy."

He was more surprised than she had expected.

"Are you?" he said finally. "Do you think our family can stand all that fine Virginia blood?"

"There's not all that 'fine Virginia blood,' Daddy. There's just David."

"Are you going to get married out there? All those fox hunting types?"

"It'll be in West Virginia. It'll have to be soon. He has to go away. I've talked to Momma. That's why I'm here. She thinks you ought to be at the wedding. She'd like you to be, but she didn't think you'd want to come."

He took her hand very tightly. "I'll come."

It was dark when Showers and Spencer got back from seeing Alixe in the hospital. Showers sat down on the steps to his porch, not wanting to go inside.

"I'll take that drink now," he said. "There should be something in the kitchen."

"I think I can be persuaded to have a drop myself."

Spencer returned with a bottle of Virginia Gentleman. He brought no glasses. Seating himself beside his cousin, he removed the cap, took a swig, wiped the mouth clean, and handed the whiskey to Showers.

"Country style," he said. "Couple of good old boys."

Showers took a pull himself, holding the bottle on his knee afterward.

"When I used to come here as a kid," Spencer said, "you and I would go out by the barn and do this."

"You've kept it up."

"They say it's habit-forming."

"Are you ever going to give it up?"

"I'm not in a big hurry, now that I've got such a charming drinking buddy."

In the hospital, Alixe had made a joke. She could hardly wait to get her wooden leg, she said, so she could fill it with Virginia Gentleman.

"She likes you."

"She's going to make it. Game girl."

"So is May."

"I'll be your best man, if you want."

"I'd like that very much."

Showers' border collie came bounding out of some distant bushes, barking, to no apparent purpose. Just enjoying himself. He

**368**

skittered to a stop at Showers' feet and sat down, waiting to be petted. Showers indulged him.

"Have you given any thought to what you're going to do?" Spencer asked, taking back the bottle.

"Yes. I made up my mind some time ago, when I was down at Fort A. P. Hill. I've already set things in motion. I'm going back into the army."

"The hell you say."

"I'm now the oldest captain in my National Guard battalion. In two weeks, I'm probably going to be the oldest major in the Third Army."

"I thought they were cutting back on manpower."

"I pulled strings. It's worth doing sometimes. I'll have a good six or seven years before I might have to retire, maybe longer. Who knows, I may end up a lieutenant colonel."

"Why not just join the French Foreign Legion?"

"It's not like that at all, Jack. I really like the military. I always have. I think I was meant for it. If it hadn't been for the farm, I would have stayed in the first time."

"Are you any good at it? I know you killed those men up there."

"I'm good enough. Perhaps killing someone helps. Not that I enjoyed it very much. But it helps to know you can do it, if it comes to that."

"How's it going to work, being married to an actress who's off doing plays and movies, while you're mucking around with a bunch of grunts in some swamp?"

"I think it will work very well. What May and I have seems to be pretty portable."

They drank. An owl swooped among the trees in the woods across the yard, disappearing into the darkness. They heard its soft call a moment after.

"What will you do with this place?"

"That's what I've been thinking about most. I wanted to talk to you about it, before I go through with my plans."

He stretched out his legs. Spencer waited.

"Do you know about Henry Showers? The man who started this farm back in the 1700s, when it was part of the frontier?"

"I'm sure mother dear must have told me."

"He was a tanner and a harness maker," Showers said. "He got this land collecting on a bad debt. We don't know much about his father, except that he was a dirt farmer in the Piedmont, and that his people had the good luck to arrive here on an English boat, and not some Irish one a hundred years later.

"Out of that they built this ridiculous notion of aristocracy, setting up the Showerses as superior beings, like all the other old dirt-farmer families out here, just because they hung on to this land and made a little money out of horses. There's a racialist component in it, too, isn't there? What's the term, Wasp? English blood and some horse-trading profits and the passage of time somehow translates into nobility, an exalted race, entitled to spit on everyone else. It's all nonsense, Jack, but that's what the *tradition* out here amounts to. The English can't help it. They've been living with their class system for a thousand years, but this country? It's no wonder people like Bernie Bloch get such grand, arrogant ideas. Look at the example we set."

"I don't recall anyone in the family committing murder, or bribing U.S. senators."

"Don't go looking in the records too closely. You might be surprised. The same is true of your side of the clan, too, Mr. Spencer. My mother's side. That sainted ancestor of ours who came over on the *Mayflower*? He was a cooper. He made barrels. And not very well, apparently. He died stony broke. It wasn't until his grandson that a Spencer began making any money, and he got his start selling fish. Yet your mother and my mother treated their listings in the Mayflower Society and the Colonial Dames and the Daughters of the American Revolution and all that garbage as though it were testament to royal descent. And the *Social Register*. That's put together by some little old lady no one ever heard of in some dingy office down in lower Manhattan."

"I'm not sure I get your point. Are you joining the Socialist party?"

"I'm not about to take to the barricades, Jack. I'm just telling you what's on my mind."

He took another sip of bourbon. He and his cousin might even go on a real bender that night. It wasn't necessarily such a bad idea—once every twenty years or so.

"I was in Boston a few years ago," Showers said. "I wanted to visit that little burying ground off Tremont Street, just down from the Common?—where the original Hester Prynne is buried. What was her name? Elizabeth Pain. Afterward, I went down the hill to where the original Spencer house is supposed to have been. There's a big glass and steel office building there now. Yet the seas haven't parted. The earth hasn't flung up the fires of hell. The firmament is still in place. And you Spencers are doing just fine, except for your drinking habits."

"And?"

"I want your permission to do what I'm going to do with the farm. I've talked to my sister, and she doesn't mind at all. You're my only other relation."

"You're going to put up an office building?"

"I'm going to give it away."

Spencer stared down at the ground. "To the Little Sisters of the Poor?"

"No. Don't worry. My father's ghost will be appeased. So will my grandfather's. I'm going to give it to the federal government."

"Cousin, I think you were in that coal mine too long."

"The house will be preserved. The local Daughters of the Confederacy will be happy to take it over. After all, Robert E. Lee had breakfast here once. John Mosby fought a little skirmish up on the hill. They can put a plaque up and call it a battle. The rest of it, all the back pasture land, it's going to be dedicated as a national military cemetery, if the local town fathers will go along, and I don't know how such patriots could object."

"Don't they already have Arlington?"

"That's nearly full. You have to be very special to get in there. Quantico is filling up, too. There's going to be quite a need, with so many World War Two veterans beginning to die off now. The Veterans Administration is looking all over the country for new sites."

Spencer took a long slow drink, then tilted back his head, completely relaxed.

"I don't mean to be giving you a hard time, cousin," he said. "I don't mind the idea at all. I've never had much interest in this place."

"Thank you, Jack."

"It's funny to think of it. Old Bob Moody could end up being buried here. He was in Vietnam, wasn't he?"

"He wouldn't go here. He won the Silver Star. He'll go to Arlington."

"Well, you could end up here, if you're serious about the army. Sooner or later. If they send you to Belize or some such place, it could be sooner."

Showers thought of May, how marvelous all the days and weeks and months and years of the rest of his life now promised to be.

"Let's hope it's later. I've spent enough centuries here as it is."

# Author's Note

This is a work of fiction. Though the story benefits from the author's experience in Washington and the horse country of the Eastern Seaboard, the story and characters, except for reference to noted individuals, are entirely fictional, and are in no way intended to resemble actual occurrences or people in Washington, Virginia, West Virginia, Maryland, or any other locale described in this book.

# Acknowledgments

I am extremely grateful to two friends and most admirable horse people, Heather Freeman of Berryville, Virginia, and Bob Welsh of Barrington, Illinois, for their help and guidance in the preparation of this book. I would know much less about the world of the horse without them. Author Dick Francis also gave splendid advice.

I must also thank a great many others in and out of government in Washington for their assistance over the years in enhancing my work as a journalist and my knowledge of the capital, including Jeffrey Bergner, Jim Coates, Torrie Clarke, Bob Funseth, Tex Harris, Elaine Povich, Arnie Sawislak, Wendy Webber Toler, and Mary Frances Widner.

My agent, Dominick Abel, and editors Ruth Cavin and Tom Dunne, have my special thanks.

I am grateful to my wife, Pamela, and my sons, Eric and Colin, as only they can know.

I owe a considerable debt to my great-great-grandfather, John Showers of Virginia, who left the Old Dominion and its slavery in pre–Civil War days to migrate to New York, and to his son, William, who died in that war fighting to preserve the Union in which this modern-day story was set. I have resided in both Virginia and West Virginia for many years now, and hope none of the fictional occurrences in this book detract from the deep and abiding affection I bear both states.

# About the Author

**M**ichael Kilian is a Washington-based columnist for the *Chicago Tribune* and the more than three hundred clients of the wire service it jointly owns with the Knight-Ridder newspaper chain. He is also aerial sports correspondent for the *Encyclopedia Britannica,* a captain in the U.S. Air Force auxiliary Civil Air Patrol, and a director of the Fund for Animals. He was born in 1939 in Toledo, Ohio, and grew up in Chicago and Westchester County, N.Y. He attended New York's New School for Social Research and the University of Maryland. He served as an enlisted soldier with the Eighth Army in Korea and the 82nd Airborne Division at Fort Bragg, North Carolina.

A former radio and television commentator for CBS and public broadcasting, he is the author of eleven books, including six other novels, as well as a contributor to several national magazines.

He and his wife, author and columnist Pamela Reeves Kilian, and sons Eric and Colin reside in McLean, Virginia, and Hedgesville, West Virginia.